# BABY BE MINE

## "I need a favour, Tucker."

"A favour." Tucker leaned back in his chair and looked at Maggie. "A big favour or a little favour?"

She bit her lip. "Pretty big. But temporary."

A big, temporary favour. He shrugged. "Sure, babe, anything for you. What's the favour?"

"I want you to marry me."

Stunned, he stared at her. Marry Maggie? He couldn't quite wrap his mind around the thought.

"You want me to marry you."

" That's right." She looked at him hopefully. "So, will you?"

First published in Great Britain 2010
Harlequin Mills & Boon Limited,
Eton House, 18-24 Paradise Road, Richmond, Surrey TW9 1SR

*A Father for Danny* © Janice Hess 2008
*Baby Be Mine* © Eve Gaddy 2008

ISBN: 978 0 263 87988 9

23-0810

Harlequin Mills & Boon policy is to use papers that are natural, renewable and recyclable products and made from wood grown in sustainable forests. The logging and manufacturing processes conform to the legal environmental regulations of the country of origin.

Printed and bound in Spain
by Litografia Rosés S.A., Barcelona

# A FATHER FOR DANNY

## "Who are you and what do you want?"

"If you'll give me a chance," Samantha said, her voice rising, "I'll be happy to explain."

He sat on the edge of the chair opposite her, leaning forward. He had the upper hand, and he knew it. "I'm waiting."

She took a deep breath. No more games. All she had to do now was give him the facts, and leave the rest to him. *Oh. And one more thing.*

She moistened her lips, wondering why she felt so nervous. He certainly didn't look as scary as his photograph. He was taller than she'd expected, and filled out more.

His eyes caught hers and she realised he knew she'd been checking him out.

"Confirming I'm the right man?"

His tone was not amused. Neither was the glint in his eye.

# A FATHER
# FOR DANNY
## BY
## JANICE CARTER

# BABY BE MINE
## BY
## EVE GADDY

MILLS & BOON

# A FATHER FOR DANNY

## BY
## JANICE CARTER

**Janice Carter** is a Toronto-based author and teacher. Her hobbies – besides writing – include cooking and reading. She is married with two grown daughters and looks forward to retirement and "grandmothering" in the near future. This is her eleventh novel and she hopes to write many more family sagas.

Dedicated with love to my mother,
Lois Gene Carter
1920–2007
And to the best father in the world,
William Henry Carter

# CHAPTER ONE

"I FIND THINGS, NOT people," Samantha Sorrenti repeated. "Things like rare books or antique coins. Art objects. Once I even had to search for an original Winnie the Pooh Teddy Bear." She grinned, hoping to lighten the mood. His brown eyes didn't flicker. Sam sighed. "What you want is a private investigator. Did you check the Yellow Pages?"

"Your Web site says you find anything."

"Any*thing*. Not any*one*."

"It didn't say you just look for stuff like old books."

"I'm sorry, but I really can't help you. My advice is to check out an agency."

He stared at her for a long, painful moment. Then he pushed his chair back and got to his feet so abruptly that it toppled over. The clatter echoed in the small room. When he reached the doorway, he turned around.

"I can't afford a private detective. Your ad says you don't charge anything unless you find it."

*It!* she felt like shouting. "Why the urgency? I mean, you could probably find him through the Internet yourself."

His face darkened. "I don't have time for that."

"But it might take only a few weeks and it's free. How can you lose?"

He took a step toward the desk. "How could I *lose?*" His voice cracked.

*He was going to cry!*

"You just don't get it. I need to find him because… because my mother is going to be dead in six weeks. Maybe less." He wheeled around.

Sam swallowed. "Wait," she said.

He stopped, turning slowly back to her. His eyes and nose were red.

"Maybe I can do something," she murmured.

He stared as if he hadn't heard right.

Sam pointed to the toppled-over chair. "Sit," she said quietly, trying not to sound as exasperated as she felt. After all, he was only twelve years old.

He didn't rush back to the chair, but shuffled instead, in that awkward walk of boys wearing ridiculously baggy pants. He slowly righted the chair and sat on it, slouching.

Sam knew this nonchalance was an attempt at face-saving, but it still rankled. He could at least *pretend* to be appreciative. "Look, I'm expecting an important call, so I can't be long, but…uh…I know someone who may be able to help." Sam stopped. Did she really want to take that step? She looked at the light in his eyes and her heart sank. She had to take it now. "Someone in the FBI."

"The FBI?" It came out as a croak.

"Do you have a problem with that?"

"No, but this is going to be just between us, right?"

"Are you talking about confidentiality?"

"Yeah. That's what I mean."

"I think you've got me confused with a lawyer. As I said, I'm not even a private investigator. I look for—"

"Yeah, you told me. Things. Not people."

Sam felt her blood pressure rise. "Do you want me to get you some help or not?"

She saw him flinch, but didn't regret her harsh tone. He might be only twelve, but he'd managed to barge into her office all on his own.

"Yes, I do. It's just that you mentioning the FBI…it sounds serious."

*More serious than you can imagine.* "Okay," she said, reaching for her notepad. "Why don't you tell me your story and I'll make some notes? Then I'll get back to you."

"When?"

"I don't know. As soon as I can."

He chewed on his lower lip for a few seconds, then began. When he finished, less than ten minutes later, Sam didn't trust herself to look his way. She stared at her notes, the words blurred by tears. She sniffed, blinked twice and finally raised her head.

His eyes met hers, and Sam thought she caught a glimmer of satisfaction in them. *He knows I'm hooked.*

She cleared her throat. "Okay, so let me review this. Your mother has had no contact with your father since you were born."

"Since *before* I was born. She says he never knew about me."

"But she never tried to contact him, to tell him about you?"

He shrugged. "I dunno. She always told me he never knew. I think he moved to another city, anyway."

"Maybe your mother can fill in some of these gaps."

"Why do you have to see my mother? Can't this be just between us?"

"Does your mother know you came to see me?"

He looked away.

"She doesn't, does she?"

"She has enough problems."

Sam had no reply to that. He was right of course. "The thing is, you're a minor. I can't legally help you without your mother's consent."

His eyes flicked coolly back to hers. "But you're not a real private detective, anyway."

*And you're no typical twelve-year-old.* "I can't do anything for you without your mother's knowledge. Anyway, you told me she was the one who suggested finding your father."

"Kinda."

"What do you mean, *kinda?*" Sam's voice rose.

His gaze dropped to his hands, interlocked in his lap. "When she first found out about the cancer, she said it was too bad my father didn't know me."

Sam felt as if she'd just plunged her other foot into quicksand. "Well, I'd have to talk to her if you want me to help," she eventually said.

"Okay, okay." His eyes met hers again. "But don't upset her. Please? She already feels bad because she knows I'll have to go into foster care after...well, after."

He didn't need to clarify. "I won't upset her, Danny, I promise. But she needs to know. Can you tell me anything at all about your father?"

"His name is Danny, too. I think my mom forgot his last name."

Or never knew it. Sam was beginning to wonder if Danny was the product of a one-night stand. Which meant the task she'd taken on would be impossible. "Anything else?"

His face brightened. "He liked motorcycles. My mom said he had a real cool tattoo on his right arm and long hair, like a rock star."

"Oh," was all Sam could think to say. The picture forming in her mind wasn't exactly a poster for fatherhood. "So Benson is your mother's name?"

"Yeah. Emily Benson." He craned his neck, looking at something behind her.

The clock, Sam realized. "You have to go soon?"

"Yeah. I told Minnie I'd be back about five and I gotta take a couple of buses."

"Who's Minnie?"

"Our next-door neighbor. I've been staying with her for the last two weeks."

"Your mother—"

"She's in the hospital."

"Oh. Is she having surgery or something?"

He shook his head. "Nope. All that's finished. Now she's just waiting. In… I can't remember the name for it. A special room in the hospital."

"Palliative care?"

"Yeah. That's it. Mom calls it the Waiting Room. She jokes about it. You know, how hospitals are always making you wait for something. She says she even has to wait to die." His voice cracked again and he turned his head toward the bookshelves at his right.

Silence shrink-wrapped the room. Sam badly wanted a glass of water. No. Make that a double of any alcoholic drink available. Unfortunately none was.

Finally he said, "Minnie says I can stay with her for now but…well, she's old, you know." He looked back at Sam. His eyes were red-rimmed. "She's living on a small pension and can't take care of me for too long."

Sam cleared her throat. "I'll need her telephone number."

Danny complied, then said, "She's in the apartment across the hall from ours, so I can go back and forth, take care of Mom's plants and stuff." He got to his feet. "So…uh, when should I call you?"

Sam knew she was sinking fast and there was no way out. Maybe a couple of phone calls would convince him she couldn't do much more. "Like I said, I have to, uh, talk to someone who may be able to help and then I'll get back to you."

"Will that take long?"

She felt her face heat. He was persistent. Not one to be put off by lame excuses. "I'll do my best, Danny."

His eyes held hers for a long moment, then he turned abruptly and walked out the door. Sam dropped her forehead into her hands. *What have you done now, Sorrenti?*

"ARE YOU SERIOUS? What in heaven's name possessed you, Samantha?"

There had been a time in Sam's teen years when she'd answer a question like that with a flippant quip. But she and her mother had finally managed to establish what they euphemistically called a "working relationship" so Sam wasn't even tempted to play the smart-ass, as her mother used to say. She regretted, however, bringing up the afternoon visit from Danny Benson during her weekly tea and chat with her mother.

"Mom, he's twelve years old and his mother is dying. He has no other relatives and…well…he almost started to cry right there in my office. What could I do?"

Nina Sorrenti set the teapot back onto the tray and handed Sam her cup and saucer. "You could have pointed him toward the many agencies available to help children in his situation."

"I know, I know," Sam muttered. "I'm a sucker for a sob story."

"I didn't say that, darling."

"But I am, I admit it. He just looked at me with his big brown eyes and I remembered—" She broke off.

"How you felt when you were his age? When your father walked out on us?"

Sam took a long sip of tea before replying. "Mother, I'm

not in one of your therapy sessions. Maybe we should just drop the subject and talk about what I really came here for—your upcoming sixtieth. "

Nina waved an index finger at Sam. "Darling, you're not going to persuade me to have a big party. I refuse to acknowledge this particular birthday."

Sam stared at her mother ensconced in the easychair across from her, one sleek leg gracefully draped over the other. She was wearing a knee-length straight skirt and tailored shirt, which highlighted her slender but shapely figure. In spite of the streaks of gray in her short hair, Nina had the face and skin of a much younger woman.

Nina went on, smiling, "Besides, you're not getting out of this so easily. I'm just pointing out something that must be obvious to you."

Sam knew the subject wasn't going to be dropped. She sighed. "What I think is that you're purposely overlooking the blatant differences between Danny's situation and mine. You're doing the psychologist thing with me and I don't like it."

"And you're still evading my question."

"Not evading so much as putting it into perspective. Of course I can relate to his problem, because I understand what it is not to have a father-figure in my life. But he never knew his father, whereas Skye and I were—"

"Abandoned."

Sam shrugged. "If you want to use that word, go ahead." She put her cup and saucer back on the table and sneaked a peak at her watch.

"*Now* who's playing therapist?"

"For heaven's sake, Mother!"

Nina laughed. "Okay, I'll give it a rest. But—"

Sam held up a palm. "Say no more. Session ended. So, tell me what's new in your life?"

Nina leaned forward to set her cup and saucer down, then smoothed her skirt as she sat back in the chair. She seemed to be taking her time to answer, Sam thought.

"Mmm, not too much, dear. I've been asked to speak at a conference next month."

"Great. Where's the conference? Anyplace exciting?"

Nina smiled. "Just here in good old Seattle. That's why I accepted. I'm not up to traveling all over the country anymore for these things. Same old, same old, as the expression goes."

"You used to love to travel."

"I know, but I don't feel the urge now. I'm all for curling up in front of a fire with a good book."

Sam laughed. "Yeah, right, Mom. Funny how I can't picture you doing that." She studied her mother for a moment, trying to see her objectively. An attractive woman, an accomplished clinical psychologist and still working at it daily.

"You're not really that upset about turning sixty, are you?"

"No, dear, not really. Though I admit it's given me much more pause than turning fifty did. But I'm hoping to make some time for myself now. I've decided to whittle down the size of my practice—I'm not taking any new patients."

Sam mulled that over. Nina had always been driven by her love for her career and her love for her children. She couldn't imagine her slowing down. But then, she also couldn't imagine her getting any older. For a long moment Sam couldn't speak.

"Well, Mom, don't think that this means we won't be celebrating your birthday," she tried again.

Nina raised an eyebrow. "I wonder where you get that stubbornness from?"

"It's genetic, I believe." Sam stood up. "What do I owe you for the consultation?"

"How about a kiss?"

Their eyes locked and they both smiled. Sam leaned down to kiss her mother.

"Will you come for dinner next Monday, rather than tea, and tell me more about Danny?"

"I'd love to come for dinner. I'm sure by then Danny will have realized I can't help him."

"Maybe your sister can be of assistance."

"How?" she asked, though Skye had automatically came to mind when she'd been talking to Danny.

"Isn't that her field? Doesn't the FBI handle missing-persons cases?"

"This man isn't really missing. I'm assuming whatever relationship he'd had with Danny's mother simply ended and he left town, not knowing he'd fathered a child."

"Skye might be able to steer you in the right direction or give you some advice."

Sam made a face.

"What's *that* for?" her mother asked.

"Nothing. I thought I might call Skye, but I'm sure she's far too busy for something like this. Besides, I have to talk to Danny's mother first. She may have a problem with him searching for his father."

"Well, of course you have to do that." Nina paused. "When was the last time you spoke to your sister?"

"Christmas." Sam leaned against one of the French doors separating the living room from the hallway and knew what was coming.

"Samantha, that was five months ago. What's happened between you two, anyway?"

"Nothing, Mother. You're reading too much into it. She lives in another part of the country."

"But you're sisters. Twins. You're supposed to be close."

"Is that what the psychology books say?"

"Don't be sarcastic, Samantha. It's not becoming and I don't deserve it."

"Sorry. But being twins doesn't mean we have to be joined at the hip."

"Don't exaggerate. You know what I mean."

"Yes, I do. It's just that whenever Skye and I are together the whole competition thing kicks in, and I'm tired of it."

"It's normal for siblings to be competitive. Especially twins, when they want to establish their own identities."

"I'm talking *perverse* competition, Mom. Obsessive. Whatever you want to call it. And Skye is always the one to initiate it."

"I've been hearing refrains like that since you both were twelve. And you're still saying it at thirty-three."

"You're right, Mother. There's no point in belaboring the point. I have to go now, anyway."

"Anywhere special?"

"Just meeting Dawn for a drink." She turned to leave, but was held back by her mother's next question.

"Any word from Todd these days?"

"Nope," she said, fighting to keep her voice level. "I told you, it's over. Finito. See you next week," she said, waved goodbye and made a quick exit before her mother could ask another question.

THE PHONE RANG just as Sam was removing the bubble-pack taped around a rare, framed Japanese print. She glanced sharply at the console but didn't recognize the number. Her client, Jean Mawhinney, pointed at the phone. "Go ahead," she said. "I can wait another five minutes."

Samantha gently set the package down on her desk and

picked up the phone. It took her a moment to recognize the high-pitched voice. Danny.

"My mother wants to meet you," he said. "Can you come to Our Lady of Mercy Hospital at ten-thirty?"

"I have a client right now, Danny. And it's already ten. Can I call you back?"

"But ten-thirty is good for Mom because she'll be finished with her bath and stuff. If you wait any longer, it'll be time for her morning nap and—"

"Aren't you supposed to be in school right now?"

There was a pause, followed by a muffled response Sam couldn't hear. She noticed Mrs. Mawhinney eyeing the package she'd been patiently awaiting for three months.

"Look, Danny, this isn't a good time. How about after lunch?"

When he finally answered, he sounded as exasperated as she did. "I wasn't going to be here after lunch."

"Do you need to be there when I talk to your mother?"

"I guess not," he muttered.

"So what time does your mother have lunch?"

"Noon."

"Okay, I can be there about one."

"She might be napping again."

Sam exhaled loudly and noticed Mrs. Mawhinney's startled expression. She smiled an apology at the petite, middle-aged woman and said to Danny, "I'll be there at twelve-thirty, Danny." Then she hung up. "Sorry for the interruption, Jean. Shall we see what we've got here?"

"Oh, yes, Samantha," Jean said as she rubbed her dainty hands together in anticipation.

HE WAS STANDING next to the information desk in the hospital lobby and wearing what Sam already identified as his trademark scowl. She felt a surge of annoyance. Wasn't *she* the one being inconvenienced by this last-minute interruption in her workday?

"She's really tired so I don't know how much time we'll have before she'll need her nap," he said as Sam drew near. "You took a long time getting here. Now I'm gonna have to miss school this afternoon, too."

"Look, Danny," she said as they moved to the bank of elevators. "Let's clarify a few things. Number one, I am not working for you in any capacity. I am here as a *favor*, got that? Second, nobody told you to skip school. I could have met your mother on my own. And last of all, you are the child and I am the adult. I don't know what your mother taught you in the way of manners, but you have no right to speak to me in that tone." Then she stopped, realizing half a dozen people around them were cued to her every word. Fortunately the elevator door opened at that very moment, and the group trooped aboard.

It was an uncomfortable ride up to the tenth floor. Samantha kept her eyes on the floor-indicator panel, wishing that she'd set Danny straight about helping him when he'd come to her office two days ago. The problem was, her resolve to say no disappeared the instant his dark brown eyes met hers.

As soon as they stepped out of the elevator and the people behind them had dispersed, Sam said in a low voice, "Listen, I'm sorry if I sounded like—"

"It's okay," he said. "You were right. Kinda." Those same dark eyes bore into hers. He wheeled around and headed into a room diagonally across from the elevators.

Sam had the unsettling feeling that the child-adult roles had been reversed, but she ceased caring about it the instant she entered Emily Benson's room.

Danny's mother lay propped against two pillows that

dwarfed her. Her hair—stringy and limp—might have been blond once upon a time but now was more the color of a mud puddle on a rainy day. Her head turned slowly toward the door as they walked in. The transparent oxygen line inserted in her nostrils moved at the same time. Sam's gaze shifted to the large red tank on the far side of the bed.

The dark-circled eyes, sunk deep in her small face, brightened when she saw Danny. Sam wondered how a simple glance could convey so much emotion. But what she knew, right then and there, was that she would not be leaving that room without making some attempt to help.

The woman ran her tongue along her lower lip, cleared her throat twice and then spoke in a voice so faint Sam had to move to the chair next to the bed.

"I'm pleased to meet you. Danny told me you offered to help him find his father."

Sam nodded.

"Are you a private detective?" Emily asked.

Sam hesitated before replying, "Not exactly, but I am experienced at finding things." She quickly added, "To tell you the truth, I'm not certain I can be any help at all."

A frown settled over the pale face. "All this has taken me by surprise. Danny just told me the whole story yesterday. How he happened to find you on the Internet and your offer to help." She paused to catch her breath.

Not quite the whole story, Sam was thinking. She looked at Danny sitting in the chair on the other side of the bed, but he was engrossed in a magazine. Or at least pretending to be.

"I don't expect you to have much luck with this," Emily added.

Danny's head shot up.

"It's been so many years. I haven't heard from Daniel since just before I..." She stopped and glanced at Danny.

"Hon, could you go get me a can of ginger ale from the nurses' station? No ice and one of those bendy straws."

He looked as if he was about to say something but changed his mind. As he left he shot Sam a glance, as if it was somehow her fault that his mother wanted to speak privately.

"I'll try to be quick," his mother said as soon as he left the room. "Just that it's embarrassing…you know…in front of my son. I met Daniel when I was waitressing at a diner up in Greenwood, not far from where Danny and I live now. You ever been to Woodland Park zoo there?"

Sam shook her head. The north end of Seattle was foreign territory to her.

"It's nice. I used to take Danny there when he was little." She broke off for a moment, her small front teeth biting down on her lower lip. Then she took a deep breath and went on, "The first time Daniel came in for coffee I was kinda put off by him, looking like a biker 'n all. But we got to talking after a while and I found out he was real nice. Different from what I expected. He talked like he was educated. You know? Anyway, one night he was still there when we closed up and he asked me to go for a drink at a bar down the street." She stopped and turned her gaze upward. "One thing led to another—if you know what I mean. I didn't even know I was pregnant until after he left."

"He *left?*"

Emily shifted her head on the pillow. Her eyes looked sad. "He just vanished. Didn't come in one day and I thought maybe he was sick or something. I waited a few more days before calling the phone number he'd given me. He was living in a rooming house. The man who answered said Daniel had up and gone. Didn't pay his last week's rent and he swore at *me,* thinking I was his girlfriend or something." She smiled wistfully.

"What was his last name?"

"Daniel's? Oh, he said it was Winston."

"Do you think that was a fake name?"

"After a few days of calling every Winston in the phone book, I figured it musta been. I wish I could help you some more but…"

"Do you have a photograph of him?"

"No, sorry." She broke into a spasm of coughing and tried to reach for the glass of water on the table next to her. Sam jumped up and held the glass for her. The very act of sipping seemed to exhaust her and she fell back against the pillows, panting as if she'd just finished a race.

"I guess Danny told you I don't have much time," she finally whispered. "He's been staying with Minnie Schwartz, our neighbor. But that's only till…well…till none of us has to wait anymore."

Sam saw tears well up in her eyes and looked away, afraid she'd start to cry herself.

"This is his idea—looking for his father," she went on. "I don't think he'll find him. But I think he should try. No harm in that, is there? For him to have a little hope for a bit longer?"

Sam blinked rapidly and shook her head. "No. No harm at all." She waited a few seconds and then asked, "Is there anything else that you know about him?"

Emily thought for a minute. "He told me his family came from Seattle. He was an only child, like me. That was one of the things we had in common." She cast Sam a rueful glance. "There wasn't much else, 'cept we had a couple laughs together whenever he came into the diner. Like I said, we only went out that one time." She paused. "He was very attractive. There was something special about him. I could see that right away." She stopped then, turning her head away.

"How about his age?"

"He was five years younger'n me. He used to tease me about being an older woman. At first, that's why I thought he left. Especially after that night. Maybe he was afraid, you know, of getting trapped into something." She gave a wobbly smile. "But looking back now, I think there was something goin' on in his life."

"Like what?"

Emily shook her head. "I dunno. Just that he didn't like talkin' about his past or his family, that kinda stuff."

"So how old would he be now, then?"

"He was twenty-four then and Danny just turned twelve so…"

"Thirty-six or -seven?"

"Yeah, I guess. I sometimes wonder what might have happened if…"

Just then he appeared in the doorway and his mother let her sentence trail off. He was holding a can of soda and he hesitated, staring first at his mother, then at Sam.

It seemed like a good time to leave. "I have to go now," Sam said, adding quickly at the alarm in Danny's face, "but I'll see what I can do to help. I have some contacts and people I can call." She saw relief wash over Danny's face. "But I can't promise anything. There's not a lot of information to go on."

"That's wonderful, isn't it, Danny?" Emily smiled at him.

Danny nodded. His eyes were red and Sam guessed he didn't trust himself to speak. Samantha watched the silent interchange between mother and son. She stood up. "I'll call you here at the hospital as soon as I find out anything."

As she walked to the door, her single thought was how much she feared breaking that slender thread of hope she knew she'd just cast out to them.

# CHAPTER TWO

SAM WONDERED how much longer she could sit and stare at the telephone. She'd put off making the call since returning from the hospital yesterday afternoon. And although she'd intended to catch up on some work, she'd been unable to do anything but sit, stare and think.

As much as Danny's attitude had annoyed her, she doubted she could have been as gutsy at twelve as he was, facing his mother's death on his own and being placed in a foster home. Making a few phone calls, as she'd told him, might be all she could do for him. Yet here she was hours later, unable to make one particular call.

Unnecessary office tasks had filled some of the hours. She'd calculated the time in Washington D.C., convincing herself that Skye would be at lunch. Assuming that she was even *in* D.C. and not out in the field "nabbing bad guys," as her twin used to say—back when they were still speaking to each other. When Sam was still engaged to Todd, blissfully unaware of what lay ahead.

Then she thought of Danny's pale, brave face and his mother's eyes. She picked up the receiver and tapped in Skye's work number, rather than her cell phone. Keep this whole thing business, she told herself.

The phone rang long enough for Sam to think the voice mail might pick up and she'd have a reprieve of sorts. Just as she was about to disconnect, Skye answered.

"Agent Sorrenti. How may I help you?"

Sam cleared her throat. "Uh, hi. It's Samantha."

There was a moment of dead silence. *"Sam?"*

"You know another Samantha?"

"Well, this is a surprise. To say the least."

Sam hesitated, then plunged in. "I'm calling for a favor," she said.

"Oh?"

The uplift at the end of the word told Sam her sister was not only doubly surprised but also apprehensive. "I met this boy—he's twelve—and his mother is dying of cancer. There's just the two of them, no other family, and he—Danny's his name—is going to have to go into foster care." She paused to catch her breath.

"Uh-huh?"

Sam quickly went on before Skye could ask what any of this had to do with her. "He wants to find his biological father and he asked me to help him."

"Oh, *yeah?*"

"You don't have to say it like that!" Sam blurted, in spite of her intention to avoid any digression.

"Like what, Sam? I'm feeling a bit mystified."

"I was wondering if you could give me any tips on finding someone." Sam pictured her sister's grin. "I told Danny that I probably wouldn't be able to do much for him, so I'm not expecting miracles. Just maybe a lead on some places I could call."

"I thought your business was finding *things.*"

Sam closed her eyes, revisiting her first conversation with Danny. "He found me through my Web site and after I met his mother, I couldn't turn him down. I said I'd see what I could do."

"So what do you want *me* to do?"

Sam stifled her frustration. "As I said, maybe you could

tell me who to call. Any agencies or places that might have records—besides the usual ones, of course."

"What's this guy's name? The father."

"Daniel Winston. But Emily—the mother—doesn't think it's his real name."

"What else have you got on the guy?"

"When Emily knew him, he rode a motorcycle, had long hair and a tattoo."

"Sounds like the real fatherly type."

Although her own immediate reaction had been the same, Sam resisted commenting, wanting to get to the point. "Emily thinks his family comes from the Seattle area."

"So if you're in Seattle and he's from there…"

"Look, Skye, if you can't help, just say so. I've already checked the phone directory and as I said, the name could be false."

"Frankly, Sam, I don't know how much I can do."

"I already explained to them it might be impossible to locate him."

"Don't suppose you got a DOB?"

"A what?"

"Date of birth."

"No, but he was twenty-four at the time and that was twelve or thirteen years ago."

"Does the guy have a rap sheet? A record?"

"I've no idea. Emily never mentioned it."

"It'd make the job a bit easier anyway. So look, why don't you see if this Emily thinks of something else and we'll talk again in a couple of days?"

"Sure. Great. Thanks, Skye." The silence that fell between them was long and uncomfortable. *How sad that I can't think of anything else to say to my twin sister.*

"So how's Mom doing?" Skye eventually asked.

"Fine. Same as always. Her sixtieth is coming up next month. Remember? She'd love to hear from you."

"I've been busy," Skye snapped. "Just got back in town a few days ago after six weeks undercover."

Sam pursed her lips. As always, the implied reprimand struck home. Finding rare art objects paled next to the dangers of her twin's job. The weight of the many months of silence between them ground the conversation to a halt. There was nothing to do but get off the phone.

"Well, I appreciate whatever you can do, Skye," Sam said.

"I'll touch base with you soon."

"Thanks, Skye," Sam said as the call was abruptly disconnected from the other end. Sam sat for a long time staring at the phone. Willing her sister to call right back? Maybe with a long-overdue apology? It wasn't going to happen. Sam powered up her computer and got back to work.

But an hour later, after she'd found and purchased online a Civil War sword for a client, she closed her laptop. She'd take her sister's advice and go back to the hospital to see Emily Benson. If she was lucky, Danny wouldn't be there and she could have a private conversation with his mother.

THE NURSE at the palliative-care station frowned.

"Ms. Benson's not having a good day," she said. "But I suppose, if you're not long…"

"I won't be. Is her son here?"

"He came in early this morning, but his mother sent him to school." The frown turned disapproving. "He shouldn't miss so much."

"His mother is dying. I imagine getting down to schoolwork is pretty difficult."

The nurse flushed. "Of course. But…you know…with

no other relatives on the scene, Children's Services could step in even before his mother passes away."

*Especially if people like you keep talking about the situation.* But Sam knew better than to alienate someone who was looking after Emily Benson. "Yes, he'll need to lead as normal a life as possible…." she said vaguely.

The nurse nodded. "And as I said, Emily's not having a good day today, so if she looks tired…"

"I'll leave. Definitely. Thanks." Sam walked down the hall and paused outside Emily's room. There was a spasm of coughing from within that sent chills up Sam's spine. When they subsided, she tapped lightly on the partially opened door and stepped inside.

Emily was stretching to reach a tissue from the box at her bedside. "Here, let me," Sam said, and leaped toward the box. She snatched up a handful and thrust them at Emily. "How about some water? Can I help you with that?"

Emily sagged back against the pillows and dabbed at her mouth. After a few seconds, she said, breathlessly, "No. It might trigger another spasm. I'm okay for now. Thanks." She closed her eyes, as if the mere act of speaking was too much.

Sam guessed it probably was. She waited until the other woman was ready.

Finally Emily opened her eyes and managed a weak smile. "Sorry about that. Not a good day."

"I should have let you know I was coming."

"It wouldn't have made any difference. I suppose it's too soon for any news?"

Sam hated to dash the hope in those sunken eyes. "I need to find out a few more things."

"It was hard to talk yesterday, with Danny here. Like I told you, I don't expect much. This is all just for Danny." She spoke in halting fragments, taking in gulps of air in between.

Sam nodded. When she felt she could safely speak, she asked, "Do you know if Danny's father had a police record?"

"He was secretive about his background, but he didn't seem like a criminal…or a biker, despite the way he looked. It made me curious about him. You know, why he acted the biker type. Made me wonder if he was running away from something…or someone."

Sam edged forward in her chair. Emily's voice was so very weak. "What do you mean?"

"I remember when I told him I had no family at all, he said that might be a good thing. I figured he'd had a falling-out with his. I mean, if he was in Seattle and they were, too, why wasn't he seeing them?"

Sam knew the question was rhetorical. She guessed Emily had asked herself it many times, especially after she knew she was pregnant.

"Did you try to find him when you found out you were pregnant?"

"Kind of. Thing is, I knew that what happened between us was just going to be one night." She turned her head to the window at her right.

Sam followed her gaze. The late-afternoon spring sun was rich and golden, ripe with the promise of summer. Was Emily wondering how many more days like it she'd see?

"When he came into Baywicks—that's the diner—the day after that night," Emily went on, "I could tell we weren't meant to be. He apologized." Her smile was more like a grimace. "So when I discovered I was pregnant, I didn't really make a lot of effort to find him. By then he'd stopped coming to the diner, and when I finally went to his place—he'd told me where he was living—I learned he'd moved out. No forwarding address. Maybe whatever he was running from caught up to him." She closed her eyes.

There was one more question Sam had to ask, though she hated to. When Emily reopened her eyes, she said, "What happens if I do find Daniel and he doesn't want to meet his son?"

"Yeah. I've thought about that a lot. Do me a favor, Sam?" Her eyes were imploring. "Don't tell either of us. Just say you couldn't find him. It would be better than knowing he wanted nothing to do with Danny or me."

"I don't know if I could do that," Sam murmured, appalled at the idea of lying to a dying woman and her soon-to-be-orphaned son.

Emily struggled to sit up. "You *have* to," she gasped. "It's bad enough Danny will be raised by foster parents. I don't want him knowing his daddy didn't want him. This way, he can always have his 'what-if' to hold on to." She fell back, exhausted. "Besides, I couldn't tell Danny the truth about his father and me—our one-night stand. I let him think we'd been dating...."

Sam studied the pattern of shadows cast on the wall by the sun filtering through the open slats of the Venetian blinds. There was no way out. She'd taken on an impossible quest and knew she couldn't live with herself if she failed. When she met Emily's gaze again, she said, "I'll do what I can for Danny. I won't hurt him."

Emily's eyes were filled with tears and Sam looked away. After a moment, she said, "My sister works for the FBI and she said she'd try to find Daniel in their database. If he has a record, it'll be easier. That's why I asked."

"Thanks, Sam, for anything you can do," Emily said quietly. "I appreciate it." Then she frowned. "Can you tell me what you charge?"

"Please, don't worry about the fee."

"I have some money set aside. I can pay."

"Let's not worry about that for now."

"But it's your business and you deserve payment. Please don't think we're poor."

Sam flushed. She'd been thinking exactly that. She saw the pride in Emily's eyes and was ashamed. "It's just that I have no idea what to charge," she said lightly, "since this kind of search is new to me. Let's see how it goes first."

Emily nodded. "Fair enough." She closed her eyes again.

Sam watched the bedcover rise and fall gently for a few moments.

Slowly Emily's face settled into repose and Sam knew she was dozing. Then she rose quietly from her chair and tiptoed out of the room.

BALANCING HER briefcase and lunch bag on one hip, Sam opened the mailbox in the small foyer of the building where she worked. It was a triplex that had been renovated five years ago into offices, and the owner was Nina Sorrenti. Her mother had bought it several years ago with money inherited from her parents.

Sam had been a regular paying tenant for the past two years, but her first year setting up Finders Keepers had been rent-free. Although she'd appreciated her mother's generosity, she was grateful to be earning enough money now to pay the same rent as the other tenants. Besides, her free year had come with strings. Lots of advice from her mother and a few digs from Skye about being on the family payroll. As if Skye had never taken a parental handout!

Sam grabbed an elasticized bundle of catalogs from her mailbox and headed up the stairs. When she reached the top landing and turned right toward her office, she stopped.

"What are you doing here? Isn't this a school day?"

Danny got up from where he'd been sitting cross-legged in front of her office door. He ignored her question. "Your sign says the office opens at eight-thirty. It's almost nine."

He had a knack for evasion that was formidable in a child his age. Sam brushed past him to unlock the door and had barely deposited her armful onto her desk when he plopped into a chair.

As she turned around, he said, "You went to see my mother yesterday."

His tone made her pause. She took her time replying, closing her office door and slinging her jacket over the coatrack. He followed her every movement, and when she finally sat down across from him on the other side of her desk, he asked, "What did you talk to her about?"

Time to set some boundaries. "I had some questions to ask your mother about your father. If you want to know what we discussed, you'll have to ask her."

"This whole thing was my idea and I was the one who found you."

"Yes, but you're a minor and can't employ someone to look for another person."

"Even if that someone just looks for *things?*" He jumped to his feet.

"I'm not going to quibble about this. I repeat—ask your mother."

"I already did and she acted like you two didn't talk about anything. It's not *fair*." He sat back down, arms folded across his chest.

In spite of that last petulant word, Sam could tell from the fire in his eyes that he wouldn't leave until he had some kind of satisfactory answer. "Basically I had to find out if your father had a criminal record, because it would make the search a lot easier."

"So what did my mom say?"

"She didn't know, but she doubted it."

He thought for a moment. "Is someone helping you?"

"Yes."

"So my mom is okay with what you're doing?"

Obviously his concern had been about informing Emily. "She's okay with it but you really need to talk to her. About everything. You two need to make plans about—"

"See, that's what really bugs me. The way adults are always telling us kids what we should do or shouldn't do, like we couldn't figure out stuff ourselves. My mom…she didn't even tell me…" He stopped, swiping at his eyes with the back of a hand.

Sam looked down at her desktop. All she could give him right now was a chance to compose himself, though she wished she could offer more.

Huskily he went on. "I never knew until things got really bad. She didn't want me to worry. And I know she's letting me do this just to get my mind off things, to make me think there's a way out of going to a foster home."

Sam looked at him in surprise. He obviously *could* figure out stuff for himself. Smart kid.

As if reading her mind, he said, "I may only be twelve but I'm no kid. Not really. So I don't really need an adult, some social worker, telling me what to do. So far no other adult—except maybe for Minnie—has really done anything for my mom and me."

Sam took in the angry face across from her. "Fair enough, Danny. All I can promise is that I'll do my very best to help you find your father."

He nodded, got to his feet and held out his right hand, which she clasped in hers. "Deal," he said, and left the office without another word.

Sam brought her hands up to her face and massaged her forehead, the faint stirring of a migraine beneath her fingertips. The day's beginning didn't bode well for the tasks she'd planned for the morning. She decided to finish some paperwork first. Perhaps she'd feel up to a cheerful conversation with her contact at Christie's in New York later in the day. Right now, she had to keep her mind on ordinary things to keep from crying over the plight of a kid who was anything but ordinary.

The tactic was a good one in theory, but emotion kept its own rules. When the phone rang an hour after Danny walked out, Sam grabbed for it gratefully. "Finders Keepers."

There was a slight muffled sound on the other end, and for a second, Sam was afraid she'd connected with a telemarketer. "Who is this?" she asked.

At last a voice replied, "It's *me,* your sister."

"I couldn't hear you."

"'Cause my mouth was full of muffin. I wasn't expecting you to pick up the phone so quickly."

"Muffin? Isn't it past your lunchtime out there?"

"Yep, but I forgot to eat breakfast, so I'm working my way toward lunch. Probably have it just before I leave for the day."

Sam kept silent. Skye's erratic schedules had more to do with her personality than her job, which was merely the convenient excuse.

"You still there?"

"Just waiting for you to stop chewing."

"Okay, okay. Listen, I'm off to a conference tomorrow and wanted to get back to you while I had the chance."

Sam clenched the receiver. "Did you find him?"

"Yes and no."

"Skye, no games please. This is important."

"Relax. I just want to explain what I did because I can't really give any more time to this. But I got a start and it looks promising. The rest you should be able to take care of."

*Yeah, right.* Sam wished she had as much confidence

in her sleuthing abilities as her sister seemed to have. "Go on."

"You told me this Emily person figured the guy was using an assumed name, and if he had no record, I figured he'd probably do what most amateurs do when they pick an alias."

"I thought you were in a hurry."

"Give me a break, Sam. Most people pick a name they're already familiar with. Makes it easier. So I decided to run a search for 'Daniel Winston', thinking at least one of those names might be the right one. I didn't get anything until I asked for all names with Daniel Winston in them and I came up with two for the greater Seattle area."

"And?"

"One was a kid and the other was for a Winston Daniel Sullivan, but…" She paused.

"What?"

"He's dead."

Sam exhaled slowly. So, it was finished almost before it began. Maybe it was better this way. Finding out your father was dead might be a preferable option to being rejected by him.

"You still there?"

"Yes. Just thinking about Danny and his mother."

"Right, well, don't go calling them up with the bad news yet, 'cause Daniel Winston Sullivan died about twelve years ago when he was sixty-six."

"*Sixty-six?* Then…"

"Not your man."

Sam closed her eyes, wishing she was close enough to grab hold of her sister and squeeze. "For God's sake!"

"There's more, though. When I called up his name I drew a flag here."

"A what?"

"A flag telling me the name was connected to an old case."

"What kind of case? Drugs or something?"

"No. Fraud. Ironically it was one of my cases when I was working there."

"You mean, when you first signed up with the agency?"

"Yep. It really wasn't much of a case though. I'm looking at it right now—downloaded the old file when I got the flag. Hmm—seems it was initiated after a couple of anonymous phone tips. Uh-huh. It's kinda coming back to me now."

"Could you just give me the basic details, Skye?"

"Relax, Sam. I'm just skimming through it here. Winston Sullivan, as he was called, was one of the owners of a company called Trade Winds—import and export operation—accused of scamming the government on contracts."

"Hold on a sec, I want to write this down." Sam reached for the pen and notepad on her desktop. "All right, go on."

"Okay, so this might have been a serious charge, but we couldn't find any real evidence. The tipster never came forward and people we interviewed had nothing much we could use."

"So why even bother? Do you normally follow up anonymous tips like that?"

"Not often, but like I said, it was my first year and my boss thought it would be good experience for me. We didn't expect anything to come of it and nothing did."

"Then why the flag?"

"Not sure… Oh, yeah. Here it is. A key witness was unavailable for interviewing. I guess I flagged it, intending to follow up, but then I was posted to D.C. shortly after and the agent who took over my caseload closed it, but kept the flag on in case the witness reported back."

Sam scribbled on the notepad. "And the witness?"

"None other than Chase Daniel Sullivan, son of Winston Daniel Sullivan."

*"Chase?"* She tried—unsuccessfully—to attach that name to her mental image of Danny's father.

"Fancy, eh? At the time he was working in the company's accounting department. When I went in to check the company's books, I found out the woman who'd been the manager had just resigned. And this Chase guy was away on a business trip or something."

Sam chewed thoughtfully on the end of her pen. "Isn't that a bit odd? That both important witnesses would be away at the same time?"

"I thought so, too, but the big bosses at the company were very open to my looking at everything."

"You mean, the father?"

"And his brother, Bryant Sullivan. They both inherited the business from their father. I just Googled the company name, and it seems the brother is still running it with his two sons."

"And what about Chase?"

"I can't tell you anything more about him. No phone listing under that name. I know someone in Transport who can check if he has a driver's license, but I haven't had a chance to call her yet. He has no credit card—at least, not in his real name and not in the alias he was using with this Emily person."

Sam closed her eyes, picturing "this Emily person" lying in her hospital bed. Sometimes Skye's professional detachment was too much. But she didn't want to get side-tracked by another quibble with her sister. "So you're tell-ing me Danny's father might be this Chase Sullivan, but you have no idea where he is."

"No, I'm not telling you that." Sam flinched at the irri-tation in her twin's voice. "He has no military record and I didn't have time to see if he's ever filed an income-tax return, but I've got one lead you can follow up easily enough yourself."

"What's that?"

"Papa Sullivan left a widow and she's a resident at a nursing home in Seattle. It's called Harbor House—in Magnolia. I'll e-mail all this to you. Her name is Martha."

"Thanks, Skye. I really appreciate it."

There was a slight pause on the other end. "I hope it helps. So, say hi to Mom for me, okay?"

"Sure. And I'm hoping you'll help plan her sixtieth."

There was a brief silence. "I'm away at a conference tomorrow and things can get busy real fast here. I'll get back to you as soon as I can about that."

Sam had heard that line before. Still, Skye had come quickly to her help regarding Danny's father, and if she had to hassle her about the party, best to do it later. "Keep it in mind, though, okay?"

When she spoke, her sister's voice was decidedly cooler. "Sure. Talk to you soon."

The line was disconnected and Sam had the unsettling feeling that perhaps she ought to have taken the opportunity to have a real talk with her sister. But once again, she'd chickened out.

## CHAPTER THREE

HARBOR HOUSE must have been a private mansion in the days of the timber barons. An imposing Victorian-style house, it perched on a hilltop far above Elliott Bay, off Magnolia Boulevard. Sam guessed that a hundred years or so ago, when the house was new, it had had a spectacular view of the harbor. Now other modern palatial homes checkered the hillside, and the nursing home's upper balconies looked down on rooftops and skyscrapers in the distance.

Still, if a nursing home was in your future, this would be the one to choose. If you could afford it. A glimpse of the circular driveway leading to a portico surrounded by large terra-cotta pots of brightly colored annuals and groomed gardens beyond confirmed the place was well-funded. Of course, inside was what really counted.

But five minutes later Sam realized she wasn't going to see any more of the inside than the large foyer with its polished marble floor and the frowning, fiftysomething woman sitting behind an imposing oak desk.

"I'm sorry," the woman repeated, "but if your name isn't on Mrs. Sullivan's guest list, then you won't be able to see her."

*Guest list?* Sam stared at the austere woman in her dark, tailored business suit and curbed an impulse to be flippant. "I don't understand. I told Chase I'd be seeing his mother and I thought he'd take care of it."

The woman abruptly raised her head from the binder she'd been referring to. Sam caught the slight hesitation in her face and quickly added, "My parents are old family friends and I'm just in town for a few days. I left a voice message for Chase to say I'd meet him here, but perhaps he didn't get it."

A narrowing of steel-gray eyes hinted that Sam may have made a mistake.

"Mr. Sullivan's regular visiting time is ten in the morning on Mondays, so he's due here tomorrow. I'll ask him if he'd like your name placed on the list." Her quick smile indicated the matter was finished.

Sam struck a thoughtful pose, extending it as long as possible. "I suppose I could arrange to stay another day. Thanks." She started to leave, eyeing the elevator beyond the desk and wondering if she could reach it before the Dragon Lady could stop her.

"What was the name again?"

"Uh…Winston. Samantha Winston."

The woman wrote a Post-it and placed it on the cover of the binder. "I'll make sure this comes to Mr. Sullivan's attention when he arrives tomorrow."

*Oh, it'll come to his attention, all right.* Sam smiled and walked out the etched-glass main door.

ON MONDAY MORNING, Chase pulled into a space on the street. He never used the Harbor House visitor parking lot at the north end of the property because he suspected the sight of a battered pickup would draw complaints. The last thing he wanted was to have any negative attention directed at his mother. Not that she'd be aware of it, but it was the least he could do, considering. He grabbed the small box of peppermint patties—his mother's favorite treat—and climbed out of the truck.

It was a bright sunny day and he hoped to be back at his workshop in time to give the cabinet he was making a last coat of stain. The oak cabinet had been a rush order and he knew it wasn't going to measure up to his personal standard, but as long as the customer was happy, that was all that mattered. The bonus for quick work was going to be a down payment on a new truck. As he walked through the gated entry to Harbor House, his attention was caught by a red Acura parked over the yellow line marking the start of the driveway.

The owner was going to get a ticket if the vehicle was left there for any length of time. He'd seen it happen many times while visiting. The management was very strict about things like that. It was one of the many reasons he'd chosen Harbor House for his mother. The rules were always taken seriously, which meant that security was never compromised. That was of utmost importance.

Chase debated informing the receptionist but decided against it. When he pushed open the massive glass door, the woman behind the front desk looked up, smiling.

"Morning, Mrs. MacDonald," he said. "How're you to-day?"

"I'm great, Mr. Sullivan. And you?"

"Couldn't be better. How's my mother?"

"Doing well, I understand. She's waiting for you in the conservatory."

Chase smiled at the phrase. As if his mother remembered his regular visiting days. Yet the routine seldom varied. All a part of the incredible pretense of the place, he thought. Forget this is a home for sick old people who don't know their own children anymore. He forced aside the bitterness, wondering what had suddenly brought it on. He'd been doing this for almost two years and should be used to it.

"Great. Thanks." He started for the elevator when she stopped him.

"Oh, Mr. Sullivan. There's someone else here to see your mother." She stood up, tilting her head slightly to the right.

Chase noticed a woman sitting in a wing chair at the end of the hallway, a few feet beyond the elevator. On cue, the woman headed his way. As she emerged from the shadowy interior, Chase realized at once this was no one he knew.

"Hello, Chase. It's been a while. I can see you don't recognize me."

Chase squinted, as if that might jog his memory. Her raven hair swayed slightly against a slender neck rising out of a crisp white shirt topped by a torso-hugging, sky-blue sweater. Her tight black jeans emphasized long, slim legs. She certainly had his attention.

"Samantha *Winston*," she said.

He felt a sudden tightening in his chest and hoped he didn't look as confused as he felt. "Uh…" He stammered, uncertain if this was just a big coincidence or something far worse.

"Relative of *Daniel Winston?*"

Chase stared blankly at the bright red lips curved in a knowing smile. No coincidence, but what exactly was her game?

"I came to see your mother, but perhaps we could have a little chat first?"

She glanced at Mrs. MacDonald, listening in from her desk.

"Feel free to use the front parlor," the receptionist said with a slight sniff.

Chase couldn't take his eyes off the woman standing in front of him, someone who had dredged up a name from the past and yet was a complete stranger. Finally he responded, "Thanks Mrs. MacDonald. Uh…I'll pop in to see my mother in a few minutes."

"Of course, Mr. Sullivan. I'll tell the nurse you'll be arriving shortly."

Chase headed for the room to the left of the elevator. The parlor, designed as a small but comfortable living room in someone's home, was one of several in the establishment for patient visits with family members and was usually full on the weekends. But on Mondays it was relatively empty, one of the reasons he chose to make his weekly visits then. As soon as he entered the room, he set the box of chocolates down on a table and closed the door behind her.

"All right," he said. "Who are you and what do you want?"

She paid him the courtesy of dropping the coy act. In fact, he was surprised to see her face redden.

"Sorry for the ruse," she said, "but I thought you might not want the receptionist to hear what I have to say." She paused. "My real name is Samantha Sorrenti."

"Go on," he said. Her unexpected nervousness calmed him. Whatever she was about to spring on him, he decided he could handle it.

"Maybe we should sit." She pointed to a grouping of furniture around the fireplace.

Chase glanced at it, then back to her. A cozy chat wasn't what he had in mind. "I'm fine." He was almost enjoying her discomfort, but he knew not to let his guard down. She had, after all, used that name for a reason.

"Contrary to what I told the receptionist, I haven't come here to see your mother. Sorry about that. It was you I wanted to meet."

*No kidding.* He waited for her to continue.

"Do you remember Emily Benson?"

He hesitated. It wasn't the question he was expecting.

"She used to waitress at a diner in the northwest part of the city. I think it was called Baywicks."

"Yes, I remember the diner. And Emily." He had a sudden image of her. Pale, almost too thin. She was a chainsmoker and always running out to the sidewalk on her breaks. But she'd been a friendly face in a turbulent time for him. And a good listener. God, how many times he must have bored her with his incessant philosophizing. In those days he'd still had something to be idealistic about—before his indulged life came crashing down around him.

"How is Emily?"

"Not good."

He frowned. "How so?"

"She's dying. Lung cancer." She cleared her throat and looked down at the Persian carpet.

It was a moment before the words registered. The Emily he remembered had been a hardworking young woman whose lack of formal education had restricted her opportunities. Yet she'd had spirit and was always positive about her future.

"I'm very sorry to hear that," he murmured at last. Their eyes connected suddenly—Emily linking two strangers. Chase turned away and closed his. He was in Emily's apartment, taking in the Salvation Army furnishings and the quirky decor. He even remembered what she'd said: *It's not much, but it's all mine.* Poverty hadn't diminished her pride. He'd liked that about her. No apologies. And now she was dying of cancer.

"Is…uh…someone looking after her?" He dearly hoped so.

"She's in the palliative-care ward at Our Lady of Mercy Hospital."

She hadn't really answered his question. "I meant… does she have someone? A family member?"

When she didn't answer, he met her gaze. There was a peculiar expression in her face. "Emily once told me she had no family," he clarified. "That's why I'm asking. Does she have a partner?" He thought he saw tears in the woman's eyes and for the first time, wondered if she was related to Emily.

"No. She's a single mom."

"Oh?"

"She has a twelve-year-old son. His name is Danny. For his father."

His eyes were fixed on her face, but all he saw was the wall shifting behind her. The framed paintings seemed to project outward and the floor moved beneath his feet. Not an earthquake, he told himself as he backed into a wing chair and sat. *Just your past rumbling toward you.*

She was talking, but he couldn't make out what she was saying over the buzzing in his head. *You have a son. Emily's dying of cancer. A son.* When he could focus again, she was standing in front of him, her eyes narrowed.

"I'm sorry if this is a shock," she was saying.

*A shock?* That was rich. "Who are you?" His voice sounded hollow, disbelieving to his own ears.

"Samantha Sorrenti."

He shook his head. "No, I mean, what's your connection to Emily Benson?"

"Well, I have this business. Kind of an agency. I look for—"

He jumped to his feet. "You're a private investigator? Who are you working for?" He was starting to put it together now. Of course. It made sense. He pointed a finger at her. "Who sent you here? What do you want from me?"

She stepped back.

"Is everything all right?"

They both looked toward the receptionist holding open the door. "Mr. Sullivan?"

"It's okay, Mrs. MacDonald," he replied.

"All right." She looked from Chase to Samantha and hesitated, as if reluctant to leave.

"If you don't mind…" he prompted, turning his attention to Samantha.

"Of course." She closed the door quietly behind her.

Chase stared at the woman standing mere inches away. Up close, he noticed her gray eyes were flecked with green and their appraisal of him was unflinching. That was good, he thought, because nothing unnerved him more than a tearful woman, and there was no way he was going to be deterred from finding out what the hell was going on. "Sit," he said, pointing to the love seat behind her.

She hesitated, as if she didn't like his tone, but did as he asked. "Look—" she began.

"No, you look," he said, cutting her off. "I've no idea what you have to do with Emily Benson, but—"

"If you'll give me a chance," she said, her voice rising, "I'll be happy to explain."

He sat on the edge of the wing chair opposite her, leaning forward with his elbows resting on his knees. "Go ahead."

HIS VOICE WAS LOWER, calmer. He had the upper hand now, Sam thought, and he knew it. She was embarrassed at how badly she'd blown the whole thing. What had possessed her to use that Winston name? There'd been no point, other than putting him on the defensive right away. Maybe the recent memory of Danny's pinched and anxious face had compelled her to take the offensive—just in case Chase Sullivan proved to be one of those deadbeat dads. Yet the sudden blanching in his face when she'd told him suggested otherwise. Plus, he hadn't rushed to deny the possibility of paternity. And, he'd seemed just as shocked and upset that she might be a private investigator.

"I'm waiting," he said.

Samantha took a deep breath. No more games. All she had to do now was give him the facts and leave the rest to him. *Oh. And one more thing.* Try to get a commitment from him to see Danny so she could report back immediately. She had a feeling that might take longer than a few minutes in the parlor of a nursing home.

Sam moistened her lips, wondering why she felt so nervous. He certainly didn't look as scary as her mental picture of him from Danny's description. The long hair was shorter, scraping the collar of his polo-style shirt and he was clean shaven. Her glance drifted to his right arm, encased in the sleeve of his worn tweed sports jacket. Tattoo tucked away.

He was taller than she'd expected and heavier. But then, she only had Emily's description, and that was from thirteen years ago. But from the way the shirt stretched across what she could see of his chest, the weight was mostly muscle. He kept in shape. His eyes caught hers and she realized right away he knew she'd been checking him out.

"Confirming I'm the right man?" he asked.

The tone was not amused. Neither was the glint in his eye.

"Who are you working for?" he asked again.

"Emily and Danny…your son." She thought she saw him flinch when she added that. "And I need to clarify something. I'm not a private investigator."

"You said you had an agency. Looking for…?"

"Things. Items people might want to buy."

"What kinds of things?"

She sighed. "Rare books. Art objects. Coins. Whatever."

"And how long have you known Emily?"

He'd skipped the Danny connection, she noticed. Maybe still processing that. "I just met her a couple of days ago. I—"

"So how come you're working for her?"

"If you'll let me explain—"

"I've been waiting for you to do that," he said testily.

"Then why do you keep interrupting?"

He didn't respond, but Sam thought she saw a trace of satisfaction in his face. Angrily, she said, "Danny found my agency on the Internet. Unfortunately he overlooked the fact that I search for objects, not people. Anyway, he persuaded me to meet his mother and later…after…well, I agreed to help him out even though this is not what I do." She had to stop to calm herself, his unblinking gaze unnerving.

"Go on," he said.

"Time is running out for Emily." She cleared her throat and waited a moment. "They're desperate." She paused, thinking he might interject. He sat so still she wondered if he'd heard her. Then she noticed one of his fingers tapping silently on his knee. A metronome keeping time with his heartbeat?

"They have no other family," she went on. "When Emily…goes…Danny will have to be placed in foster care. That's why he decided to look for you."

He got up and moved to the large bay window in the center of the room. It looked onto an enclosed garden patio, and for the first time Sam realized there were some people sitting outside, bundled up against the fresh spring air. She wondered if his mother was one of those people and had a sudden pang of conscience. Had she spoiled *her* day, as well as her son's? Too late for guilt now, she told herself.

"Okay," he said, without turning around. After a long moment, he added, "You can go, then."

*"Pardon?"*

He pivoted on his heel. His face was set in stone. "Your job is finished now, right? You've done your bit."

"Well I…I suppose…I guess…"

"So you can go."

Reluctantly, she got up from the love seat. "What about Danny?"

"Danny's my business now." His expression was so intimidating she turned meekly toward the door and pulled it open.

His voice stopped her. "Unless you feel you're owed something more."

Frowning, she looked back at him. "What?"

"Maybe you think you ought to be paid more money. In that case…" He paused to dig into the inner pocket of his sport jacket and pulled out a small billfold.

"For your information," she said, fighting to keep her voice even, "I haven't been paid a cent and don't expect to be. I came here for Danny and Emily because I wanted to help them. They don't have some wealthy, blue-blood family to fall back on like you do." She spun around and walked out, slamming the door behind her.

Her brisk march along the carpeted hall to the main door was met by raised eyebrows from Mrs. MacDonald, sitting behind the reception desk. Sam passed her with scarcely a glance and exited onto the front steps, where she stopped to catch her breath.

He was right, of course. That was what bothered her so much. She'd completed the task she'd been asked to do and had no further reason to stick around. It was his peremptory dismissal of her that rankled. As if she were a delinquent student and he the school principal. She felt embarrassed at how passively she'd left, without a single word of reproach. But then, she'd never been good at the smart comeback. That was Skye's forte.

She continued on to her car, wondering exactly what she'd tell Emily and, especially, Danny, about Chase Daniel Sullivan. She wished she'd pinned the man down, made him say exactly when and where he'd meet Danny. Then she pictured that meeting. A cool, perhaps reluctant father and his desperate, vulnerable son. *Someone a lot stronger than Emily Benson needs to be on the scene, too.*

By the time Sam reached her car, she'd decided to be that person, and even the sight of a parking tag fluttering beneath her windshield wiper failed to dampen her resolve. Then she realized that she had no idea where Sullivan lived or, worse, if he would actually follow through and meet with Emily and Danny. She snatched the parking tag off the window and got into the car.

Her options were to go back and demand some kind of commitment from the man or drive on meekly home. Not much of a choice. A third option occurred to her. She quickly started up the engine, backed out and drove to the street, where she parked about fifty feet from the Harbor House driveway. When he left, she'd see him and follow.

She saw the front door of the nursing home open. A tall figure stood in the doorway, his back to the street. It was him. Sam slouched down in the seat as Chase headed for the sidewalk. She raised her head enough to watch him through her side mirror. He stopped for a second at the foot of the circular driveway, and Sam stiffened when she saw him look at the space where she'd originally parked. There was no way he knew what her car looked like because she'd arrived at the home ahead of him.

After a few seconds, he strode up the street away from her. Sam sat up and watched him. He seemed to be examining all the vehicles parked on both sides of the street. Looking for her? she wondered. Would he turn around and come back her way? Her heart thumped a bit more vigorously. But he stopped beside a pickup truck, his hand on the door. Suddenly he spun around and headed her way again.

Sam ducked her head enough to watch him walk back up the circular driveway and into Harbor House. She considered her next move. Assuming the truck was his, at least she could get the license-plate number for Skye to check out. She turned over the Acura engine and, with one last glance at the nursing-home front door, drove toward the pickup.

She stopped just short of it, jotting down the plate number on the back of her parking tag before driving off. She had no doubt at all that she'd be meeting up again with Chase Sullivan. No way was he going to have the last word. Metaphorically, anyway, she thought, recalling her last words to him. Something about wealthy blue bloods. Judging by the sad shape of that pickup truck, the "wealthy" bit wasn't apt.

"DID YOU FIND what you were looking for?" Mrs. MacDonald asked pleasantly as Chase entered the front door.

"Hmm?" he asked, preoccupied with how Samantha Sorrenti had vanished so quickly. He still had no idea why he'd run after her. Just that the instant she'd walked out the door he'd realized he really knew nothing about her. He hated the feeling of someone having information about him while he was left in the dark. Suppose he wanted to get in touch with her—God forbid!—or at least needed to contact her?

"Whatever you left in the truck?" Mrs. MacDonald prompted.

"Oh." He'd already forgotten the excuse he'd given her for his sudden rush out the door. "I was afraid I'd left the keys in the truck, but I hadn't. A bit forgetful today," he explained, and started down the hall to the conservatory.

"Mr. Sullivan?"

He turned around. The receptionist was standing up and grinning. In her right hand was the box of patties. Chase hoped he didn't look as ridiculous as he felt.

"Thanks," he said, striding back to the desk to collect the chocolates.

"She'll be expecting them," she said with a soft smile.

"For sure. Thanks again." He was grateful for the long, winding hallway to the conservatory, as it gave him time to compose himself. His mother was keenly sensitive to the moods of others and would mentally shut down if she detected a whiff of stress.

He stood at the entrance to the room whose decor mimicked a small concert area, with a highly polished piano in one corner and a musical stand beside it. Several folding chairs were stacked along one wall to accommodate patients and their guests when musical events were held. But now the area was scattered with wheelchairs, their occupants staring passively out the floor-to-ceiling bank of windows that looked out on the grounds behind the home.

Spotting his mother, whose chair was angled inward, Chase headed her way. Although he waved his fingers as he approached her wheelchair, she didn't focus on him until he was standing directly in front of her.

"Hi, Mom," he said, leaning over to kiss her cheek.

She didn't respond to the kiss, but at least she didn't flinch, as she did occasionally. "For me?" she asked as she noticed the box of patties in his hand.

Chase smiled. The weekly routine had begun. "For you," he said, handing the box to her. He unfolded one of the chairs and set it beside her wheelchair. Then he reached over to help her take the plastic wrap off the box. After he opened it and she held a patty in one trembling hand, her watery blue eyes met his and she asked, "Who are you again?"

He stroked the back of her other hand, resting on her lap. "I'm Chase, Mom."

She frowned. The name obviously triggered some faint memory, but not one she could connect to the man sitting next to her.

"The peppermint patty man," he clarified.

She smiled sweetly. "I love peppermint patties," she said, and nibbled delicately on the one she was holding.

Chase watched her savor the chocolate. He still remembered the first time he'd brought her a box and the gleam of delight in her eyes. The confection was the only bond between them. That fact had saddened him in the beginning, but now he accepted it and was content to simply watch her enjoy herself. He knew the nursing staff, for nutritional and health purposes, managed to spirit away the leftovers every week. His mother likely forgot about them, anyway, the instant they were out of sight. But he clung to the ritual, afraid of losing even that link with her.

When she finished eating a couple, he dabbed her lips with a tissue from one of the ubiquitous boxes in every room and made an attempt at conversation. But as always, her attention drifted. After a few minutes, he bent over to kiss her goodbye. "See you next week, Mom," he whispered. He set the box with the remaining patties on a table and headed out the door. He never looked back to see if she noticed he was leaving.

By the time he got to the truck, he'd decided to forgo his weekly latte fix. He needed some quiet time away from people to think about what had happened that afternoon. Driving away, he impulsively made a right at the first intersection.

The tree-lined street wound up the hillside above Harbor House and Magnolia Boulevard. He hadn't been along this route for years, but little had changed. Some of the larger homes had been subdivided into apartment units, but the cul-de-sac he turned onto hadn't changed at all. Especially the house at the very end. Chase pulled over and switched off the engine.

Funny that he could view the vine-covered stone exterior and the wrought iron gate with so little emotion. Even now most of the memories of the place were unhappy ones. He wondered who lived there now. Not that it mattered. When he'd been away all those years after his father's death, sleeping in grungy boardinghouses or sometimes in the rough, he'd often imagined the dark, wood-paneled interior and polished hallways. The quiet, too.

As a child he'd seldom had friends visit. His mother had suffered from migraines and couldn't bear the noise and exuberance of children. When he was a teenager, he began to spend more and more time away until he'd eventually disappointed everyone—or perhaps no one—by moving out altogether. Then he couldn't get enough noise and bright lights and loud, raucous people.

Chase wiped a hand over his face. He'd awakened that morning anticipating the customary routine of his weekly visit. Mother first, then a stop at the nearest Starbucks for his latte. On to his favorite hardware store to browse or perhaps pick up an order. If he had time, he'd stop at the market and buy croissants at the bakery he loved best.

Over the past few years impulse and spontaneity had given way to order and routine. He'd made a new life for himself. Not the one he'd expected to have as a teenager, but still…a life he could handle. Now it was going to be blown apart, shattered and reformed into something he had no vision of, much less feeling for.

He'd given up on the notion of a family for himself years ago. That acceptance had led to a couple of broken relationships, which he'd regretted at the time. It was ironic that the one-night fling he'd had with Emily Benson had produced exactly what he'd sworn never to have. A child. Chase lowered his forehead onto his hands, clutching the steering wheel. Omigod. *A twelve-year-old son.*

# CHAPTER FOUR

SAMANTHA WAS DUE at her mother's for dinner by six, so, figuring that would give her enough time for a visit with Emily Benson, decided to drop by the hospital on her way. As she rode up to the palliative-care ward, she hoped that Danny would not be there. She thought he might have a lot more questions than his mother and she wanted to avoid having to answer one in particular. *Why didn't you get Chase Sullivan's address and phone number?*

Of course, she could explain that she'd immediately called her FBI sister and left a message asking her to get an address from the license plate. But she had a feeling Danny would consider the excuse lame. And it was.

Sam was relieved to find Emily alone, sitting up in bed and leafing through a magazine. She looked a hundred percent better than she had the last time Sam had seen her.

"Hi, Emily."

"Sam, I wasn't expecting to see you so soon," Emily murmured, a look of apprehension in her face.

"Mind if I close the door?"

"Leave it open a crack. The nurses like to be able to look in on me."

Sam did so. She ought to have thought of that. A patient in palliative care could have a crisis at any moment. When she sat down, Emily turned the magazine over on her lap and quietly asked, "Good news or bad?"

Right to the point, Sam thought, just like her son. "I've found a man called Chase Daniel Sullivan whom I believe to be Danny's father."

*"Chase?"*

"Yes. His father was Winston Daniel Sullivan, but he died about thirteen years ago. He lived here in Seattle and was an owner of an import-export business."

"Uh-huh. And this man…Chase? Have you met him? What makes you think he's Danny's father?"

"I have met him. Same eyes," Sam said at once. "Hair color, too. Plus, he remembered you."

Emily looked away. Sam waited for her to digest this very significant piece of information. Finally Emily asked, "How did he look?"

The question didn't really surprise Sam. Most women would have wanted to know what an ex had said about them. Not Emily. She either didn't care or knew it was irrelevant. Likely the latter, Sam thought.

"Short hair. No sign of a pierced ear, but I can't report on the tattoo because his arms were covered."

Emily smiled. "I remember that tattoo. Some kind of Tibetan prayer, I think. You'd have thought from his appearance, that it would be a snake or a big heart with MOM in the center." She waited a moment. "So…uh…what did he say when you told him about Danny? Or did you?"

"He was obviously shocked, but he didn't deny the possibility of being Danny's father."

"But what did he *say?*"

Sam played back the scene mentally, but it came out as a swirl of emotion rather than facts. She recalled her frustration when he peremptorily dismissed her. "He was more concerned about you," she said finally, telling herself that wasn't really a lie so much as an assumption.

Emily looked away toward the window again. "I've

been thinking about all of this the last couple of days. Now I'm not so sure I want Danny to meet him."

Those quietly spoken words bounced around the room. "Why not?" was the only response Sam could manage, but she was thinking, a bit late for second thoughts now.

Emily gazed out the window a few seconds longer, then returned her gaze to Sam. "I don't know if you'll understand."

"I can try." *Or I could scream,* which wouldn't do in a palliative-care ward.

"As much as I hate the thought of Danny being in foster care, I'm scared about him being with a man who may be torn about having a son suddenly forced on him. I mean, unless Danny—Chase—has drastically changed, I know he'd do the right thing by my Danny."

Sam thought back to Chase's end-of-conversation remark that Danny was his business now. *Business.* "I got that impression, too," she understated.

"So that's not the issue. It's more…what if he comes to resent Danny later? This is going to affect his whole life. And maybe he already has a family."

That hadn't occurred to Sam, and not for the first time, she marveled at how she'd screwed up. When Danny had pressed her to look for his father, he'd certainly had far more faith in her investigative skills than she deserved. Plus, there was the other thing—the small matter of an old FBI inquiry into the family business. She really knew nothing about Chase Sullivan. Maybe Emily was right. On the other hand, there was Danny, clinging to his dream.

"But isn't this about Danny? He's so determined to find his father and if Chase is his father, then he'll do the right thing. He'll adapt. Isn't that enough?" Sam's gut feeling was that Danny had to know.

"*Adapt.* I think Danny deserves more than a father who

just adapts. And he's a tough kid, you know? I think he can adapt, too. There are a lot of great foster homes out there and hopefully I'll have time to be involved in helping Children's Services look for one."

"But it's not the same, is it? As being with your own father?"

Emily's sigh indicated more fatigue than frustration. "No, it's not the same. But it may not be worse if that father really doesn't want you. And I don't want Danny to have to deal with that. I won't be here to help him."

Sam stared at the floor. She could say nothing about the undeniable truth of that last sentence, but she had to make one last pitch. "I just think Danny deserves to know. He's old enough to handle the problems that will come with this change in his life."

Emily thought that over for a moment. Finally she said, "Yes, but he's still learning how to handle losing one parent." She stopped then and looked down. A huge tear landed on the magazine on her lap.

Sam wanted to comfort her. But she also knew words would change nothing and, besides, she knew what Emily was saying. Losing his mother was going to be traumatic enough for Danny. Realizing the father he'd been looking for might be less than enthused about his newfound son would be devastating. Still…

"Emily," she said once she could trust herself to speak. "Give the idea some more thought."

Emily dabbed at her face with a tissue. "All right. I suppose I need time to absorb this, too. So let's not tell Danny just yet."

"No. But soon we have to tell him something."

Emily nodded. "Soon." She sank against her pillows.

Sam got out of her chair. "I'll come by in a couple of days, all right?"

Another nod.

Sam closed the door gently behind her. On the elevator ride down, she realized something that made her catch her breath. She'd have to find Chase Sullivan before he found Emily and Danny. And she doubted he'd be happy to see her again.

SAM KNEW the question would come but still braced herself when it did.

"So what's the latest with that boy?" Her mother was pulling items from the refrigerator and missed the look on Sam's face. "The one whose mother is dying. And how is she doing, by the way? How much more time does she have?"

As usual, Nina was tossing out questions too quickly for Sam to answer any of them. "I don't know, medically, anyway. I visited this afternoon. She looked better than the last time I saw her." *At least until I had my talk with her.*

Nina glanced up from salad preparation. "Does that mean you've decided to take on the case?"

"Yes, Mom, it does. And I took your suggestion and called Skye. She gave me some information."

Nina appeared to mull that over. "Good for you. So what's happening now?"

"Well, thanks to Skye, I think I've found Danny's father."

"Already?"

"It wasn't that hard."

"You said, 'think.'"

"There's been no DNA test, but he looks a lot like Danny and he didn't deny that he is the father."

"Still, it's not an indisputable fact."

Sam chewed the inside of her cheek. "No, it's not. Want me to set the table?"

Nina raised an eyebrow. "I thought we'd eat right here, at the counter. If you don't mind."

Sam shrugged. "Fine with me."

While she retrieved cutlery from the drawer beneath the work counter, Nina added, "So what now?"

"Well, it's complicated."

"How?"

"Now Emily isn't sure if she wants Danny to know I may have found his father. She's worried that the dad— his name is Chase Sullivan—will feel pressured to take him and will eventually resent Danny."

"Sounds like Emily's a smart woman."

"Oh, she is, but she's only looking at it from her point of view."

Nina frowned. "Yes, but she's the mother and she's dying. She wants what's best for her son."

"Even if it means Danny not knowing his father?"

"Sometimes those sacrifices must be made for the good of the child."

Sam stared at her mother. She wondered if they were still talking about Emily and Danny. "Is that why you didn't take Dad back when he asked?"

Nina paled, but didn't hesitate to answer. "Yes, because I didn't want my children to grow up in an atmosphere of distrust and betrayal and bitterness."

"But maybe Skye and I could have handled that."

"Perhaps, but I knew *I* couldn't. And I thought better to have one parent and live in peace and harmony than to be around two adults who'd grown to dislike one another. I had to make a choice, Samantha. Just like Emily."

"But what if it's not the right choice?"

Nina sighed. "Maybe it won't be. People can only go with their instincts. With what feels right to them."

"Is that what you did?"

Nina placed her hand on top of Sam's. "I hoped it was the right choice." She looked into Sam's eyes. "What do you think?"

Sam wasn't sure she wanted the talk to go this way, but it was too late to back out now. "I'm not sure. I never had the chance to find out otherwise."

"No, you didn't. But I never stopped your father from seeing you girls."

Sam bit down on her lip. It always came to that. The irrefutable fact that he never had.

"Does it still hurt?" her mother asked.

"I don't know, frankly. It shouldn't, now that I'm all grown up." She forced a smile.

"Maybe that's why you care so much about Danny. Why it's important for you to have him connect with his father."

Analyzing again, Sam thought, but she had to admit how close to the mark her mother might be. "Maybe," she whispered.

After a few seconds her mother said, "I think the lasagna's ready."

SAM LEFT her mother's condo early. She had an appointment at ten the next morning, but needed to make a few phone calls to organize the final details of the sale and shipment of a Thai Buddha for the client. The report confirming the provenance of the Buddha was supposed to be e-mailed to her office before nine and her transatlantic phone call agreeing to the vendor's terms had to be placed by nine-thirty. The adrenaline rush of such tight scheduling was a part of the job that Sam loved and a contrast to the long, sometimes dull, hours spent searching the Internet or obscure catalogs for items.

When she noticed she had voice mail, she was tempted to ignore it. Her gut feeling was that Danny had found out she'd visited Emily and wanted to pump her for information. Not that she *had* to return his call until the next day, anyway, but she bet he'd be waiting by the phone and she doubted either of them would get any sleep if she didn't call him back.

But the message was from Skye. "Hey, Sam, got your call about the plate number for Chase Sullivan. I must admit, I am impressed. Didn't take you long to rustle him up at all. Maybe you missed your calling. So here's the info. The guy lives on Bainbridge Island. Cool, eh? Remember how we always wanted to open up a little toy shop there when we were kids? Anyway, he has a carpentry business called Sullivan's Fine Furniture on Primrose Lane, wherever that is. I don't imagine the island has grown too much in the last few years, so it shouldn't be too hard to track him down. Listen, kind of off topic, but I've got an idea. My conference sucks, so I've decided to blow off the last two days, go back to the office and schedule some holiday time.

"I haven't seen Mom since…um…Christmas, and you said you'd like some help with her sixtieth, so I think I'll fly out there for a week or two. And like I said, since you've tracked down Chase Sullivan, maybe I'll pop into the office there and have a look at the old case, see if anything's been done on it since I left. So I'll call Mom and tell her she's going to be having a guest for a week or so. See ya soon. Bye."

Sam jotted down the address, deleted the message and slumped onto the sofa. Great. All she needed was Skye added to the mix of Emily, Danny and now, Chase Sullivan. It was typical of her sister to butt into her business. *First she compliments me on my detective work and then she decides to come and take over.*

And in spite of the recent phone calls, Sam knew she couldn't go through the whole Christmas thing again with Skye. The accusations and the expressions of wounded innocence. *How could you think that? What kind of sister do you think I am?* The kind who kisses her twin's fiancé. With passion. That kind.

Sam groaned and headed for bed, sensing that the next few days were going to get a lot more complicated.

CHASE WAS IN THE BACK of the shop when he heard the tinkle of the doorbell, indicating someone had just entered. He'd hated the cuteness of that bell when he'd bought the place a year ago, but knew he'd be spending a lot of time in the workroom and common sense—*business* sense—had prevailed. He was clamping two sections of a chair together and rather than have to stop, he leaned forward to peer around the door frame. A woman was closing the door. Something familiar about her. When she turned around, Chase quickly withdrew his head. It was *her.* He couldn't believe it. And how had she found him? Irrationally he convinced himself that if he stayed quiet, she just might leave.

"Hello?" she called out.

Any second she'd wander into the back and catch him perching on his stool. Chase swore under his breath, set the clamp down and headed into the showroom part of his small shop.

"Oh," she said. "I wasn't sure if anyone was here."

She was either a skilled liar or a fool, and Chase doubted the latter. "Bainbridge isn't so far from the city that we can leave our businesses unattended," he said dryly.

"Oh? But it has the reputation of being such a tight-knit community. Neighbors looking out for each other."

The look she gave him indicated she was up to the challenge of a sparring contest. Chase was having no part of it. "Miss…uh…"

"Sorrenti. Samantha Sorrenti." Her tone and the look

on her face told him she knew he hadn't really forgotten her name.

"I've no idea why you're here," he said, leaning against one of the handmade oak display cases. "I'm sure you're not just touring the island, and I have nothing more to say to you. If you've come to hound me about contacting Emily's son—"

"And *your* son."

"If you say so."

"That's not what you said yesterday."

"I don't recall saying anything about being the father of the boy."

"His name is *Danny*."

Chase held his breath, fighting to keep calm. She was doing it again, drawing him into a verbal wrangle that he knew could only end badly for him. It wasn't his kind of game.

"And you know in your heart he's your son," she added.

He did, but he wasn't going to admit that to her. "I told you I would contact Emily and I will. Now I'd like you to leave my shop."

The features in her face seemed to tighten and she turned her head. Bingo, he thought. That got to her.

After a moment, she quietly said, "I went to see Emily yesterday afternoon and told her about our meeting."

A surge of anger rose inside him. What was it about this woman that she felt no impunity at all about interfering in his personal life? "I specifically asked you—"

She held up a hand, cutting him off. "I know what you *told* me. I also know that I don't take orders from you. Once again you're not letting me explain."

"But that's the issue here, isn't it? Why you feel you even need to explain. You found me and you passed on some information to me. Yes, significant information that affects me in a deeply personal way. And the key word there is *personal*, Miss Sorrenti. So now that I have that information, my question to you is, why are you still around?"

"I'm still *around*, as you so nicely put it, because Emily made a request of me that meant I'd have to contact you again."

Judging from her expression, Chase guessed the request was not one she'd agreed with. He waited for her to continue, refusing to be drawn into any more talk than necessary. Besides, he could see that she was struggling to keep her voice steady and he wasn't certain if that pleased him—in a petty way—or not.

Finally she said, "Emily isn't certain now that she wants you to meet Danny. She'd like some time—not that she has a lot of it—to think things through. And she definitely wants to talk to you first, alone."

It wasn't what he'd expected. He'd spent the whole night tossing and turning over in his mind all the scenarios of a face-to-face with Danny. *His son.* By daybreak he'd accepted the very real possibility of Danny being his son and had even begun to accept that he'd have to bring him into his life in some way. The suggestion that this might not happen was something he couldn't take in, at least not at the moment. He turned his back on her, hoping she'd leave. He needed to be left alone with this news—to digest it and decide what his options were.

After what seemed an interminable length of time, she said, "So now that I've done what Emily has requested, the ball is back in your court, Mr. Sullivan. Goodbye."

He waited for the door to close before moving nearer to one of the windows to see her climb into a small red Acura parked in front of the shop. So that was *her* car parked illegally at Harbor House.

WHO WAS SHE KIDDING? Not that there was anyone else around to impress, anyway, but there was work to do. It was just that for the past few days she'd done little more than go through the motions. She seethed every time she thought back to the beginning of the week and her visit to Bainbridge Island. Her intentions had been good, she rationalized. She was doing Emily a favor and had expected that she'd be bringing a message he'd be happy to receive. But all expectations ceased the second she stepped out of her car.

She'd had to double-check the address because the chic simplicity of Sullivan's Fine Furniture didn't fit with the battered pickup truck he'd been driving. And the austere, almost stark exterior of the place also jarred against the whimsical cuteness of the neighboring stores, decorated with fake gingerbread and seafaring motifs. But the real surprise was what was inside.

The carvings of birds and pieces of exquisite hand-crafted furniture were as good, if not better, than any she'd seen in online catalogs, or even in any exclusive furniture shop. The place was a gem tucked away out of public view on Bainbridge Island. Sam doubted the locals could afford his pieces and wondered how Sullivan advertised off-island? Perhaps he didn't. Perhaps clients found him by chance. Perhaps he preferred it that way.

The thought reminded her of Skye's investigation into the family business. Maybe part of Chase Sullivan's hostility had more to do with that than with the discovery that he'd fathered a son. Whatever the reason, he obviously couldn't get rid of her fast enough and she was all too happy to oblige. Though why she was still fuming about the visit three days later mystified her. She'd called Emily right away, giving her an edited version of events and passing on the address of the place. There was no directory listing for Chase, but she decided to check out the Internet and found a Web site for the shop that was as austere as the place itself. An e-mail address and phone number were also provided.

Sam gave up pretending to work and decided to leave for the day. The phone calls she needed to make could be done at home and besides, she was happy to defer the last step in her most recent job. A man from Portland had e-mailed photographs of a twelfth-century Indian Buddha he'd recently purchased and wondered if she could find another one for his collection. She'd forwarded the picture and description to a curator at a Seattle museum who moonlighted as an appraiser. Her report indicated the Buddha was most probably a fake. Now Sam not only had to inform the man that he'd spent a small fortune on a twentieth-century reproduction but convince him of that fact.

She locked up, thinking her trip to Bainbridge had left her "prickly and snarly," as her sister used to say in their adolescence, when arguments were a daily occurrence. Thoughts of Skye reminded Sam to call her back and tell her not to bother coming home just yet. As far as Sam was concerned, the whole Sullivan-Benson affair was finished, and their mother's sixtieth was still a month away. She was still forming the voice-mail message she'd leave Skye when she stood in front of her condo door and realized it was unlocked. Either she'd forgotten to lock up when she'd left that morning or someone had broken in. Well, not exactly broken in, since there was no sign of forced entry. Someone with a key, then. And only two other people had keys to her condo. No, wait. Three? Had Todd returned his after their breakup? Damn.

She cautiously opened the door and noticed two things. The shower was going full blast and a black duffel bag was sitting on the foyer floor. She didn't recognize the bag but wasn't alarmed. Burglars didn't usually shower. Still, she tiptoed toward the bathroom and reached it as the door swung open. Sam felt her stomach plummet.

It was like looking at her mirror image. Almost. Except this one was wrapped in her bath towel and dripping on the tiled floor.

"Hey, sister," Skye said, flashing a big smile.

# CHAPTER FIVE

"My surprise evidently has left you speechless," said Skye.

"I wasn't really expecting you. I thought at first someone had broken in."

"And taken a shower while burgling the place?"

"Ha ha," Sam muttered.

"Come on, lighten up," teased Skye.

"You might have let me know you were coming."

"I left a voice mail."

"You said you were coming home. Not to *my* place."

Skye stared at her long and hard. "So I guess I should get dressed and leave you to *your* place." She went back into the bathroom and closed the door behind her.

Damn and double damn, thought Sam. We haven't seen each other for six months and we're already pushing each other's buttons. She retreated into the kitchen and put the kettle on for tea. When Skye emerged from the bathroom minutes later, Sam called out, "Want some tea before you go?"

Skye appeared in the doorway. "Tea? It's almost five. Got any wine?"

"I'm surprised you haven't already checked."

"I was going to do that after my shower."

Her sudden grin tugged Sam back to their childhood, before adolescent rivalry had reared its ugly head. Sam turned off the stove. "Wine it is," she said, pulling the refrigerator door open. She glanced at her sister while opening a bottle of Riesling. "When did you cut your hair?"

"A couple of months ago. When did you cut yours?"

"About the same time."

They smiled at each other, understanding the weird connection of coincidence with identical twins. Their lives had been full of such parallels, until distance made any comparisons impossible. Distance and the fact they'd scarcely spoken to each other in the last six months. Sam frowned.

"Okay, so what's *really* the problem?" asked Skye, picking up her wineglass.

Now wasn't the time, Sam knew. "Nothing. I wasn't expecting you so soon. Just wondering if Mom knows you're here already. "

"Not yet. Thought I'd—"

"She hates surprises," interjected Sam.

"I was going to say I planned to call her from here."

"Oh." Sam peered into her glass, thinking she was always making assumptions about Skye and having them fizzle in her face. *Maybe the problem is with me. No. I wasn't going behind her back with* her *fiancé.*

"Living room?" Sam cocked her head toward the L-shaped area off the galley kitchen. She led the way, taking the armchair opposite the couch.

"No changes here," said Skye.

Sam glanced around the small apartment and its simple furnishings. In spite of a couple of expensive art pieces— an eighteenth-century Chinese porcelain bowl and a one-of-a-kind Lalique vase—the place was almost spartan. She thought suddenly of Chase Sullivan's shop and the few pieces of furniture she'd seen there the other day, wondering what his reaction might be were she to turn up again, only this time as a customer.

"Why the smile?"

"Hmm?" Sam looked across at Skye. "Oh, nothing, really. I was just thinking that except for a few things, the apartment is pretty bare."

"Yeah, but the few things are really beautiful."

"I guess." Sam sipped her wine. The dead stop in the conversation was merely another confirmation of the widening gap between them. The Christmas-Todd thing seemed destined to be the "elephant in the room" no one would talk about, consigning their conversation to small talk. She wanted to say, "Look, if you'll just say you're sorry, then I can forgive you," but she knew Skye was no more capable of apologizing then she was of forgiving. They'd established this pattern sometime in early childhood, and age had only entrenched them.

"What're you thinking about?" Skye suddenly asked.

Caught out, Sam felt her face heat up. "Oh, nothing much," she said, turning her head toward the window. She glimpsed Skye's face as she did so, noting her sister knew she was lying. The silence stretched.

Finally Skye said, "I guess I should be going."

"Are you going to call Mom?"

"I'll call her on my cell in the taxi."

Sam hesitated, then said, "I can give you a ride."

"It's a bit out of your way, Sam. Unless you were planning to see Mom tonight, anyway."

"No, I wasn't."

"Well, then." Skye slapped her palms on her thighs and got up from the couch.

Sam sat motionless, listening to Skye gather up her things from the bathroom and when she heard the zip of the duffel bag, she forced herself out of the chair to say goodbye.

Skye was standing at the door, her bag in hand. She looked expectantly at Sam.

"Sure you don't want a ride?"

"Nah. I can grab a cab at the corner." Skye paused. "I like your hair."

Sam smiled. "Thanks. I like yours, too."

"Almost identical."

"Almost."

Skye opened the door and suddenly stopped. "I got side-tracked a bit. Meant to ask how that case of yours is going."

"Case?"

"You know—the boy, his father and the dying mom."

Sam felt her skin prickle. *Trust you to phrase it so casually.* "Uh, well, okay."

Skye leaned against the door frame, obviously in no hurry to leave. "I took some holiday time—I think I mentioned that in my voice mail. If you like, I could give you some help with it."

Sam looked her sister in the eye. "I'm fine, but thanks, anyway. Case is solved—or resolved."

"Oh? Father acknowledging paternity?"

"Basically."

Skye nodded thoughtfully, then said, "Well, that's good for the kid…I suppose. I'm still curious, though."

"About what?"

The sharpness in her voice made Skye straighten up. She gave Sam a puzzled look. "About the fraud thing. With the guy's family's business."

Sam waved a hand. "That's history. The important thing is Danny linking up with his father."

"Maybe. Unless…"

"Unless what?"

"Unless the father could potentially be a felon."

Sam stared at Skye in disbelief. "No way."

Skye arched a brow. "You sound so convinced, sis. Is he attractive, this Sullivan?"

"What are you suggesting, Skye?"

"Nothing. Just picking up a certain tone in your voice."

"Not everything boils down to the simple equation of man and woman," Sam retorted.

Skye's gaze traveled across Sam's face. "You sure about that?" She stepped into the hall, adding, "Anyway, as I said before, I've got some time on my hands. Might be worth checking out." She closed the door before Sam could reply.

Not that she had anything to say. Except for a slow mental count to ten to calm herself. She downed the rest of her wine and pondered her next move. Knowing Skye, she wouldn't be distracted from her goal. The key was to preempt her somehow. But then, what if Skye was right and Chase Sullivan *was* guilty of some past crime?

If Emily were in good health, Sam could discuss the problem with her and let her decide. Introduce the man to Danny and take a chance that he wasn't going to be hauled off to jail, or wait and see. Maybe Skye wouldn't find anything linking him to a crime. Hadn't she already investigated the family business—what was it called? Winds something—and ended up dropping the matter for lack of evidence?

Sam took the empty wineglasses into the kitchen and rinsed them. *You worry too much, Samantha Sorrenti.* That was what Skye always used to say, and some of the time, she'd been right. Yet in her dealings with others—especially her family—Skye herself didn't seem to worry *enough*. Chances were this idea of hers would never get off the ground. No point in keeping Danny from his biological father on some whim of Skye's. Sam reached for the phone to call Emily at the hospital and find out if she'd made a decision about seeing Chase. If things sped up a bit, Skye might backtrack or change her mind. *Maybe.*

When a young voice answered, Sam almost hung up. *Danny.* "Uh, could I please speak to Emily?"

There was a brief silence, followed by, "Who's calling?"

"Samantha Sorrenti."

"Have you found out something?"

The blurted question sounded both excited and apprehensive. Sam closed her eyes, debating whether to lie or evade. She opted for the latter. Emily could do the lying if it came to that. "I really need to speak to your mother, Danny," she said in a voice that permitted no argument.

His silence was long enough for her to consider other strategies when Emily abruptly came on the line. Sam heard her telling Danny to please leave the room *now*.

A few moments passed, then, "Samantha?" Emily sounded tired.

"Sorry. I didn't think Danny would be there."

"It's okay. Not your problem. He keeps forgetting I'm still his mother." There was a weak laugh. "I think we've reversed roles a bit these past few weeks."

"I guess that's understandable," Sam said, "and I suppose he's been anxious to hear some news."

"Mmm." A pause, then Emily said, "I feel bad, you know? I've been kinda lying to him. I tell myself they're important lies to protect him, but I've decided I can't do it much longer. If you hadn't called me, I was going to call you and tell you to go ahead."

"Go ahead?"

"You know, tell Daniel—I mean, Chase—that I'd like to see him."

Sam hesitated, wondering if she ought to tell Emily about Skye and what *she* was thinking of doing. But Emily had enough to deal with right now—keeping Danny from finding out about Chase until Emily had a chance to meet with him first. "Okay. I suppose that's a good idea."

"You sound doubtful."

Sam sighed. How to explain that contacting Chase Sullivan again was the last thing she wanted to do? "Not about him seeing you." She paused, knowing there was no way out of this one. "I guess I could call him for you."

"Would you mind? I'm not good with phone talk—especially for something emotional. And I don't think they're going to give me a day's leave to visit him." There was a sharp cackle of laughter mixed with the dry, uncontrollable cough that often overcame her.

When the horrible hacking finally stopped, Sam asked, "Meanwhile, what will you tell Danny?"

"That he'll just have to be patient."

Right. He'll really buy into that. "I'll get back to you then," Sam said.

When she hung up, she sank into the chair and dropped her head into her palms. *Was this ever going to end?*

"HE'S NOT OPEN YET."

Sam turned to the fiftysomething woman watering the flowers in the window boxes of her souvenir shop.

"Ten," the woman said, gesturing with her free hand to a sign on the door that Sam only just noticed.

Sam checked her watch. It was barely past nine and she was already regretting her decision to see Chase Sullivan, instead of calling him. On the ferry ride over, she'd wondered why the impulse had struck her at all. Hadn't she found the man totally irritating the last time she'd been on Bainbridge? Furthermore, she had to get back to the city in time for a noon phone call from an East Coast client. Perhaps she wanted to see his face when she told him Emily wanted to meet with him. She didn't have to be a real private investigator to know you could tell a lot from someone's face, especially at an emotional moment.

The woman stepped closer to the knee-high picket fence surrounding her tiny storefront and said, "If it's really important—and I know Chase can use the business—he's down the street having his morning coffee. Make a right just before you hit the main intersection. A few doors in from the corner. The Primrose Café. He's there every morning."

"Thanks, I appreciate it." As she headed for her car, the woman called out, "Easier to walk. It'll take ten minutes and parking in that section can be a hassle."

"Okay, thanks again." Sam hitched her shoulder bag higher and walked briskly toward the central shopping and tourist area of Winslow, the island's official town.

The short walk brought back memories for Sam, when she and her sister came here on school visits and, sometimes, with Nina and out-of-town guests. The community, with its arts-and-culture focus, pretty marinas and tourist shopping was a convenient thirty-five-minute ferry ride from the Seattle docks and many people who lived on the island commuted into the city to work.

Until yesterday, Sam hadn't made the trip to Bainbridge in more than fifteen years. The noticeable changes were along the main drag, with a profusion of tourist shops competing for space with longtime stores that provided the basic necessities. If Bainbridge was bigger, Sam guessed the big-box stores would start sprouting up as they had on the mainland. Perhaps they already had, somewhere beyond the central area. Still, she could see why someone with artistic talent and a penchant for a quieter life might opt to live here. Or perhaps someone with a past he wanted to forget.

As soon as she spotted Primrose Café, Sam stopped to think about how she was going to tackle the meeting. He'd be surprised of course, and not pleasantly. So he'd either take the offensive right away and try to get rid of her as

quickly as possible, or he'd refuse to speak to her altogether. Her best strategy would be polite insistence. Besides, he didn't seem the type to make a scene in a public
place.

She saw him as soon as she stepped inside. He was sitting in a corner booth, facing the door and reading the
*Seattle Times*. She hesitated, reminding herself that she
was here for Emily and Danny, not to score points in the
game of getting the last word. And if she managed to keep
the talk polite, she might even find out something about
his past. Something she could use to persuade Skye to
leave the man and his family alone.

He didn't look up from his paper for a full thirty seconds
while she stood in front of him. When he did, his expression of shock was immediately followed by apprehension.
No, thought Sam, more like fear. *He thinks I'm stalking
him.* Although the notion amused her, she didn't dare
smile. Instead she got right to the apology.

"I'm really sorry to bother you again, Mr. Sullivan, especially here in the middle of your...uh—" she glanced
down at the half-filled coffee mug and plate of crumbs
"—breakfast, but I spoke to Emily Benson last night and
she's changed her mind."

He frowned, but said nothing.

"She would like to see you, after all, as soon as possible."

His face remained impassive, though she noted a slight
tightening around his jaw. He folded the paper and set it
on the bench beside him. "You came all the way here to
tell me that?"

Sam shrugged. "Unfortunately I neglected to get your
phone number yesterday." It was almost the truth, she
told herself.

"Getting the facts must be lesson one in the private
eye's manual," he said.

She forced a smile. "Probably, but like I said, I'm not a private investigator. Mind if I sit?"

"Suit yourself, but I have to open up at—"

"Ten. That gives us forty minutes."

He raised an eyebrow.

"The woman who runs the store next to your place."

"Ah, that would be Marjorie."

"Very helpful," Sam said as she sat on the banquette seat across from him.

"Our local neighborhood watch," he muttered. He was about to say more when a waitress appeared to ask Sam if she wanted coffee.

"Chase?" She turned away after getting Sam's order. "More coffee?"

"Sure, Laura." After she left, he placed his elbows on the table, intertwining his fingers while studying Sam. "Why the sudden change of mind from Emily?"

He was getting right to the point—and beating her to it, as usual. "She can't put Danny off much longer. Plus, she doesn't like deceiving him."

"What do you mean?"

"He doesn't know about you yet. I mean," she added at the confusion in his face, "he doesn't know that I found you."

He frowned. "This is all very very strange. Almost disorienting. I keep thinking I'm going to wake up to find it's all been a…"

"Bad dream?"

"Yes. And I don't mean because my life has suddenly been turned upside down or that I'm afraid to accept responsibility for a foolish act when I was younger—none of that. Just that I don't have a clear picture of any of this. I don't know how or where it started."

The dark circles under his eyes and his sober, unshaved

face said it all. The man was suffering and, unexpectedly, Sam felt sorry for him. Until she wondered how Emily would react to the description of Danny's conception as a "foolish act."

"Look, Mr. Sullivan…"

"Make it Chase. We may not be friends, Miss Sorrenti…"

"Samantha. Or Sam."

He nodded. "Samantha, but it's apparent you know much more about me than the average acquaintance."

*And maybe more than you think, Chase Sullivan.* "Not really," she lied, "but you're right. I should start from the beginning. I think I told you when we first met that I have this business—I find things for people—and Danny found my Web site when he was searching for local private investigators."

"And he persuaded you to help him."

"He's a pretty persuasive kid," she said. The waitress came then with a mug for Sam and the coffeepot. Sam thought he looked grateful for the interruption. Chase insisted on paying and after she left with the money, Sam went on to say, "Once I met Emily, I couldn't refuse. They were both so desperate for…for something to hang on to. Some hope."

At that, she busied herself with her coffee. She didn't dare look up, fearing he'd think she was trying to pull his emotional strings. But when she risked a peek, she saw that he was still stirring his coffee, staring into the mug.

After a long moment, he raised his head and asked, "So how did you manage to find me so quickly? I'm not in the phone book."

*Now comes the tricky part,* thought Sam. Keeping Skye out of the equation. "Well, I Googled 'Winston Sullivan' and got your father."

His coffee mug stopped midway to his mouth. "Why that name? Emily knew me as Daniel Winston."

"Why the alias?" she countered.

His face took on a faraway look. "It's a long story," he said, sipping his coffee. When he set it down again, he checked his watch. "And there's no time for it today, I'm afraid. You've got fifteen more minutes to fill me in."

Sam felt a surge of annoyance. "And likewise mine is a long story. Let's just say I have some connections."

That got his attention. "Oh? What kind of connections?"

Sam decided the talk had taken a wrong turn. "Is that really important right now? The fact is that Emily would like to see you and time is running out."

He rubbed his forehead. "I don't really know what she expects, other than child support. And if Danny is my son, of course I'll pay it. Somehow."

She recalled the neighbor's comment about how Chase could "use the business". Still, the man must have some money if he was paying for his mother's care at Harbor House. She watched him fidget with his spoon. He seemed nervous. But then she pictured Emily, pinning her hopes on this man.

"I think Emily's not worried too much about money, though I'm sure her medical bills are huge." Sam leaned forward, stressing the point she wanted to make. "I believe she and Danny are more interested in *father* support."

He looked up, his dark brown eyes large in his drawn face. "*Father* support. Yeah, I can relate to a kid wanting that." Then, as if he'd said too much, he finished off the rest of his coffee and stood up. "I have to go."

Sam followed him out of the café. His stride was long and brisk and she trotted at his heels like a puppy. "When do you think you'll be calling her?"

He stopped. The look on his face made her add, "Just that she'll be waiting to hear from you."

"What's your stake in all this?"

The question took her aback. She wasn't sure she could even explain. "I just…as I told you…I was touched by both of them." She stepped aside for a woman pushing a stroller and when she turned her face to him again, something in his eyes made her blurt, "I don't know why. I can't seem to let it go."

He nodded. "Well, that may be the first honest thing you've said to me this morning." He resumed walking.

Sam was speechless. She slowed her pace, not trusting herself to say another word, assuming that was even possible. A few feet shy of the shop, Chase halted again. His neighbor, Marjorie, was sweeping the sidewalk in front of her store.

He waited for Sam to catch up to him and in a low voice asked, "What floor at Our Lady of Mercy?"

"Ten. The palliative-care unit."

"Thank you," he said, and marched up to the front door of his shop. Marjorie said something to him while he was unlocking the door, but Sam could tell he wasn't interested in making small talk. He nodded at her and stepped inside, closing the door.

Sam stood on the sidewalk, feeling as if she'd been ditched on her high-school dance floor.

Marjorie looked her way and smiled brightly. "Changed your mind?" she asked.

"Hmm?" Sam frowned. "Oh…er…yes."

"That's a shame," the woman said. "He does wonderful work."

"I'm sure," Sam murmured, and headed for her car, catching a glimpse of Marjorie's curious face as she did.

CHASE PAUSED in the open doorway. Emily was lying propped against two pillows and watching something on the small overhead television. He took in the oxygen tank at her bedside, the tangle of translucent plastic tubing and the solitary plant perched on the windowsill. A confusion of emotions overwhelmed him. *Thirteen years ago I would have hightailed it.* It was a shameful admission, but he also knew he was no longer that self-centered young man. He'd made amends in many ways. This was just one more.

Inhaling deeply, he tapped lightly on the door frame. Emily's head slowly swung his way. Her face paled even more. Chase cleared his throat. "Hi, Emily," he said, and walked toward the bed.

Her blue eyes were huge in the sunken cheeks of her face. Chase stood staring down at her, at a complete loss for words. Then he pulled a chair closer to the bed, sat down and gently lifted her hand from the bed, wrapping it tenderly in his.

# CHAPTER SIX

SAM WAS PRINTING out a bill of sale for a client when the phone rang. As she reached for it, she noticed Our Lady of Mercy Hospital on the call display. She stared at the number, letting the phone ring twice more before summoning the courage to pick up.

"Sam?"

"Hi, Emily. Everything okay there?"

"Yes. Great. He came to see me the day before yesterday."

"Chase?"

"Chase. Daniel. I'm still not used to calling him that."

"Has he met Danny yet?"

"Yesterday. I told him Danny would be by after school and he came, too, just a bit later. Gave me time to tell Danny he was coming."

"And how did it go?"

There was a long pause, followed by a sigh. "Not the way I expected."

"What do you mean?"

"Danny seemed real subdued. When I told him you'd found Chase, he seemed almost scared and when they met, he barely said a word."

Sam wasn't surprised. "I think that's a natural reaction, don't you? I mean, now that his fantasy has been realized, he may be questioning if it's what he really wanted, after all."

"You think? I never thought of it that way. Another reason I was calling you is that Minnie came to see me today and—"

"Minnie?"

"My neighbor, the one who's taken Danny in while I've been here."

"Oh, right."

"She got a call from his school—seems he's been playing truant a lot more than I suspected."

That didn't surprise Sam.

"Anyway, the principal wants Minnie—or Danny's guardian—to go to some meeting about this. The problem is that Minnie has real bad arthritis and to tell the truth, I think she's at the end of her rope with Danny. I'm not sure how much longer I can impose on her."

Sam had a bad feeling where the talk was going. She decided to step right in. "Then I guess it's a good thing you've found his father."

There was another silence. "Yeah, but…it seems unfair to put this on Chase, don't you think? I mean, he's still getting used to the idea of having a son at all, much less having to deal with a problem and I was wondering, since you know Danny already…" Her voice trailed off.

"Emily, I hardly know Danny. Don't you think he's better represented by a school counselor or someone?"

"I was thinking more of someone not connected to the school who could, you know, advocate for him."

"Where and what time is this meeting?" She jotted down the details and before hanging up, said, "Please tell Danny I'll meet him in the principal's office."

"Of course and, Sam, thank you so much. Really."

"Glad to do it, Emily."

"And you know what?"

"What?"

"He's really changed. Not at all like he was thirteen years ago."

Chase, she meant. "I guess that's a good thing."

"For sure. I mean, he was always a decent person, but now he doesn't seem so uptight."

*Really? I hadn't noticed myself.* Sam wondered how Emily felt emotionally about seeing Chase again but didn't have the nerve to ask.

"Anyway, seeing and talking to him made me feel that he'll do right by Danny." Her voice fell. "I don't know what the future holds for them, but I think things will work out. And it was good for me in another way—made me realize the Daniel I knew would never have been a good match for me." Her chuckle ended in a coughing fit.

Sam waited, wishing there was something she could do to ease the woman's suffering.

"Sam," she said when she'd recovered somewhat, "please let me know what I owe you—"

"Emily, I'm not even a real P.I. Forget about it— please!"

"It could never be enough, know what I mean? You've made the next few weeks more...more hopeful for me and Danny."

Sam reached for a tissue on her desk and dabbed at her eyes. "That's more than enough payment right there, Emily."

"Thanks, Sam. Listen, I'm kinda tired now. Call me tomorrow—after the meeting, would you? And again, Sam, thank you."

The line disconnected abruptly. Sam sat very still for a long time before calling the one person in the whole world she wanted to see right then. Her mother.

"I'M IN THE KITCHEN, dear," Nina called out as Sam, shouting a hello, walked in the front door.

Sam threw her purse and jacket onto the closest chair and joined her mother, who was arranging flowers in a vase.

"Those are pretty," she said.

"Yes, they are. I love the first tulips of spring. Skye brought them."

"Oh? Is she here now?"

"Not yet, but I'm expecting her soon. After you called, I thought it would be nice for all of us to have dinner at Domani's."

"I wasn't expecting to stay for dinner."

Nina looked up from her flowers. "Do you have plans?"

"No, but—"

"Then you must come. The three of us haven't been together since Christmas."

*Christmas.* "Look, Mom, I need to talk to you about something."

Nina moved closer to Sam, concern in her face. "Are you okay?"

Sam smiled. The serious business of the world always faded in importance when Nina's daughters might be in trouble. "Yes, I'm fine. It's about that boy and his mother—Emily and Danny Benson."

"Oh, yes! Skye said you met the father."

*She did, did she? What else did my meddling sister have to say?* Sam's jaw tightened.

"Is there a problem?" her mother was saying while anxiously searching Sam's face.

"It's Danny," she said.

"Uh-huh. Look, dear, let's sit in the solarium. Shall I put the kettle on? Or would you like something stronger?"

The Sorrenti family cure for whatever ailed you. Tea and talk. Sometimes something stronger than tea. Sam thought back to the other day when Skye was at her place.

For a few minutes the tension had been lifted by the chit-chat and wine—until Skye's parting comments.

"Nothing, Mom," she said, deciding to try to finish the talk before Skye came home.

They sat in the small solarium in the L at the end of the living room. A small terrace separated this area from the kitchen, and as Sam sat on the love seat she realized she was facing the same view as she had been at Christmas. When Skye was finishing the last of the pots and pans and Todd had crept up behind her, encircling her waist with his arms and spinning her around to plant a long—very long—kiss on her lips. Lips that were identical to Sam's. *But not Sam's.*

"What is it?" her mother asked. "You look so pensive."

"Emily called me this afternoon and apparently Danny's been truant from school. She asked me to go to a meeting with his principal—as his advocate."

"Surely the father…"

"Exactly what I said, but Emily thinks it's too soon to drag him into a problem with Danny. Maybe she's worried it'll put him off—you know, make him rethink the whole parenthood thing."

"A bit late for that."

Sam smiled. "Yes, I agree. But I feel obliged to help."

"Dear, what's the basis of this relationship you seem to have established with Emily and her son?"

Sam slumped back onto the love seat. "Mom, I really don't need any analysis at the moment, trust me. I think Danny needs counseling and I want to know if you can get him a referral to someone. Hopefully someone inexpensive."

"Unless Emily has private insurance…"

"I think she must have some kind of plan—she's got a private room in the palliative-care ward. But all that can be worked out later."

"Obviously her son has a great deal of anxiety about what the future holds for him, hence the acting out at school."

Sam couldn't resist teasing. "Gee, Mom, you think?"

Nina smiled. "Stop mocking me, Samantha. All right. I'll see what I can do. I mean, I'd offer to help the boy myself, but I don't think it's appropriate."

"Not arm's length enough?" Sam quipped. It was a line she and Skye had trotted out as teenagers whenever Nina tried to counsel them.

"No, and now I'm going to speak to you as your mother. I believe you've taken on quite a lot with the Bensons. Don't interrupt. Let me have my say before you dismiss well-intentioned advice. Part of me is pleased that you're a caring person willing to help someone at such a painful time, but another part is worried that you're becoming embroiled in that family's troubles and you may have difficulty extricating yourself from ongoing responsibility for them. When the time comes—when this tragic situation unfolds, as you and I both know it will—will you be able to deal with it?"

Sam reached over and took her mother's hand. "Mom, I assure you that I'll be fine."

"What do you think of the father? Is he a decent man? Will he stand by his obligations?"

Sam smiled. Nina often reverted to her own rearing with its focus on old-fashioned values when dealing with personal issues. She recalled many would-be boyfriends being grilled in just such terms. *And one who probably ought to have been.*

"I haven't quite figured him out, but he hasn't shirked the whole paternity thing, so I've a feeling he'll be there for Danny."

Nina's gaze was fixed on Sam. "Well, that's a start.

But don't you think you've done all you can do for that family now?"

"Of course. The rest is up to them."

"Yes." Nina paused a second. "Then why did you agree to go to this meeting about Danny?"

"Did I say I agreed to go?"

Nina smiled indulgently. "Yes, dear. You said you felt obliged."

Sam smiled ruefully. "I did, didn't I. I don't know why exactly I felt obliged, but I'm sure that'll be the extent of my ongoing responsibility."

"How can you be sure?"

"Because Danny now has a father to support him."

"That's not a certainty. And then there's Danny. He may reject this new person in his life."

"But it's what he wanted! He was obsessed with finding his father."

"That's when the letdown can happen. After the finding part."

Sam sighed. "I came here to feel better, not more confused."

"Confused? Who's confused?"

Sam and Nina turned as one to where Skye was standing in the entrance to the solarium. "Have I interrupted something?"

For once Sam was grateful for her sister's timing. "Nope. We were just discussing a mutual acquaintance," Sam quickly said. "And Mom's treating us to dinner. At Domani's."

"Ah, just like old times."

Sam kept her eyes fixed on Skye. She had no intention of bringing Danny, Emily and especially, Chase Sullivan, into any further conversation with Skye. She also knew her mother's professional discretion would kick in. Nina had always managed a fine balance in negotiating arguments between her daughters while respecting their confidences. It was a trait Sam had learned to appreciate over the years.

As Nina got up to get ready to go out, she turned to Skye. "And how did you spend your day, dear?"

"Catching up with some old friends," she answered, following her mother into the living room.

It wasn't until much later, on the drive back to her apartment, that Sam realized during the entire dinner Skye had not referred to her day again. Nor to the "old friends" she'd supposedly contacted. By the time she was turning out her bedside light, she'd convinced herself that those friends might have been former business colleagues. Skye was up to something, and she had a feeling it was going to end in another quarrel. Or worse.

THE NEXT MORNING Sam was almost out the door of her office to go to the meeting at Danny's school when the phone rang. She paused, debating whether to let it go to voice mail. She was running late and didn't want to get stuck in a long conversation with a client. On the other hand, she'd been expecting important information from a dealer in New York and hated to extend the matter with an endless game of telephone or e-mail tag. She strode back to her desk and looked down at the phone. The call display flashed Sullivan.

Sam froze, then grabbed for the phone. "Chase?"

"Hello, Samantha." He got right to the point, as usual. "I was talking to Emily last night, arranging for Danny to spend the weekend with me, when she mentioned the meeting you're going to this morning. I'd like to tag along."

"How did you get my number?"

There was a slight pause followed by a low chuckle. "Well, I guess you're not the only one good at sleuthing. I helped myself to a Seattle directory."

"You're his father. Why don't you go to the meeting instead of me."

The voice became a bit chillier. "I suppose I was thinking of Danny. He's only met me once. I thought maybe he'd feel more comfortable if you were also there. I simply wanted to be kept informed on what's happening."

Sam had to give him credit for that. "Does Emily know you want to go, too?"

"No. I didn't think of it until after I talked to her last night. I assumed she wouldn't mind."

Grudgingly Sam said, "I'll meet you at the school then. The meeting's in forty-five minutes. Can you make it from the island in time?"

"I'm already in the city."

Sam gave him the address for the school and rang off. Traffic was light, but the school was in the northeast area of the city, in Greenwood. A long way from Emily's hospital. Sam thought of Danny going all that way on his own on public transit. The kid had gumption.

The idea that she was attending a school meeting as a substitute parent for a boy she'd known less than a couple of weeks was bizarre. The Benson family business had taken up a lot of her personal time, but then again, what would she have been doing otherwise? It was a sad commentary on her life post-Todd.

Yet, it struck her that as much as her life without Todd was more solitary, except for the first few weeks after the Christmas debacle, it hadn't been unhappy. The thought had slowly been forming that she might be better off without Todd. Hadn't she sometimes thought they had little in common? If she was really honest with herself, hadn't she occasionally suspected he was a little too attentive to other women? That he might even have cheated on her? Of course, none of that excused her sister. Todd might not have known which one he was kissing—as he'd protested—but Skye most definitely had.

Sam spotted the two-story, yellow, stucco school building on her right. She swung into the semicircular driveway that fronted the school, parking right behind a rusting white pickup. As she got out of the car, Chase was climbing out from the truck.

He'd obviously taken some effort with his appearance. He was clean-shaven, and his gray crew neck pullover was topped by the pale-yellow collar of a shirt. Black jeans accentuated long, lean legs, which Sam noticed for the first time. All her other encounters with the man had been centered on her mission for Danny and Emily. Now, in such a neutral context, she could see that he was a very attractive man. If only he'd lighten up a bit. The smile he gave as she walked toward him was promising, suggesting this meeting with him might not begin as badly as the others had.

"Shall we go in?" he asked without any preamble. He headed for the door, holding it open for her.

A sign requesting visitors to report to the office and with an arrow pointing straight ahead was posted on the wall opposite the main door. They walked silently along a corridor lined with bulletin boards displaying samples of children's art and writing until they reached the glass-walled office.

A fortyish secretary sat at a desk behind the office reception counter and looked up. "May I help you?" she asked, smiling.

"We have a meeting with the principal," Chase said. "About Danny Benson."

The secretary got up and walked to the counter. "Oh, yes. And you are…"

"Chase Sullivan," he said, pausing slightly before adding, "Danny's father."

"Oh. Very good. Danny's mother called to say someone would be coming in on her behalf. Please have a seat Mr. and Mrs. Sullivan, and I'll let the principal know you're here."

Sam couldn't help smiling, though she didn't dare look at Chase. When they were ushered into the inner office, she quickly introduced herself as a friend of Danny's mother. The principal, a short, stocky man in his early fifties, shook hands and asked his secretary to call Danny from class.

As the door closed behind her, the first thing he said was, "We're aware of Danny's situation at home and have been giving him plenty of latitude regarding his behavior. But I regret to say there's been little improvement. Unfortunately Danny was involved in a physical altercation yesterday and I have no option but to suspend him for a couple of days."

Chase leaned forward in his chair and asked, "What was the reason for the fight?"

"I believe he was called a name and he retaliated physically. We try to teach our students to use words to express their feelings, rather than fists but…"

Sam's immediate thought was that Danny must have been pushed to the limit. She didn't see him as a child who'd use violence. She was about to ask what name he'd been called when Chase beat her to it.

The principal looked embarrassed. "I believe the boy who provoked Danny called him a bastard. And although he was the one who was injured, he was reprimanded very severely for using such language."

While the principal was talking, Sam watched Chase's reaction with interest. He paled visibly at the word *bastard*. Then a dark stain crept up from the collar of his shirt, suffusing into his face. His fingertips curled under his hands, resting on his thighs as if he were struggling not to leap across the desk and grab the other man. Or so it seemed to

Sam, but when Chase finally did speak, he sounded very much in control.

"I will certainly speak to Danny about the appropriateness of his actions and will have him write an apology to the boy he attacked. And I would like that boy to write an apology to Danny for what he called him."

The principal nodded. "Yes, of course. But given the physicality involved, I'm afraid the suspension still stands. Danny may return to school on Monday." He buzzed the intercom on his desk to have Danny sent in.

Danny walked in, closing the door behind him. He saw Sam first and flashed a sheepish smile. When he noticed Chase, the smile vanished. He perched on the edge of a chair next to the door. While the principal reiterated their conversation, Sam noticed that Danny kept taking sidelong glances at Chase.

As soon as the principal finished, Chase stood up, extended his hand and said, "Thank you sir, for informing us about this matter. I'll see that Danny's letter is sent off right away." Then he tapped Danny lightly on the shoulder, signaling him to stand.

Sam blurted a thank-you, as well, and followed Danny and Chase out of the office. When they reached the front door, Chase abruptly turned around and asked Danny if he needed to get anything from his classroom before leaving.

Danny's sullen no was a surprise to Sam, who'd always seen a much spunkier side to the boy. Chase simply said, "Fine, then let's get on our way."

Once outside, he stopped again. "You've got two days before the weekend. I spoke to your mother yesterday about your coming to my place on Friday, staying for the weekend. However, given that you can't go to school and your neighbor..." He paused, obviously forgetting her name.

"Minnie Schwartz," mumbled Danny.

"Right. Anyway, it sounds as if she might need a break from, well, supervising you so—"

"I can stay by myself at our apartment. I've done it before," blurted Danny. His face was red and he was frowning.

Sam couldn't tell if he was on the verge of tears or an angry outburst.

Chase looked down at Danny's bent head. "I don't think so, Danny. That's not an option."

No one spoke until Sam couldn't hold back any longer. "Actually I was wondering if Danny might want to come to my place. Or rather, my mother's house. She told me she'd like to meet you and—"

Chase shot her a withering look. "Perhaps the three of us should grab some lunch and talk about the next step."

Feeling foolish now, Sam said, "If you like. How about it, Danny?"

He shrugged.

Chase expelled a loud sigh. "Okay, lunch it is. There used to be a takeout burger place in the park at Greenlake. Not far from here. At any rate, I'm sure there's some kind of fast-food place around the lake. Danny, why don't you ride with Samantha? I'll lead the way." Without awaiting a reply from either of them, he headed for the pickup, climbed in and started the engine.

She shook her head, wondering why she'd come to the meeting only to have him very competently take charge. "C'mon, Danny."

As she followed the truck out the driveway and onto the street, Danny said, "Sorry you had to come all this way, Sam. But that guy had it coming. He's been bugging me for weeks."

Sam glanced at the boy, slumped on the seat beside her. "It's okay, Danny. I'm sorry you didn't tell anybody about that boy if he's been bullying you."

"I tried to, but no one would listen," he said, his voice rising. "Anyway, none of that matters anymore. I'm just sorry I made problems for my mom."

Sam reached out a hand to pat his arm. "Your mom understands."

"Yeah, I guess." He turned his head to look out the window. After a moment, he said, "What do you think of him?" He jutted his chin to the windshield and the truck in front of them.

She had no idea what to say. The question was so similar to her mother's she opted for a similar answer. "I'm not sure, to be honest. But I think if he didn't care about you, he wouldn't have come to the meeting today."

He thought about that. "Maybe. He's probably pissed— sorry—ticked off about me. Maybe he's even wondering how he can get out of, you know, the whole thing."

He didn't have to clarify what the "whole thing" was. And Sam didn't have the courage to insist otherwise. Danny might be right.

As the truck pulled into a parking lot adjacent to a burger stand, Sam turned to him and said, "I meant what I said about meeting my mother, Danny. She's a psychologist and knows a lot of people who are trained to counsel kids who…well, kids who…"

"Whose mothers are dying?"

She parked beside the truck and turned off the engine. "Kids who need to talk about their feelings. People need to do that, Danny. When they're grieving."

He raised his head, flicking back the hank of hair that seemed to perpetually droop across his forehead. "I'll think about it," he said, opened the door and got out.

Midweek, the park was virtually empty except for a few dog walkers and joggers. But the burger place was open. They took their orders to a picnic table under a tree and wolfed the food down silently. Danny finished first and, after tossing his refuse into a bin, wandered along the edge of the water. Hands in pockets and shoulders slumped, he seemed small and vulnerable against the larger backdrop of the lake.

"I sometimes forget he's only twelve," Sam said, watching him.

"It's a pivotal year," Chase said. "Once he's a teenager, greater expectations and responsibilities will be heaped on him."

He sounded so wistful Sam turned to him and asked, "Is that what happened to you?"

"How do you mean?"

She was startled by the suspicion in his voice. "Was more expected of you when you became a teenager?"

"There was more expected of me the instant I was *born*."

Sam looked at him, caught by the bitterness in the reply, but he was staring off into the distance. Or into the past, she decided. Except for the scraps of information Skye had passed on, Sam knew little about his background. Scion of an old wealthy Seattle family. Hint of scandal or wrongdoing in the family business. Mother in exclusive nursing home. The only paradox in the whole mix was Chase himself.

Former motorcycle rider and current fine-furniture maker. Owner of beatup truck. Bearer of tattoo, now hidden under long sleeves. New father.

Not exactly the markings of a rebel, but Sam supposed that, set against where he came from, Chase Sullivan was a bit of an anomaly.

Her curiosity about him prompted her to ask, "I assume Greenwood is where Emily and Danny live, since his school is here. Is this where you were living and working when you met Emily thirteen years ago?"

"Yes," he said, still gazing out at the lake and Danny. "She was working in a diner when I met her. I was working at a construction site nearby."

Construction. Not the family business. She wanted to know more, but he abruptly stood up and said, "We should call Danny back and figure out where he's going to be for the next few days."

"I was talking to him about my mother on the way here," Sam said. "Mom is a clinical psychologist and she might be able to refer Danny to someone. Just so he can talk about Emily and…and everything." She felt suddenly nervous under his scrutiny.

Finally he said, "Yeah, that'd be good for him. He may not think he needs it now, but he will later." He glanced at Danny, slowly walking toward their picnic table. "But I guess he'll have to be the one to decide."

"Yeah, I'll leave it up to him—he has enough pressure right now."

"For sure."

The moment stretched between them and Sam felt an urge to fill it. "You were good with him, in the principal's office. Setting the record straight about the other boy's part in the fight. And you didn't jump on Danny."

He turned sharply from the lake to her. "I'd no right to jump on Danny. I may be his biological father, but I've yet to become the father he needs. Besides, if that had been me in Danny's place, I'd have done the same thing."

He flashed a smile that altered his whole face and Sam felt herself smiling back. When Danny reached them, they briefly discussed the next few days, finally agreeing that he would stay with Minnie until the end of the day on Friday and then go to Bainbridge with Chase for the weekend. Chase also suggested Danny ride home with him in the truck now, so that he could see where Danny lived, and the boy agreed. Reluctantly, it seemed to Sam.

"Don't forget to call if you decide to take me up on my offer," Sam reminded Danny as he was about to get into Chase's truck. "You know, what we discussed on the way here," she added at his frown.

"Oh, yeah, sure," he said. Then he grabbed her arm. "Hey, why don't you come to Bainbridge this weekend, too?"

"Oh, well, heavens, Danny…" Sam was at a loss for words. She glanced quickly at Chase, whose face was impassive, though she thought she saw a flicker of alarm in his eyes.

"Please?" He looked at Chase. "It would be all right, wouldn't it?"

Sam realized the boy was nervous about the trip. "I don't know, Danny. This is a chance for you to get to know your…well…Chase."

The man in question finally spoke up. "Why don't you come for lunch—maybe Saturday?"

Danny smiled expectantly at her as Sam struggled to find a way out. In the end, she could think of no excuse that wouldn't sound lame or mean-spirited. "Sure, that would be nice."

As she waved goodbye, she recalled her promise to her mother only yesterday. *That's it for my involvement with the family. Now the rest is up to them.* Yeah, right.

# CHAPTER SEVEN

SKYE TOSSED the photocopied file onto the passenger seat of her mother's car and, starting up, pulled out of the parking lot of Seattle's FBI field office. She'd had no trouble getting the file, especially since she'd been the investigating agent thirteen years ago.

Many of the agents who'd been working there with Skye then had either retired or been transferred or promoted elsewhere. Except for the clerk in Records who'd teased, "Tying up loose ends, eh, Skye?" when she'd requested the file.

"You never know," she'd replied. "Anyway, gives me something to do in my holidays." She'd instantly regretted that because the clerk had given her a pitying look and said, "Don't tell me you've turned into another workaholic agent."

"Occupational hazard," she'd joked as she scooped up the file and headed for the copy machine.

If only it were a joke and not the pathetic truth, she thought as she drove. Although she'd tried to convince herself and Sam that she had to make the trip west for her mother's birthday, anyway, she knew arrangements could have been done by e-mail. The birthday itself wasn't for another month, and Sam had had every right to be suspicious of her motives for returning home so much earlier.

She bet her twin was seething about the interference

with her current project—the Benson/Sullivan family—and she couldn't blame her. Skye would never have thought of looking into the old inquiry if Sam hadn't called up asking for assistance. It was a lot easier for Skye to use that as an excuse to spend holiday time at home without having to spell out the main reason—she was tired of the estrangement from her sister and was hoping to put the whole Christmas-and-Todd fiasco to rest.

Yet now she was home, she had doubts that any reconciliation was possible. Whenever they were together they were like two alley cats. Fur raised, claws bared. Sam took everything she said the wrong way and all conversation inevitably led to that thing with Todd. The bane of Skye's life for the past six months. And it hadn't even been a good kiss.

Skye took another swig from the plastic coffee cup in the holder and contemplated her next move. A good cup of coffee seemed the first step—it was a crime that the office coffee could be so foul in the birthplace of Starbucks. Then she'd go back home, reread the file and make some notes. Next, she'd pay a little visit to Trade Winds, the import-export company Chase Sullivan's father had partly owned. After that, Bainbridge Island. In the original inquiry, she'd never interviewed Chase. He'd been off at a conference or out of the country somewhere. And after observing Sam's face when she'd teasingly suggested she might be attracted to the man, Skye's curiosity was significantly aroused. *Yes. Haven't been to Bainbridge in years.*

The light changed and she made a sharp turn, heading for a coffee outlet two blocks away. A large latte, cozy up on the couch in the solarium for a good read and then she'd toss a coin to see which came next. Trade Winds or Bainbridge. Sounded like a plan.

CHASE STOOD BACK for a better view of the room. He had two more days to rig up space for Danny and the task was proving to be a real challenge. No matter where he moved things, the problem remained. His place was just too damn small. Ironically it had been the size that appealed to him almost two years ago when he signed a lease agreement to rent the shop and the cottage behind it. It was definitely a huge change from his childhood home in Magnolia. That fact alone—as well as the price—had clinched the deal.

He'd spent most of the morning moving things from the small room off the kitchen that had served as storage and distributing them between the cottage and the shop. His neighbor, Marjorie, had watched from the backyard of her gift shop.

"You're not moving, are you?" she'd asked, peering over the waist-high fence.

Chase had stopped, shifting the carton in his arms. There was no point in being too vague about what was happening, because Marjorie would keep digging until eventually she'd mined all the gossip potential she could. After a few seconds, he'd explained, "I'm having company for the weekend—maybe longer."

"Oh? Someone from out-of-town?"

"No, someone from the city." He'd seen right away she wasn't going to be satisfied with that, so he'd set the box down and walked over to the fence. "My son." The words bounced around in his head. Their meaning had yet to sink in.

She'd gaped. "I'd no idea you were even married."

"I'm not—not anymore," he'd added quickly, recalling the epithet that Danny had been taunted with at school.

"My goodness! How old is he?"

"Uh…twelve…going on thirteen."

"For heaven's sake! Aren't *you* the dark horse!"

Chase had had no doubt that the news would spread rapidly up and down Primrose Lane, which was probably a good thing, saving him from making the explanation over and over again.

Most of the day had been a write-off. Even Marjorie lost interest after a while. By late afternoon, Chase had emptied the storage room of everything but a small table. He'd have to go into the city tomorrow to one of the chain stores to buy a cheap single bed and mattress, along with some other accessories to make the place look like a room and not a renovated storage area.

Still, the work had been a good physical diversion from the questions that had been plaguing him since the day he first met Samantha Sorrenti at Harbor House. Questions like, how did he get to know a twelve-year-old boy who, a week ago, was a complete stranger and who, now, was his son? Or, what would the two of them do for a whole weekend? And the biggest question of all—how would his life change?

He knew the answer to the last one. *In more ways than you can even foresee.* He was ashamed to admit to himself that a mere few years ago, that realization would have filled him with self-pity. But now that the initial shock had passed and the truth had registered—the instant he saw Danny, Chase knew he was his son—he'd come to accept that this was one responsibility he would not be able to walk away from. He remembered an old saying his father had thrown at him several times—"You've made your bed, now lie in it."

As a teenager, he'd loathed hearing that. Not just for its implicit dismissal of any and all troubles, but for its cold-ness. The underlying message was always clear: *You'll get no help from me.* The adult Chase Sullivan had grown to understand the reasons his father had uttered it. Which led to the question Chase feared the most.

Would he be a better father to Danny than his own father was to him?

He checked the time. A tourist was dropping by just after five to pick up a carving of a great blue heron. He'd started carving birds and other animals in the dark days of winter more than a year ago and had been surprised at their popularity with tourists. It made sense to diversify a bit. Not many people wandered in off the main drag to buy a cherrywood cabinet or a black walnut table. Most of his furniture sales were orders or commissions from specialty shops in New York or San Francisco. Some pieces had been sent as far away as Toronto, Canada. He could live modestly on Bainbridge on the sales of just three or four of these commissions, but the carvings drew the tourists into the shop.

He thought about Marjorie's reaction to the news he had a son and guessed that most of the residents on the lane would be equally surprised. He'd lived on the island for almost two years and had had no visitors. In fact, he seldom had company at all. When he'd first arrived, Marjorie had tried to set him up with a couple of women, but she'd eventually given up. Other than a handful of acquaintances, there was really no one else to be shocked—or pleased—at this new person in his life. The only person he knew who would have loved to know Danny was his mother. Sadly she didn't even recognize her *own* son anymore.

He closed the cottage door and walked up the stone path to the shop. He still had a few minutes to make up a shopping list for his trip into the city in the morning. The first thing he did was to turn over the Closed sign and unlock the front door. He noticed a car parked in front of Marjorie's place and wondered if she, too, had a late customer. The tourist season wouldn't pick up until late May so many stores closed at five, rather than six or even nine.

He recalled his remark to Samantha Sorrenti the other day about Marjorie as the local neighborhood watch and realized that he himself wasn't very good at noticing the comings and goings of the people on Primrose Lane. In many ways, full-time residence on Bainbridge was like living in a village. Especially given that the permanent population was only about twenty-five thousand or so, and most of those lived in Winslow.

He was just finishing the list in the workroom when he heard the doorbell tinkle. "Be right with you," he called out. There was no reply, so he set the paper and pencil down and peered into the showroom. When he saw a woman looking at a carving, her back to him, his immediate response was annoyance.

Samantha Sorrenti. What now? They'd already agreed that she'd come for lunch on Saturday. The woman was impossible. And obviously she wasn't here for any emergency, because she now had his phone number and so did Danny and Emily. Which meant she'd probably come to belabor some point or remind him to do something. Determined to hide his irritation, he forced a jocular tone into his greeting.

"Samantha," he said, walking toward her, "you're a full three days early. You're—"

She turned around, smiling.

He stopped. She looked like Samantha, though the hair seemed a bit different.

"Chase?"

She sounded like Samantha. She tilted her head and the smile became a tease.

"—not Samantha," he finished. He felt disoriented. How could she not be Samantha?

"You're quite right," she said, extending her hand. "I'm her twin sister, Skye. And you must be Chase Sullivan."

"Samantha didn't tell me she had a twin," he said.

"No? Well, perhaps she felt it wasn't important."

And of course it wasn't, he thought. Most of their talk had been centered on Danny or Emily. He searched her face for any telltale difference, still not quite sure how he'd guessed.

"And you are very good," she went on, "because few people can tell us apart, especially so quickly. Tell me," she said, moving closer, "what were the clues?" She fixed her gaze on his.

That was one right there. That almost provocative boldness.

"Just intuition, I guess."

"Uh-huh," she said. She studied him a bit longer and then, indicating the showroom, added, "You've got some wonderful pieces here. How're sales?"

That was another one. He doubted Samantha would have been so blunt. "Not bad, Miss Sorrenti."

"Please, under the circumstances, call me Skye."

"And what circumstances are those, Skye?"

"Well, you know Sam and…" For the first time, she seemed to falter.

She'd come to check him out, he realized. But why? For her sister? "Are you touring the island, or visiting my shop in particular?" he asked.

"I'd like to see around the island—it's been years since I was here last. But unfortunately I don't have the time today. And although your place is lovely, I actually came to speak to you."

Aha. She was checking him out. Anxious to ensure that her sister was not getting involved with some deadbeat dad? Or maybe this was some trick cooked up by the two of them. Fool Chase and see what admission he might make about…what? That was what stumped him. It wasn't as if he denied being Danny's father.

"About what?"

"About your family's business—Trade Winds."

Her reply was so unexpected that for a moment he couldn't speak at all. Every nerve and pulse in his body came to a complete halt.

When he failed to answer, she said, "In particular, an inquiry instigated some thirteen years ago by the Seattle FBI field office."

Ignoring the drumming in his ears, he asked, "What does my family's business have to do with Samantha?"

She smiled. "Not much. The big coincidence here is that *I* was the investigating agent at the time."

He'd have sat down at that, except he didn't want to appear weak. Besides, there was nothing handy.

"I no longer work out of that office," she went on, "but recently…well, a decision was made to reopen the inquiry."

"What? Why?"

She shrugged. "Maybe the office is just reviewing some cases, who knows? Anyway, since I never had the chance to interview you back then, I thought I might be able to ask you a few questions now."

His mouth was dry and his head teemed with far too many questions of his own. And he didn't want to address any of them to Skye Sorrenti. What he wanted was to get rid of her as quickly as possible.

The front door swung open then, the bell echoing in the silence.

"Hello," said the woman hesitantly, standing in the doorway. "You're still open, aren't you?"

Chase could not have greeted a customer more

warmly. "I've got the bird all packed up," he said, moving away from Skye.

"That's great. I hope I'm not taking you from anything?" She glanced from him to Skye.

"Not at all." He turned toward Skye, noting the pursed lips and frown. "Perhaps we could talk again, another time?"

She either didn't hear or was refusing to budge. He was about to repeat himself when she nodded curtly, muttered, "Definitely" and strode out the door.

Later, with a double scotch in hand, Chase sat down in his cottage and reflected on an afternoon that far outweighed, in potential for calamity, his first confrontation with Samantha at Harbor House. He had no idea why his past had been resurrected and was now poised and ready to dash his current life to pieces.

He didn't believe for a second that Samantha Sorrenti's twin sister—*an FBI agent!*—was coincidentally on the scene less than two weeks after the whole nightmare began. Obviously they had planned and prepared this, but to what avail? There was no connection that he could see between Emily and Danny and Trade Winds. Except, of course, that if the FBI inquiry had never occurred, he would never have met Emily. *And never had a son.* The endless possibilities of *if* spiraled through his mind. He downed the scotch and turned off the CD player. In three days he'd be seeing Samantha. Then he'd get some answers.

SAM KNEW SOMETHING was wrong the instant she walked into the shop on Saturday. Chase was talking to customers and his eyes flicked over her as she entered, but shifted without trace of a welcome immediately back to the couple. Not that she was expecting an effusive greeting, but a quick smile would have been nice. Perhaps the visit with Danny was not turning out well and for some reason, he held her responsible. No, she thought at once, he's not that petty.

She browsed idly around the display cases until Chase, on his way to the cash register, muttered, "Danny's in the cottage, behind the store. Go out the rear door in the work-room and along the path."

"Okay. Thanks," she muttered back, thinking, *you were the one who invited me for lunch!*

When she stepped outside, she felt as though she'd entered another world. A narrow but long yard, bordered on one side by a fence draped with a flowering vine and on the other by a row of tall pine trees, sloped gently down to what seemed to be a narrow river or channel. A stone cottage stood at the end of the pine trees, a few yards from the water. As Sam drew closer, she saw a makeshift wooden dock and an overturned red canoe.

The day was warm for early May and the screen door of the cottage was open. It was the kind of old-fashioned door Sam had seen in country-home magazines, with white-painted scrollwork framing the mesh. Perhaps Chase had made it himself. She walked up two stone steps to the door and tapped lightly.

"Danny? It's me, Samantha."

"I'm in the kitchen," he called out. "Straight through the living room and to the right."

Inside, the cottage was all that the screen door had suggested. Simplicity, style and comfort. The floors were hardwood and instead of a fireplace, there was a black woodstove against a wall lined with shelves of books. A tan-colored sofa and matching armchair were the only places to sit, though a magnificent, gleaming round coffee table, on which sat an enamel pitcher of daffodils, was definitely the showpiece of the room. The whitewashed stucco walls were bare except for a poster-size framed photograph of a northern landscape. A floor lamp stood beside the armchair and the stack of books and magazines on the floor next to it suggested this was where Chase spent time.

The living room ended in a large picture window that overlooked the river. A door to the right led into a sunny kitchen where Danny stood at a counter, chopping vegetables. The kitchen was half the size of the living room but large enough to contain a small harvest table along one wall. There was an exterior door, opened to reveal a screen door identical to the one at the front of the cottage.

"Well, Chef Danny," said Sam, smiling. "Are you preparing lunch today?"

He gave a token scowl, but Sam could tell his heart wasn't in it. "Just the salad. Does…uh…Chase still have customers?"

Sam heard the hesitation. At least he wasn't calling him Mr. Sullivan. "Yes. So, how's it been?"

He shrugged, but didn't look up from his chopping. "Okay, I guess."

"What did you do last night?"

"Not much. He doesn't even have cable! He said maybe we could rent some DVDs today."

"Has it been boring, then?"

Danny raised his head. "At first. But last night he helped me with a carving, and then today's been okay. We went out in the canoe early this morning and saw some neat birds. Stuff like that. And he said maybe sometime he'd teach me how to do some things around his workshop. You know, like sanding."

"That would be interesting."

The scowl returned. "I guess." He went back to the salad.

Sam waited a few moments before asking, "Have you thought some more about the counseling idea?"

"Yeah, but I haven't decided yet."

She knew not to push the issue. At least he was thinking about it.

"Can I help?" she asked.

He turned his hands, palms up. "I don't know. Chase said to chop this stuff for salad and there's a bowl on the counter over there. I don't know about dressing or anything."

"I'll look in the fridge." It was well stocked for a bachelor, she thought, but then realized he must have shopped with a teenager in mind as there was a lot of milk and a big bottle of cola. A platter with an assortment of cheeses was on a shelf and she pulled it out, along with a bottle of salad dressing.

Danny had finished his task and was leaning against the table, his head bowed and his arms folded across his chest. He seemed a bit lost, and Sam knew that the events of the past week must be overwhelming. She set the items from the fridge on the counter and went over to Danny, touching his forearm.

"It'll be okay, Danny. One day at a time."

He raised his head, his eyes shining with tears. "Yeah," he said huskily, "that's what Mom says. And I try to do that, but sometimes, you know, in the middle of the night I wake up and…"

Sam pulled him into a hug. They were still standing like that seconds later when Chase walked into the kitchen.

He paused, then went to the fridge. "Salad looks good," he said as he pulled out some cold meat and condiments.

Sam patted Danny's back and withdrew, then helped to transfer the lunch items from the counter nearest the fridge to the table.

"What would you like to drink?" Chase asked. "I've got wine, iced tea, milk, water, soda, juice. The usual."

"Iced tea sounds good," said Sam.

"Water," said Danny, adding "please," a second later.

Chase put a bread board with two crusty loaves on the table and gestured for them to sit. Sam couldn't recall the last time she'd felt so uncomfortable. She tried to kickstart a conversation, but every attempt fizzled.

Suddenly Chase suggested that Danny go up to the workshop and bring the carving he'd started the night before. The instant Danny left the kitchen, Chase said, "I had a visitor a couple of days ago."

"Oh?" Sam was more mystified by the expression on his face than the comment itself.

"Your sister."

"*Skye?*" Sam dropped the piece of bread she was buttering onto her plate.

"That's the name she gave. And I admit it was a bit of a shock, since I didn't know you had a twin."

The accusation in his voice rankled. "Look, it's not as if we've exchanged CVs or anything."

"True enough, though I think you already know quite a lot about me. Maybe it's time you reciprocated."

"Is that necessary now? I mean, you know I have a twin."

"A twin?" Danny stood in the doorway. "Cool. How come you never told me?"

Sam caught Chase's smirk as she looked from him to Danny. "'Cause it never really came up, Danny. What's that you've got?"

He held up a block of wood roughly shaped like a boat. "I started it last night." He handed the piece of wood to Sam.

"It's gonna be a tugboat."

"Why don't you get the drawings for it?" Chase suggested.

Danny looked from him to Sam and back again. "Sure," he mumbled, and headed out again.

"You haven't asked the big question yet," Chase said to Sam.

She knew at once what he meant but was hoping Danny would return fast and save her from answering. "What question?"

"Why your sister was here." He kept his voice low.

"I've no idea why she came here," she replied.

"Oh, I think you do." He glared at her across the table.

"Actually, I don't."

"You expect me to believe that? You have a twin who *happens* to be an FBI agent who *happens* to have investigated my family years ago. If you're telling me this is all some weird coincidence, I'm not buying it."

Sam stood up and pushed back her chair. "I don't know why she came to see you. And I have no intention of being grilled like this. I'm not the criminal here."

*"What did you say?"*

She didn't dare look at him. "I better leave," she muttered. She reached for her purse slung over the back of her chair.

"Sam? What's the matter?" Danny stood in the kitchen doorway. He looked very upset.

"I'm sorry, Danny. I have to leave. Something's… come up."

She scarcely glanced his way as she brushed past him. "I'll call you Monday. Good luck at school." As she marched into the living room, she heard Danny's voice behind her.

"What happened, Chase? What did you say to her?"

## CHAPTER EIGHT

SAM GOT AS FAR as the sidewalk and stopped, still hearing the dismay in Danny's voice. She was behaving like a child, running off when things got tough. She couldn't do that to Danny, and whatever Skye was up to, she owed it to Chase to at least set the record straight.

So she turned around and followed the path along the side of the building, back into the yard and down to the cottage. Humiliation time. The kitchen was so quiet at first she thought they'd left. They both looked up, surprised. Danny's grin made up for her embarrassment.

"I...uh...changed my mind," she said. "I don't have to get back after all. I see you haven't gone on to dessert yet, so that's a good thing." She slung her purse back over her chair and sat down. Chase got up and without a word, set another plate in front of her. Danny passed her the salad and they finished the lunch with a minimum of small talk. After a dessert of fruit salad, Danny insisted on washing up.

"Chase will show you around the yard," he prompted.

"That won't take long," Chase said, "but there's a bench by the river."

Sam got the hint. "Well, it's a lovely spring day and I'd like to see the river."

When Chase closed the door behind them, she added, "Almost thirteen and going on thirty."

"I'm beginning to think so. Maybe thirteen is the new thirty."

Sam laughed. When he grinned back, she was struck by how much he resembled Danny. And because of that, she felt a sudden connection with him.

But then his face turned serious. "Thanks for coming back. I was worried for a moment that the whole weekend was going down the tube."

"It was silly of me to run off like that, as if I'd done something wrong."

He just kept looking at her. "Shall we head for the bench?" he finally asked and, without waiting for her reply, led the way to the river's edge and a small white bench under a sprawling willow tree.

When they were seated, Sam stared at the narrow river with its weedy shore, then at the cottages and homes jutting out of the trees on the other side. Craning her neck, she could see a bridge downriver and the beginning of the large marina that served the town.

"It's very pretty here," she said. "When I came to Bainbridge as a child, I only saw the main drag and regular tourist places. Though once we came by car and drove out to the one of the beaches. I can't remember the name."

"Tell me about your sister," he said.

*Okay, so small talk isn't going to distract him.*

"She's an FBI agent and once was stationed in Seattle. Now she's in Washington, D.C."

"She said she investigated my family. What do you know about that?"

"Not much." Sam met his eyes. "There was an allegation of fraud or something. She said the inquiry didn't turn up anything and the case was closed. End of story."

"I wish," he muttered.

"Look," she said, "whatever happened years ago has nothing to do with you and Danny."

He looked across the river. "Maybe not, but I'm confused by the timing of all this. Why now?" He turned back to Sam. "Danny's told me some of it—how he found you and so on. What bothers me is your sister's part. You said she no longer works in Seattle, so why has it happened that when she visits Seattle, the case is suddenly reopened? I can only think that it was at *her* initiative. What's she after?"

Sam took a deep breath. "To tell you the truth, I don't know. You've got to believe me," she said at the change in his face. "I called her to ask for some help right after I met Emily. I wasn't really expecting to find you at all, but finding you turned out to be much easier than I thought."

"Because of what your sister told you," he said quietly.

"Yes. I probably would never have found you on my own because the only name Emily knew you by was—"

"Daniel Winston."

"Right. Why did you use an alias? Did it have something to do with the case?"

"In a roundabout way. Frankly, I don't want to discuss that at the moment. I just want to find out what your sister intends to do."

And that was the crux of the problem, Sam thought. "I don't know. Skye is one of those people who—you know the saying—marches to the beat of her own drum. She and I haven't been as close as we were when we were kids. And until she arrived a couple of days ago, I hadn't seen her since Christmas."

"Really? Why is that?"

"I don't want to get into that right now."

"So we both have our secrets." His dark brown eyes revealed no hint of irony.

"I guess we do," she said. "But the important thing in all this is Danny. He needs to know that he'll have a father to look after him when Emily…"

"Precisely," he said. "Which is why I'm asking you to find out exactly what your sister is planning and to do whatever you can to prevent her from pursuing the case."

His face was dead sober. Sam had the feeling that the request was more of an order. Then Danny's shout broke the spell. They both turned toward the cottage. He was standing just outside the cottage back door. "I'm finished," he announced.

Chase waved, signaling they were coming. He stood up and offered a hand to Sam, helping her to her feet. His grasp was strong and his fingers callused from his trade. He continued to hold on to her hand.

"Danny wants us to go to the center of town with him. Perhaps we can get back to our conversation later?" He applied more pressure and Sam knew for sure that his request was an order.

She wrenched her hand free. "Of course," she said.

Danny gave her a questioning look as she came up to him. Wanting to know if whatever had happened between her and Chase was now resolved? she wondered. Sam tousled his hair and said, "Let's go do some sightseeing."

"You two go ahead. I should probably open up the shop again," Chase said as he caught up to them.

"Are you sure?" Danny asked.

"Of course." Chase looked from him to Sam. "Don't forget to pop in and say goodbye before you head back to the city."

She almost saluted, but settled for a quick "sure" as she looped her arm through Danny's and headed up to the street.

They walked silently for a bit until Danny said, "I'm

glad you came back, Sam." He paused, then added hesitantly, "Did he say something to upset you?"

"It was a misunderstanding," she said, "and it had nothing to do with you."

"But I thought you hardly knew him."

"Well, that's true. Oh, look, isn't that cute?" She pointed at a window display of a miniature fishing village.

Danny either saw through her diversionary tactic or wasn't interested, because he scarcely glanced at the window. "I guess you must know more about him than I do, because you searched for him."

She knew right away what he was hinting at. "Danny, the best person to ask about Chase is your mom. And of course, the man himself."

"He's pretty quiet," Danny said. "He asks me stuff about myself and my mom, too, but he never talks about himself. Just about his business mostly."

"Where did he learn to carve and make furniture?"

"He said he traveled around a lot after he and my mom broke up. He lived in Alaska for a long time and worked for a carpenter there. That's when he learned how to make furniture."

Like Emily, Chase had apparently given Danny a version of the relationship that made him feel part of something real, not just the byproduct of a one-night stand. It was obvious the man was both insightful and sensitive—which certainly was a major contrast with the way he grilled her about Skye. Definitely a man of contradictions.

"He must have told you something about his own family," she said.

"Only that his father is dead and his mother is in a nursing home."

"I see." But she didn't really. Why the mystery? Sure, his family business had been investigated for fraud, but hadn't Skye said Chase wasn't even questioned? That there hadn't been enough evidence to take the inquiry further? What could the man possibly be hiding?

"Sam?"

"Hmm?" She looked down at Danny's frowning face.

"I asked if you'd like an ice cream from the best place in all of Seattle."

"Oh. Sorry, Danny. Yes, I'd love to. How sweet of you."

He gave a sheepish grin. "It was actually Chase's idea. He gave me the money."

"In that case, I think a double is in order. Lead on."

They ate their waffle cones while walking back to Primrose Lane. Just as they reached the front of Chase's shop, a woman from the adjacent store was saying goodbye to someone in a car at the curb.

Sam recognized her immediately from her last visit to the island.

The woman turned to them as the car pulled away. "Hello, there," she said. "You must be Chase's son," she said to Danny and, smiling at Sam, said, "We haven't officially met, but I've seen you a couple of times."

"Oh, right. I'm Samantha Sorrenti and this is Danny."

"I'm Marjorie Lawrence. Chase told me he had a son coming for the weekend. Such a private guy, isn't he? I mean, we've been neighbors for almost two years and I just found out he had a son the other day!"

Sam smiled, but said nothing, recalling Chase's referral to the woman as the "neighborhood watch."

"How do you like Bainbridge so far?" Marjorie asked Danny.

"It's cool. Different."

"Not as much to do here as in the city, I suppose."

He shrugged. "The city can get boring, too," he said.

"True enough," she said, laughing. Then turning to Sam,

she said, "I know you like it because you keep coming back. That's a good sign. I waved at you when you were here the other day, but I guess you didn't see me."

*Skye.* Rather than get into a tiresome explanation—and she'd had enough of Skye for the day—Sam said, "No, I didn't. Sorry about that." She looked at Danny. "We'd better let your father know we're back," she said, ushering him up the sidewalk.

Chase was in the back of the shop working and got up to greet them.

"Thanks for the treat," Sam said, holding up the remains of her cone.

"Glad you enjoyed it," he said.

Rather than have to go through another question-answer period about her sister, Sam said, "I should get going. I have some work to do in the city. Thanks for inviting me. Lunch was great."

They walked her out to her car and while Danny's attention was caught by a passing group of teens, Chase quickly spoke in Sam's ear. "Don't forget to talk to your sister."

Sam pulled her head back to look him in the eye. "As soon as I can."

He nodded. "And, uh…I'm sorry if I seemed a bit intense earlier. It's…" He paused, as if at a loss for words.

"A long story?"

He gave a half smile. "Yeah. Someday I hope to fill you in on the rest of it."

The admission took her by surprise. She smiled back. "Good. I'd like that."

It was a strange end to a strange day, she thought as the ferry headed back to the mainland. She couldn't say for certain that she knew Chase Sullivan any better, but she'd definitely learned more. As soon as the ferry docked she headed straight for her mother's place to see Skye.

Fortunately Nina wasn't home. Sam knew how much Nina disliked bickering, especially between her daughters. When they were teenagers, she'd often remind them that friends would come and go in their lives—as would lovers, but a sister would always be there. Sam wasn't sure that was a good thing.

She got to the point as soon as she found Skye in the kitchen making a pot of coffee.

"I've just come back from Bainbridge Island."

Skye looked up from the coffee machine. "Oh?"

She sounded nonchalant, but Sam noted the quick flash of guilt. "You might have told me you saw Chase, instead of setting me up like that."

Skye set the coffeepot on its stand and pushed the start button. When she turned around, her eyes were blazing. "Why is it always about you, Sam? This has nothing to do with you, okay? There was no setup, no entrapment. I went to see him in a line of inquiry—"

"That you established, Skye. You have no official backing for any of this. It's your own personal obsession."

"Obsession? What kind of psychobabble are you spouting now?"

"You didn't find anything thirteen years ago, yet you still can't let it go."

"That's ridiculous. I came home to see Mom and hopefully patch things up with you—though I'm beginning to realize that's an impossibility—and I decided to spend some of my free time reexamining an old file. Where does *obsession* fit into that scenario?"

Sam counted to ten. Skye had always been an amazing spin doctor, and her rationale would have convinced anyone who didn't know her as well as Sam did.

"Skye," she said, purposely lowering her voice, "you know very well that Chase Sullivan would never have entered your FBI radar if I hadn't asked for some assistance."

"What are you suggesting, Sam? That I'm doing this out of some desire to get back at you? A personal vendetta or something? Do you realize how that sounds?"

They were on the brink, but Sam refused to back off. She couldn't now. "I know how it sounds and how it looks, Skye. We've been through this many times since we were teenagers."

Skye turned away to get a coffee mug from the cupboard. "Yeah, yeah. The old competition thing. I was the bad twin and you were the good one."

"You were the only person who thought that, Skye. No one else did. Not ever."

Skye remained silent, just poured the coffee and gestured to the pot.

Sam shook her head but didn't take her eyes off her sister. They were going to finish this years-old argument at last.

Skye took a long sip, staring thoughtfully at Sam the whole time. "I *am* competitive," she finally said. "It's true. But I'm like that with everyone and everywhere. Not only with you."

"Okay, but there are times when you're supposed to back off."

Skye set her coffee mug down on the center island counter. "I know that, too. But…I can't explain it. I just can't seem to back off. My life's a constant race. Every situation I'm in, it's as if there's a guy waving a checkered flag in front of me."

"Come on, Skye. That sounds like the 'just can't help myself' syndrome."

Her sister's eyes flashed. "And you sound like Mom."

"That's a low blow. Beneath even you."

Skye grinned. "We did promise never to quote Mom to each other, didn't we?"

Sam felt a rush of warmth for her sister, remembering suddenly the times when they giggled late at night in their bunk beds. Way back when. Then she remembered other promises they'd made. One in particular—*thou shalt not steal your sister's boyfriend*—that Skye had blatantly broken. The surge of affection was instantly replaced by despair. Were they ever going to get on track again as sisters?

"So where do we go from here?" Sam asked.

"Regarding?"

*Us,* Sam wanted to say. But there were other priorities. A twelve-year-old boy who'd just found his father. It would be too cruel if Danny were to lose Chase, as well as his mother.

"Chase. His family's business. That whole thing."

"Oh." Skye moved away, flicking off the coffee machine and putting her empty mug in the sink. "Right. Back to that."

Sam heard the disappointment in her voice. Had she misread her sister? "There's a time limit here, Skye. Danny's mother. She needs to know he'll be okay. That his father will be around for him. That he won't have to go into a foster home."

"Sounds like a Dickens' novel," muttered Skye.

"Don't trivialize this."

Skye raised her hands in surrender. "Okay, okay. What's your point?"

"I'm asking you to drop it. To forget about reexamining the case."

Skye kept her eyes on Sam as if waiting for her to change her mind or to back off. Then she abruptly spun around and left the room.

Sam headed for the sink to splash water on her face. What was her next step if Skye refused?

Seconds later Skye was back, holding a large brown envelope in her hand. She tossed it onto the counter by the sink.

"Here," she said, her voice sharp and decisive. "I'll let *you* decide what to do. Read this and get back to me."

Sam picked up the envelope and pulled out the papers inside. The cover page was stamped with the FBI logo and file number. Beneath was a date from thirteen years ago. Sam looked up, but her sister had already left the room.

SAM POURED HERSELF a second cup of coffee and sat in her favourite chair, staring at the thin sheaf of papers on the table next to her. She hadn't had the nerve to read the photocopied file at her mother's place, not wanting Skye looking over her shoulder. So she'd waited till today— Sunday—just to prove to herself that she, unlike her sister, was not obsessive and the file was no big deal.

And after reading it, she thought perhaps it really wasn't a big deal. The gist was that the FBI's Seattle field office had received two anonymous phone calls from two different public phone booths. A male voice had suggested the office might want to investigate a local import-export company called Trade Winds, which had received several government contracts. The caller said the company was defrauding the government.

A memo recommended that, in light of other recent cases of government fraud, the calls should be followed up on. A case number was assigned and the file handed over to the new recruit, Skye Sorrenti. The remaining reports on file belonged to her.

Sam was fascinated by the terse, bureaucratic jargon that her sister had used. At the time, she'd only been in the Seattle office less than a year, and Sam knew Skye didn't talk like that in her personal life. But somewhere in the past thirteen years her professional and personal styles merged, so that her speech and mannerisms at work and at home were the same now. The realization saddened Sam. Had Skye's job changed her that much, or had the potential for such a change always been there in Skye? Perhaps it didn't matter how the change occurred. The real issue was, could the old Skye—the one she remembered from their early adolescence—be resurrected?

A few employees had been interviewed, along with the two men who owned and ran the company—Winston and Bryant Sullivan. Sam was intrigued by the notation that Bryant and his two sons actually ran the business. Though only in his midsixties, Winston was considered semi-retired due to a heart condition.

A sample of contracts, along with invoices and receipts, were also reviewed. People who'd signed some of the receipts were interviewed, but one person whose name appeared on a few papers had been unavailable. Chase Sullivan, only child of Winston. Sam picked up the file and shuffled through the loose papers until she found a handwritten note by Skye to contact Chase Sullivan on his return. It was dated two weeks before Skye was transferred out of Seattle. The last memo on file was a recommendation to take no further action in the inquiry.

It didn't take an FBI agent to see that there wasn't much of a case. Sam knew her sister had been right to close it. So why all the fuss now? she wondered. And why was Chase so insistent that Skye drop it?

Sam had no answers to either question. What she did know was that she needed a break from it all.

# CHAPTER NINE

CHASE HUNG UP the phone. What rotten luck. A big order, one for a cabinet, and he'd had to turn it down. Mainly because of the timeline. Or so he'd began to tell himself as the customer described what she wanted. After he made his excuses and rang off, he realized that time was indeed the factor. Only it was Emily and Danny's time he'd been thinking about. The kind of cabinet the woman wanted would take at least three months. How could he devote himself to an intricate piece when Emily didn't have three months? Not according to her doctor, whom he'd spoken with after introducing himself as Danny's father.

That was why he'd invited Danny for the weekend right away, rather than allow for a slow and steady period of adjustment. They didn't have time for that, which was also why he'd panicked after Sam's sister dropped in on him. If the whole thing had come up six months or more from now, he might have been able to deal with it. But when he'd promised Emily he'd take care of Danny—*no matter what*—he'd no inkling that *all* of his past was going to come back with a vengeance.

He hadn't heard a word from Sam since she'd left on Saturday. Okay, he told himself, it's only been three days. She needed time to talk things out with her sister, and having met the sister, he figured that would be a challenge. She didn't seem the type to capitulate easily. They might be identical physically in almost every way—except that Sam had green flecks in her gray eyes and her sister didn't—but in personality they were different. He scarcely knew Sam, but could clearly see that difference. Chalk and cheese. Angles and circles. Maybe it was Skye's career that had created that edginess, or maybe she was simply made that way.

All he knew was that unless Sam could persuade her sister to drop whatever she was doing, his whole life could change. Again. And not just his, but Danny's. He hoped that Sam had some luck. A lot depended on that. More than anyone knew.

He'd realized almost at once that Sam hadn't known about Skye's visit, but something had driven him to keep at her, to find out exactly what was going on and how much she was involved. It was partly because he didn't *want* to believe that Sam was in on it with Skye; but if she was working with her sister, he didn't want Danny affected by it. Chase could see how much Danny liked her, and he didn't want the boy to get hurt.

The weekend had turned out better than expected, considering his stress after Skye's visit. He and Danny had apparently made the same vow: keep things as neutral and friendly as possible. Danny had phoned Emily a few times, filling her in on what they were doing. He'd heard the excitement in Danny's voice as he told his mother about their paddle along the channel and how Chase was going to teach him the J-stroke. It had seemed like a small thing to Chase, but he'd forgotten that Danny was a city kid who'd had little exposure to nature.

On the ride back into the city, they'd talked a bit about plans for the future, both of them shying away from the long-term and focusing on the day-to-day. Danny wanted to stay with Minnie until school ended, if she agreed. He wouldn't have to change schools and would be closer to the hospital. But he would spend weekends with Chase, giving her a break. Neither of them mentioned the summer or a time when Emily would no longer be there.

When Chase had dropped Danny off at Minnie's, there'd been a moment when Chase thought Danny expected a goodbye hug. But Chase held back, recalling himself at the same age and the embarrassment of public displays of affection. So they'd shaken hands, instead.

It was amazing how the mind adapts, Chase thought. Three weeks ago he had no clue how his life was about to change. His only connection to family was his weekly visit to a mother who no longer knew him. He hadn't been involved romantically with a woman since his sojourn in Alaska, and when he'd found out his mother had Alzheimer's and was in a nursing home, he'd left the state and the relationship quickly and permanently. Proving what he suspected about himself long ago—the whole idea of commitment to a family structure terrified him. One dysfunctional family in a lifetime was more than enough. Why risk it happening again?

Now he had a twelve-year-old son. The start of a family. The idea attracted and frightened him at the same time.

The doorbell drew him from the workroom to the front of the shop. Chase froze when he saw the man in a business suit looming inside the doorway. It had been years since he'd seen his cousin and, although Howard Sullivan had filled out considerably, Chase immediately recognized the patronizing smirk.

"Nice place you got here, Chase," said Howard. "Long time no see." He moved forward, extending his right hand.

Unless Howard had undergone a huge personality change, Chase knew the gesture was pure formality. And considering their last meeting, hypocrisy, as well. "What do you want?" he asked.

The other man dropped his hand. "Not very friendly for cousins."

"Cut it, Howard."

"Sure. Okay by me. It's not as if we were ever close."

"So, what do you want?" Chase repeated.

"The old man wants to talk to you. Got a minute?"

"What about?"

"I'll let him tell you."

"Where is he?"

"Outside in the car."

"Tell him to come in, then."

"He can't. Bad legs. He's got diabetes and a heart condition. Be better if you came out to him."

"I'm working."

"Don't look too busy to me. C'mon, it won't take long. Then you can get back to your *work*." The sneer summed up his opinion of Chase's vocation.

There was no point in arguing. "Give me a second." He returned to the workroom to turn off the carving tool he'd been using. The sudden appearance of his cousin and uncle in almost two years was no coincidence. He had a sinking feeling the impromptu visit was connected to Skye Sorrenti, which meant that Sam had either been unable or unwilling to act on his request. He hoped the former, hating to think he'd misjudged her.

"Best lock up," his cousin said as Chase followed him out. "We're taking a little drive."

Chase flipped the sign to Closed and locked the door.

There was a large black Cadillac sitting at the curb. The front passenger-side window rolled down and Howard's brother, Terence, greeted him. Like his brother, Terence had grown in girth, though his receding hairline and wire-rimmed glasses gave him an air of maturity his brother lacked.

Chase hesitated. There was an implicit threat in the whole scene. His cousins had always been bullies, who had refined veneers they assumed in social settings. But he doubted his uncle would permit any harm to come to him. At any rate, there seemed little choice but to do as instructed. He opened the rear door nearest the sidewalk and climbed inside.

"Uncle Bryant," he said as Howard closed the door behind him and walked around to the driver's side.

"Chase," Bryant Sullivan rasped. "I see you got a haircut. Still got the tattoo?"

"What do you want, Uncle Bryant?"

His uncle ignored him, turning to the front seat. "Howard, take us somewhere nice and quiet. Preferably with a view."

"Sure, Pop. Any recommendations, Chase?"

Chase said nothing, keeping his eyes on his uncle. He'd always been a larger version of his brother, Winston, and Chase figured his father would have looked much the same had he still been alive. The past two years had aged the man dramatically. Ill health seeped out of every pore in his sallow face.

Chase had always been fascinated by his cousins' utter lack of social skills. Bryant and Winston, Chase's father, were the only sons of a Seattle family that was socially prominent at the turn of the twentieth century. Old money. Traditions. Etiquette. Chase had been indoctrinated from birth, and he'd assumed his cousins had been, too. But their parents had divorced and a string of stepmothers had failed to do what a nurturing mother like Chase's had done to act as a buffer against the father's bullying ways and teach the boys the niceties.

The car cruised down Primrose Lane, made a right onto the main drag and headed out of town. After a few minutes Bryant said, "We had a business agreement, Chase. I hope you haven't broken it."

"I keep my promises."

"We hope so," said Terence.

Chase ignored him. "What's this all about, Uncle Bryant?"

"I had an unexpected visit last Friday afternoon. End of the day. I was about to head to my club when a young woman insisted on an appointment."

Chase had a sickening feeling about what was coming. He swung his gaze to the window at his right, feigning disinterest.

"A woman from the FBI," Bryant said, "telling me she was heading an investigation into the business."

Chase closed his eyes. He couldn't have spoken if he'd wanted to.

"Do you know anything about this, Chase?"

He took a deep breath and looked at his uncle. "Not a thing."

"So you haven't been making any more phone calls like the one you made thirteen years ago?"

Chase didn't flinch from the watery-eyed stare. "No, I haven't. Now can we go back to town? I have work to do."

His uncle studied Chase's face long and hard. Finally he said, "Take us back, Howard."

"That's it?" asked Howard. "We could've settled this on the phone."

The tight smile that came and went in Bryant's face never quite reached his eyes. "Nothing like a one-on-one, Howard. The need to see for yourself. That's a business maxim you should know by now."

"Sure, Pop," he muttered, scowling at Chase.

Chase stared out the window on the short ride back to Primrose Lane. He knew his uncle might find out eventually about the connection to Skye Sorrenti. He just hoped he'd have time to plan what he could do about it, if anything.

When the Cadillac purred to a stop in front of the shop, Chase immediately opened the door. But his uncle stopped him one last time.

"How's your mother doing? I haven't seen her for ages. Must drop by for a visit."

Chase continued out the door, slamming it behind him.

SAMANTHA KNEW she couldn't put off contacting her sister and Chase any longer. She hated the position she was in, caught between two people who had a strong interest—for whatever reason—in something that happened years ago. The last couple of days had been spent catching up on some of the work she'd deferred as long as possible and frankly, she'd appreciated the break from the whole Trade Winds thing. Yet she'd found herself thinking about Chase at odd moments, picturing him on his stool at his workbench or putting together lunch in his small, sunlit kitchen.

Her opinion of him had altered dramatically since that first meeting at Harbor House, when she'd feared he'd deny all possibility of being Danny's father and find a way to absolve himself from any responsibility. And in spite of the fact that he'd been abrupt and almost hostile toward her in the next couple of meetings, she felt he was beginning to warm up a bit. What surprised her was how much that pleased her. And it wasn't just because she needed a positive relationship with him to maintain her connection with Danny and his mother, which was something she now realized she wanted. It was more than that, though she couldn't have said what, exactly. The only problem in the equation was Skye.

Sam stood up and stretched. She'd managed to get caught up on most of her calls and e-mails and knew she really could not postpone getting back to either Chase or Skye any longer. But which one? The phone suddenly rang, and when she looked at the caller display, she knew the decision had been made for her.

"I need to talk to you," he said, skipping a greeting.

Maybe she was deluding herself about the warming-up bit, Sam thought. "About?" she asked, though she knew even before he answered.

"Your sister. Meet me at the Starbucks at Pikes' market. I have some shopping to do there. Half an hour?"

As if he gave her a choice. Sam said, "Sure," and he hung up. She stared at the receiver for a moment in disbelief. The man was definitely challenged when it came to social niceties. She filed some papers and was about to leave when the phone rang. Caller display indicated it was Chase again.

"Listen, I—" she began.

"Just heard from Minnie Schwartz. The hospital called her to say Emily has taken a turn for the worse. I'm heading there now. Want to meet me?"

"I'll be there as soon as I can. Does Danny know?"

She heard him swear softly. "I'll call his school and arrange to pick him up on my way to the hospital."

"Is it bad?"

"Her lungs are filling up with fluids and they've had to put a chest tube in. That's as much as Minnie knows."

"I'll get there as soon as I can," Sam said, and hung up. She moved mechanically and quickly, grabbing her purse, cell phone and, at the last moment, a paperback, though she didn't expect she'd be relaxed enough to read.

The ward seemed especially quiet as Sam stepped off the elevator. Emily's door was partially open, so she was able to peek around it to see if she ought to enter or not. Emily was lying propped against two pillows, an oxygen mask covering the lower part of her face. The bedcovers were carefully arranged over a clear, plastic tubing system that went from her chest to a container hanging off the side of the bed. Her eyes were closed and Sam hesitated, almost afraid to go into the room. A nurse came along and stopped next to Sam.

"Are you family?" she asked.

"Not really."

"There's a waiting room down the hall," the nurse said, pointing.

"Her son will soon be here. Will he be able to see her?"

The nurse smiled. "Danny? For sure. She's come around quite a bit since this morning, but she's tired. Every crisis, no matter how small or big, is exhausting for her. Have Danny check in at the nurses' station before he goes in."

She started to walk on when Sam asked, "What does this mean? In terms of her ongoing condition, I mean."

"You'll have to talk to her doctor about that. He'll be making rounds in an hour or so. But unless you're an immediate family member..."

"Of course, I understand." As the nurse walked away, Sam realized that her unexpected feeling of exclusion arose from the fact that she felt as if she *was* family. She headed for the waiting room and halfheartedly skimmed her paperback, constantly checking the bank of elevators that opened into the area for sign of Chase and Danny. Half an hour later an elevator opened and the two exited.

Danny looked pale and dazed. He headed automatically for Emily's room, brushing past Sam as she stood to greet them. "Danny!"

He spun around. "Honey," Sam said, lowering her

voice, "the nurse said you should check in with them first. Your mother might be sleeping."

"Is she okay?"

She ached to wrap her arms around him, but knew what he needed right then was information—and his mother. "The nurse said she'd improved since this morning."

She caught Chase's eye over Danny's head, wanting him to step in.

"Come on, Danny. I'll go with you," he said, and placing a hand on the boy's shoulder, steered him toward the nurses' station down the hall.

Sam watched them, a lump forming in her throat. She noticed that they had the same way of carrying themselves. Straight-backed, shoulders squared. Resolute in the way they walked side by side, but somehow vulnerable, too. And in that moment a flood of affection for the two flowed through her. Crazy. On one level, she scarcely knew either of them, yet the connecting link of Emily and what she was going through had forged a bond.

They stopped at the counter and Sam watched as a nurse escorted them to Emily's room. They stood in the doorway a few seconds and then followed the nurse inside.

Sam began to pace. Moments later there was a flurry in the hall and a group of white-coated men and women trailing behind an authoritative man with a clipboard emerged from a room and headed toward Emily's. The doctor and his students making rounds. Sam watched as they stood briefly in the hall outside Emily's room while the doctor spoke to them. They went inside and once again, Sam was left waiting and wondering.

After what seemed ages, the medical group left the room and continued on down the hall. Just as Sam was considering going in to see Emily, Chase came out and headed her way. He was pale, his face drawn. He sank into a chair.

"How is she?"

"Better. But the doctor told me that these crises will escalate. Her lungs fill with fluid and have to be drained."

Sam sat in the chair next to his and bowed her head, overwhelmed by the implication of what he'd said. Escalate. Emily's suffering would increase. She felt his hand pat her upper back and then make slow, circular motions that were comforting and warm. She let herself drift with the movement until he suddenly pulled his hand away. She raised her head.

"We have to talk," he said.

She knew instantly he wasn't referring to Danny and Emily. "Yes," she said.

"Your sister went to see my uncle, at his place of business. She asked him some questions and then he came to see me." He rubbed his brow with an index finger. "Did you talk to her?"

Sam shook her head. "I tried, but it's still up in the air. To tell you the truth, I just wanted to forget the whole thing. Make it go away."

"Yeah," he said. "You and me both. I've spent the last thirteen years reconciling myself to the fact that I played a big part in the breakdown of my family and even my father's death. These past two years I finally managed to put together a life for myself and the promise of a future."

Sam didn't know what to say. The blunt facts in the FBI file she'd read had certainly not addressed the personal and emotional toll on the Sullivan family. She wished she could make it right for Chase, but knew it was too late for that.

"What happened?" she finally asked.

"It's…it's complicated, Sam. This isn't the time or place for explanations."

"I understand and I'm sorry, Chase," she said, pausing,

"but isn't it a good thing that you were still able to overcome all that?"

He got to his feet, and forked a hand through his hair. "That's the point. Things were going well until…"

"I came into the picture."

"Not just you. All of it. Emily and Danny and then your sister. Now my uncle and cousins have turned up and suddenly my whole damn past is right in my face." He strode over to a window overlooking the hospital parking lot.

"Of course it is. What did you think? That you could just live your life and never have to account for what happened? That all those unresolved issues would simply vanish?"

After a long moment, he said, "I paid for all of that. I exiled myself from my family—my mother—and tried to make amends as best I could. If it wasn't for your sister—"

Mentally she agreed totally. But loyalty to her twin surfaced. Sam walked over to where he stood, his back still turned to her.

"Don't put this on Skye. She's doing her job. I don't know why she's decided to resurrect the whole thing with your family's business, but she has. If you're innocent, you have nothing to worry about, do you?" *Are you?* she wanted to add.

He turned to face her. "You don't know anything about my worries. You come into my life, playing the Good Samaritan or whatever, reuniting a boy with his father and then blithely set loose someone who can ultimately destroy everything."

The unfairness of his words angered her. "Set loose? Skye is my sister, not some pack dog. And if you'd dealt with these things the way you ought to have years ago, you wouldn't be in this situation now."

He grabbed hold of her forearms, holding her so close

she could smell the breath mint he must have been sucking on moments ago. "You know nothing about my problems nor what I've done about them."

"You walked away from Emily when she was pregnant."

He drew back, dropping his hands. "That's beneath you."

Sam flushed and bit her lip.

"I didn't know about Danny," he said. "If I had, I'd have…"

"What?"

The unexpected voice drew their attention to the entrance of the waiting area and Danny, staring at them. "What would you have done?" he asked again. His face was red and his eyes glistening. "Would you have married my mom and made her whole life different? Maybe she wouldn't have had to work so hard. Maybe she'd have quit smoking, because she wouldn't have been so stressed about making money and looking after me all by herself."

"Danny—" Chase moved toward him.

"No. It's too late to say you're sorry!" he cried. He spun on his heel and ran toward the bank of elevators. One opened and he jumped on.

Sam hurried after him. "Danny, wait! Come back." But the door closed.

"Please don't tell me this is my fault, too," Sam said, looking at Chase.

"No," he said with a sigh. "I should have talked to him honestly about Emily and me."

"He'll come back," she said, feeling suddenly sorry for him.

But when Danny didn't return after fifteen minutes, Chase went downstairs to the cafeteria and gift-shop area to look for him. While he was gone, Sam took the opportunity to see Emily. She was sleeping, but Sam tiptoed into the room. She stroked the back of her hand, resting on top of the covers, and whispered, "Don't worry, Emily. Danny will be fine. Chase will take care of him. And I will, too," she added. Then she left the room to return to the waiting area, arriving as the elevator opened and Chase walked out.

"Any luck?"

He shook his head. "I called Minnie to warn her he may show up there, angry and hurt. She promised to call if he did."

"Where could he have gone?"

"I don't know. I know so little about him. Who his friends are or where he hangs out." Chase chewed on a knuckle thoughtfully. "The park. Where we went last week, after the interview at his school. Greenlake."

"It's a long way from here. He'd have to take a bus."

"Yeah, but it's still on his way home. Anyway, he's been gone half an hour. We have to do something." He started for the elevators.

"I'll come with you."

He turned around. "You don't have to."

"I know. I want to. Is that okay?"

"There's not room for three in the truck."

"Why don't we take my car? I'll bring you back here for your truck."

"Sure. Let me tell someone at the nurses' station to call in case Danny comes back here."

They walked out to the parking lot. Sam thought back to everything they'd said, wondering how much Danny had heard. She was ashamed to think she'd accused Chase of running out on Emily when she knew he hadn't known she was pregnant. And as for her rebuke that he ought to have resolved the problems in his past, rather than flee from them…. *Well done, Samantha. Why haven't you taken your own advice?*

She was glad to be driving. Concentrating on the traffic meant no conversation, and she figured she and Chase had said enough for one day. Occasionally she glanced his way, watching him stare out the window, lost in thought. Yet some part of him seemed to be constantly moving. His fingers tapped on his thighs and his leg jiggled impatiently, as if he were mentally racing the car to the park himself. Fortunately she managed to hit every green light.

When she finally pulled in to the same parking area they'd been at a few days ago, Chase had the door open before Sam even turned off the engine. She watched him cover the asphalt lot with long, purposeful strides. He didn't bother looking back to see if she was following. By the time she reached the picnic area beyond the take-out burger stand, Chase was heading along the water's edge. In the distance, she saw a small figure hunched against the wind.

Sam stopped by a picnic table and watched as Chase caught up to Danny. Chase put a hand on Danny's shoulder and bent down, obviously talking. Danny threw off the hand and moved away. Chase waited, then extended an arm and drew the boy closer. Sam perched on the tabletop, shivering. It was past six and the temperature was dropping as the sun dipped toward the western sky.

Eventually the two began to walk her way. Danny's head was hanging and he shuffled along beside Chase, whose arm rested lightly across his shoulders. When they reached Sam, Danny looked up. His eyes were red and swollen.

"I'm sorry I ran away, Sam," he said.

Tears welled up in Sam's eyes. She opened her arms and wrapped them around Danny as he climbed up onto the table next to her. He lowered his head onto her lap and sobbed. Sam rubbed his back with one hand, using the other to wipe her own tears away. Chase sat on the other side of Sam and, without a word, draped his arm around her shoulders, drawing her closer to him. They sat like that long after the sun disappeared beneath the horizon.

## CHAPTER TEN

IMPULSIVELY, driving out of Greenlake Park, Sam suggested, "Maybe Danny would like to spend the night at my place."

She looked at Chase, in the passenger seat. He caught her gaze and nodded. Turning to Danny in the rear, he asked, "That okay with you?"

Danny mumbled something that sounded like a yes.

"Thanks, Samantha," Chase said.

"My family and friends call me Sam."

"Sam it is."

She felt his eyes on her and wondered what he was thinking. She hoped that he no longer thought she'd been conspiring with Skye. When they arrived at her place and Danny got settled in front of the television, Sam decided to do something to prove to Chase that she wasn't teaming up with her sister against him.

They were having a glass of wine, sitting at the small table for two in a corner of the kitchen when Sam excused herself, went into the bedroom and returned with the file Skye had given her. Chase frowned as he registered the name on the cover page.

"Where did you get this?"

"My sister copied it from the archives at her old office."

His face told her he was wrestling with that. "Have you read it?"

She nodded.

"And?"

"I didn't see anything incriminating."

"May I?" he asked, indicating the file.

"Of course. That's why I'm showing it to you. And I'm hoping…"

"I can explain it?" His face cracked in a half smile, as if he doubted he'd be able to.

"Yes," she said, smiling back at him.

He opened the file and thumbed through it. "You're right, there's not much here. Nothing incriminating, as you said. But what's here raises a question, and the answer to that is what your sister missed when she investigated Trade Winds."

Sam was almost as intrigued by the fact that Skye might have made a mistake as she was by Chase's cryptic reply. "How so?"

He shuffled the papers, extracting two or three and showing them to her. "Here are two reports and an invoice all signed by me."

"Uh-huh." She felt an urge to tell him to get to the point, but was beginning to realize he needed to work through the steps himself.

"So if I were investigating this, I'd ask myself why a low-level clerk in a company was signing reports and invoices." He paused for a long moment and said, "I guess I should start from the beginning."

"That would be good. Let me just see if Danny needs anything." Sam went into the living room to check on him, though she really wanted to make sure the television was loud enough to drown out their conversation. But Danny had fallen asleep. She clicked off the TV and covered him with the throw on the back of the couch.

"He's sleeping," she said on her return.

"He's had a rough day." Chase rubbed his forehead. "We all have. Especially Emily."

She liked that he'd highlighted the person who made all the rest of their bad days seem minor. *We must never forget Emily.*

"Okay," he said, sighing, "to begin. My father and his younger brother, Bryant, inherited Trade Winds when I was just a toddler. It's been owned by Sullivans for more than a hundred years and was originally a shipping company. But at some point, my father and uncle decided to get into the import-export business. They got commissions and contracts from various agencies and companies to import or export goods. Basically to act as brokers. Something like what you do, I think, but in a broader context."

He flashed a smile that, unexpectedly, warmed her.

Then the smile faltered. "I don't want to digress by getting too far into the dynamics of my family, but they're relevant to what happened. I had a rocky relationship with my father. When I graduated from university—in arts, not business as he'd wanted—my main goal was to get as far away from Seattle as I could. My mother was secretly on my side, but she didn't have the wherewithal to stand up to my father. She gave me money for graduation and told me to see the world. I did, and came back two years later, broke. I couldn't get a decent job, so when my father urged me to work for the company, I caved in. His health hadn't been good and while I was away, he'd been diagnosed with angina. By the time I came home, he'd handed over the daily operations to my uncle, though he kept his title of president. Most of his time, however, was spent on the golf course and at his men's club." He paused to sip his wine, running a fingertip around the edge of the glass.

"What did you do in the company?" Sam asked.

"While I was away, my uncle's two sons—Terence and

Howard—came into the business. They started out in the mail room and spent time in every department. My father wanted me to do the same. Of course, by then they were already supervising—Terence was in accounts and Howard oversaw the administration part. Trade Winds has always been a family-run business. Back then, there were fewer than fifty employees. The smallness is important, because it meant that virtually all the important aspects of the business were controlled by family. Anyway," he said, "I started out in the mail room and after a couple of months was moved into accounting. Because I had no background in that, I was basically a file clerk." He grimaced. "My cousins felt I needed a lot more practical experience. I hated working there, but my mother persuaded me to give it some time. My cousins took every opportunity to give me a hard time."

"They were bullies," Sam said.

"Yeah. Always had been, even when we were little. They'd gang up on me and lie when I tried to tell my parents what they'd been doing. My mother suspected, but my father always took their side. I needed to toughen up, he'd tell me."

Sam recalled the school bullying incident with Danny and Chase's refusal to rush to judgment about Danny's role.

"That part's important, too," Chase continued, "to what happened later. One day Uncle Bryant came up to me and asked me to sign a document. He told me it had to be signed by a family member, someone other than the CEO. I didn't even get a good look at it and to tell you the truth, I didn't care. That happened a few more times and probably I'd have continued to blindly sign away until one day the chief accounting clerk, a woman who'd worked for the company for several years, came to me with one of the invoices I'd signed.

"It was from a company that Trade Winds had hired to do some consulting work as part of a government contract. Terence and Howard had both gone to private schools and had maintained a lot of powerful contacts. After they got into management, they used those old friends to secure some very lucrative government contracts. It was another thing my father threw up at me. They'd been networking for the business while I'd been backpacking around Asia. And I'd come home with nothing to show for my world travels but long hair and a tattoo." He grinned. "Both of which I've since outgrown, though the hair was the easiest thing to change."

He lapsed into thought. Thinking of other changes? Sam wondered.

"Anyway," he went on, "the accounting clerk approached me about this invoice and wanted to know what kind of company it was. She wanted to ask about a figure on the invoice but couldn't contact the company."

"What do you mean?"

"The phone number on the invoice was phony and when she sent something by mail, it was returned. She went through her records and found a handful of invoices from the same company and I had signed all but one of them. She was shocked when I told her I didn't know anything about it. She said my signature indicated that I had received the goods and paid the company. Then she asked me why I would sign something I knew nothing about." He sighed. "It was a good question and I had no answer except for my own ignorance and stupidity. That plus the fact that I really didn't care at all. But when Big Nance—"

"Who?"

Chase smiled. "Nancy Wicks, the accounting clerk. Those of us she considered friends called her that. If you saw her, you'd get the irony. She's a tiny thing, but very tough. Anyway, Nancy said that there might be something going on and if I had signed off on everything, I'd be implicated. So I thought about it and gathered up all the documents I'd signed and took them in to my uncle. He assured me everything was kosher and not to worry. But there was something in his manner that made me think he was lying. Things started happening quickly after that. I was sent off to a trade show in Portland, which surprised me because no one had had any confidence in my business sense up to that point. While I was gone, an FBI agent dropped in to the office—your sister, Skye. She told my uncle they were investigating a complaint of fraud against the business. Apparently there had been an anonymous phone tip. In the meantime, Nancy Wicks was advised that she'd been made redundant. I knew none of this until I came back from the show."

He rubbed his eyes and yawned. "It's getting late. I'll try to wrap this up quickly. To sum it up, I came back to find Nancy gone and my uncle, father and cousins furious about the inquiry. Uncle Bryant accused me of tipping off the FBI and my father believed him. Uncle Bryant spun the whole thing to make it look like I'd been involved with what was going on. And my name was on a lot of those documents. There was a huge fight and my father accused me of betraying the family. I took off, leaving the whole mess behind me. Running away from my problems." His mouth twisted bitterly. "I hung out in the city for a bit, got a construction job and that's when I met Emily. A month later, my father had a fatal heart attack." He stopped. Then, "I never had a chance to prove my innocence. After the funeral, I wanted to get as far away from Seattle as I could."

"When did you come back?"

"Two years ago." He stretched and yawned. "And that's another story, which I'm much too tired to get into now. I should go—have to get my truck."

"Oh, right, I'd forgotten all about it. I was going to drive you there, but now that Danny's asleep—"

"Leave him be. I can take a taxi."

She almost invited him to stay over, too, but held back. Although she now had a more complete picture of his past and who he was, it was best to not rush their developing friendship.

On his way out, Chase asked, "Are you busy in the morning?"

"At some point I should check in at my office, but I can drive Danny to school if that's why you're asking."

He frowned. "Oh, right. School. I guess I have a way to go before I automatically think like a parent."

Sam patted his arm. "You're doing just fine, Chase. Give it time."

His eyes connected with hers. "Thanks. But the reason I asked is that I'd like you to meet someone. Danny, too. I'll call his school to say he'll be in later."

"All right." She was intrigued.

"Great. Meet me at Harbor House about nine-thirty. You remember where that is?" His grin was teasing.

He wants us to meet his mother. "I do." She smiled.

"Okay, then," he said. "Tomorrow."

He grasped her hand and Sam stiffened, thinking he was going to pull her toward him. But instead, he held it lightly, as if he were about to lead her onto a dance floor. Then he gently let go, turned and left.

Sam stood by the closed door a moment, thinking that something had just happened between them. Exactly what, she couldn't say. But she realized a barrier had been removed. He was no longer an adversary, but someone she wanted to work with to help Danny.

Yet sometime in the middle of a restless night, she asked herself if perhaps she'd simply been conned. After all, she'd heard only one side of the story. As she finally dropped off to sleep, she could hear Skye's more skeptical voice reminding her that people—especially criminals— tell you only what you want to hear.

HE GOT THERE EARLY, mainly because his mother had good days and bad days. Plus his routine was off, this being midweek.

"She's having a good day so far, Chase," the receptionist told him. "Nurse Andrew said she ate some breakfast, and right now, she's sitting in the solarium. Do you want to visit with her there?"

"Yes, thanks, Mrs. MacDonald, but I'm expecting a couple more visitors, so I'll wait for them in the hall."

When Sam turned up with Danny in tow, Chase was amused by the expression in Mrs. MacDonald's eyes. She obviously remembered Sam—and not kindly, judging by the downturn of her mouth. But her professionalism took charge and she managed a thin smile as they passed her desk on the way to the solarium.

Outside the entrance, Chase paused to say, "My mother has Alzheimer's, Danny. I don't know if you know what that is but—"

"Yeah, I do," he snapped. He obviously wasn't happy about the visit.

Chase bit back a retort. He tried to think how he'd have felt at the same age, being forced to go to a nursing home to see an old woman he didn't know. But this old woman was Danny's grandmother, and like it or not, he was going to meet her. His gaze met Sam's, above Danny's head. She shrugged and gave a sympathetic smile.

"Why don't you go in first and we'll follow a minute later, give you time to greet her?" Sam suggested.

He felt an unexpected warmth for her, realizing not for

the first time in the past couple of days, how badly he'd misjudged her. "Good idea. She might be alarmed if we all troop in at once." He glanced at Danny, who was busy surveying the paintings on the wall. Chase smiled inwardly at this new interest in art.

He stepped into the solarium, scanning the small group of elderly people in wheelchairs until he saw his mother sitting in a wing chair in a corner. It was her favourite place, giving her a clear view of the gardens outside and angled away from the rest of the room. Martha Sullivan had always been an introvert and even now, in the mental fog of Alzheimer's, that part of her personality remained. He walked toward her, and as he drew near, said, "Hello, Mother," as he always did, so as not to startle her.

She turned her head slightly and he squatted to be at eye level with her. Her pale eyes stared blankly at him, as they always did, but he no longer felt the pain at her lack of recognition.

"I'm Chase," he said. "How are you today, Mother?"

"I'm fine," she murmured. "How are you?"

"Good. I've brought you a couple of visitors. Would you like to meet them?"

Her face remained impassive, though when he mentioned visitors, she glanced over his shoulder. He turned to see Sam close behind him, Danny ambling slowly in their direction.

Chase stood up. "This is my friend Samantha."

"Hello, Mrs. Sullivan," Sam said as she moved closer. She extended her right hand, but Martha ignored it, as Chase knew she would.

"Hello," said Martha.

She looked back at Chase and for a second, he thought he saw recognition in her eyes.

"Are you the man who brings the peppermint patties?" she asked.

"I'm sorry, I didn't bring you any this time."

Chase pursed his lips. Just then, his mother's eyes widened and an expression of absolute delight filled her face as she looked beyond him.

"Chase!" she cried, raising her arms in greeting.

Chase turned to see Danny, who was only two feet away. The boy stared at Martha.

"Come here, son," said Martha.

Chase caught Sam's expression and moved aside, gesturing at Danny to come forward. And when his son did so and stood before Martha, Chase couldn't tell if what he felt was pride that Danny didn't hesitate or pain that the first time he'd heard his mother say his name in two years had not been for him. All he knew for sure was that he couldn't speak over the lump in his throat.

He watched Martha reach out and stroke Danny's arm. He couldn't recall the last time he'd seen his mother smile like that. After a couple of minutes, he managed to say, huskily, "We can't stay long, Mother. Danny, er, Chase, has to get to school."

Danny looked at him, then back at Martha.

"Are you going, Chase?" asked Martha, beaming at Danny.

"Yes, I have to go to school," he said, "but I'll come back another day."

"Please do," she said, then looking at Chase, said in a sterner voice, "Don't forget my peppermints the next time."

He caught the glint of amusement in Sam's eyes, but nodded soberly. "I won't," he said, and leaned over to kiss her on the cheek.

As he ushered Danny and Sam out the door, he took one last glance at his mother. She was staring blankly out the solarium windows. *We're already forgotten,* he thought.

When they reached the foyer, Chase made a decision. "Danny, would you mind going on ahead for a couple of minutes? I'd like to have a word with Sam."

Danny's gaze flicked from Chase to Sam and back again. His expression shifted, too, from neutral to suspicious. "I'll wait outside, by the front door."

"Thanks, buddy," Chase said. "We won't be long."

As he headed for the entrance, Chase turned to Sam. "I don't mean to be mysterious," he said at the question in her face. "I just want to fill you in on some background about my mother, and I feel uncomfortable talking about it in front of Danny."

Sam touched his arm. "Okay, but maybe you should explain to Danny when we get outside. He hates being left out."

Chase nodded, but he kept seeing the look in his mother's face when she spotted Danny. "I left Seattle after my father died, but I kept in touch with my mother," he began. "She begged me to come home, but I'd promised Uncle Bryant I'd stay away from Seattle. He'd convinced me everyone was better off and that if anything happened to the business, my mother's livelihood would suffer as much as his own—her main source of income after my father's death was his share in the business. So I kept my word until about two years ago. I'd begun to think something was wrong with her while talking to her on the phone. She seemed more forgetful than usual. The letters she sent me became almost nonsensical. Finally I contacted Uncle Bryant and asked him to check up on her. A couple of weeks later he called to say she'd been found wandering the street outside our family home and had been hospitalized. I was living in Alaska at the time, but I left as soon as I got the call."

"Is that when she was admitted here?"

"Yes. To his credit, my uncle didn't leave her. He got her in here right away and she was already settled by the time I arrived. She didn't know me, of course—the disease had reached that point—but she was obviously content. My uncle wasn't happy about my intention to stay in Seattle. He made it clear that he was happy to pay for my mother's accommodation and care as long as I refrained from making any claim on the family business. I had no choice but to agree. So if he cuts the purse strings, she'll have to be moved to a state hospital." He paused. "I couldn't bear that."

"Chase, you have to do something about this situation."

He looked at her, unsure what she was referring to.

"With your uncle and the company. If there was something illegal going on, it'll come back to haunt you."

"Are you telling me this because of your sister's interest in the case?"

"No. But if it wasn't her asking questions, it'd be someone else."

He felt a rush of annoyance. "Why can't people just let it be?"

"Do you want to spend the rest of your life with this hanging over you?"

She was right, of course. There were days when he could forget all about it and others when he was filled with anger—at his father and uncle and especially, himself. He'd been prepared to carry the burden to protect his mother and perhaps, after she was gone, then he'd put things right. But now he felt differently. Things had changed.

"Oh, Chase," Sam murmured. He felt her hand touch his. Instinctively he clasped her hand and held tight. For the first time in a long time, he sensed a connection with another adult. He liked the feeling and didn't move away until he saw Danny looking at them from the other side of the glass front door.

"You have to do it for Danny, Chase," Sam said. "He's in your life now."

He watched Danny—his son—gesture impatiently. *I owe this boy something,* Chase thought. *Most of all, I have to start being a father.*

SKYE WAS BEGINNING to regret coming home. The fact was, she was bored. And as always, when boredom struck, her mind wandered to other tasks she'd rather do or other places she'd rather be. She'd been waiting two days for Sam to get back to her about the Trade Winds file and refused to call her.

Surely Sam had found what she'd noted in the file thirteen years ago. That the documents had been signed by Chase Sullivan, who had been little more than a file clerk at the time. And although she had no new evidence to warrant a request to reopen the case, she was still intrigued by Sullivan's role.

Skye sighed heavily, blowing out all her pent-up frustration. She leaned back in the swivel chair at her old desk and stared at the notes on her laptop screen. The conundrum was that if she stirred things up at the field office and the case *was* reopened, her own neglect of it would be all too obvious. If she hadn't been in such a rush to leave Seattle for her transfer to Washington, she would have followed up with Chase Sullivan on his return. Instead she'd left the task and the file to her replacement, who apparently had screwed up, too.

Now she was left with the same question she'd asked herself years ago. Why had Chase's signature been on those reports and invoices, as innocuous as they seemed, if he had not been in management? She wanted the answer to that question but knew it would inevitably lead to trouble.

In spite of her sister's vehement denial that she had no interest in Chase Sullivan beyond his role in his son's life. Skye had seen the color in her cheeks. No one knew her sister better than she did. And no way was she going to be blamed for another ruined relationship. Although, did she want her twin linked to someone who might be a cheat? She thought about last Christmas. Maybe responding to Todd's kiss had been a regrettable impulse, but underlying the impulse was a desire to reveal him as the consummate womanizer she sensed he was.

When the phone rang later that day, Nina called Skye to pick up. It was Samantha.

"We need to talk," she said. "You, me and Chase Sullivan."

"Okay. When and where?"

"My place, tonight at seven."

"Okey-dokey," Skye said. She hung up with a satisfied smile. The decision had been taken right out of her hands. Good.

# CHAPTER ELEVEN

"WHAT, NO WINE?"

Sam hid her grin from her sister. "This is a business meeting, not a social one." She switched on the coffee-maker and began pulling mugs from a cupboard.

"You aren't dressed for a business meeting," Skye pointed out. "That top is a tad sheer, isn't it? And those jeans very tight, I must say."

"Cut it out. Here, put some of these cookies on a plate." Sam handed her a box.

"Store bought? Couldn't you at least have baked?"

"Ha ha." It was a family joke—no one in their family baked. Sam hoped the light mood would last, but had her doubts. She'd invited Skye to come earlier than Chase—she wanted to fill her in on what she'd learned from him yesterday.

Chase had dropped Danny at the school, but called Sam from his cell phone to continue their discussion about Trade Winds. Eventually Sam had persuaded him to talk to Skye, informally and off the record. Now she had to convince her sister likewise.

"He seems to be a bit late," Skye said, checking her watch.

"No, I asked you to come earlier."

"Oh, yeah?"

Sam saw the instant wariness in her sister's eyes.

"Come and sit down," she said, leading the way into the living room.

Skye perched on the edge of the couch. "What have you cooked up, Sam?"

"Come on, Skye. Surely when I said we were meeting with Chase, you figured out what it was going to be about."

"So I gather the two of you are going to try to persuade me to drop the inquiry." Her expression suggested she was up for the challenge.

"Not really. I was hoping you'd agree to work with us to find out the truth."

Skye's eyes narrowed. "The truth? Are you prepared for that?"

"Why wouldn't I be?"

"Just that—you know—you seem a bit attached to this guy and his kid."

Sam held up a hand. "Hey. They have names and I want you to use them. Okay?"

Surprise flickered across Skye's face. Then she shrugged and said, "Fine."

"Good. Now let me tell you Chase's story. I'd like you to think about it before he gets here. If you're not into helping us, there's no point wasting everyone's time."

Skye leaned back into the couch, crossed her legs and said, "Go ahead."

Sam wasn't fooled by her nonchalance. She'd caught the flash of anger in her twin's eyes. But she gave a condensed version of the story, because she wanted to finish before Chase arrived. To her surprise, Skye didn't interrupt once, and she managed to relate the gist of what happened years ago, ending with the visit to Martha Sullivan.

When she finished, Skye didn't speak for a long time, obviously digesting everything she'd heard. "So you're telling me Chase had no idea what was going on in his own family's business?"

"It seems unbelievable, but he was younger—twenty-three then—and he had no interest in the company. He didn't even want to work there and was just biding his time until he'd had enough saved to travel again."

"The woman who went to Chase with her concerns—what was her name again?"

Sam scanned the notes she'd made. "Uh…Nancy Wicks."

"Okay, so she couldn't find any record of a company that had been contracted by Trade Winds for these government commissions."

"Right, and when Chase confronted his uncle with the invoices, he was told everything was aboveboard."

"Huh. Sort of, butt out and don't worry your pretty little head about all this."

Sam smiled. "In this case, your handsome little head."

Skye arched a brow. "Like that, is it?"

Sam regretted the remark instantly. "Just joking. Back to business."

Skye stared at her a long moment before saying, "All right. Was there any mention of Nancy in my notes?"

"No, she'd already been let go by the time you went there."

Skye frowned. "So they could have purposely left me in the dark about other employees to interview. It does make sense if she was there when the scamming was going on."

"Scamming?"

Skye leaned forward. "This is what I think was happening. Trade Winds had received a lot of lucrative government contracts, right?"

"Right. Apparently Chase's cousins had government connections."

"Whatever. The point is, a company like Trade Winds simply contracts jobs and goods. They'd get some other business to provide the stuff they've been hired to obtain, pay them and then collect from the state or the federal government."

"Chase said it was similar to what I do."

"Yeah, it is. But suppose the company that provides the service doesn't exist? Suppose it's a company on paper only and is actually 'owned' by Trade Winds."

"But they have to provide something, don't they, in order to get the government to pay them?"

"I hate to tell you how easy it is to cheat the government, Sam. People do it all the time. Think about it—governments are huge bureaucracies with a lot of people working in them. Half the time, one department has no idea what another is doing. You wouldn't believe the stories I've heard or the scenarios I've seen."

"Are you saying that one department could be paying off an invoice without actually checking to see if the job was done?"

"Exactly. Or if the goods were provided in full. Perhaps only half of what was requested was received, but full payment was made." Skye reached out a hand. "Let me see my file for a sec."

Sam handed her the file and waited while Skye rifled through it.

"Here's something," she said, retrieving a slip of paper. "This invoice is for something called 'inventory consultation' by a business called H. J. Weiner and Company."

"What is that? Inventory consultation?"

"Who knows? My guess is that it's something to do with business investing. Maybe checking out business markets somewhere." Skye flipped through the file again. "Here's a report connected with that particular invoice. H. J. Weiner was contracted by Trade Winds to study import-export markets in China. You know, like the kinds of goods that would sell well over there and vice versa. And," she added, skimming the report, "it's been signed by none other than Chase Sullivan."

"Because his uncle, or maybe one of his cousins, got him to."

Skye shot her a withering look. "So he says."

"I believe him. He signed things without bothering to read them. He didn't care."

"Relax, Sam. I'm just reminding you there is another perspective here. In spite of what Chase told you, there's no proof that he's telling the truth."

"And there's no proof that he defrauded the government."

Skye waggled the invoice and report at her. "His name is on both of these documents. If it could be proved that there is no such business as H. J. Weiner and Company, then he's in big trouble."

"But…" Sam stopped, overwhelmed by the implications.

"There may be a way out of this for Chase," Skye said. "If we could persuade the local FBI office to reopen the case, new evidence may turn up."

"How?"

"Presuming the uncle and sons were cheating the government twelve years ago, they may still be doing so. And obviously Chase won't be connected to those new cases."

"Well, you've more or less been doing that, haven't you? Reopening the case?"

"More or less."

Sam waited. "Well, which is it?"

"I've been researching the file on my own time, Sam. I don't work in Seattle anymore. I don't have official sanction to review the case."

"But you could get it, couldn't you?"

"Not without new evidence or information turning up to warrant a review."

"Then why have you been checking this out on your own?"

Skye looked away. "I'm not clear on that."

"What's that supposed to mean?"

Skye's gaze shifted back to Sam. "Well…for one thing, I knew I'd need something to do while I was in town. Also, I was curious. Your phone call brought it all back and I wondered if I could find anything new. Plus…" Her voice trailed off.

"What?"

"Just that I knew I hadn't done a great job with the inquiry the first time around. I was a rookie and tended to believe what was staring me in the face and not question what I didn't see."

Sam was surprised at this admission of weakness from Skye. She didn't know how to respond, but was saved from doing so by the front-door buzzer.

"That must be Chase," she said, getting up to ring him in. "Help yourself to coffee while I get the door," she said over her shoulder. She thought she heard Skye mutter "Whoopee" on the way.

Sam didn't expect the sudden flutter in her midsection when she saw Chase standing in the doorway. He held out a bottle of wine and said, smiling, "Hello again."

"Hello, to you. Come in. Skye's already here. And thank you for this," she said, taking the wine and closing the door behind him. "How'd it go with Danny?"

"Okay, I guess. I was hoping he'd open up a bit about his mother but maybe I'm expecting too much too soon. But I did tell him more about my mother and gave him an edited version of my falling-out with my father."

"Good for you. Did he say anything about the visit to Harbor House?"

"He said I must feel bad about my own mother not knowing me anymore."

Sam placed a hand on his forearm. "In spite of his often contrary manner, I think Danny is a sensitive boy. Like his father," she impulsively added.

Chase put his hand on hers. "Thanks, Sam."

The mood was broken by a voice behind them. "Coffee's ready," Skye said, "but perhaps you'd prefer wine?"

"I believe you two have already met," Sam said.

"Indeed we have," said Chase solemnly, his gaze fixed on Skye. "And coffee's fine with me."

Sam wondered if this meeting was a mistake. She was about to suggest opening the wine, after all, when Chase smiled and extended his right hand to Skye.

"At least now I know whom I'm speaking to," he said.

"Oh, I think you were pretty quick figuring that one out before," Skye said, shaking his hand.

Sam breathed an inward sigh of relief.

They settled into the living room with coffee and Skye got right to the point. "Sam's filled me in on what you discussed with her, Chase. I told her that unless new evidence or information comes to light, the case probably won't be reopened. So I'm not exactly sure what you two—or the three of us—can do."

While Sam appreciated her sister's frankness, she was annoyed at the negative slant she was giving. "Let's not rule out anything yet," she quickly said.

"Was there anyone else in the company besides this Nancy Wicks who suspected what was going on?"

Chase shook his head. "It was—and likely still is— basically a small business. There were only a handful of people in the office."

"So your uncle and cousins were the only ones really running the business." She thought for a moment. "It wouldn't hurt to talk to the Wicks woman."

"Wasn't that already done when the inquiry was going on?" Chase asked, reaching for one of the cookies on the plate that Sam had set on the coffee table.

To Sam's surprise, her sister blushed. "I didn't know about her." Then she added, "But I should have come back to question you."

"Yeah. Maybe it would have all come out right at the time, instead of thirteen years later."

There was no sound but the gentle crunch of cookie. Finally Sam could stand it no longer. "Look, there's nothing to be gained by imagining what might have been or should have been done back then. Let's work with what we know now." She looked at Chase. "Would you be able to find Nancy?"

"If she's still at the same address, yes."

"Then we'll start with her. Why don't you confirm her address and we can go see her tomorrow. And, Skye, maybe you could find out if there have been any other inquiries or suspicions about Trade Winds since."

"Presumably they'd have been cross-referenced with the old file," she said.

"Still, there might be something somewhere."

"Maybe."

Sam glanced sharply at her sister. She obviously wasn't pleased at the way things were moving along or simply didn't like being told what to do.

"There is one other matter," Chase said.

Both sisters looked at him.

"When I came home two years ago, I found out that my mother had sold her share of the company to my uncle. I know she didn't get what she ought to have and I argued with my uncle about it, but he basically told me the sale was final. I think my mother had already been diagnosed with Alzheimer's by then, so…"

"He took advantage of her," interjected Sam. "Wouldn't that make the sale invalid?"

Skye sighed. "I think Chase would have to hire a lawyer to look into the details. Unless he has definite proof of wrongdoing." She stood up. "I should go. Mom wants me to go shopping with her in the morning."

*"Shopping?"* Nina's dislike of shopping was legendary in the family.

"Yeah, go figure. I think there's a man in her life."

Sam didn't know if she was more shocked by this revelation than by the fact that Skye, who'd been home only a week, knew before she did. It also made her realize, sadly, how seldom she and her sister communicated.

She walked her to the door, where Skye leaned forward to whisper, "Don't forget what we talked about before Chase arrived. His part in this," she said when Sam frowned.

"And don't you forget you promised to do some checking around."

"Watch yourself," was all Skye said, closing the door behind her.

Seething, Sam headed into the kitchen for the bottle of wine. "Would you like a glass of wine?" she called out.

"Love to."

She spun around to find Chase standing in the doorway. "Heavens, you startled me. Here, you open it while I get the glasses." She handed him the corkscrew, reached for two goblets in the cupboard above the sink and hastened into the living room. She couldn't explain why she felt so nervous, but sensed it had a lot to do with her increasing change of mind when it came to Chase Sullivan.

When he joined her, she was sitting in her chair, leafing through the file again. He sat on the couch. "Thank you," she said as he poured the wine. "Can you think of anything else we could do?"

"Hmm, yes, I can."

She raised her head. "I…uh…was talking about the case."

"Oh." His gaze didn't falter.

Sam knew her face was red, but sipped her wine, pretending she hadn't caught the nuance in his voice.

After a moment he said, "Sorry, I didn't mean that to come out like a bad line in an even worse movie. It's just that our conversations always have to do with Danny or my past. I was thinking on my way over here that I really know little about you. Certainly not as much as you seem to know about me."

She looked straight at him and said, "I agree with you about the first point, but as for knowing a lot about you, I hardly know more than…well, more than my sister."

He cocked his head, clearly puzzled.

"I mean," she went on, discomfited by his stare, "what I know about you are *facts*. Things other people know— or could find out. Your history."

"My history," he repeated softly. "Let's not go there tonight. Tell me about *your* history—especially with your sister." He reached for another cookie and settled back into the couch.

"Not much to tell." Sam shifted in her chair. "Identical twins raised by a single mother who is also a practising clinical psychologist."

"Divorced?"

"Yep. When we were two. My father couldn't take the impact of twins on his personal life."

"Do you have contact with him?"

"None at all. I think he made a halfhearted attempt at

maintaining contact for the first couple of years, but then he met someone else, started another family and so the story goes."

"Maybe it was better that way, being with only one parent, but someone whose love you never had any doubts about." He folded his arms across his chest, looking disarmingly like a psychologist.

Sam considered what he said. She'd never really looked at their abandonment by their father that way, but she saw that he was right. Nina had more than made up for a missing parent. "I suppose," she murmured, drinking more wine and wishing he'd fasten his eyes somewhere else.

"I gather you and your sister have a…well, I guess you could say a communication problem."

Sam's laugh was derisive. "I guess you could say for sure. We look alike, but we're very different."

He nodded. "That was my first impression when she came into my shop. Now I'm not so sure."

"How do you mean?"

"I noticed when we were talking tonight that you and she seem to have some kind of mental connection. I can't explain it. She'd say something and your body language signaled a reaction. Then you'd both look at each other at the same time. Am I making any sense?" He grinned suddenly, unfolding his arms and relaxing against the cushions. "Maybe it's a twin thing."

"I've been edgy around Skye lately, so perhaps that's what you're seeing."

"Edgy?"

"We had a falling-out some months ago," she said dismissively, hoping he'd drop the matter. But no such luck.

"What about? It's none of my business, but I'm curious." He leaned over to refill her wineglass, adding a bit more to his at the same time.

All of a sudden, Sam found herself wanting to tell him about it. "The story behind the story really goes back to high school," she said. "When we were in twelfth grade, I was dating a guy I didn't really like all that much, but at the time, having a date seemed to be more important than *who* you were dating. My sister and I had this rivalry about, say, who would snag the first date for the monthly school dance, that sort of thing. Anyway, Skye and I had an argument one day about dates and I'm not sure which one of us suggested the idea or maybe it hit us both at the same time—that mental thing we had going, as you said. So we decided that the next time he asked me out, we'd trade places and see if we could fool him."

"Ah, the old switcheroo trick," he said, raising an eyebrow.

"Yes, and Skye was always a good actor, which is why I think she's so good at undercover work. Anyway, the poor guy had no idea and was incredibly embarrassed when she finally told all. Especially after a rather heavy make-out session."

"Uh-oh."

"When she came home that night, we had a laugh about it, but I felt really guilty afterward and apologized to him the next day. He told me very bluntly what he thought of both of us and never asked either one of us out again. But the prank taught me something about respecting other people and I refused to use my twin-hood to play any more tricks again. Not even on our mother—because we'd done that as children. I made Skye promise never to pretend to be me and vice versa." Sam paused to take another sip of wine.

"So fast forward to last Christmas. I was engaged to be married to Todd—I'd been dating him for a while and I thought I loved him and he loved me. Skye was living in

D.C. then, as she still is. We were all at my mother's for dinner and I offered to do the dishes. Skye came into the kitchen as I was starting and said she'd take over, that I'd done a lot of the preparation so I should take a break. So I did. I joined my mother in the solarium—it's across the patio from the kitchen. Todd had gone outside to get something from the car."

"I think I'm getting the picture."

"It was like a scene in a French farce. Fiancé mistakes twin, kisses the wrong one."

"But it was a bit more than a simple kiss," he said quietly.

She sighed. "Yes. So much so that I couldn't forget about it—as my ex so diligently tried to persuade me to do."

After a moment, he asked, "And now?"

Sam smiled. "Now I don't even know what I saw in him."

He smiled back. "But you're still angry at Skye."

"I'm not sure. I thought I was, but maybe I'm more angry at myself. That she obviously saw something in Todd I missed. That worries me."

"I gather you haven't settled the matter with her, then." He finished the last of his wine and set the glass on the coffee table.

"No, though I want to. But we both seem to keep skirting around the whole thing. Or we argue about some trivial incident when…"

"What you really want to say are all the things you never said at Christmas."

She nodded. There was nothing more to say. After a few seconds, she quietly asked, "More wine?"

He looked at his watch. "Thanks, but I should get going. I've got an order to finish tomorrow and it's getting late."

She felt a rush of disappointment, hoping her story hadn't bored him or put him off completely. At the door, he paused and took hold of her hand.

"Personally I can't understand how any man could mistake you for your sister." He pulled her closer, lowered his head and kissed her.

His lips were soft, but demanded more than a chaste good-night kiss. Sam brought her arms up around his neck and held him against her, giving in to the warm, sweet rhythm of his body pressed into hers. When he pulled away, she sagged into him. He chuckled softly, steadying her with his hands.

"Thanks for the history, Sam…and for other things I hope to share with you in time. Good night." He closed the door behind him.

Sam felt stunned. Her life had just taken a sharp turn in a very unexpected direction. She ran her tongue along her lips, still tasting him. She wanted the sensation to last as long as possible.

## CHAPTER TWELVE

SAM WAS AWAKENED by the buzz of the front door. She shot up, disoriented, and looked automatically at her clock-radio. Nine. In the morning. On Saturday. She groaned and fell back onto the pillow, but the caller persisted. She reached for the phone on her bedside table and connected to the person at the door.

A muffled voice answered her sharp hello. High-pitched but assertive. When Sam repeated her "Who is it," the caller shouted, "Danny!" She closed her eyes, wishing she was simply dreaming. She crawled out of bed, threw on a robe and waited, bleary-eyed.

"It's Saturday," she said as she flung open the door. "Aren't you supposed to be with Chase?"

He brushed past her, his bad mood hunkering on his shoulders like a raven in an Edgar Allen Poe story. Sam stared speechlessly as he swept through the living room and kitchen, pausing outside the bathroom. Although his eyes darted toward the open bedroom door, he held back, obviously reluctant to cross that particular barrier.

"Can I ask what the heck you're doing?" she snapped.

"Is he here?"

"Who?"

"Chase," he said, looking her straight in the face.

"And why would he be here?"

For the first time, Danny faltered. Glancing away, he

muttered, "He left a message at Minnie's to say he couldn't have me this weekend 'cause he had to finish an order or something."

Right. He'd mentioned that last night. "And?"

His shoulders rose up and down under the oversize hoodie. "I thought maybe he was here, that's all."

"But why would he be here?"

Danny's eyes widened, incredulous. "You two were really deep into it the other night when I stayed over. I thought…well…when I heard he was copping out on me, I thought maybe he was with you. *You* know."

Sam knew if she hadn't been fantasizing about that very *you know* for part of the night, she'd have been far angrier at the suggestion than she was. She closed the door and moved past him to the kitchen. "Have you had breakfast? Want some orange juice or something?"

"I'm not hungry and you can't just change the subject, okay?"

Sam spun around. "Listen, Danny. You wake me up on a Saturday morning—my sleep-in day—to accuse me of…" she sputtered, "whatever…."

"Whatever." He sneered. "Are you—"

"No, I am not. I know what you were going to ask and although it's absolutely none of your business and I can't believe I'm explaining myself to a *twelve-year-old boy,* I will say once and for all, no. Satisfied?"

He remained silent, but Sam noticed his stubborn chin relaxing a bit. He averted his face. "I was gonna say 'dating.'"

"Yeah, right," she muttered. Then she caught his eye and grinned. "Why do I feel like my mother just barged in on me?"

He might have smiled back, she figured, had she used any other word but *mother.* "I was serious about breakfast,

Danny. Let's have some juice first and then decide what we can cook up." She went on into the kitchen before he could stop her. By the time she carried two tumblers of juice into the living room, he was slumped, legs sprawled out in front of him, on the couch. He took the juice with a mumble that Sam guessed was a thank-you and she sat across from him in her chair.

She sipped her juice slowly, wondering what to say to him. Danny had definitely misinterpreted their quiet talk the other night in the kitchen while he slept—she thought—on the couch. And while her attitude toward Chase had changed drastically in the last week, she was only now beginning to realize that her feelings for him had changed, as well. A single kiss had certainly confirmed that. *But it was only a kiss.*

The memory of Skye's sheepish expression when Sam confronted her at Christmas rose in her mind. It was only a kiss, she'd said, with such dismissal Sam had wanted to strike her. *Funny how little I care about that now.*

"So let me get this right. You thought your father and I were dating and that maybe he'd spent the night here."

Danny couldn't meet her gaze. "Yeah," he muttered into his glass.

"Well, we're not and he didn't. Okay?"

He shrugged.

"Anyway," she went on, imagining there might be a future possibility of that very scenario if his kiss was anything to go by, "would it be so terrible if we were?"

Danny's head shot up, his eyes narrowed. "Not terrible for you but maybe for me."

"Why?"

"Oh, forget it. It doesn't matter, anyway, now that I know what's what."

"But it *does* matter because I can see you're upset about

it—or about something. Why don't you tell me what's bothering you?" She set her glass down on the table and leaned forward in her chair.

Rather than answer, he concentrated on finishing his juice. When he did, he seemed to drift off, lost in thought, as he ran his fingertip along the rim of the empty glass.

"Danny?" she prompted, softening her voice. "What is it?"

He uttered an impatient sigh and looked as if he'd rather be anywhere else. "Now I see how silly it is, but I was thinking, what if you and Chase…you know, liked each other and wanted to get together. And that would be nice, I guess, for you, if it did happen." He paused. "Even though it won't, 'cause you're not dating, anyway." He stressed the last few words.

Sam wished he'd get on with it, but didn't dare interrupt.

"But suppose it did happen. I know some kids whose parents split up and they have stepmothers and fathers and all that. My friend Jeff tells me things are okay for him now, but he still misses the way his family used to be." Danny raised his voice. "I know my mom is going to die. Nobody really talks about it, but I know, okay?" He shot her a defiant look.

It was all she could do not to get up and go over to him. In spite of his expression, he fairly screamed pain. She couldn't speak for a long moment. "We don't talk about it, Danny, because—like you—no one wants to think about it. Maybe people do that, hoping the reality is never going to happen. All of this—knowing someone who's dying— is all new to me, too."

He seemed to mull that over. "Yeah, I guess. But see, the point of looking for my father was so I'd have someone after Mom…and so I wouldn't have to go into a foster home. If my…if Chase meets someone and falls in love and gets married and has kids…well, he may not want me around anymore. I'm not a cute little kid and I have problems at school and things on my mind and all that kind of stuff."

Sam knew right away what he was getting at. "You're worried that your father may want to start a new life with someone and you won't fit into it. Your mother will be gone and you'll have no one," she said softly.

He looked up. His eyes were red. "Yeah," he whispered.

Sam fended off an overwhelming urge to cry. She took a deep breath and said, "Chase would never in a million years do that, Danny. And I'm not talking about just accepting responsibility for you. He wants to *know* you—as a person and as a son. You're both still in the process of finding out about each other. It takes time. But believe me, if Chase didn't care about you, he'd simply write a check and hand it to your mother. Why do you think he took you to Harbor House the other day to meet his mother?"

Danny flushed. "I wasn't very nice that day, not when we first got there. I didn't know why he dragged me to an old people's home. But then after I met Martha, I kinda figured it out."

"What did you figure out?"

Another shrug. "That he wanted me to know something about him and his childhood." He stopped for a minute. "It was weird how she thought I was him as a kid. Afterward I wondered if it made him feel bad."

"Maybe he felt sad for a few seconds, but then I think he felt really good about how nice you were to Martha. And how you didn't correct her about the confusion. I think he was very proud of you."

"Really?"

Sam nodded. She felt a lump in her throat at the hope

in his voice. "And there's another thing, Danny. You may have started out as my client—" she paused, smiling "—but you've ended up as a friend. Friends stick together, right?"

"Yeah," he whispered.

After a moment, Sam said, "I have an idea and you can say no if you like. How about coming with me over to my mom's place for the day? I'll introduce you to my twin and we can all hang out."

When Danny agreed, she smiled. "Here," she said, handing him the TV remote, "entertain yourself while I dress and call my mother."

On the drive to Nina's, Sam filled Danny in on a few basic particulars of her life.

"What's it like being a twin?" he asked. "Do you dress the same?"

Sam laughed. "Heavens no. I think our mother did that when we were babies, but she wanted us to develop our own personalities. We were always put in different classrooms at school, if possible, so we would focus on making our own friends and not rely on each other for companionship."

"That sounds like a good idea. Do you ever do stuff together?"

"We used to, when we were younger and still living at home. But we went to different colleges and now Skye— that's her name—lives and works in Washington, D.C."

"Yeah? Skye, that's a neat name."

"She always said she got the best name because she was born first. She's fifteen minutes older than me."

"Samantha's a nice name, too," Danny quickly said.

"She's an FBI agent."

"Cool!" Danny turned her way, his jaw dropping. "Does she have a gun and everything?"

"Oh, yes, though I've never seen it. She may not have

it here because she's on holidays." *Supposedly.* Sam wondered if Skye had made a decision yet about helping her and Chase get evidence against Trade Winds.

She found out soon enough. "He's cute," Skye whispered as Danny headed farther into the foyer to meet Nina. "So are we babysitting today or what? Mom said our shopping expedition was on hold."

Sam turned to face her sister. "I think Danny would be very offended by that suggestion, Skye. He's been looking after a terminally ill mother for the past six months."

"Sheesh, lighten up. But seriously, what's happening? I thought you and Chase were all hot to track down Nancy Wicks."

Sam pulled her by the arm to an alcove at the end of the hall. "Are you going to help us with this or not?"

"I don't know. The thing is, I'm in a bit of trouble over the Trade Winds thing."

"What do you mean?"

"I had a call from my section head this morning."

"This morning?"

"Well, it was noon his time but still Saturday."

"What about?"

"He had a call from the head of the field office here, who apparently had another call from some muckety-muck in the state government who just happened to be an old buddy of…"

"Bryant Sullivan?"

"You guessed it. Anyway, Sullivan has accused me of harassment and since the case hasn't been officially opened, I was warned off."

"How?"

"Keep away from the place and the people or risk suspension."

"Oh, Skye. That's serious."

She looked away. "Especially since it would be my second suspension."

"Your second! When was the other time?"

"Just before Christmas. Another reason for my bad behavior."

Sam narrowed her eyes. "I hope you're not trying to justify what you did."

"No, I'm not," Skye said angrily, turning toward her. "I'm only saying it was just one more problem I was dealing with at the time. Can we drop it now? Mom's headed our way."

"I asked Danny if he'd like us to take him sightseeing," Nina said as she came up to them. "He would. Can you believe he's never been to Chinatown or up the Space Needle? So is that okay by you, Sam?"

"Sounds great," Sam said.

"Wait a minute, Sam," Skye said. "You and I were planning a little expedition, weren't we?"

"Shopping?" Nina asked.

"Sort of. Just checking out something," Skye said.

Sam gnawed on her lip. She knew if she turned Skye down, her sister might not give her a second chance. "Do you mind taking Danny on your own, Mom?"

"Not at all, but you'd better speak to Danny, Sam, because he thinks you're spending time with him today." She walked off to join Danny, who was wandering through the living room.

"What kind of expedition are you talking about?" Sam asked Skye.

"Going to see Nancy Wicks."

"But I did tell Danny we'd do something together."

"Come here." Skye pulled Sam by the arm to the entrance to the living room. Sam could see Danny and Nina deep in conversation in the solarium at the end of the room. "I think Nina's got you covered for part of the day, at least."

"What about that suspension thing?"

"I'll stay in the background. Besides, this Nancy doesn't know me at all. We don't even have to *mention* the FBI."

"You mean, *I* should ask the questions?"

"Don't sound so horrified. We'll talk about what to ask on the way."

"I don't even know where she lives."

Skye rolled her eyes. "Really, Sam, you make a lousy P.I. She's in the phone book."

"We have to see if Chase can come."

"Why? We can do this on our own."

"But he knows Nancy. And this concerns him most of all. He has to be there. Why the look? Do you have a problem with him coming?"

Skye turned away, heading for her bedroom. "No, just that I'll feel like a third wheel or something."

"What? Tell me you don't mean what I think you do." She marched after her sister.

Skye stopped and turned away. "You know exactly what I mean. I was only with the two of you last night for an hour, tops, and it was like dodging blanks on a maneuvers course."

"Oh, come on."

"The looks, Sam. The checking each other out. Whatever you want to call it. I'm surprised our hair wasn't standing on end with all the electricity zinging around the room."

Sam dropped her hand from Skye's arm. "If I seemed to be looking at Chase a lot, it was because I wanted to see his reaction to what you were saying about the fraud scheme and all that."

Skye smirked. "Please, Sam, that's real lame. If you haven't figured out yet that you're attracted to the man, there's not much I can do for you. Except stay out of it."

"See, that comment is what bugs me. What do you mean by it?"

"Been there, done that. I'm not going to be blamed for any more of your failed relationships."

It wasn't anger that choked Sam's reply, but pain. Pain at the realization that she and Skye had drifted so far apart that her twin could believe, much less utter, such a cruel remark. She stood still, taking slow, calming breaths to fend off a rebuttal that would only take them both down a path Sam knew she dared not go.

Lowering her voice, she said, "I'm not going to respond to that now, Skye, but we will go back to this, trust me." She started toward the solarium to tell Danny about the change in plans, then stopped and turned around. "Maybe you've given up on our relationship, but I haven't." Inwardly shaking, she spun on her heel before Skye could say another word.

Danny was graceful about the change in plans. "Will you be seeing Chase? I thought he was busy this weekend."

Sam hesitated. It wasn't her place to inform Danny about what was happening with his father and Trade Winds. On the other hand, she didn't want him to think she'd lied when she denied being romantically involved with Chase. "Yes, he does have work to do, but we have some business to discuss that's very important and he may decide to meet with us, after all. I know he'll explain it all to you at some point. I can tell you it's not about you or your mother, but about Chase and…uh…a legal matter Skye and I are helping him with. I'm sorry if that seems vague, but for now…"

Danny's dark eyes bored into hers, and Sam sensed he knew more than he was letting on. "Sure. If you're talking to him, can you tell him my mother's feeling much better, but she'd like to see him again—soon?"

His message resonated. While she and Skye were carrying on with their petty arguing and plotting with Chase to rectify the past, Emily and Danny were clinging to their last times together. Sam placed a hand on Danny's shoulder, giving it a squeeze. "I will, Danny, and tell your mom I'll be in to see her, too, as soon as possible." Impulsively she bent down to give him a quick kiss on the top of his head. "Bye then, see you later."

On her way to the kitchen to call Chase, she met Nina, carrying a tray of muffins and juice. "I talked to Danny, Mom, and he's okay with my going off with Skye."

"What's going on, Sam?"

"Mom, I'll tell you all about it soon, but not now. It's something to do with Chase and his family's business."

"You know that Danny is very fragile right now." Nina's stern face suggested nothing else mattered.

Sam pursed her lips. "I do, Mom. And the matter that we're trying to resolve will actually benefit Danny someday. So even though it may seem as if we're not thinking of him, we are."

"Of course, dear, I wasn't suggesting otherwise. I'm simply reminding you that he needs a lot of support. After we finish our sightseeing, I plan to go with him to the hospital and meet Emily."

Sam recalled her mother's reaction to the Benson-family plight when she'd first told her about Danny's office visit. How she'd advised her not to get emotionally entangled. "Thanks, Mom," she said, thinking how many things had changed since that fateful day. She kissed her mother's cheek. "I'll give you a call later."

Skye was nowhere to be seen, so Sam went on to the kitchen to call Chase. He picked up right away.

"I was wondering when you'd call," he said. "I've re-arranged my work plans so I can be free to go see Nancy Wicks. Still up for it?"

Sam marveled how a voice that signalled trouble mere

days ago could elicit such pleasure now. "Yes, but there's a small glitch. I'm here at my mother's with Danny, but he's going to spend the day with her."

She heard a muffled curse. "What's he doing there? I left a message at Minnie's before I came over to your place last night that I'd meet him at the hospital on Sunday."

Reluctant to clarify the real reason for Danny's impromptu visit, Sam said, "He just showed up at my place this morning. I think he needed some company. Anyway, I've been wanting to introduce him to Mom, so this works out okay. Why don't you give me Nancy's address and I'll meet you there."

"Sure. I'm already in the city so I can be there in about half an hour."

After jotting down the address, Sam disconnected and went looking for Skye.

She was in her old bedroom, working on her laptop. The room served as a den now, with a pull-out couch, but remnants of high-school days could still be seen. Yearbooks were lined up sequentially on the built-in shelves and, in one corner, a framed poster of the senior-year musical that both of them had performed in.

"I called Chase and we're meeting at Nancy Wicks's place. Are you coming?" When Skye swung her chair around to face her, Sam tried not to show surprise at the redness in her sister's eyes. She couldn't remember the last time she'd seen Skye cry, and she wondered if the argument they'd just had was the cause. Although she still needed to tell Skye about her anger and sense of betrayal over the Todd business, she felt bad. "We'll manage on our own if you'd rather not come."

"I'll come. Last night, you asked me to find out if there have been any further inquiries about Trade Winds since the last investigation, but since I'm forbidden access to the files now, I won't be able to do that. Maybe Nancy can add something to what we've got." She paused to shut down the computer. "Is that okay with you?"

Sam felt a rush of warmth for her sister. "Of course it is. I'll wait for you at the front door."

When Skye joined her a few minutes later, Sam noticed that she'd washed her face and applied a touch of make-up. As Skye walked out the door, Sam patted her lightly in the center of her back—a reassuring touch they'd often used on each other as children. *When all this is over,* she thought, *I'm going to do whatever it takes to get my sister back.*

# CHAPTER THIRTEEN

CHASE WAS SURPRISED to see both sisters climb out of Sam's car when he pulled up in front of Nancy's place. He watched them walking toward the pickup, thinking that, in spite of the difference in their clothing styles, it was damn difficult to tell them apart. He knew that Skye had slightly deeper lines in her forehead, maybe from frowning at criminals the past few years, and Sam's voice was gentler than her twin's. But those subtleties aside, he understood how easily they could fool a person. Like the high-school romance Sam told him about last night.

He smiled, thinking of the goodbye kiss for the umpteenth time since leaving her place. It had been impulsive and, initially, meant as a sign that he appreciated her confidence. But as soon as his lips touched hers, he knew it was no platonic gesture. He hadn't experienced such desire in a long time. Far more than merely sexual, there was also warmth and comfort in the kiss, as if it had been the most natural thing in the world to do. As if he'd been kissing Samantha Sorrenti for years. When he woke up, her face was the first thing he saw in his mind's eye and he could still taste her lips.

He got out of the truck and met them on the sidewalk. "I called Nancy after I spoke to you, Sam, to give her a heads-up. She sounded mystified when I mentioned we wanted to talk to her about Trade Winds, but I reassured her I wasn't here representing my uncle."

"Why would she think that?"

"I don't think she ever found out what happened after I returned to Seattle." He looked at the wood-frame bunga-low before them and headed for the front door. "I thought Skye was doing some other fact-finding today," Chase said in a low voice as Sam caught up to him. Skye was a few feet behind her.

She turned toward him, so close he could have leaned in an inch more and touched her skin with his lips. The thought made him feel almost light-headed.

"Skye's been warned off the case." She glanced back at Skye. "I'll fill you in later," she whispered.

*Warned off the case.* He had a gut feeling that Bryant was responsible for that, knowing his uncle had connec-tions in local and state government. The futility of what they were attempting swept through him. His uncle had money and contacts, while he had a few scraps of paper that didn't prove anything.

He stopped on the doorstep. "Is there any point in going through with this?"

"It's worth a shot," she answered immediately. "For Danny."

He wanted to kiss her on the spot, but rang the doorbell instead.

When the door opened, he was transported back thirteen years. Nancy Wicks hadn't changed a bit. Tiny as a sparrow and sporting a huge smile, she cried, "Chase!"

He bent at the waist to receive her hug. "Hi, Nancy, it's good to see you again. Let me introduce you to Samantha Sorrenti and her sister, Skye," he said, gesturing first to Sam at his side and then to Skye, coming up behind them onto the porch.

"Whoa! I haven't even had my daily glass of wine and already I'm seeing double."

"I see you've still got your sense of humor," Chase said as he and the twins followed Nancy into the front hall.

"It's certainly improved since I left the company. Come into the den. Tom's made coffee. Everybody want a cup?"

Chase heard either Sam or Skye—which, he couldn't be sure—murmur assent as he trailed after Nancy down the hall. Her wiry, steel-gray hair bobbed around her head with each step. She'd always walked with such bouncing exuberance, ready for anything and everything. No employer in his right mind would have let Nancy Wicks go. At least, no one but Bryant Sullivan. They entered a small den where a tall, white-haired man carrying a tray of coffee mugs met them. "Just put it on the table, Tom," Nancy said, and turning to them, introduced her husband.

After a few minutes of polite conversation, sipping hot coffee and complimenting Nancy on her homemade oatmeal cookies, Chase got right to the point. "Nancy, we came to talk to you about what happened at the company thirteen years ago."

Nancy's smile disappeared. "Has Bryant sent you?"

"No, no, as I told you on the phone, I'm not here representing him."

"I heard via the grapevine that you resigned soon after I left," she said.

"Actually I was fired, but I would have quit anyway."

"Was it about those companies?"

Chase locked eyes with Sam over Nancy's head. "Yes."

"I've been waiting years for someone to ask me about those companies," Nancy said. "I heard there was an investigation, but no one came to talk to me."

"Why didn't you call the FBI yourself, then?" Skye asked.

Nancy looked across the room at Tom. There was an awkward silence until Tom said, "Actually, I called the FBI—twice."

Chase glanced from Nancy to Tom. "I don't understand," he said.

"Nancy was stressed out over this thing," Tom said. "She was convinced there was something underhanded going on, but when she tried to get answers from her boss, he just put her off. She talked to you about it, Chase, but in the meantime I couldn't stand seeing her come home every night worried sick that she was involved in something illegal. So I decided to stir things up a bit."

"It was *you!*" Chase was stunned, thinking back to the day he'd returned from the trade show and his father's accusation of betraying the company and the family.

"Maybe I caused some trouble for your family?" Tom asked hesitantly.

*Like maybe blasted it apart.* But the past was long gone, Chase reminded himself, and the family held together by strings, anyway.

"Nancy—and Tom—Chase hasn't mentioned yet that my sister, Skye, was the FBI agent who went to the company to make inquiries after…uh…your anonymous phone call," Sam put in, saving Chase from having to respond to Tom's revelation.

Nancy's jaw dropped. "No kidding."

"We came to find out exactly what your suspicions were before your husband made his phone call and what evidence you saw to confirm those suspicions," Skye put in.

"Well," said Nancy, drawing her five-foot frame up straight in her chair, "you may recall my talking to you about a couple of companies, Chase. We'd hired them to fill some government contracts and I had a question about one of the invoices. Contacting the company was just like spinning wheels. Going in circles. I'd get a voice mail to tell me to call another number and that one would be out of service. That kind of thing. I talked to you about it,

Chase, before I went in to see your uncle. He was a gruff man and I avoided him as much as possible. Anyway, you'd only been in the department a few weeks and didn't know much." She grinned mischievously. "Window dressing, the girls in Shipping called Chase," she said to Sam and Skye.

Chase saw the amusement in Sam's eyes and felt himself redden.

Nancy went on. "When I did get up my nerve to talk to Mr. Bryant, he didn't seem concerned at all. Basically told me his sons had given the jobs to those companies and they would look into the matter. Not long after that, I think you went and talked to him, Chase, because we couldn't track down some numbered company. Everything started moving very quickly after that. Tom here called the FBI—and I want to say right now that I had nothing to do with that." She glared at her husband.

"She didn't," asserted Tom.

"Then Chase was sent off to that trade show and the very next day, Mr. Bryant told me my job was being made redundant. He said Chase was going to share my work with his cousins and…well…that was the end of more than ten years with Trade Winds. I figured out what was happening, but had nothing to hold against them but suspicions. And we didn't have the money to hire a lawyer to appeal my dismissal." She stopped, her eyes glistening.

Tom reached over to pat her hand.

"But to Bryant's credit," she added, as if not wanting to offend Chase about his relatives, "he was very kind about my severance package. It was a nice one."

Chase pursed his lips. Kindness had definitely not been his uncle's motive and he bet Nancy knew that, too.

Sam pulled the folder out of her large shoulder bag. "Skye managed to get a copy of her old file. Can you take a look at this and see if you recognize or recall any of the companies mentioned?" She handed the folder to Nancy, who sifted through them carefully.

"This one," she said, holding up a slip of paper. "H. J. Weiner and Company. It was the first one, I think, that I couldn't trace. See the invoice? They billed us nineteen thousand dollars for consultation. I never did find out what *kind* of consulting and why it should have cost us so much. Mr. Bryant gave me the order to pay it and I did. But I wasn't happy about it." She folded her arms across her chest indignantly.

Chase realized right then that they'd gotten all their answers. "Is there anything else you can tell us, Nancy?" he asked.

She shook her head. "No, I'm sorry. If I'd known what was going to happen, I'd have photocopied some things, or gone to the FBI myself. But it all came so quickly. They gave me a check and one of the boys—Terence, I think—watched me like a hawk while I cleared out my desk. That really ticked me off. As if I was the one who'd been stealing from the company, instead of the person trying to save them money."

Chase looked across at Sam, raising his eyebrow. She got the message and rose to her feet. "Nancy," she said, "thank you so much for meeting with us."

"I don't think I told you anything you didn't already know."

"It was important to confirm our suspicions, Nance," Chase said.

"You *are* going to look into this, then, are you?"

"Definitely," Chase said. He bent his head to kiss Nancy on the cheek. "It was good to see you again."

"Don't stay away so long this time," she said, poking him in the chest. "Come back and fill us in on everything. I want the whole story next time."

Chase smiled. "For sure, Nance."

Moments later, standing on the sidewalk with Sam and Skye, he asked, "What now?"

Sam was still looking back at the Wickses house. Finally she turned around and the flash of uncertainty in her face made him want to pull her to him. The desire to toss the whole business aside had never been stronger.

"Well…" she began, looking from him to Skye. "I think we can't do too much more until we find out if one of the companies is fake. And if so, then we have to prove somehow that Trade Winds just made up that company. Have I got it right?" She turned to Skye.

"I have a friend who might be able to help me track down the Weiner company."

"Can you do it without getting yourself into more trouble?" Sam asked.

"Keep your fingers crossed. How about I borrow your car, Sam, and you can go back with Chase?"

Chase glanced away, not wanting either of them to see the eagerness in his face at the proposal. He waited anxiously until he heard Sam say, "Um, sure, if Chase doesn't mind."

Keeping his voice as neutral as possible, Chase replied, "No, not at all."

"Okay, then, give me your keys, Sam," said Skye, "and I'll phone you if I find out anything."

Chase watched her climb in the car and start up the engine. The car made a fast three-point turn and as it zipped past them, he could have sworn he saw Skye sporting a huge grin.

He looked at Sam and said, "I don't know about you, but I haven't had any lunch. Are you interested? I know a great little place near the market." Her face lit up with pleasure, and he knew—for now—the past was history. All that mattered was exploring this new and exciting development in his personal present.

LUNCH, though every bit as delicious as Chase had promised, was merely a backdrop to the far more enjoyable pleasure of tracking every movement of his long fingers or his lips as he talked quietly and earnestly about his life on Bainbridge. The entire hour was a full sensory production, excluding the actual eating part, and Sam could have sat hours longer, taking in even more of Chase Sullivan. But unfortunately, the waiter had other plans and brought them their bill.

After Chase insisted on paying and sent the waiter away, he said, "After your call I contacted my client and got a couple of days' grace on that rush job. Since we have some free time, would you like to come back to the island with me for a bit—see my carvings?" His grin was teasing.

"How could I refuse?" Then Sam remembered Danny. "There might be a tiny problem. I'm not sure how Danny's going to take the news that I'm with you."

Chase frowned. "What's up with Danny?"

Sam quickly filled him in on Danny's morning visit, too embarrassed to look at him when she got to the part where Danny had suspected Chase might be in her bedroom.

*"What?"*

Sam held up a hand. "It's okay, Chase, really. I had a talk with him. The whole scene was driven by anxiety about possibly being rejected by you. Someday."

He was shaking his head in disbelief. "Haven't I proved myself yet? What more do I have to do to persuade him that I accept him as my son—he *is* my son—and that I won't shirk that obligation?"

Sam waited a moment before saying, "I don't think he wants to be merely an 'obligation' to you."

A stain of red crept up his neck. "You know I didn't mean that to sound so cold. It's just that mentally, I know he's my son and I have no problem accepting that. But emotionally…" He looked down at the table.

Sam placed her hand on his forearm. "Chase, no one expects you to suddenly love Danny as a father just yet. That will come. Just keep on doing what you're doing. Connect with him as an adult and eventually you'll both fall into the roles." She sighed.

He raked a hand through his hair. "You're right. Relaxing and letting things just happen is the best strategy. But I'm curious—what precipitated his impromptu visit?"

"Uh, well…it seems he was paying more attention to us the other night than we thought. He obviously misconstrued our hushed tones as we talked about Trade Winds and all that."

Sam didn't have to fill in the blanks for him. She saw that he guessed right away what Danny imagined they were talking about.

The waiter returned with the change and as soon as he left, Chase said, "Come on. I think we could both use a break from Trade Winds and—hell—even from Danny. How about it? Let's get impulsive."

"Why not?" She grinned.

"Okay, let's go to the island." He ushered her out of the restaurant and when they could walk side by side, he casually clasped her hand in his, a move so natural Sam felt as though she'd been linking hands with him forever.

The truck was parked in a lot near the market and as they reached it, Sam decided to make her phone call right away. Chase stood aside while she pressed the speed-dial button for her mother's, but Sam couldn't take her eyes off him. He caught her looking and she flushed, grateful to have the excuse to turn away as her mother answered.

"Mom, it's me, Sam. I just called to say that I'm going to be a bit later than I thought. Is Danny still with you? Or did you take him to Minnie's?"

"Yes, he's still with me. We've just come back from the hospital and I've been waiting for your call. I have an engagement this evening, Sam."

"Oh, sorry, Mom. I should have thought to ask before we left. Um, is it something flexible or…?"

"A dinner date, actually. With Bill Carter."

Sam digested that. Bill Carter was the family lawyer. And perhaps the mystery man Skye had alluded to? "Oh…well…would you be able to take Danny back to Minnie's place for the night? He can give you directions." She paused, took a deep breath and added, "Chase has invited me back to his place for a bit." There was a long silence. "Mom?"

"Yes, dear. I'm just processing that. So what shall I tell Danny?"

"The truth, Mom. I'm not asking you to make excuses for me."

"Is something going on I should know about, Sam? I mean, I don't want to keep things from Danny and at the same time I don't want to seem completely ignorant about my children's lives."

Sam had to smile. It was so typical of Nina that nothing could be unfettered by questions. "He and I need to talk over some things, Mom. About the possible legal trouble Chase might be in."

Another pause, followed by, "Ah, yes. The legal trouble."

Sam ignored the irony in her mother's voice. "Do you think I should speak to Danny myself?"

"No, no, that's all right. We had a little chat this afternoon about his visit to your place and the feelings that prompted it. He's a pretty amazing young fellow. And his mother is remarkable. I can see why you were compelled to stay with them, Samantha, in spite of the personal commitment involved."

Sam felt a rush of affection for her mother. "Could you tell Danny that Chase will call him in the morning?"

"In the *morning?*"

She saw right away what her mother was hinting at. "He plans to go to the hospital and I'll probably join him there."

When her mother responded, there was a hint of disapproval in her voice. "All right, Samantha."

"Oh, and is Skye at home? She has my car."

"She's here, but I haven't seen her for hours. She's been holed up in her room working on her computer. Do you want to speak to her?"

"No, it's okay." She hoped Skye was busy researching information on Trade Winds.

"Goodbye, then."

As Nina rang off, Sam thought about how quickly her mother had always been to come to their aid when they were teenagers. Not quite *no* questions asked, but few. And she was beginning to realize that perhaps the self-centeredness of her youth had continued on into adulthood. Why hadn't she considered that her mother might be seeing someone? In spite of her surprise at the news, she was happy for Nina. Bill Carter was not only a longtime family friend, but a warm and wonderful man. She tucked her cell phone back into her purse and turned to join Chase, standing by the truck.

"Everything okay with Danny?"

"Sounds like it. My mother's going to drive him to Minnie's."

"That's really great of her."

"Yes, it is. I think we don't really appreciate our parents until we're adults, do we?"

His face sobered. "I suppose." He lapsed into silence.

For a moment Sam thought she'd broken the spell between them but suddenly he brightened and said, "Let's talk about families on the way to Bainbridge."

"You've only heard the very tip of that gigantic iceberg from me."

"I'm all ears," he said quietly, opening the truck passenger door and, cupping a hand firmly around her elbow, helping her up into the cab.

The truck moved slowly through traffic around the market. "Saturday's the worst day," muttered Chase. "I should have known."

"The lunch was worth it," put in Sam.

He turned to her. "I hope so."

Sam wasn't certain if he was referring to food or company, though his expression suggested the latter. Personally she didn't mind sitting at a standstill in the cramped cab of a pickup if Chase was the man behind the wheel.

Five minutes later, Chase gave up. "I'll cut off at the next intersection. I know a shortcut to the ferry through some side streets. It takes us near the Trade Winds office. Are you interested in seeing it?" He shifted his attention from the traffic to Sam again.

"Yes, I am." She thought back to what Skye had told her about the history of the family-run company. "When was the last time you saw the place?"

"Two years ago, when I came back to Seattle from Alaska. My uncle and I had a *business* meeting." He snorted at the word. "So he called it. But it was basically a settlement deal. Stay far and clear of Trade Winds, drop any claim to it and your mother spends the rest of her life in comfort at Harbor House."

"The other night you said your mother had sold her share of the company to him."

"That's right. Bryant's lawyer showed me the paper-work and wasn't very subtle about informing me I'd have no chance of getting it back."

"Even if you could prove Bryant coerced an Alzheimer's patient?"

"Proving things like that cost money, Sam."

And that was that. Sam mulled over his predicament, while Chase finally managed to make his turnoff and wind through back streets toward the ferry docks. The truck crested a hill and Sam could see the harbor a few blocks below.

"This area was once solidly commercial," Chase said. "When Trade Winds was established as a shipping com-pany, the port and dockyards were much closer. My father once told me the neighbourhood was alive with merchant marines, dockworkers, tradespeople and, of course, the taverns and boardinghouses associated with all that. Now it's mainly residential, with some office buildings." The street was lined with stately homes, some of which had been turned into apartment units and offices, with a hand-ful of nondescript two- and three-story buildings scattered amongst them.

"It's a bit farther along," he said, slowing the truck down.

Sam stared out her window, trying to imagine what the street might have looked like in the late 1800s when Chase's ancestors set up business. Some of her own family had come to America from Italy a little more than sixty years ago, just before her mother was born.

The truck coasted into an empty parking space and Chase shifted into Park. "There it is," he said, pointing to a large, three-story stone edifice that fit in perfectly with its palatial neighbors. Except for a brass plate next to the door, fronted by a set of stone steps and wrought iron handrail, there was no indication that it was a commercial building.

"It's quite beautiful," said Sam, adding, "in a Gothic sort of way."

"Yeah, well, that was the style way back then. In the beginning, my great- grandparents lived upstairs, but later the family moved to Magnolia and changed this place into offices. When I was really little, my father sometimes brought me here on a Saturday morning. I got to explore the nooks and crannies—and there are a lot of them—while he had meetings or made phone calls."

He sounded so wistful that Sam turned her head. "So there were some good memories?" she asked softly.

His eyes met hers. "Some," he said. "A lot changed when I hit my teens. By then, my father had changed, too."

"How?"

He shrugged, looking uncomfortable. "Living the high life. Clubs. Drinking. Women."

"It must have been…difficult," she said, aware of the understatement but at a loss for another word.

"Very diplomatic, Sam. Frankly it was hell. Especially for Mother. But I got to leave." He stared blankly beyond her at the building.

Sam wanted to reach out to him, but he was miles away, lost in the past. Suddenly his expression altered into one of pure hatred. Sam turned to see a man in a business suit standing in the now-opened front door of Trade Winds.

Not as tall as Chase, but large-framed, he seemed to be talking to someone inside. Suddenly he pivoted and looked straight at them.

Chase swore.

"What is it?"

"My cousin Howard. He's…well…let's just say he's

not a nice person. I'm kind of breaking the agreement with my uncle by being here."

"We're just looking at the place," Sam said, staring at the man.

Howard moved slowly down the steps, speeding up as he seemed to recognize who was parked there.

"Let's get out of here," muttered Chase as he shifted into Drive and cranked the steering wheel.

The truck screeched out into the driving lane and Sam could see Howard lumbering to the curb, waving a fist at them, shouting something.

"He looks pretty ticked off."

Chase didn't reply. In profile, Sam thought he looked just as furious. More than that, she thought with a shiver, he looked dangerous.

The truck sped down the street and squealed to a stop at the first intersection. Chase turned to her, a bleak expression in his eyes. "This is going to sound lame, but do you mind if we blow off the trip to Bainbridge? I…" He gave up, looking away.

Sam thought she understood what was going on inside his head, but wasn't certain. All she did know was that the mood had shifted and a trip anywhere now was one headed for disaster. "Of course I don't mind. It's probably better that I go home, anyway. Do you mind dropping me off at the nearest transit stop?"

"Don't be silly. I'm taking you to your place."

There was little conversation after that. He drove slowly, as if in a trance. Sam couldn't figure out if he was replaying what had just happened or if he was trying to calm himself. Perhaps a bit of both, she decided.

By the time he pulled up in front of her duplex, she was relieved that the day had made an abrupt turnaround. Maybe things were moving too quickly between her and

Chase. Maybe there was still an awful lot more to learn about him.

"Thanks for lunch," she said, smiling. She started to open the door when he grasped her by the shoulder and pulled her to him.

"I'm sorry," he whispered in her ear. "I'll make it up to you. There'll be even more carvings to see the next time."

She giggled. "Don't be—" Silly, she was going to say. But the word was stifled by his lips landing on hers, his hands coming up to cup her head, holding it gently but firmly in place. No chance of escape. Not that she wanted one. Kissing him was like diving into a whirlpool, a breathless submerging. Salty lips and heat, her tongue tangling with his. Sun glittering ripples behind closed lids and wave on wave of pure pleasure cascading through her body.

His hands slipped down and under her sweater and she heard someone gasp—was it him or her?—as he touched bare skin. She pressed into him, but he suddenly tore his mouth from hers, gasping for air. Sam held on as long as possible, gradually drifting away from the kiss and his arms.

She sagged against the door, hoping her grin didn't look too hungry. "Wow," she murmured when speech returned.

"Wow," he echoed. He reached over to tug her sweater back into place, then clasped her hand in his.

"Funny how things have changed," she said.

"Funny and wonderful." His eyes bore into hers. "We're going to continue this," he promised, "as soon as possible."

"Yes," she whispered. Reluctantly, she slipped her hand out of his and opened the door.

"I'll call you later," he said as she stepped down onto the sidewalk.

He started up the engine and she stood for a long moment, watching the truck move away and down the street. Finally she turned to head inside and as she did so, noticed a car creeping past the duplex, its driver looking her way. Sam squinted into the late-afternoon sun, trying unsuccessfully to see who was so interested in her building. *Or her.*

## CHAPTER FOURTEEN

CHASE SET HIS CHISEL down on the worktable and went to answer the phone. He was hoping it might be Sam, changing her mind about coming to dinner. When he'd called to invite her late last night, he'd heard the hesitation in her voice and wondered if she was concerned about how the dinner might end, or if Danny might find out about it. But he'd decided he was being paranoid and that she might simply have a lot of work to catch up on, as she'd explained. He was in the same position and could relate.

It wasn't Sam. "Oh, hello, Mrs. MacDonald. Has something come up with my mother?" He felt anxiety rise inside him. Harbor House had only called him once in the two years he'd been back, and that was after his mother had locked herself in a bathroom.

"Not exactly, Chase. And I'm sorry to bother you on a Sunday morning, but the phone call was most unusual so I thought I'd better. At least, before I talked to Mr. Klein about it."

Chase frowned. Klein was the manager of Harbor House. "That's quite all right," he said as patiently as he could.

"Your uncle, Mr. Sullivan, phoned to say that from the first of next month he'd no longer be responsible for your mother's account. He said you'd be paying it. I thought I'd better confirm with you before talking Mr. Klein and changing the paperwork."

Her message bounced around meaninglessly in his head. "Sorry, but when did my uncle call to tell you this?"

"Just an hour ago."

Chase tried to focus over the hammering at his temple. He closed his eyes and suddenly saw his cousin outside the company yesterday afternoon, staring angrily at the pickup truck. Howard. "Um, could you hold off on the paperwork for me, Mrs. MacDonald? To tell you the truth, my uncle hasn't contacted me about this yet."

There was a brief silence on the other end. "Oh, dear. I hope everything's okay. I assumed you knew."

"If you could give me some time—maybe till tomorrow?—I can settle this misunderstanding."

"Certainly, Chase. Give me a call when you have. The changeover doesn't happen for another week."

Chase hung up, passing a trembling hand across his face. Bryant was definitely playing hardball. He had no doubt that Howard went running to his father about the visit, as innocuous as it was. Never had he dreamed his uncle could be this petty and mean. Yet he ought to have known, having been witness to such acts before. But he wasn't going to let them get away with any more intimidation.

He tore off his canvas work apron, searched quickly for his keys and headed out. The worst part was waiting for the ferry. The half-hour ride was interminable, but at least afforded him the chance to think about what he'd say. He already knew what he wanted to do, but breaking the law was a last resort. And he tried not breaking any on the drive into the hills up to Magnolia where Bryant still lived, a mere eight blocks away from Chase's childhood home.

Fortunately the gate was open. Chase doubted he'd have been able to wait for someone to let him in. He wheeled the pickup around the circle, braking hard right at the front door. He banged on the steel-enforced panel with his fist and stuck his left index finger in the fancy door buzzer at the same time.

The door swung open while Chase's fist was raised, about to come down on the panel one more time. A matronly woman, no doubt a housekeeper, stood in the doorway, a look of fearful apprehension in her face.

"May I help you?" she asked, the words almost choking her.

Chase dropped his arm. "Yes. You can tell my uncle Bryant that his nephew, Chase, is here and wants to see him. Immediately."

"Your uncle isn't well today. He's resting. Perhaps if you came…"

Chase brushed past the woman. He hadn't been in the house for several years, but it hadn't changed much and he remembered the basic layout. Standing in the center of the gleaming foyer, he debated where to begin his search for Bryant.

She saved him the trouble. "He's in the solarium, off the den and to the right of the kitchen."

"I know where it is," Chase said, and spun around, leaving the woman speechless before the still-open front door. The house was huge and Chase doubted his cousins lived at home. Bryant's last wife had died a few years ago and, except for a couple of staff, he was all alone in the mausoleum.

In spite of the size of the place, it didn't take him long to find the solarium. His uncle was sitting in an armchair, his legs up on a footstool and covered with a blanket, reading a newspaper. His head shot up, shock in his face as he saw Chase.

"You know why I'm here," said Chase, standing in front of his uncle, hands on his hips.

"How dare you storm into my house like this?" Bryant blustered. "Get out now, before I call the police."

"Maybe that's a good idea, Bryant. Go ahead. While I'm at the station, explaining away my surprise visit to my dear uncle, I'll drop a few hints about Trade Winds."

"I doubt that, boy. I doubt that very much," said Bryant. "We had an agreement and you broke it."

"By parking in front of the company building for thirty seconds?"

Bryant frowned. "You know what I'm talking about. I refuse to discuss the matter further. I'll give you two minutes to clear out." He raised the newspaper and began to read again.

But Chase saw the paper shaking in the old man's hands and, for the first time, realized that fear had changed sides. It didn't make him feel any better, but it did make him determined to stay. "I don't know how you can sit there, knowing what you're doing to my mother. Knowing what you've done to my family, you and your offspring."

The paper dropped onto his lap. Bryant's eyes flashed. "You mean, what *you* did to your family. You shattered your father's trust and love when you made that call to the FBI."

"For the record—*again*—I did not make that call. Besides, the whole scene thirteen years ago was a set-up concocted by you and your sons. You know that. So please have the decency to drop the act."

"*You* have the decency to think about your mother for a change. If you were so concerned about her welfare, why did you break your promise? You knew what would happen."

"I didn't break any promise and you know it. Just tell me this—how long did you and my father carry out your scam? For all the years you both ran the company or just when you started getting those government contracts?"

"Your name was on those invoices," retorted his uncle.

"Not all of them," said Chase. "It won't take much to reopen the case."

"My friends have taken care of that," he said, dismissing Chase's implied threat with barely a sniff.

"Friends can be embarrassed by bad publicity."

Bryant retrieved the newspaper, but this time, didn't even pretend to read it. Instead he lapsed into silence, staring off into space.

"You didn't answer my question," pressed Chase. "When did you and my father cook up the fraud scheme?"

A peculiar expression flitted across Bryant's face. Chase puzzled at it for a few seconds until a tiny lightbulb illuminated in his mind. "My father didn't know about it, did he?"

The paper fluttered to the floor. His uncle looked up at him, suddenly a vulnerable and very old man.

"That's why our fight was so horrendous," said Chase, seeing the scene in his mind. "His mistake was to believe you, rather than his own son. Because you were his only sibling. His business partner. Supposedly his best friend. How much easier to believe you than his rebellious son."

Bryant's chin trembled. "Get out now or I *will* call the police."

"You're contemptible. I don't know how you can look yourself in the mirror. You screwed your own brother and now you're doing the same to his sick and defenseless wife. You disgust me." Chase turned and strode to the door.

"*You* can look after your mother now," cried his uncle. "Time to be a man, instead of a boy running from your problems. You should've thought of the consequences before you teamed up with that woman." His laugh pitched.

Chase didn't trust himself to look back. He made his way to the front door in a daze, thoughts and emotions fighting to trip him up any second. There was no sign of the housekeeper. A good thing. The poor woman had been frightened *before*. He shoved the door with the flat of his hand and stood on the threshold, blinded by the sun.

"What the…?"

Chase watched as his cousin closed his car door and headed his way. Terence, not Howard. Probably another good thing. Chase kept right on going toward his pickup.

"What are you doing here?" Terence asked, frowning.

Chase opened the truck door and climbed inside. Starting the engine, he saw Terence moving closer toward him. So tempting, Chase thought. A slight swerve of the steering wheel. He killed the image. Reversed away from his cousin, spun around and shot down the circular driveway to the main road. He didn't stop shaking until he reached the closest Starbucks.

It wasn't until later, on his way to the hospital to see Emily, that he recalled part of Bryant's rant as he was leaving. *Teamed up with that woman.* What woman? He'd been with Sam, but how would they know…? Uh-oh. They thought she was Skye. And that explained the extreme reaction. Howard told Bryant he'd been with the FBI agent.

SAM STOPPED outside Emily's door. She felt guilty about not coming sooner. She hadn't seen her since the day Danny stormed out. How long ago was that? Only days, but it felt like weeks, so much had happened. Such as, *I think I'm in love with your son's father.* How awkward was that? Sam exhaled, then took a quick deep breath and gently pushed open the door.

Emily was propped up on pillows, staring listlessly at the muted television suspended from the ceiling in the corner opposite the bed. She half-turned her head at Sam's approach and gave a wan smile.

"You're the very person I wanted to see," she said in a voice so low Sam had to strain to hear.

Sam smiled back and perched on the bedside chair. She patted the back of Emily's hand, resting at her side. "How are you today?"

"Not too good," Emily said. "Slight fever. I met your mother yesterday," she went on, changing the subject. "She's a wonderful woman. You're very lucky."

Sam nodded. "I am."

"She was so great with Danny. I could tell right away how much he liked her."

"Yes, she's good with kids." Sam heard herself say what she'd never have admitted in her adolescence. But it was true, she realized. She'd just never seen it.

"And Danny agreed to meet the counselor your mother recommended." Emily closed her eyes.

Sam watched her chest rise and fall beneath the cover. The time between each breath seemed long. There was a fine sheen of perspiration in her face and her skin color had a yellowish tint. Sam felt a surge of apprehension. Emily's condition was rapidly deteriorating.

Her eyes flicked open and she looked up at Sam as if she were seeing her for the first time that day. Then she must have remembered, because her expression shifted and she frowned. "Sorry. Sometimes the fatigue just takes over. I wanted to see you, Sam, because I have a favor to ask."

"If it's about Danny, not to worry," Sam quickly said. "I will most definitely stay in his life."

"Yes, please. It means so much to me…knowing he'll have a woman's influence. And I know Chase is going to take him in. He's been talking to Minnie and Danny about it." She paused again, taking slow breaths.

"Chase told me they'd arranged for Danny to spend

weekdays with Minnie until the end of the school term," Sam said. "Then he'll move permanently to Bainbridge, with Chase."

Emily nodded. She started to speak, but had to stop.

"Not to worry, Emily. All of us are going to take very good care of your son."

Tears welled up in Emily's eyes and spilled over. Sam took a tissue and dabbed them gently, trying desperately not to cry herself.

After a long moment, Emily said, "I'm hoping for something more for him, Sam. Something he's never really had."

Puzzled, Sam asked, "What?"

"A family, Sam. That's what I want for my boy. A family of his very own."

"We'll do the best we can there. Danny will be a part of my family, now, too."

Emily's head rolled slightly from side to side. "Not what I mean," she whispered.

Sam leaned closer to the bed to hear. "What do you mean?"

"I may be dying, but my eyesight and intuition are in full working order." Emily smiled weakly. "When Chase mentions your name, or you say his…I can hear it in your voices. See it in your faces." Her chest pumped slowly from the labor of such a long speech.

Sam felt her face heat up. She knew what Emily was hinting at but didn't know how to respond. *Yes, I think I'm in love with him. But it's all happened so fast and I'm not positive he feels the same or if it's all just physical lust. And heaven knows where any of this is going to go….*

"Uh…you're right, Emily. I have changed my mind about Chase—drastically." She smiled. "But I simply don't know how it's all going to end."

"Just…let it happen," murmured Emily. "Don't fight it. You two were made for each other." She stopped and closed her eyes.

Sam watched Emily drift off. When she realized she was sleeping this time, she stood up, leaned over to Emily and whispered, "Whatever happens, I will make some kind of family for Danny." She kissed Emily on the forehead and quietly left the room.

Outside in the hallway, she sagged against the wall and searched in her purse for a tissue. A nurse came by and stopped to ask if everything was all right.

"I'm fine, thanks. I've just been in to see Emily Benson. She's not doing well."

The nurse shook her head. "Are you family?"

"Kind of."

"Well, I'm not permitted to talk about her condition unless you are, but we're calling in family today."

Sam nodded mutely, understanding the subtext of that statement. The nurse patted her on the arm and walked on. Sam dug blindly into her purse for her phone and called Chase. He didn't pick up, so she left a message to say she was at the hospital, but leaving for home. Could he call her when he arrived at the hospital? Last night they'd planned to meet there, but Sam didn't think she had the emotional stamina to stay longer. Besides, the nurse had said *family* and right now, that meant Danny and Chase. She took the elevator down and headed for the transit stop to take the bus home. Skye still had her car. It was typical of Skye to assume Sam would manage in the meantime. Sam mentally scolded her twin while waiting for the bus. When it finally came, disgorging many hospital visitors, Sam decided to go to her mother's, instead.

The bus ride was interminable, with at least three route changes. By the time she got off at the stop two blocks from her mother's, Sam was ready to have it out with her sister.

"She's not here," Nina said, seconds after Sam walked in the door. "But she left a note for you, in case you called or came by."

"Why did she take my car? Couldn't she have taken yours?"

Nina gave her a sharp look. "I've no idea, dear. I thought you knew all about it."

Sam slumped onto the couch in the living room. "I expected her to drop it by last night or even this morning. I had to take the bus to the hospital."

"I hope that's not a whine in your voice," Nina teased.

In spite of her frustration, Sam had to grin. "Sorry. I think it was. It's just that Emily's not doing well at all—a nurse told me the hospital has called her family. That sounds serious, doesn't it?"

Nina sat on the edge of the couch next to her. "I'm afraid it does, dear. If you want to go back to the hospital, you're welcome to use my car."

"Thanks, Mom, but the nurse emphasized the *family* part. Besides, I think it's better for Chase and Danny to have time alone with Emily."

Nina took Sam's hand. "Emily and Danny are very lucky to have you for a friend, Samantha." She paused a moment, then stood up. "I'll get that note."

Sam headed for the kitchen and a glass of water. Standing at the sink, she glanced to her right, into the solarium across the patio. She saw herself sitting in the armchair there, facing the kitchen sink—and Skye. How insignificant that whole incident seemed now. And how many light-years away from Todd was the man she'd now come to love. She set the empty glass onto the counter and turned at her mother's entrance.

"Here you go, dear."

Sam took the note and sat at the table, while Nina continued emptying the dishwasher.

Hi, Sam.

Sorry about the car. You're probably ready to throttle me! I have an errand and will pop by your place later this afternoon. I spent most of yesterday searching listings of government contracts on the Internet and making phone calls. I managed to come up with an interesting piece of information. A numbered company that's received two recent orders from Trade Winds (for contracts for supplies to the Defense Department) turns out to be owned by H. J. Weiner and Company. Sound familiar? Anyway, a buddy of mine has just let me know that Weiner and Company is registered under the name Terence Bryant Sullivan. No kidding. The old circle game. We got them, sis. Now to gather what we've got and persuade someone at the field office to check it out. Got my fingers crossed. See ya later.

Sam felt excitement rising inside. All nasty thoughts of Skye vanished. Her sister had really come through. "Mom," she said, raising her head, "I'm going home now. Skye said she'd drop the car around later today."

"Shall I give you a lift, dear?"

Sam hesitated, tempted to say yes. But at the moment she didn't feel like exposing herself to Nina's inevitable questioning about Chase. Her feelings for the man were too new, something she wanted to hold tightly to her chest—for now. Her mother must have inferred the truth, because as Sam walked to the door, she said, "We'll catch up later."

"Okay, Mom. And I may have some questions for you, too." She grinned teasingly. "About Bill Carter."

Nina smiled. "I guess we both have some catching up to do."

"Yep," Sam said, and gave her a quick goodbye hug. The hike to the bus stop was interrupted by her cell phone. Chase. A delicious warmth flowed through her at the sound of his voice.

"Hi, there," he said. "Got your message. Where are you now?"

"Heading home on the bus. Skye still has my car." She paused a beat, almost afraid to ask. "How's Emily?"

"They think she's got pneumonia. Doing some tests."

Sam closed her eyes. Pneumonia. She doubted Emily would have the strength to battle this last assault on her poor body. When Sam could speak, her voice was husky. "Where's Danny?"

"Still at Minnie's. I'm going to go pick him up right now."

She hesitated, wondering if this was the time. Still, he needed to know. "I have some news, too."

"What?"

Sam gave him the gist of Skye's note. He didn't respond for a moment.

"This is big, Sam," he finally said. He told her about the visit to Bryant and the phone call that had precipitated it.

"That's awful," Sam said. "What will you do?"

"Well, given what you've just told me, I think I've got a huge bargaining chip."

"But you're going to let the authorities handle it, right? I mean, we have to call in the FBI now."

Another pause. "I suppose. But it'll mean the end of the company—my family's business."

"Chase, it hasn't been your family business for thirteen years."

"Yeah, I guess you're right. Funny, I just never thought this whole thing would be resolved. I was resigned to carrying it with me the rest of my life."

Sam wished she was with him, to wrap her arms around him. "Some of it always will be with you," she said, lowering her voice.

"Right. Sam, I…"

Static buzzed the signal and she couldn't hear the rest of what he said. "Say again?"

"I said I thought about you all night."

Sam shivered. She glanced quickly at the two other people waiting at the bus stop, then moved farther away. "Me, too," she whispered.

"Can't hear you, Sam. You're breaking up."

"Me, too!"

"Ah. Good. Listen, I got a call coming in. I'll get back to you."

Sam closed up her phone, thinking the day was going to be a long one. The bus arrived and she stepped on. But surprisingly, the trip home wasn't too bad because she spent the forty-five minutes with thoughts of Chase's promise to continue the kiss begun yesterday, alternating with worry about Emily and Danny.

The first thing she spotted as she rounded the corner to her duplex was her car parked in the No Parking zone. She smiled, thinking Skye might at least have placed a sign in the windshield. Officer on duty or some such thing. Sam bent down to check inside as she drew near, noting that her sister had also not locked the car.

Impulsively she withdrew her cell phone from her purse. She'd get her to come outside and move the car herself. That is, if she was up in the apartment. Sam leaned against the passenger door and looked up at her apartment window. The phone rang and instantly, another chime joined in. Sam

frowned. She jumped away from the car and looked around.
The muted but distinct peal of Skye's cell phone was com-
ing from inside the car. Sam opened the passenger door.
Skye's black leather handbag was lying on the floor.

## *CHAPTER FIFTEEN*

CHASE SWITCHED off his phone and leaned against the wall of the hospital waiting room. Minnie's call was disturbing, to say the least. Danny had left her apartment while she'd been at church. Chase told her to have Danny call if he came back. He checked the time on his phone again. It was almost three o'clock. Where the heck was he?

He debated calling Sam again but guessed she was still making her way home. Besides, it was his problem, not hers. He began to pace, trying to figure out where the boy might be. Anger surged in him. Danny's timing couldn't be worse. Minnie had insisted he'd been fine when he went to bed last night, so whatever prompted this disappearance occurred in the night or early morning. And he couldn't call any of Danny's friends because, except for a single reference to someone named Jeff, he had no idea who they were. A sense of inadequacy about how he was handling the job of parenthood rolled over him.

He wished he could ask Emily if she had some idea of where he'd be, but she was sleeping. Besides, she couldn't afford to expend any energy in worry over Danny. Deciding to wait a bit longer before driving out to Minnie's he headed down to the cafeteria for another coffee. As he stepped off the elevator, he bumped into a tall, white-haired man in a lab coat. Emily's doctor.

"Ah, Mr....uh..."

"Sullivan."

"Yes, I was hoping you'd arrived. I want to have a word with you about your wife."

Chase didn't bother correcting the mistake. He followed the doctor to one of the few vacant tables in the cafeteria. When they were settled, Chase had to lean forward to hear the man over the hubbub of people's voices, clinking dishes and cutlery.

"Emily's prognosis isn't good and that's why we called you. I need to inform you that we have a DNR on her file."

"A what?"

"A 'do not resuscitate' instruction. Emily signed it when she was admitted to the palliative ward. It basically means that we don't take any heroic measures. If she goes into cardiac arrest, say, we don't try to revive her."

Chase turned away for a second, gazing blankly at a weary-looking couple at the table next to theirs. "I see," he finally said.

"The thing is, I'm worried about your son. He was in a highly agitated state the last time he saw his mother. I don't want him to be alone with her."

Chase nodded. He couldn't speak over the lump in his throat.

The doctor stood up and patted him reassuringly on the shoulder. "We'll make sure Emily doesn't suffer."

He didn't see the doctor leave. The room swam in a watery haze. Chase blinked, wiped his eyes and forced himself to his feet. He needed a quiet corner to think.

SAM RAN UP the stairs, taking them two at a time. Hopefully Skye was there, totally ignorant of the fact that she'd left her purse in an unlocked car in a No Parking zone. But the apartment door was locked. She fumbled for her keys, then let herself in.

"Skye? Skye?" Sam wandered from room to room, but the silent apartment offered up no clues. Tossing Skye's purse onto the couch, Sam immediately called her mother. The line was busy. She left a terse message asking Nina to call her right back. Impulsively, she tried Chase, but the line was busy.

Frustrated, she pocketed her phone and began pacing. Knowing her sister, she'd probably decided to dash to the corner convenience for a soda or something. Sam ran to the purse and rummaged in it. Skye's wallet was still there. Okay. No impromptu shopping. The car keys were also in the purse, suggesting Skye had been on her way out of the car when something—or someone—stopped her. Perhaps she'd been accosted by one of the other tenants and was chatting merrily away while her twin sister was freaking out.

Sam picked up her phone and called the tenant in the ground-floor unit. No answer. Skye obviously wasn't in the building. So where was she? When she tried Chase's number again, she got his voice mail.

"Can you call me as soon as possible? Skye seems to have disappeared."

Sam rang off and headed for the kitchen and a glass of cold water. She needed to calm down and consider where Skye might have gone. *Without her purse and phone.*

Wherever Skye was, Sam was dead certain she hadn't gone willingly.

SHE TRIED not to give in to the panic, so focused on anger instead. Anger that she'd so foolishly ignored the man getting out of the car parked behind her. Not that she'd had any reason to be suspicious of him. Even her realization that he was moving swiftly toward her hadn't sounded any alarms because she knew she'd parked Sam's car in a No Parking zone. She'd gotten out of the car and had been bent over, reaching for her purse on the passenger seat when he suddenly came at her from behind.

The hard pressure of a gun's barrel against her lower back was a sensation she'd experienced only once before and had hoped never to experience again. He'd grabbed her by the collar of her jacket, pulling her against him and the gun. She'd turned her head, looking for someone on the street to help her. But, impossibly on a Sunday afternoon, there hadn't been a single person around.

When he'd marched her toward his car and she'd seen that the trunk was already popped open, her stomach heaved. By then she'd recognized him. Everything fast-forwarded. The push into the trunk, so swift she had no chance to fight back. He was big and strong. Silent, too.

*Does he know about Sam?*

Skye guessed they drove about fifteen minutes. He drove fast around curves and she had to cling to the spare-tire unit to keep from being tossed around. The car braked sharply and she was thrown hard against the metal plate holding the tire in place. The blow to her head brought tears, but she welcomed the pain. It sharpened her senses and her anger. As soon as she heard the trunk latch unlock, she braced herself to leap out at him.

But he was quicker than he looked and perhaps smarter, too. The trunk flew up and just as Skye was about to uncoil and spring up, a fist punched her right in the solar plexus. She fell back into the trunk, gasping to catch her breath. When he swiped a piece of duct tape across her mouth, panic overwhelmed her. Whatever his plan for her had been, Skye knew she was in serious trouble. He rolled her roughly onto her side, jerking her arms out from under her and to her back, squeezed both wrists together with one of his hands and then wound a long swath of duct tape round and round them. She lay helplessly in the hollow of the trunk, staring up at him as she tried to control her breathing. The smile on his face was chilling.

"I just want you to know that I personally have had it with you people," he said. "Pop's in intensive care right now because my jerk of a cousin started butting his nose into things. And I can't really tell you how long you're gonna be around here—Terry and I have to make some plans. So before I drag you outa there, I want to warn you that if you do anything to attract attention, your stay will most definitely be cut very short. Understand what I'm saying?"

She nodded.

"Okay, so I'm gonna pull you out and we're going to walk into the house as quickly as we can." He took one last look around him before reaching down to grab her under one arm and pulled.

Skye winced as her legs scraped over the edge of the trunk. Her knees gave slightly as she put her full weight onto them, but he wrapped one arm around her waist and half-dragged, half-walked her to a closed door. She knew where they were. The Trade Winds building that had once been the family mansion. She certainly hadn't imagined a few days ago that she'd be back so soon, and under such circumstances. The thought might have made her laugh, had the duct tape not been so tight over her lips.

He unlocked the door, holding her against him with his other arm. When it swung open to reveal a dark staircase leading into a basement, she braced her heels against the landing step, refusing to move. He shouted at her and a door leading from the landing to the ground floor suddenly opened. A man stood in the frame, his jaw gaping. Must be Terry.

"Howard, what the hell…"

"Help me get her down into the wine cellar."

"Are you crazy? Do you know what you've done? Do you think this is going to help Pop?"

"It's going to make me feel better," Howard said, his face reddening.

Terence backed up. "You're on your own, then. I'm not getting involved."

"Yeah? We'll see about that." Howard jerked her away from the landing and took two steps at a time down into the basement, pulling her behind him.

She had no choice but to comply, knowing that if she resisted, he'd simply throw her down. And breaking a bone would mean the end of any chance to get away. She couldn't see over his wide back and shoulders, but heard him breathing heavily as he worked at some door mechanism. Then he turned abruptly and pushed her forward into a small, unlit room. Or closet, more like it, she thought, just before she landed with a thud on the concrete floor.

As he closed the door behind her, he shouted, "You shoulda stayed out of it. It's all your fault—and my cousin's."

Skye tucked her legs up beneath her and maneuvered herself into a sitting position. If he'd been foolish enough to bind her wrists in front of her, she could have started working away at the tape on her mouth. She heard his heavy footsteps lumbering up to the ground floor. Doors slammed and voices raised. *Guess they're arguing about me.* Skye breathed deeply through her nose, forcing herself to be calm. Giving in to panic would achieve nothing. She lowered her forehead onto her knees and tried to think. Tried to zero in on some kind of twin telepathy to summon her sister.

Would Sam figure it out? And in time to save her? Those were two questions she decided to tuck away. The answers were just too much to consider at the moment.

NOT KNOWING where to begin looking for Danny, Chase called Nina Sorrenti. She'd been with Danny yesterday and could maybe shed some light on where he might have gone. The fact that she was listed in the directory was a bonus. Of course, he could have gotten her number from Sam, but he was reluctant to drag her into this. And Nina was every bit as gracious as he'd hoped she'd be.

First he apologized for calling her without a formal introduction.

"That's quite all right," she said. "I feel as though I know you, anyway."

That gave him pause, wondering whether she'd garnered information about him from Sam, Danny or Skye. "Danny seems to have taken off," he said, giving her a summary of Minnie's phone call and the need for Danny to get to the hospital.

"Oh? Samantha told me that Emily wasn't doing well."

"She has pneumonia."

After a few seconds, Nina murmured, "Oh, dear." Her tone said it all.

"I don't have any idea where to start looking for him and was wondering if you could give me any suggestions."

"Hmm. Let me think." The line was silent for so long Chase wondered if he'd lost the connection. Finally she said, "Yesterday when we were out sightseeing, we went to the Space Needle, which he loved, and afterward I drove through Queen Anne for an even better view of the skyline. He loved it and said his mother would have loved it, too. I regretted not having a camera, but told him I'd take him back as soon as possible to get a photo of the view for his mother."

"So whereabouts in Queen Anne were you?" Chase tried to hide his impatience. The neighborhood she was referring to was huge.

"There's an overlook at Kerry Park where we stopped to see the bay and city."

Chase swore under his breath. Kerry Park was a long way from Minnie's place. Still, Danny had no qualms about traveling around the city. "Okay, that's a start. I'll check it out."

"Is there anything else I can do?"

He thought for a moment. "Danny's going to need some professional help, Ms. Sorrenti. I know you've been facilitating that and I appreciate it. Emily talked to you about it yesterday, I believe?"

"Yes, a bit. But I could see she wasn't having a good day. Please feel free to call me anytime. And please, it's Nina."

"Thanks. I will…Nina."

After tucking his phone back into his jeans pocket, Chase went to the nurses' station on Emily's floor, leaving his phone number and a request to call him should Danny arrive at the hospital. He called Sam, but her line was busy and, rather than complicate things more, decided not to leave a message. He had a rough idea where Kerry Park was. He just hoped Danny was still there, if indeed that was where he'd gone.

THE MORE SAM LOOKED at the evidence, the more convinced she was that something bad had happened to Skye. She finally got through to her mother, who told her Chase had called about Danny's whereabouts.

"Have you caught up with your sister yet?" asked Nina.

Sam opted for a white lie. "No, I haven't, but I'm sure she'll show up."

"She left here ages ago. Let me know when she does. I want to find out if she'll be home for dinner."

Sam was torn between laughter and tears. She knew

Nina would want to know what was going on, but she didn't want to frighten her mother just yet, at least not until she'd contacted Chase. "I'll call you soon," she promised, and hung up.

By the time she reached Chase, she was on her way to her car. She quickly filled him in.

"Chase? Are you still there? Did you get what I just said?"

"Yes, Sam. Listen, I'm on my way to Kerry Park. Your mother said he really liked the place, and so I'm thinking he might have returned there. Now, about Skye. Are you positive she simply hasn't taken off on her own?"

"Without her purse or wallet? Her cell phone?" Sam heard her voice rising with each word.

"No, I guess not. This doesn't look good. But there's something I should tell you. Yesterday, when we stopped in front of Trade Winds and my cousin Howard saw us? I thought he was reacting to my being there, but this morning I learned it was you he was angry about."

*"Me?"*

"Not you, but Skye. He saw you and thought he was seeing your sister. He figured I was in cahoots with the FBI and freaked out."

"Oh." Her mind raced, sorting out the implications of what Chase was telling her. She'd reached her car and climbed inside. She ducked her head, searching the floor for any clue to Skye's disappearance. Nothing. This wasn't a fairy tale, she told herself. No trail of bread crumbs to follow.

"You still there?" Chase asked.

"Yep. Just getting into my car. Listen, I thought of something. After you brought me home yesterday, when we were out front…uh…well…saying goodbye?"

"I vaguely recall that," he teased.

"Right. Anyway, when you left, another car crawled past as I was standing on the sidewalk. The sun was in my eyes, but I could tell the driver was looking my way. As if he was checking out my building—or me. Do you suppose it could have been Howard? Maybe he followed us."

"Maybe." Chase paused. "Probably. This is really not looking good. Call the police."

"Skye's an adult—don't they make you wait twenty-four hours or something for missing adults?"

"There are extenuating circumstances. Her purse and things were left behind, you said."

"I'm betting one of your cousins has taken her. You said they were ticked off—maybe seeing us together was the last straw. Maybe they found out we've got information about those companies."

"I can't believe one of them would be crazy enough to kidnap an FBI agent."

"Say they did. Where would they take her?"

"I've no idea. Anywhere."

"But if it was an impulsive act, maybe they'd want to just keep her somewhere till they decided what to do with her."

There was a moment of silence. "Maybe you should have been the FBI agent, rather than your sister."

"Ha, ha. Think, Chase."

"Okay. Supposing you're right. Maybe the best option would be the Trade Winds building."

"Okay, I'm going there."

"No, wait. Not by yourself. As soon as I get to Kerry Park and hopefully find Danny, I'll call you back and we can sort this out together. Don't do anything till I call you. Promise?"

Sam hesitated. She hated to jeopardize this budding relationship with a lie, but her sister might need her. "Uh, sure. Okay. Call me when you find Danny."

As soon as they disconnected, she started to press 9-1-1, but then stopped. Trade Winds wasn't that far away. She'd check it out first, then call the police.

CHASE REACHED the Kerry Park overlook ten minutes after talking to Sam. His palms were sweating and his heart racing. He had a feeling she wasn't going to heed his advice and that scared him. He'd always considered his cousins liars and fraud artists, rather than major criminals. But he knew from experience that Howard had a mean streak and little impulse control. What Sam had suggested was a more likely scenario than Chase wanted to admit. Especially after his visit to Bryant.

He parked the truck on a side street and walked briskly through small knots of people taking photos or simply looking at the view. There were quite a few tourists and locals at the site. It was a Sunday in mid-May and a clear, sunny day. Mount Rainier thrust above the city.

Chase strode along the fence barrier, eyes scanning from left to right. Then he doubled back. This time he stopped to look out and below, noticing a set of stairs leading down the slope to a playground and tennis courts. He squinted, searching amongst the scattered people for someone who might be Danny. Just when he was considering using one of the telescopes, a familiar shape moved into his line of vision.

He took the steps two at a time, brushing rudely past people, ignoring their protests as he kept his eyes fixed on Danny. The boy had moved to a bench and was watching some children playing on the climbing apparatus in the playground.

Breathless, Chase could barely speak when he reached the bench. Danny turned, but hardly seemed surprised to find him there. Chase sat down on the bench and waited until he'd caught his breath.

"I was worried about you, Danny."

"Oh, yeah?"

"No one knew where you were."

Danny frowned. "How'd you find me, then?"

"I called Nina Sorrenti. She told me how much you liked it."

"She's pretty nice."

"Yes." He craned his head, noticing the camera on the other side of Danny. "You wanted to take some photos for your mother."

Danny just nodded.

"It's a good day for picture-taking. I haven't seen Rainier that clearly in a while."

Another nod.

Chase grit his teeth. He was desperate to call Sam back, but knew he couldn't rush Danny. He thought about telling him what was happening, but decided the kid had enough on his mind. "Get many pictures?" he asked.

"Enough."

"Shall we go show them to your mother?"

Danny's head swiveled. "Now?"

"Why not?"

He shrugged. "No reason. Thought maybe you'd be angry."

"I wasn't angry, Danny. I was scared."

Danny searched his face. "You don't look scared."

"Adults are good at hiding their feelings."

"Yeah. I've learned that." He stopped for a minute. "Yesterday, Nina and I talked about my mother and some other stuff. Nina gave me permission to call her that," he quickly explained.

Chase tried not to smile. "So do you think you might be interested in talking to one of her colleagues?"

"I think so," Danny said. He looked back at a group of

children chasing some others, laughing. Suddenly he got to his feet. "Maybe we should go now."

Chase followed him up the stairs, one hand resting lightly on his shoulder. When they got to the top, Danny said, "One more picture, okay?"

"Sure. How about I take one of you with the Space Needle behind you?"

"Okay. Did you know Mom and I never went up there? Yesterday was my first time."

Chase pretended to be setting up the camera. He wished, suddenly, he'd been around before, when Danny was younger. He fought tears. *Well, you're here now. And here to stay.* When he could safely raise his head, he smiled at Danny, who was leaning against the fence. "Move a bit to your left," he said.

As he raised the camera, a woman beside him said, "Would you like me to take a picture of you and your son together?"

Chase glanced at Danny. Their eyes locked. "Yes, we'd love that," he said. He walked over and stood beside Danny, draping one arm loosely across his son's shoulders.

SAM NOTICED a small side street about half a block from the Trade Winds building and turned onto it. She guessed there might be parking behind the buildings and she was right. An alley led off to her left, running parallel to the main street. When she got out of the car, she stood for a moment, planning her next move. The predominantly residential area was quiet, with few people around. It was almost five. She checked her phone again but no messages. Had Chase not found Danny yet?

She put that worry aside for the moment and focused on her missing twin. Now that she was here, she might as well check the place out. She stowed her purse under the driver's seat and locked up. Set her phone on vibrating mode and tucked it into her shirt pocket. Took a deep breath and walked into the alley. Most of the houses were enclosed by tall fences, but at the rear of the Trade Winds building was a small parking area. Sidling along the fence, she reached the place where the fence ended and the parking began. She stopped short of it, protected by the neighboring fence, to see if anyone was around. So far so good. Then she poked her head out for a quick peek.

Two cars were parked at strange angles in the small space. Behind one of the cars was a windowless door. Sam froze. Her phone was vibrating in her pocket. Keeping her eye on the door, she flipped open the phone. It was Chase.

"I've found Danny," he said, his voice low.

"Speak up," she hissed.

"Can't. He's too close. Wait."

Static, followed by Chase, a bit louder now. "It's okay. He's gone to look at some flashy sport car parked near us. I'm taking him back to the hospital, but I can't just leave him there. He's bound to be upset when I tell him Emily has pneumonia."

"Call my mother. She'll meet him at the hospital and take him home for a sleepover, if necessary." She waited. "Did you hear me?"

"Yes. Okay. I hate to do it, but it's the best option right now. I'll come by your place right after."

"Uh…well…don't do that."

"What? Why not? Where are you?"

"Um…at Trade Winds. In the little parking lot behind the building." She heard him swear.

"Look, go wait by your car," he said. "In fact, get inside it and lock the door. I'll get there as quickly as I can. We'll figure out our next step then."

"Uh-huh. Say, remember telling me how you used to

play here when you were little? You said you explored all the nooks and crannies?"

"Yeah. Why?"

"Where were some of them? Think you could still find them?"

"For sure. But wait for me, okay? Promise?"

"I'll do my best," she said, and disconnected before he could say another word.

She put her phone back in her pocket. Checking the rear door once more, she took a deep breath and crept across the parking space.

Heat emanated faintly from the first car she passed, but the car closest to the door was cool. When she reached the windowless-door, she saw that the latch was resting lightly on top of the frame. Someone had been in a big hurry. Sam splayed her fingers on the edge of the door and gently tugged.

Somewhere in the building two men were arguing, loudly and fiercely. She pulled the door open wide enough to squeeze through onto a small landing. A set of stairs at her right led to the ground floor and another, down to a basement. The voices were definitely up, so Sam took the other route.

She made sure the door was left in the same position as she'd found it, in case she needed a fast exit. The stairs descended into darkness, but there was enough light from the small gap in the door to orient herself. She waited at the bottom for her eyes to adjust. There was a long, narrow hall with closed doors off each side. She moved slowly ahead, her fingertips running along what felt like a wood-paneled wall at her right. If there was a light switch, she didn't find it. Reaching the first door, she turned the handle. Locked. Likewise for the second and third. Sam stopped at the end of the hall.

The voices above were muted by the thick basement walls and ceiling. She dreaded the possibility of having to go up there, but she would if necessary. Skye was in the building somewhere. She could feel it.

Her cell phone vibrated again. She flipped it open and whispered a hello as loudly as she dared.

"Sam? Where are you? Why are you whispering? No, no. Please don't tell me…"

"Yes, I am," she hissed. "I'm in the basement. I can hear men's voices upstairs. They seem to be arguing."

"How many cars in the parking lot?"

"Two. One got there just before me, I think."

"I've left the hospital and your mother is there with Danny. Why don't you go back out and wait for me at your car? I can get to you in about fifteen minutes."

"All the doors in the basement are locked. Is there another way in or out of here?"

"Where exactly are you?"

"At the end of this corridor. It's a dead end." She heard a muffled exclamation. "Chase?"

"It's not a dead end. There's a secret panel in the wall— not sure if it's to the left or right. I found it when I was a kid. Face the wall dead center and press your fingertips against it, up high. Try left and right. There'll be a click and the panel will open. Small room behind. It was a storage room for booze during Prohibition."

"Okay. I'll call you back."

"Wait—"

Sam disconnected before he could tell her again to leave. *Sorry, Chase, I've got to do this.* She reached up and ran her fingers along the wall to her right, pressing lightly in a line. Back and forth and again. The voices upstairs seemed to be lower now, with longer pauses. That worried Sam. As long as she could hear arguing, she knew where they were. She decided to try the left side, but had no success there, either.

Her underarms were damp with perspiration and her pulse pounded in her ears. Chase must have got it wrong somehow. She went back over his instructions. *Found it when he was a kid. When he was much shorter. High then, lower now.* Starting at shoulder height, she repeated the process, reading the wall with her fingertips. And by the time she had scrolled down to just above her waist, she felt a slight give.

She stopped, wiping her forehead with the back of her hand. This had to be the place, but the panel wasn't swinging open the way secret doors did in the movies. She pressed harder. The wall here was definitely spongey and as she moved along, it began to give slightly. When she was almost at the center starting point, a small section of the wall shifted left and under the exterior panel. *Aha. A sliding door, not a swinging one.* Footsteps thundered from above her head, seeming to move in her direction. She had to hide.

There was just enough light at the entrance to expose notched shelving on both sides of a narrow room. Wine racks? she wondered. More shouting from upstairs. Heart racing, she set one foot into the dark interior. Just as she turned to close the sliding door behind her, she heard a faint humming sound. Unable to see even her hand, she inched forward in the dark until her right foot stubbed against something soft. She bent down, feeling with her hands. Finding cloth. She ran her fingers up the fabric to smooth, warm skin. Hair. Her stomach lurched and she bit down hard on her lower lip so as not to cry out.

"Skye?" she whispered.

# CHAPTER SIXTEEN

SAM FELL to her knees, fingers scrabbling at the tape across Skye's mouth. She made low shushing sounds as Skye struggled to communicate, digging her nails under the tape and pulling it down inch by inch. First one side, then the other. She felt her sister flinch once, and realized she'd either scratched her or the tape had caught some hair. Small injuries, she told herself, as she worked away at the binding. The instant the tape came way enough for Skye to talk, Sam clapped a hand on her mouth.

"Let's get out of here." She paused, almost afraid to ask. "Did he hurt you?"

"No. Just my pride. So stupid," Skye whispered back. "He was at your place, waiting for me. I got out of the car and he came up behind me with a gun. Made me get into the trunk of his car. In broad daylight. No one around." She stopped, catching her breath.

"It's okay, Skye. Relax."

"He taped my hands, too." She gave an awkward half-turn, showing Sam her bound wrists.

Sam muttered an expletive. She tried to dig her fingernails underneath, but there was no gap between skin and tape. "I can't find the join!" she cried. "It's too tight."

"Never mind," Skye snarled impatiently. "Let's just get out of here."

Sam placed her hands under Skye's armpits and pulled

her sister up. Gasping, she leaned against the wine racks with Skye swaying into her. They crab-walked between the wine racks to the panel door. The voices upstairs were louder now, shouting. A door slammed and heavy footsteps reverberated through to the basement. Sam, her arm around Skye, froze.

"Did you call the police?" Skye asked.

"Not yet."

"Call them."

Sam recognized that tone. Skye was rallying. She dug out her cell phone and pressed 9-1-1. As soon as Sam gave the address, the dispatcher informed her there'd been a call about a burglary on the premises.

"Burglary? No, there's no—"

"Give me the phone," said Skye, raising her taped hands. Sam placed the phone at her sister's ear.

"This is Agent Skye Sorrenti speaking. We have a possible hostage situation with an abduction of an FBI agent. Two suspects, one armed. Approach with caution. Rear entrance." She gave her badge number and jerked her head, indicating for Sam to take away the phone. "Let's go."

They scurried along the dark corridor, but as they reached the bottom of the cellar stairs, someone thundered down the steps to the landing above. Sam pulled Skye into the stairwell. The back door slammed shut and silence fell over the entire building. Except for their ragged breathing. After a painfully long moment, Skye whispered, "We have to go now. Me first."

"No. Your hands are tied. Me first."

"No, I can use my feet."

"Yeah, just like you did when he got you."

"Are you going to rub that in for the rest of my life?"

"Maybe. If I have to."

Skye drew her head back to look Sam in the face. "You're serious."

"Yep."

They both grinned at the same time. Sam teared up. They were still in danger, but she had her sister.

"So much for the big FBI agent," Skye murmured.

"You said it, not me."

Skye nodded.

"Let's go," said Sam, heading for the bottom step.

"Wait. About last Christmas."

"Geezus, Skye. *Now?*"

"It had nothing to do with taking Todd away from you or that competition thing. I had this gut feeling about him, that he wasn't good enough for you. I tried to tell you before, but I thought you wouldn't believe me. Whenever I was alone with him, he was always making these suggestive remarks. Finding excuses to brush against me. I should have just come out and told you, but—"

Sam placed two fingers on her sister's lips. "Shh. It's ancient history. You did me a big favor." She paused, adding, "Just keep your mitts off the one I have now."

"You don't have to worry about that one, Sam."

Sam kissed her sister on the cheek. "Me first," she said, and led the way up the stairs to the landing.

The rear door was fully closed. Sam swore under her breath. She heard Skye coming up behind her, and as she turned to tell her to wait, a man's voice sounded from her right. She spun around. Howard was standing in the doorway at the top of the other set of steps. The gun in his right hand wavered slightly as he looked from Sam to Skye and back to Sam.

"Son of a bitch," he muttered. "There's two of you."

CHASE WANTED to throw his cell phone out the window in frustration. Traffic was typical for a balmy Sunday afternoon. Tourists, shoppers and gawkers. He wove the pickup in and out of lanes, feeling and hearing the outrage behind him as he cut drivers off and braked hard for the occasional jaywalker. He had one goal—to get to Sam as quickly as possible.

He couldn't pinpoint the day or the moment when Samantha Sorrenti ceased to be an adversary and became a friend. Well, not exactly a friend, he qualified, because what he'd been feeling for her the past few days had little to do with friendship. He wasn't certain he could call it love yet, though it was far more than physical desire. He simply wanted to be with her. To see her green-flecked eyes light up or the tiny crease of worry between those eyes when she spoke about Emily or Danny. The soft sibilance as she whispered his name. Her full, sweet lips and… He groaned. *Focus,* he told himself. *Drive.*

At the intersection before Trade Winds he turned onto the side street and then the alley. A few yards in, he spotted Sam's car and pulled in behind it. He was reaching for his phone on the passenger seat when he heard a gravel-spitting roar and looked up to see a car fishtailing out of the parking area behind the building. He couldn't see the driver, but the car looked like the one at his uncle's that morning. Probably Terence.

He jumped from the cab, shoving his phone into his jeans pocket and ran to the rear door, passing another car that surely belonged to Howard. The door was locked. He stood back, staring up at the second-floor windows. No sign of life anywhere. He considered dashing around to the front, but hesitated, recalling a security camera there years ago. No sign of police yet, either. Still, he had to do something. About to head for the front, he noticed the door handle rotating.

"DOUBLE THE TROUBLE," said Howard. "Just what I need. Okay. So be it. Terry told me I was on my own with this." He pointed the gun at Sam. "You open the door."

"You can end this right now," said Skye. "Plea bargain, mental breakdown. It could make a big difference to your sentence."

"You must be the agent," he said. "At least I got the right one. And thanks but no thanks. There's too much to lose now. I'm thinking a car accident or something. I'll sort out the details while we're driving."

"You won't get away with it."

"Shut up!" he shouted. "Open the door!" He jerked the gun, and Sam didn't have to be told twice, turning the knob and pushing. Before it was fully opened, he rushed down the steps, grabbed a clump of Skye's hair and pulled her backward against him. She gasped in pain. Sam spun around, trying to grab his arm. He raised the gun, pointed it at Sam and then pressed it into Skye's neck. "Get moving," he ordered.

Sam hesitated.

"Do it," gasped Skye.

Sam stepped out and stopped, blinded by the sunlight. Howard pushed her with his free hand and she stumbled forward. Suddenly a hand grasped her by the forearm and yanked her off to the side. She fell back against the owner of that hand, craning her neck sharply to see.

She opened her mouth to say Chase's name, but was stopped by his finger on her lips. Then Chase moved behind the open door.

Skye burst out followed by Howard. Realizing what was going on, she aimed a hard kick backward at Howard's shin. He shouted in pain, pushing her away from him. Chase lunged forward, knocking the gun from Howard's hand.

Chase's fist landed squarely on his jaw. Howard fell

backward against the hood of his car. He shook his head, then came at Chase. But Skye was ready for him, kicking out her right leg and hitting his knee with enough force for all of them to hear a loud crack. Screaming in pain, Howard crumpled to the ground, facedown. Chase ran to him and placed a steady foot on his back.

"Well done, Skye. That was some kick." He locked eyes with Sam and smiled.

When the first siren wail rang through the alley, he stepped away from Howard, extended an arm and folded Sam into his side, pressing the top of her head into the curve of his neck. She snuggled close, waves of relief and peace flowing through her.

After Howard was taken away and the duct tape snipped from Skye's wrists, Sam and Chase sat in the back of a patrol car while Skye talked to the police.

"I'm sorry…" Sam began to say until Chase leaned over and kissed her on the forehead.

"Not now. I'm hoping we'll have many days—and years—to go over all this. I just want to hold you close." He wrapped his arms around her and Sam gladly sank into them. She was almost asleep when the peal of cell phones jarred her. They looked at each other and dragged their phones out.

"My mom," said Sam.

"The hospital," said Chase.

Sam kissed him once more, knowing the peaceful interlude was over.

A PATROL CAR drove them to the hospital, siren blaring. Every second counted now, in the time left for Emily Benson. When the elevator door opened on the palliative ward, Danny was standing in the hall, Nina a few feet behind. He ran into Chase's arms, burying his face in his father's chest. Nina gestured to Sam, indicating the waiting area at the end of the hall, and left them alone.

Danny led the way into Emily's room, Chase's arm across his shoulders. Sam followed, but stayed in the doorway. An oxygen mask covered the lower part of Emily's face and her eyes were closed. Yet it seemed to Sam that she stirred slightly as Chase and Danny sat in the chairs next to her bed. Danny placed his hand on hers, while Chase wrapped his arm around him.

Except for the whirr of the oxygen machine, silence filled the room. Sam watched, a lump swelling in her throat. She was about to go down the hall to join her mother when Chase glanced up and smiled, cocking his head to the empty chair beside his. She hesitated. Did she really belong in that family grouping?

But when Danny turned and beckoned, Sam tiptoed into the room. Chase extended his free hand, clasping hers, and squeezed gently. The three of them sat silently, a tableau locked together in Chase's embrace, watching Emily.

And Sam knew she did belong.

# EPILOGUE

SAM STACKED the last few dessert plates from the dining-room table, gathered up the cloth napkins and started for the kitchen. Then, on impulse, she decided to take a peek into the living room, where Chase was going through some legal papers. The four weeks since Emily's death had been difficult for everyone, especially Danny. But now the healing process had begun and their lives were settling into a kind of normalcy.

Chase was sitting at the end of the couch, a briefcase opened on the floor at his feet and files of papers beside it. He looked up when Sam entered the room and smiled.

"Hi, beautiful," he said.

The familiar and delicious fluttering set off by his voice, his smile, his touch, seeped through every part of her. "Hi, to you, too," she said softly. "How's it going?"

He set the sheaf of papers he'd been reading onto the couch. "It all looks more complex than it really is. Basically, my cousins and Uncle Bryant were pilfering from the company and various agencies for years, as we all suspected. I had an interesting talk earlier with Bill while you and Skye were getting the cake ready."

Bill Carter had offered to look into the sale of Martha Sullivan's shares in Trade Winds on Chase's behalf. He'd joined them for Nina's birthday dinner that night, but had to leave early. "Oh? Did he say anything about your chances of getting the proper sale price?"

"Yep. He said we have a solid case and Mother will have a large sum of money coming to her...well, to Harbor House, for her care. But there's something else no one knew about. It came out when Bryant's lawyers were probating his will."

Chase's uncle had suffered a fatal heart attack less than twenty-four hours after Howard and Terence were arrested. The likely convictions of the pair and the scandal resulting from the newly opened fraud investigation had sent Trade Winds into receivership. Sam had thought there'd be no more surprises.

"What is it?" she asked, intrigued.

"Although my uncle owned the whole business after he swindled my mother out of her shares, he apparently didn't own the building itself."

"What do you mean?"

"I told you before the building was the original Sullivan family home, two generations back. It turns out it was never part of the company's holdings, but privately owned. The oldest son of each generation inherited it."

"So your father..."

"Yep. As the older son, he inherited it from his father and he rented it to the business for a nominal fee. When we had our big fight years ago, he threatened to disinherit me. When he died, I never received any money, but apparently he kept me in his will as the next and rightful owner of the house. Uncle Bryant was the executor and my father's lawyer was also Bryant's. He managed to convince the lawyer that he'd informed me and that I'd agreed to let the company rent the building. Of course, it was all a lie."

"He was a calculating man, wasn't he? But that's wonderful about the building."

"Yeah. I wish I'd known much earlier. I could have turfed them all out of there." His laugh was harsh.

"The property's very valuable. That's good for you and Danny."

"For the three of us," he murmured.

Sam liked the sound of that. *The three of us*. She smiled, her gaze locked with his.

"Are you almost finished in there?" he asked.

"Yes. I'm going to change into my sweats and relieve Skye with the pots and pans."

"Hmm. Can I watch?"

She laughed. "What? Watch me wash dirty pots?"

"I was thinking about the changing part."

Heat rose into her face. Memories of the previous weekend—their first alone together—surfaced. They'd arranged for Danny to spend the time with Nina, and she and Chase had gone into seclusion at Sam's place. "Hold on to that wish," she said. "We're definitely going to have a repeat of last weekend."

"I can hardly wait."

Knowing she'd either have to take the dishes to the kitchen or put them down, Sam reluctantly said, "Same here. See you in a few minutes."

As she turned to go, he said, "I love you, Sam."

She stopped. "I love you, Chase."

She was still glowing when she entered the kitchen.

Skye was loading the dishwasher. "Thought you got lost," she said.

"I did, kind of."

"The telltale heart."

"Hmm?"

"It's written all over you, sis. You're an open book, as they say."

"Maybe I am," Sam murmured.

Skye rolled her eyes. "Oh, God. I think you'd better join me in a run after we finish in here. Cool down."

"I'd like that."

They smiled, thinking back to two days ago, when they'd talked late into the night after Skye had arrived for Emily's memorial and Nina's birthday dinner. They hadn't seen each other since a few days after *That Day,* as everyone had begun calling the day Emily died.

"Chase has some great news."

"He's going to make an honest woman of you?" Skye teased.

"Ha ha." Sam told her about his family-home inheritance.

"That *is* great, Sam. I'm happy for him. He deserves something after what his relatives did to him."

"Yes, he does." Sam handed the dishes to Skye. "I see you helped yourself to my old clothes."

"Fortunately you had a couple of track suits in your drawers. Who'd have thought we'd have a cool snap in mid-June?"

"It's supposed to warm up tomorrow. We're taking Danny back to Kerry Park in the morning. He wants to scatter some of Emily's ashes there."

Skye stood up from loading the dishwasher. "Is he up to that?"

"Chase thought so. He's adjusting very well, according to Mom." Sam looked across the dark patio to the solarium opposite. Danny and Nina were heavily into a chess game.

"Mom's been fabulous," said Skye, coming up beside her.

"No kidding. It was so good of her to forgo a big party and let us have just a family birthday dinner, instead. My appreciation for her has multiplied over these past few weeks."

"Mine, too," said Skye and added, "And for you, sister."

Sam hugged her twin. "I'm glad you could take a few more days to come home for Mom and for Emily. Danny was excited about your visit. Apparently you promised him a tour of the local field office."

"All arranged for tomorrow afternoon."

"Thanks, Skye."

"No problem. He's a great kid. I really like him."

Sam looked across to the solarium again. "Me, too."

"Do you think Emily knew how things were going to work out?"

Sam teared up. "Yes, I do. There was something in her eyes when she realized the three of us were there together."

"She was an awesome woman."

"And a good mother."

"Yeah." Skye looked toward the solarium. "Like ours. I'll finish the pots and pans. You go get changed."

"Are you sure? You've done most of the cleaning up."

"Of course I'm sure. Do what I say. I *am* your big sister."

"And I love you for it."

Skye bent her head, rolling up the sleeves of her sweatshirt. When she looked up, her eyes were damp. "Sam, I give thanks every single day for what you did for me."

Sam bit her lip. "I do, too, Skye, for having luck on my side."

Skye shook her head. "It wasn't luck, Sam. You were amazing." After a long moment, she said, "Okay, pots and pans and then a nice run around the neighborhood. Sound good?"

"Very good." Sam started to leave, but remembered something. "How has it been for you, Skye? At work?"

Skye sighed. "Things are fine now. Lots of questions about everything." She flashed a sheepish grin. "I've endured a lot of ribbing about the abduction, I can tell you that. But I also got a lot of praise for finding the evidence to reopen the case."

"I'm glad. And…uh…any more news on the romance side of things?"

"I've been seeing someone very different from the others. He's a chef and he loves to cook for me." She chuckled. "That's why I've taken up running again."

Sam laughed. "Be with you in five."

She hurried to her room and was back within the promised time, walking into the kitchen just as Chase was approaching Skye, finishing up the pots at the sink. Sam froze, heart thudding painfully against her ribs.

"Sam?" Chase said.

Skye turned around and before she could utter a word, Chase added, "Oh. Do you know where Sam is, Skye?"

Skye grinned, pointing her index finger at her twin. "Right behind you."

He turned, his face breaking into the wonderful, heart-breaking smile Sam had come to love so much. "Hi, beautiful."

Sam rushed into his open arms, caught her sister's gaze over Chase's shoulder and winked.

\* \* \* \* \*

# BABY BE MINE

## BY
## EVE GADDY

**Eve Gaddy** is an award-winning author of more than fifteen novels. She lives in east Texas with her husband and her incredibly spoiled golden retriever, Maverick, who is convinced he's her third child.

This book is for Mary Ellen Brown, my best friend
through so much and for so many years.
I'm blessed to have you in my life.

Acknowledgements

Many thanks to Dr Nancy Lieb for once again
being my source for all things obstetric and
gynaecological. And many thanks to
Meridith Hayes for answering my legal questions.
As well as many thanks to Justine Davis for
answering my questions about cops, women in
particular. Any mistakes about any of these things
are mine alone. I also want to thank
Kathy Carmichael and Kathy Garbera
for critiquing and listening, and especially
for helping me when I get stuck. Y'all rock!

# CHAPTER ONE

THE LOVINGLY RESTORED, guardsman-blue '64 Ford Mustang convertible blew into town doing fifty-two in a forty. Twenty seconds later Maggie Barnes nailed him. Lights flashing, siren wailing, the sweet, high sound cops loved and everyone else feared, she drove up behind him and pointed to the curb when he looked in the rearview mirror. She read his lips and laughed out loud.

Sometimes she really loved being a cop. When the speeder was Tucker Jones it only made life that much sweeter. Her old friend Tucker could always make her laugh. And since today was Friday and Valentine's Day, Maggie could use some entertainment.

Valentine's Day was highly overrated, in her opinion. The fact she was single and not dating anyone had nothing to do with it, she assured herself. She didn't like it because it was a stupid holiday designed to make money for florists, jewelers and producers of chocolate. Besides that, work usually sucked on Valentine's Day. You could never tell what crazy thing someone would get into their head to do and then she would have to clean up the mess.

Seeing Tucker Jones's beautiful blue eyes and listening to his latest excuse about why he was speeding seemed like a much better alternative to wondering what new disaster was waiting for her later that evening.

Since it was a near-record warm day for February, he'd been driving with the top down and was waiting for her when she reached the car, his fingers beating a tattoo on the car door. The car, like its owner, was bad, gorgeous and sexy. She knew all about that badass car of Tucker's, because he'd told her in exhaustive detail on more than one occasion how he'd rebuilt and restored it.

"Hey, Maggie."

"Hey, Tucker."

"Is there a problem?" he asked. Of course, he knew perfectly well why she'd stopped him.

She took off her sunglasses and hooked them on her shirt pocket. "Well, now, there sure is."

"I wasn't speeding. Your radar must be broken."

"I didn't say I pulled you over for speeding."

"Why did you, then?"

"Because you were speeding. Again." Maggie looked him over and smiled. "Fifty-two in a forty. You're busted, Tucker. License and registration, please." She reflected that she ought to have that information memorized by now.

"I know a good lawyer. I'll get out of it. Save yourself the trouble." He handed her his driver's license and reached in the glove compartment for the vehicle registration.

Maggie laughed. Tucker was a lawyer and he undoubtedly would get out of the ticket. That fact never stopped him from arguing, though. Or her from giving him a ticket if she wanted. "You know what they say about a lawyer who defends himself."

"Having a fool for a client? Witty. Very witty. Have I mentioned I really go for a woman in uniform?" He gave her a wicked, sexy grin.

Damn, he was cute. And he knew it, too. She started writing information on the ticket. "Only every time I've ever pulled you over. Too many to count."

"Have I ever said I really go for beautiful redheads in uniform? Especially a cop uniform?"

She nodded. "Also every time I've pulled you over." She glanced at him and added, "Funny thing, that's the only time you ever mention it."

"It was worth a try." He gave her his most charming smile, which she admitted was something to see.

"Did you have a reason for speeding?" He almost certainly didn't. Unless it was because he liked his cars as fast as he liked his women.

"Why do I need a reason? No one can drive this car and not speed. It's unnatural."

Maggie snorted.

"Doesn't the fact that we've been friends since high school make a difference?"

"Tucker, if I only stopped people I didn't know, I'd never stop anyone. Then the chief would fire me and what would I do? Sell shoes?"

"Come on, Mags, have a heart."

"Don't call me 'Mags,'" she said. He knew she hated it and did it to annoy her. "Cops give tickets. Cops don't have hearts."

"I know one cop who does. You." He looked at her soulfully and, she hated to admit, it was proving effective.

She handed him the warning ticket. "You could be right. But don't let it get out."

He grabbed her hand and kissed it lavishly. "You're one in a million. Run away with me and be my love. We'll go to Mexico." He kissed her hand again. "Or Aruba. Or Tahiti. We'll go—"

Laughing, she pulled her hand away. "Stop that, you fool. I'm on duty here."

"You won't run off with me?" He looked incredibly disappointed.

Maggie shook her head. "Sorry. You'd be flirting with another woman before the plane touched down. Possibly before it left."

"Oh, come on, Maggie. I'm not that bad."

"Ha."

"I'm not. You sound like my mother."

"Gee, thanks." Maggie didn't much care for Tucker's mother, and the feeling was more than mutual. Eileen Jones always looked at Maggie as if she were something nasty stuck to the bottom of her shoe. "What's she done this time?"

"Same thing she always does. 'Darling, you must stop this incessant womanizing and settle down. I know just the girl,'" he said in a fair imitation of his mother's accent.

"How many women has she introduced you to over the years?" Maggie asked. "Hundreds?"

"I've lost count. I've been going out with the latest in a long list. Several times."

Maggie raised an eyebrow. "Sounds serious."

"Well, it's not." He scowled. "Damn it, that doesn't mean I'm a womanizer."

"Seems a little harsh," Maggie agreed. "I'd call you a player, myself, but incessant player-izing doesn't have quite the same ring."

"Very funny. The woman has an obsession with having grandchildren. You'd think she had one foot in the grave."

"You can't blame your mother for wanting grandkids. You are her only child and you'd have pretty babies."

He put his hand over his heart and patted. "Be still. Maggie Barnes just paid me a compliment."

"Don't let it go to your head," she advised him. "It's fat enough already."

"I think the term is *swelled*."

"Fat, swelled, makes no difference to me." Surprisingly, Tucker wasn't conceited, she just liked to tease him. Oh, he knew he was good-looking and that women liked him. They'd been after him since high school so he could hardly help knowing it. But Tucker believed most women pursued him because he'd grown up with money and then made a bundle on his own, when he'd practiced in San Antonio before moving back to the Aransas City area. She suspected there was a story there, but beyond an odd comment or two, he'd never told her.

Her radio squawked and she pressed the button down in response. "Crap," Maggie said when she heard the code. "I've got to go. Cheer up, Tucker. At least you don't have to go break up a domestic disturbance."

"Maggie." He put his hand on her arm. "Be careful, okay?"

"Always am," she told him. "But thanks for worrying."

TUCKER WONDERED NOW and then what would have happened if he and Maggie had ever hooked up. They wouldn't still be friends, that was a given. He'd remained friendly with women he'd dated, but never what he'd call truly friends. Since he valued his friendship with Maggie as much as she did, she was probably smart to make sure it stayed that way.

He watched her walk back to her car, admiring the way she moved. Most of the time, he just saw his old friend Maggie when he looked at her, but every once in a while he remembered she was a woman, and a damned attractive one to boot.

He started the car and pulled onto the road, heading for his parents' place in Key Allegro to drop off some legal papers. He thought about Maggie again and the call that had come in for her. He knew she could take care of herself. She was a good, experienced cop. But shit happened. A year or so ago she'd had to shoot and kill a man who had already shot a friend of hers and who was also trying to kill his estranged wife. Domestic-violence calls could get out of hand quickly and he didn't want another one to go sour on Maggie.

She'd handled it in the past, though. He had to trust she'd handle whatever happened in the future.

Maggie wasn't a girly-girl, but she was definitely feminine. She was a Tae Kwon Do black belt, and although he was as well, she'd kicked his ass on more than one occasion. He'd also heard rumors that she'd taken up boxing lately, though he hadn't verified that.

Twenty minutes later he pulled up to his parents' waterfront home, parked and went up the walk.

"Darling, you're late," his mother said as she opened the door and enveloped him in a scented embrace.

"Late? You didn't know I was coming."

"But of course I did. You told your father and he told me." She put her arm through his and led him into the living room. "And someone else you know is here with me," she added meaningfully.

A woman stood with her back to them, a spill of long, red hair waving to her shoulders. *Maggie? Impossible…. He'd just left her, and she hadn't been headed this way.*

"Isabella?" He realized who she was as she turned around. "I wasn't expecting to see you here."

Isabella was the woman he'd mentioned to Maggie. They'd gone out a number of times since his mother had introduced them. She was beautiful, cultured, sweet and intelligent. There wasn't a reason in the world he shouldn't have taken her to bed, but he just hadn't been ready to take the relationship to that level. If they became lovers, Isabella would read more into it than he was ready for.

She smiled. "I came by to see Eileen on opera-committee business. When she mentioned you were coming by I thought I'd stay and say hello."

He took the hand she held out and, because she expected it, kissed her cheek. Turning to his mother he said, "I just stopped by to leave you these papers. Don't forget to tell Dad," he said, walking over to lay the packet down on the grand piano.

He stayed and talked a while, then, since his mother and Isabella both expected it, made a date for the following night. Isabella left shortly thereafter, and he congratulated himself on successfully getting his mother off his back once more.

"Tucker, stay a moment," Eileen said when he would have left. "Isabella is a lovely girl, isn't she?"

"Sure, she's pretty," Tucker said warily.

"Her family is from Fort Worth, originally. Her parents are on the boards of a number of museums."

Tucker tilted his head. "Mom, why would you think I give a flip about what Isabella's family does?"

She made the *tsk* sound that generally annoyed the hell out of him. "You seem very interested in her. I thought you'd like to know something about her background, in case she hasn't told you, that is. I believe her family is quite wealthy, which I'm certain she won't have mentioned."

He bit down on the urge to say, *No, that would be vulgar, wouldn't it?* "I'm not sure why you're telling me all this. I've dated her a few times. Nothing serious."

"But it could be. Oh, Tucker, she's exactly the type of woman I can see you with."

Tucker pinched the bridge of his nose, wondering how he could get out of the house without telling his mother to butt out. Because if he did that she'd get her feelings hurt, and while she wouldn't cry, she'd make him feel like the biggest jerk on the planet.

Before he could think of a good response, Eileen said, "I simply want you to think about the fact that Isabella would be a perfect match for you. And that you're certainly old enough to consider settling down."

He wasn't in love with Isabella, though. But then, he didn't really believe he'd fall in love again. He'd been burned badly enough to make him a little cynical about love. He wasn't going into that subject with his mother, however. She'd find a way to demolish his arguments. She always did, at least on this subject.

"I'll think about it," he said. Which, of course, he wouldn't. He had no desire to get married, but he knew better than to argue with the brick wall of his mother's will. Much easier to avoid her for a while.

He got away without too much more trouble. But instead of thinking of Isabella, he found himself thinking of an entirely different woman all the way home. A certain redheaded cop he'd known since high school.

Maybe he could talk Maggie into being friends with benefits. He thought about that a moment. Then shook his head regretfully. No, their friendship was more important to him than any momentary pleasure. Besides, she'd laugh herself sick if he proposed it. And then she'd invite him to spar with her and kick his ass for good measure.

# CHAPTER TWO

"I CAN HELP YOU and your kids get into a women's shelter," Maggie said. "Just say the word and I can arrange it. You and the children could be there and safe before your husband returns."

"I don't need a shelter," Sara Myers said. "Jasper would never hurt me or the kids."

*What do you call that shiner he gave you?* Maggie wondered. *A love tap?* That must have hurt like hell. Maggie didn't hold out much hope that the woman would leave her abusive husband. She'd had too much experience with this sort of thing and she could see the woman wasn't ready to admit the guy would likely only get worse over time.

"I told you I fell," Sara insisted. "Jasper didn't lay a hand on me. I'm sorry for your trouble."

Maggie sighed, acknowledging defeat. The neighbors had called this one in, reporting a disturbance in the apartment next door. By the time Maggie arrived, the woman's abusive spouse was long gone. Probably drunk and gone off to get even drunker, Maggie thought, and then he'd come home and whale on the poor woman some more.

"Call us if you need us. And here's my cell number in case you change your mind about that shelter." She handed the woman her card.

Sara showed her to the door. "He's a good man, he really is. He's upset about losing his job. That's all."

Maggie didn't reply. What could she say that she hadn't already told the woman during the half hour she'd spent with her? Certain that the beating had been "just this once," the lady wasn't listening. Maggie hated domestic-abuse cases. Hated that she couldn't do more to help the victims. But Sara had refused to admit the truth, and with the abuser not even being present, Maggie's hands were tied.

Happy Valentine's Day, she thought grimly, walking to her cruiser in the deepening twilight. An annoying day, topped off by an abused woman who wouldn't accept her help. She'd been a cop too long to jinx herself by saying the day couldn't get worse, because in police work, it could and frequently did.

As she neared her cruiser she heard a baby crying. She looked around but didn't see another soul in the parking lot. The noise sounded as if it was coming from near her patrol car. As she reached it, Maggie stopped short, nearly tripping over the car seat that sat beside the driver's door.

"Well, what do we have here?" she said as she squatted down to see the baby in the car seat. "What's wrong, sweetheart? Where's your mother?"

The infant was a girl, judging from the pink blanket she was wrapped in. She couldn't be more than two

months old, if that. She touched the baby's cheek. It
didn't feel too cool so maybe she hadn't been here long.
She looked around again but whoever had left the child
was either long gone or hiding.

She scanned some bushes a short distance away, but
couldn't see much in the gloom. She started to walk over
to look more closely, but the baby was cranked up and
crying in earnest now and clearly needed her attention.
She squatted down again, spotted a pacifier and put it
in the little girl's mouth. That quieted her, at least for
the moment.

There was a note pinned to the blanket. Maggie shined
her flashlight on it to read the printed block letters.

Please take care of my baby.
He said he'd kill her if I
keep her. Her name is Grace.

Holy moly. Maggie stared at the baby, who was
fretting and looked like she was winding up to cry again.
Probably hungry, poor little thing. Then she noticed
there were a couple of bottles in the car seat as well as
some diapers.

Maggie stood, torn between wanting to check out
possible witnesses and the fact that she couldn't leave
the child. She sure as hell didn't intend to cart the baby
with her while she talked to people.

She popped her trunk open and pulled out a pair of
thin latex gloves and put them on. Then she took the
note off and bagged it, to take it to the police lab. She

would probably have the car seat and bottles dusted for fingerprints, and she didn't want to contaminate the surfaces with her own.

She picked up the car seat and put the baby in the cruiser since it had gotten a little chilly. Then she keyed in the mike and said, "Requesting backup at the Wayside Apartments, two-seventy-five Fifth Street. I have an abandoned infant."

"What's that you say?" Allison, the dispatcher, said. "A baby?"

"That's right. I found her sitting in her car seat right beside my door. I need some help to check out the building for witnesses." Just then the baby—Grace, the note had said—spit out her pacifier and began to wail. "Send me the backup as quick as you can. I have to go."

Turning on the interior light, she took the baby out of the car seat and settled her in the crook of her arm. When she gave her the bottle, Grace sucked on it greedily. Maggie wondered if the mother was still hanging around, trying to see what was going to happen. Or had she simply set the carrier down and walked off, trusting the cops would come back to the car before long? Either way, Maggie didn't like it. Abandonment was a crime, plain and simple.

Grace was a beautiful baby. Fine blond hair, dark blue eyes like all babies had at first, perfect rosebud mouth. She looked well cared for, Maggie admitted. And she was so sweet. But then, all babies were sweet. Her nieces and nephews certainly were.

She stifled a pang, remembering she wouldn't be

seeing either her sister Lorna or her kids—Bobby, Jeannette and baby Summer—as often as she had in the past. Her sister's husband had recently been transferred and the whole family had moved away. To Florida, of all places. If Maggie saw them at holidays from now on, she'd be lucky.

Now Maggie's parents were thinking about following them. Her dad was a fisherman but he'd been talking about retiring and doing something else. Maggie couldn't imagine it, but her mother sounded set on moving.

Maggie loved her mother but sometimes she really resented knowing that her mother didn't think she'd ever get married and have children of her own. "You're just not domestic, Maggie." A refrain she'd heard from her mother and sister for years. Her dad never said it, but then, he didn't talk a lot anyway.

Although Maggie admitted she wasn't a regular domestic goddess by any means, she didn't see why that precluded her having a family of her own. Of course, she had to find a man in order to do that, and that didn't seem likely anytime soon.

After Grace finished the bottle, Maggie burped her. She thought about putting her back in her seat, but there was still no sign of backup, so she simply held her until Grace fell asleep. "Don't you worry, honey," she murmured to the sleeping baby. "Maggie will make sure you're taken care of while we look for your mama."

AN HOUR LATER Maggie held a crying baby Grace in one arm, while holding a phone receiver against her ear.

"No, we haven't located the mother," she told her friend Nina Baker, a social worker at Child Protective Services. "We've barely had time to question anyone. There were no witnesses. Or at least, no one who'll admit to seeing anything."

"Have you identified the baby yet?"

"No. I'm about to take her footprint and see if we can find a match at any of the area hospitals. But even if we identify the baby that doesn't mean I can find the mother. I couldn't get any useable prints from the note or the car seat or the bottles she left."

"Sounds like it might take a while to find the mother, then."

"You got that right. This baby needs someplace to stay as soon as possible. She's exhausted and needs somewhere to sleep besides in her car seat at the police station."

"I'll get right on it, Maggie," Nina said. "I'll call you back as soon as I've located foster care for her."

"Do you think that will be a problem?"

"Oh, no, I'm sure it won't be. I'll call you back as soon as I find a home."

Thirty minutes later, Nina still hadn't gotten back to her so Maggie called her. "Nina, what's going on? This baby needs to get out of here."

"I'm sorry, but I'm having a little problem finding someone to keep her on such short notice. The foster parents we usually turn to in this situation are ill and I'm having to call all around the area."

"You haven't found anyone?"

"Well, not yet," Nina admitted. "But I've contacted another—"

"Look, let me take her home with me," Maggie interrupted. "This is stupid. She needs a bath, she needs some food and she needs to get the hell out of here so she can sleep. I'm telling you, the poor little baby is exhausted."

"Well… Are you sure? I could take her myself, but—"

"Just let me take care of her, Nina."

"I suppose that would be all right," she said, still hesitant. "But aren't you on duty?"

"I cleared it with the chief to go off shift early. I'll take her home with me and you can let me know when you've found a foster family for her."

"Thanks, Maggie. You're a lifesaver."

"Come on, sweetheart," she said to the sobbing baby. "You're going home with Maggie. We're going to get you all fixed up."

JUST BEFORE SHE LEFT the station Maggie called Delilah Randolph. Delilah and her husband, Cameron, owned the waterfront restaurant and bar The Scarlet Parrot.

"Delilah, it's Maggie," she said when her friend answered. "I need a favor."

"Sure, Maggie. What is it?"

"I need to borrow some diapers and formula and bottles until I have a chance to buy some. And maybe a playpen or something else for the baby to sleep in."

"What baby?"

"I found an abandoned baby a few hours ago and CPS couldn't find anyone to keep her tonight. I'm taking her home with me and thought maybe you could help me out."

"Someone abandoned their infant? How terrible."

"It happens," Maggie said. "Although it's more often newborns who are abandoned. This little girl is a couple of months old, I think."

"I'll bring some things and meet you at your house. I've got some clothes, too. A footed sleeper and something for her to wear tomorrow. Any idea what size she is?"

Maggie checked the outfit Grace wore and told Delilah the size.

"Got it. I'll see what I have and borrow whatever else we need from my sister-in-law."

"Great—thanks, Delilah. See you in a few."

An hour later Maggie put a bathed, fed and freshly clothed baby Grace to bed in the borrowed playpen turned crib. Delilah had stayed to help her and was waiting for Maggie in the kitchen.

"I put her on her back," Maggie said, walking into the room. "That's what they tell you, isn't it?"

"That's right. Until she can turn over she should sleep on her back."

"Want some hot chocolate?"

"If you're having some."

As Maggie took out the mugs and ingredients, Delilah asked, "What's going to happen to Grace now?"

"She'll go into foster care until we locate the mother. If we don't find the mother…" Maggie poured milk and chocolate into the mugs and stirred them. "I suppose she'll eventually wind up being adopted. Who knows how long that will be, though?" She stuck the mugs in the microwave and turned it on.

"It's odd, but the baby didn't look neglected. Or abused. I looked for bruises or other signs when we bathed her. I'd say she'd been well taken care of."

"That's what I thought, too. No signs of abuse at all."

"Why would her mother abandon her? I can't imagine abandoning Johnny."

"She left a note saying 'he' threatened to kill the baby and asked that she be taken care of. Thought the police should be able to do that, I imagine. That's why she left her by the patrol car."

"I'd have left him, then. Not the baby."

"Not everyone's as brave as you were, Delilah. Or as smart to get out while you could. But yeah, that's what I'd have done, too."

Delilah laughed. "I wasn't brave, I was scared for my life. That's why I ran."

Delilah had fled an abusive marriage. A man who had already murdered his first wife. She was on the run when she'd met Cameron and eventually married him after her husband was killed. By Maggie.

The microwave dinged so she took out the mugs and set one in front of her friend.

"It still bothers you, doesn't it?" Delilah said. "That you had to shoot him. And that he died."

"No." She shook her head. "I've made peace with it. He gave me no choice but to shoot him. I just wish there had been another way to settle things, that's all."

Delilah reached for her hand and squeezed it. "You

saved all of us that day, Maggie. Me, Cam and Gabe. I said it then and I'll say it now. Thank you."

"Why are we talking about that?" Maggie said gruffly. "I did my job and there's no gratitude necessary." She took a sip of hot chocolate. "Now let me ask you something."

Delilah sat back, smiling. "Okay. What?"

"Do you think it would be totally crazy if I applied to be Grace's foster mother?"

# CHAPTER THREE

THE NEXT DAY, Nina still hadn't found foster care for Grace, so Maggie kept her that day and night. It didn't take long to realize that keeping the little girl had turned her heart to mush.

She'd always loved children. Once, she'd imagined that someday she'd find a man, marry him and have a family with him. But she was thirty-four and beginning to think that scenario was never going to happen. Even so, with one notable exception, she'd never considered single parenthood. Until now.

The crazy idea she'd shared with Delilah had really taken hold in her mind. Delilah hadn't thought it sounded too wild, and had urged her to go for it if that was really what she wanted. But although Delilah herself had been in the foster care system briefly, she knew no more than Maggie did about becoming a foster parent.

Why shouldn't she apply to care for Grace? She had a good job and was perfectly capable of caring for a child. She'd have to work something out about her hours and child care while she was at work, but there were working single mothers everywhere. Her idea was only bolstered by the thought of the precious little girl adrift in the system.

Maggie believed there was a very good chance the police would track down the parents, but who knew what would happen once they did? Even if they found Grace's parents, she could very well still remain in the foster care system, depending on what the judge decided about the charges of abandonment that were sure to be brought against the mother and possibly the father, as well.

She'd talked to the chief and he'd agreed to give Maggie a few days off to take care of the baby until a more permanent solution could be reached. And in the meantime, Maggie was falling hard for baby Grace.

The morning after that, Nina called. "I found a foster home for Grace. When would be a good time for me to come pick her up?"

*Never,* Maggie thought, looking at the baby in her arms. Grace was smiling and blowing bubbles. "I can keep her longer. It's not a problem."

"Oh, that's sweet of you, Maggie, but I need to get her into a licensed home. Technically, I shouldn't have let you keep her, but I was in a bind, and besides, I know you."

"Nina—" She started to say something but decided what she wanted to talk about would be better discussed face-to-face. "Never mind, I'll see you in a little while."

"Any news about locating the mother?" Nina asked after she arrived at Maggie's house.

Maggie sat in her easy chair to feed Grace while she talked to Nina. She refused to think about the fact that it might be the last bottle she gave the baby.

"We know her name. The footprint matched a child born to a Carol Davis, nine and a half weeks ago. Father unknown. She named the baby Grace, which is what the note said. No luck on her last listed place of residence. She was long gone and no one remembered much about her. Or said they didn't. It was marginal housing, a hole-in-the-wall apartment complex in Corpus Christi in a bad part of town.

"According to the officer who checked all this out, Carol Davis lived there with a man, but no one knew his name or admitted to knowing anything about him. The officer got the impression he might have been a gang-banger and they were afraid to talk."

"Which would help explain why she abandoned the baby. If she's involved with a gang member who doesn't want the child it must have seemed safer to give the baby up."

"But why didn't she go through other channels? Legal channels? Why just abandon her? I'm telling you, Nina, the child has been well cared for. I don't think she was neglected in any way. So why would the woman suddenly be willing to simply walk away from her child, abandoning her in a parking lot, for God's sake?"

"I don't know. There can be a number of reasons why she might abandon the child. But until you find her we won't know. You have no idea where she went after she left the apartment complex?"

Maggie shook her head. "My department is pursuing leads, as is the Corpus Christi police department, but it's not looking good. The mother seems to have vanished.

If she's living with a banger we may never find her." She burped Grace and leaned back to hold her in her arms. A rocker, that's what she needed.

"But she delivered the baby at a hospital. Seems like you could get some information through them."

"Yes, but we didn't. Carol Davis came in as an indigent through the E.R. There's no way she had the money to cover hospital costs, and she sure as heck didn't have insurance."

"No, I suppose not. Well, good luck. It sounds like you'll need it." Nina glanced at her watch. "I need to be going. I told the Petersons I'd bring the baby over as soon as possible."

"Yeah, Nina, about that. Could I talk to you a minute?"

"Of course."

Maggie hesitated, wondering how to broach the subject. "If I were licensed for foster care, is it possible I could take care of Grace?"

Nina stared at her a moment. "You've never mentioned wanting to be a foster parent before."

"It's something I've been thinking about for a while now," Maggie said. Which wasn't a lie if a couple of days could be considered a while. "Taking care of Grace made me realize I really did want to become licensed." But she had to admit, she didn't want to be just anyone's foster mother, she wanted to be Grace's foster mother.

"Even if you do, there's no guarantee you'll be allowed to foster Grace."

She must be pretty transparent. "But there's a chance."

"Yes, of course there's a chance. Maggie, are you really serious about this?"

She nodded. "Foster parents get first shot at adopting the child, right? Assuming she comes up for adoption?"

"Yes, but—" Nina looked troubled. "First of all, you don't know that Grace will ever come up for adoption. And it's not that simple. There's a long process involved in becoming licensed as a foster parent. Training and assessment of your ability to care for children, background checks, that sort of thing. And then there's an even more intensive process to be approved as an adoptive parent. Intensive and invasive. The people who assess you pry into every part of your life. Your present, your past, your relationships with friends and family. Everything."

"I don't have any skeletons." Not just a lie, but a whopper. But her secrets were buried deep. "I'm a cop. I have a good, steady job. I'm a respectable, responsible person. Doesn't that count?"

"Well, of course, but—"

"I want to start the process now," Maggie interrupted. "Help me do this, Nina."

Nina seemed distressed. She hemmed and hawed and finally said, "You're single."

"What does that have to do with anything? I looked it up online. It says single people can be foster and adoptive parents."

"That's true." Nina bit her lip and sighed. "I wouldn't tell just anyone this, but since it's you… If there's a choice between giving a child to a single parent and giving her to a couple, the couple wins almost every time. The party line is that your marital status doesn't matter, but take it from me, it does."

"You're saying I have to be married to be Grace's foster mother. To be a foster mother, period."

"No, not at all. I see no reason why you won't be approved as a single foster parent. But I am saying your chances of getting to keep Grace are better if you're married." She hesitated. "The thing is, Grace is the type of child who everyone wants to foster or adopt. She's an infant and she's healthy. Now, if she had some sort of mental or physical problem, then that might be a different case. I'm telling you the truth, Maggie, even though it shouldn't be that way." She stood and added, "The Petersons are a great couple. Grace will be in good hands."

But she wouldn't be in Maggie's hands. It wasn't fair, damn it. It wasn't as if she could go out and stop the next man she saw and ask him to marry her. She wasn't even dating anyone, much less talking marriage. The only single men she knew very well were committed bachelors.

Single man. Committed bachelor. An idea hit her, stunning in its simplicity.

"You're not seeing anyone seriously, are you, Maggie?"

"Actually, I am. In fact, I think he's going to propose any day now." *Liar, liar,* her mind chanted. *Minor detail,* she decided. *I can fix this.*

Nina looked like she wasn't sure she believed her. "Isn't this kind of sudden? I don't remember you talking about seeing anyone special."

"But you haven't seen me in a couple of months,"

Maggie reminded her. "He's an old friend of mine. We started dating fairly recently, but we've known each other forever."

"Does he have a name?" Nina asked drily.

"Tucker Jones," Maggie said, stepping into deep, deep trouble.

SINCE SHE WAS still off for the day, Maggie decided to put her plan into action immediately. Anything was better than sitting around looking at all the baby stuff…and no baby to go with it. She'd watched Nina take Grace away with her heart heavy and tears threatening. At least she would be able to see the baby, though. Nina had said she'd fix it with Grace's foster parents for Maggie to visit and she'd let them know Maggie wanted to care for Grace as soon as she was approved.

As a rule, Maggie didn't cry. Since she'd become a cop there were only a handful of times she could remember crying. A couple of times when she'd worked in Dallas and a particularly brutal case had come along. She hadn't cried on the job but she sure had once she'd gone home.

Another time had been when she discovered the man she'd believed wanted to marry her had lied to her. Not only was he not divorcing his wife, but his wife was pregnant with his child. And to put the whipped cream on that dessert, the wife had gotten pregnant while Maggie was dating him.

She'd cried over him, and over her naiveté in believing his lies when he'd been stringing Maggie along. After that, she vowed never to get involved with a man who wasn't completely free. She'd kept that vow until she'd met and fallen for the love of her life. What a disaster that had been.

But Tucker Jones was as free as a bird. Well, he did say he was dating someone, but he also said he wasn't serious. Surely he hadn't managed to fall madly in love with the woman in the space of a few days. Not Tucker. He enjoyed his freedom too much.

Which could be a problem, she admitted. But it wouldn't be a real marriage, after all. He could resume all his normal activities as soon as they divorced. After she had custody of Grace.

First she had to see him, though. Since it was Sunday and she knew he rarely went to church, she called him at home. Maggie waited as the phone rang, tapping her pen on the table.

"Hey, Maggie. What's up?"

"Oh, not much," she said, keeping it casual. "How about meeting me for lunch today?"

"Today?"

Her heart sank. She really wanted to put her plan in action. "Yes. Why, do you have plans?"

"I could rearrange them if it's important."

"If you wouldn't mind, I'd really like to see you today."

"All right. When and where?"

"The Scarlet Parrot, about twelve-thirty."

"See you there."

TUCKER HAD HAD TO cancel a lunch date with Isabella but he'd done it willingly. There had been something in

Maggie's voice that he couldn't quite describe. She'd sounded a little bit anxious, he thought. Something was going on with her.

He was waiting for her at the table when she walked in. Damn, she knew how to make an entrance. She wasn't in uniform and she looked nothing like a cop. Nothing like one of the guys, either. Today she wore her long, wavy red hair down around her shoulders, a light-weight white sweater that molded to her generous curves and a short, tight black skirt that made her world-class legs hard to miss, even for a man who didn't normally think about said legs.

Now he knew something was going on. Maggie didn't often dress up, at least that he'd seen, but when she did... Wow. He stood as she reached the table.

"Hi, Tucker. Thanks for meeting me," she said as she sat in the chair he'd pulled out for her.

He sat down, too. "Wouldn't miss it. You look great, Maggie."

"Thanks," she said, looking pleased.

He considered her a moment. "What are you up to?"

She smiled and flashed him a look brimming with mischief. "Now why would you think I'm up to something? Just because I asked you to lunch?"

He'd noticed before that Maggie's hazel eyes often changed color with her mood. Tucker wasn't sure what kind of mood went with that brilliant emerald-green, but he found it more than a little fascinating.

"That's one reason," he said. And because she'd gone to some trouble to look like one of his ultimate fantasies. The thought made him feel...weird. This was Maggie, after all. "Is this like a date?" he asked suspiciously.

"Not exactly," she said, with a laugh in her voice.

"Last I checked you swore you'd never date me. You said you'd been cured of that in high school." Even all this time later, he still felt like a jerk whenever he thought about what had happened the one and only time she'd agreed to go out with him, when he'd asked her to homecoming her junior year. Even so, it was a long time to hold a grudge, in his opinion.

"I'm sure I didn't say never." She busied herself spreading her napkin out and putting it in her lap. "Besides, I told you, this isn't exactly a date."

The waitress came and took their drink order, returning shortly with two iced teas. When she asked if they were ready to order, Maggie told her they'd like to wait.

Mystified and curious as hell, Tucker waited for Maggie to get to the point…which she didn't do.

She stirred sweetener into her tea and took a sip. "How was your date with the latest audition?"

"The latest what?" he said blankly.

"You know, the woman your mother set you up with. The one you said you'd been dating. The latest auditioner for the part of Mrs. Tucker Jones. The future mother of your children."

"Oh, Isabella. She's…nice." He took a sip of his drink, wondering where she was heading. If she was heading anywhere, which he was beginning to doubt.

"Just nice? Are you seeing her again?"

"I'm not sure. Why?" he asked. Maggie didn't normally quiz him about his dating habits. A suspicion entered his mind. "Are you trying to set me up with someone, Maggie?"

She laughed. "I guess you could say that. I just wanted to make sure you're not involved with anyone."

"You ought to know I'm not. You saw me three days ago and I wasn't then." He took another drink and continued, "If you want me to go out with a friend of yours, why didn't you just ask me over the phone? Why the lunch and all the mystery?"

"It's not that simple."

It never was. He wondered what was wrong with the woman, because there almost had to be something seriously weird about her. "Who is this woman?"

"Well, Tucker—" She met his gaze and held it with dancing green eyes. "It's me. But I don't exactly want to date you."

"Color me confused as hell. What are you talking about, Maggie?"

"I need a favor, Tucker."

A favor? Why didn't she just ask? Why all the lead-up? But knowing Maggie, she must have a reason for how she approached him. "A favor." He leaned back in his chair and looked at her. She seemed a little anxious now. "A big favor or a little favor?"

She bit her lip. "Pretty big," she admitted. "But temporary."

A big, temporary favor. He shrugged. "Sure, babe, anything for you. What's the favor?"

"I want you to marry me."

Stunned, he stared at her. Marry Maggie? He couldn't quite wrap his mind around the thought.

"You want me to marry you."

"That's right." She nodded happily, as if pleased by his perception. "So, will you?"

"Maggie…?" She looked at him hopefully. "What are you smokin'?"

# CHAPTER FOUR

MAGGIE SCOWLED AT HIM. "Very funny. I'm not on drugs and you know it."

"You want me to marry you and we've never even been on a date. How crazy is that?"

"It's not crazy," she insisted, though she realized it did sound a bit...well, strange.

"Why?" When she didn't answer, he said, "Are you pregnant? Did the son of a bitch run out on you?"

"Don't be silly. Of course I'm not pregnant. It's nothing like that."

He put his face in his hands and laughed. And continued to laugh. When he finally stopped laughing he wiped his eyes and looked at her. "Okay, you really had me going for a minute. What's the joke?"

"It's not a joke. I'm dead serious."

Delilah stopped at the table. "Hi, Tucker. Hey, Maggie. Has Rachel taken your order?"

"I told her we'd wait but would you mind sending her back over?"

"I'll do better than that. What do you need?"

They both ordered the shrimp plate, a dish the Scarlet Parrot was famous for.

"How's the baby?" Delilah asked as she picked up their menus.

"She's good. They found her a foster home. Took her this morning."

"What did you decide to do?"

"I'm working on it," Maggie said, and couldn't resist glancing at Tucker. He looked thoughtful, not confused. Damn it, the man always had been quick.

Delilah smiled but didn't say anything else as she left.

"What baby? And am I to assume she has something to do with this cuckoo idea of yours?"

She ignored the jab about her idea being cuckoo. "I found an abandoned baby on Friday. Her name is Grace," she told him, and plunged into the story, including what she'd learned from Nina about her chances of keeping the child.

"She's just so precious," she said in conclusion. "If you saw Grace you'd know why I want to keep her. That's why I need to be married. But obviously, I'm not dating anyone seriously so…that's when I thought of you. You're not interested in being married, and besides, we're friends. I couldn't exactly ask a stranger to marry me. Which makes you the perfect person to be in a sham marriage with me."

Tucker had listened intently, only interrupting her to clarify a point or two. The waitress had come and left their food and Maggie was picking at hers, since she'd been too busy talking to eat much. Normally Maggie was good at reading people, it came with her job. But she couldn't tell what Tucker was thinking at all. He just sat there, staring at her with an unblinking gaze.

Tucker rubbed the back of his neck and frowned. "I'm

not questioning why you want the baby. But you know it's illegal for CPS to discriminate against you on the basis of your marital status. You don't have to be married to be a foster parent. Or to adopt, for that matter."

"I'm aware of that. But like Nina said, if it comes to a choice between a married couple and a single parent, guess who wins?"

"Legally—" he began.

Frustrated, Maggie interrupted. "It's not about the law, Tucker. We both know that. This is about what really happens. And I can't take the chance that I'd lose her just because I don't happen to have a ring on my finger."

"Maggie, this is insane."

"Please, Tucker." What would she do if he refused her? And if she lost Grace because of that? Pleading wasn't in her nature, but if that's what it took, she'd do it. "It will only be until I can get custody of Grace and for a short time after that. We'll have to stay married for at least a few months, and by then I might know whether I can adopt her. As soon as that's settled we can get a divorce."

"You're nuts, you know that? You're doing all this for a baby you might not even get to keep. Have you thought about what you'll do if the mother shows up?"

"I'll deal with that if and when it happens. In the meantime, Grace needs foster care and I want it to be me. And you, if you'll help me."

"It won't work."

"It will. I know it will work. And it's not like we'll have a real marriage."

"Yeah, about that." He pinned her with a sharp look. "Does this fake marriage have any fringe benefits?"

"What do you mean?"

He arched his brow and smiled. "What do you think I mean? Does this phony-baloney marriage include sex?"

Stupidly, she hadn't even considered that. She'd been totally focused on her goal of caring for Grace. But now that he mentioned sex, she felt her stomach flutter. She couldn't deny that she'd always wondered what it would be like to go to bed with Tucker. But it would be a mistake. A huge mistake. "No sex," she said decisively. "And no sex with other women, either." No way would she put up with that, fake marriage or not.

"I'm supposed to be celibate for the duration? For what, months? Forget it."

"Cheer up, Tucker. I'll be celibate, too."

"Now I know you're nuts. No, forget it."

But he didn't sound definite to Maggie. She tried another tack. "Marrying me will get your mother off your back. Have you thought about that?"

He seemed struck by the thought and then he started laughing, though he wouldn't tell her why. Maggie had an idea she knew, however.

"I know she doesn't like me but at least if you're married she can't expect you to go out with all the women she's been parading in front of you."

"That part's not really a hardship," Tucker said. "Unless they want to go to the opera."

"I hate opera, too," Maggie said hopefully. "And we do have things in common. We both enjoy Tae Kwon Do and action movies and...well, we've been friends for a long time."

"I don't know. I'd have to be certifiable to agree to this scheme of yours."

He was wavering. She knew it. She could feel it. She put her hand over his. "Don't decide right now. Take some time to think about it." *But not too long.*

"Thinking about it won't make this idea any less insane." He searched her eyes and smiled. "You really want this baby, don't you?"

"More than I've wanted anything in a long time. I can't explain it. She just…something about her calls to me. I have to try."

He sighed. "All right. I'll think about it."

She had to restrain herself from throwing her arms around his neck. "Okay, that's all I ask." He was still regarding her suspiciously, so she added, "Are you busy after lunch?"

"No, why?"

"Come with me to see Grace."

He hesitated for a moment, then shrugged. "All right."

She breathed a sigh of relief. Seeing Grace might not seal the deal, but it couldn't hurt. Tucker was a nice guy. Surely once he saw Grace and saw how much Maggie wanted to keep her, he'd go along with her plan. And Grace was such a charmer, how could he resist?

*BIG MISTAKE,* Tucker thought. He'd known it even as he'd agreed to go with Maggie. And now here they were alone with the kid, who he admitted was pretty as could be with her wispy blond curls and dark blue eyes. The foster mother was obviously comfortable with

Maggie, because she'd gone off to do laundry or something the minute they showed up. And now Maggie was holding the baby and cooing at her and looking like the complete marshmallow he'd always suspected she was. Tough cop Maggie Barnes was gaga over the kid.

Maggie looked at Tucker and smiled that big, heart-in-her-eyes smile. "Do you want to hold her?"

Hold her? What if he broke her? But he didn't see a way out of it. "I don't know anything about babies," he said without much hope.

"That's all right, I'll show you." She placed the baby in his arms, then stood close by while he held her.

She was so…little. She yawned, blinked at him with those big blue eyes and waved a tiny fist in the air. A fist the size of a walnut. Good God, how did people take care of anything so fragile and helpless? He made another mistake and looked at Maggie. She met his eyes and smiled again. Damn, she was totally gone over this baby.

"Isn't she precious?" Maggie said, still with the sappy look on her face. And her voice… He'd never heard her sound like that, so tender and, face it, so damn vulnerable. *Vulnerable* wasn't really a word he'd have picked when he thought of Maggie. Until today, that is.

Even Tucker had to admit there was something about the baby that got to him. Something…not needy. More like trusting. "You'd better take her," he said.

Maggie took her back and said, "I'm going to put her down for her nap. We can leave after that."

*You're an idiot. You're thinking about doing it. You*

*are actually considering marrying Maggie,* he thought as he watched her walk out.

Shortly after that they left and he went back home. But he didn't get a single one of the chores he'd been planning to do accomplished. His house was in a newer subdivision of Aransas City with some fairly substantial homes, though nothing approaching the scale of his parents' waterfront home in Key Allegro. He went out on the deck to sit in the warm February sunshine and think about Maggie's proposal.

He kept seeing Maggie's face when she'd held the baby. She'd looked so happy…and so wistful. Her smile had touched him and the hope in her eyes made him wonder how he could stand to disappoint her.

And they *were* friends. Maybe not as close as they'd been as kids, but he cared about Maggie and had enjoyed renewing the friendship when he'd moved back to town. Still, marrying her seemed a little excessive.

It hit him that he was actually *seriously* considering doing it. She wanted this kid so badly. Otherwise she'd never have proposed such a scheme.

He thought about his parents' reaction and had to grin. His dad would be fine with it, if that's what Tucker wanted. But then his dad had never shared his wife's ambitions for Tucker. His mother would blow a gasket if he told her he was marrying Maggie Barnes. Especially since she'd been pushing Isabella at him as hard as she could.

Maggie was a cop and the daughter of a fisherman, not the sort of woman his mother had dreamed of him marrying. Maggie had no patience for the social scene or any of the other things Eileen Jones held near and dear. And while Tucker loved his mother, he had to admit, one of her major faults was that she was a snob. Cops and fishermen were not genteel, not in Eileen Jones's world.

If he did marry Maggie, he'd have to come down hard on his mother. He wouldn't allow her to disrespect his bride, even if she was a fake bride.

But could he live with Maggie and not have sex? Wouldn't that be too weird?

Tucker spent the rest of the afternoon and evening thinking. By the next afternoon, he knew he wouldn't get anything accomplished until he'd taken care of the problem.

He called Maggie's home and got no answer, then tracked her down at work. "When are you off?"

"My shift's over in an hour. I came in early today. Have you decided?"

He didn't answer that directly. "We need to talk. I'll come to your house after your shift."

"All right. I'll see you then."

He'd made his decision. Now all he had to do was convince Maggie to change the game plan. Not in a major way. Just one little detail.

TUCKER WAS WAITING for Maggie on her front porch when she came home so she went in that way instead of through the kitchen as she usually did. She hadn't been able to tell on the phone, but she suspected he was going to turn her down. So she'd spent the rest of her shift trying to brace for it.

"Hey, Tucker."

"Hey, Maggie."

He followed her in and she tossed her keys down on the hall table. She hung the jacket she hadn't needed on the hook by the door. Walking into the living room, she took her Glock out, checked it, then laid it on the coffee table. Next came the equipment belt, which went on the table beside the Glock.

If she ever did get to keep Grace she'd have to lock up her weapon. That would be one of the first things CPS made sure of. She stretched and wished she'd had time to have a little workout with the punching bag before Tucker arrived. It might have relaxed her.

"What?" she asked because Tucker was staring at her.

He grinned. "I've never seen you take off your cop stuff before. It's kind of…sexy."

Maggie laughed. "Right. Are you hitting on me, Tucker?"

"Well, that's what I came to talk to you about. That and your proposal."

"You decided not to, didn't you?"

"No, I decided I'd marry you."

She stared at him. "Really?" Her heart thudded painfully. He wouldn't joke about that, would he?

He stuck his hands in his pockets and walked away a few steps. "I'll marry you but I'm not sure about one of your conditions."

"What condition is that?" she asked warily.

"I don't think we can live together and pretend to be married and never have sex. It just won't work, Maggie."

"You're saying if I want to marry you I have to have sex with you. That's blackmail."

"Don't be ridiculous. And that's not what I said, exactly. I said it wouldn't work."

"Sex would be a mistake. Think how messy it would be once we divorced."

"I don't see why. If we both know going in this is temporary, why shouldn't we enjoy ourselves?"

She was appalled to discover she was considering it, and not simply because she wanted to be married. "You don't really want to sleep with me, Tucker. You just don't want to be celibate for months."

He walked over to her, reached out and gently played with her hair. "You're wrong about that, Maggie." He paused and added, "Did you know I had a thing for you in high school?"

"Liar," she said a little breathlessly. She was finding it hard to breathe. The man had no right to be so gorgeous. And when he smiled at her like he was doing now… Oh, baby. What had ever made her think Tucker Jones would be safe? That she could marry him and not want to sleep with him? Stupidity, that's what. Still, she hadn't come this far to give up now.

"Yeah, you had a thing for me all right. Is that why you stood me up for the homecoming dance?"

He frowned. "I knew you still held that against me. I was eighteen and stupid, Maggie."

"You were a slime," she stated categorically, moving away from him. "You stood me up because Annette Carson said she'd sleep with you if you took her instead of me." At least, that was the story she'd heard. She'd never found out if it was truth or rumor. But judging by Tucker's expression, it held more than a grain of truth. "I cried about you, you jerk."

He winced at that. "I didn't sleep with her," he said. "And I knew I'd made a mistake as soon as I did it. You never gave me another chance after that."

"Once burned, you know. But it doesn't matter now, anyway."

"Doesn't it? Would it help if I told you I regretted it ever since I did it?"

"Huh. Because she wouldn't put out, I imagine."

"No, because I hurt you and you never forgave me."

"I forgave you. We were still friends after that."

He laughed. "After you made me grovel. Yeah, I guess we were friends."

"You have a point," she conceded. "Living together and not having sex might not be easy, but we're both adults. We should be able to put our glands on hold if necessary."

"That's just it. Why is it necessary?"

Part of her wished it wasn't. But she had to be realistic. "Because sex would make the marriage too real. And neither one of us is ready for that."

He didn't look convinced. He'd put his hands in his pockets and was studying her. He still wore his office clothes, tailored khaki slacks and a powder-blue dress shirt with the sleeves rolled up over muscular forearms. Her mouth went a little dry just looking at him. She wondered why she didn't simply agree and make it easy on both of them.

"Admit it, Tucker. You don't want a real marriage any more than I do. Sex would complicate everything."

"Maggie—"

She broke in before he could shoot her down. "There's another reason. I'm not cut out for meaningless sex."

"This might come as a shock to you, but I don't much care for it, either. But I don't think making love to you would be meaningless, Maggie."

"That's as much of a problem as if it *were* meaningless. What if one of us fell for the other? That would bring nothing but pain to both of us."

"I don't know." He shook his head. "I see what you're saying, but that doesn't change the facts."

Her heart sank. He was trying to let her down gently. Maybe he was right. A fake marriage was too much to expect from him. But she wanted Grace so badly she'd been willing to try anything to get her. Almost anything. She knew herself too well, though. If she went to bed with Tucker, she'd fall for him. And she couldn't risk that. "What facts?" she asked, clamping down on her emotions.

"We're going to have to pretend to an intimacy we haven't experienced. It won't be easy."

"No, but we can do it. I know we can."

As he looked at her a rueful smile twisted his lips. "I care about you, Maggie."

Hope burgeoned. "I know. I care about you, too. What are you saying?"

"What the hell. I'll marry you."

"Really?" She wanted to throw her arms around him but she restrained herself. "Marriage and no sex?"

"If that's the way you want it."

"I think that's best for both of us, considering the circumstances." She held out a hand. "Shake on it?"

Tucker looked at her hand, then at her face and smiled. "Don't you think we should seal this deal with a kiss?" He took her hand and tugged her closer.

His mouth curved upward, his eyes were smiling, but there was understanding in them, too. She hesitated, torn between doing what she wanted and doing the smart thing. But damn it, a woman didn't get engaged every day. Sham or not, she was still talking about marriage.

"You don't want our first kiss to be at the wedding when the preacher says 'you may now kiss the bride,' do you?"

"That would definitely be safer," she said, and he laughed.

He pulled her closer, their joined hands pinned between them. She slid one hand up his arm and around his neck. His other arm came around her to hold her lightly at the waist. Maggie was a tall woman but Tucker was several inches taller than her and she had to look up to see his face.

"Are you sure about this, Tucker?"

"About kissing you?"

"No, about the whole thing."

He smiled and his arm tightened around her. "Let's get married," he said softly, and then he kissed her.

## *CHAPTER FIVE*

HE'D ONLY MEANT IT as a friendly kiss. But her lips were soft, and tempting, and when he traced the bow with his tongue, they parted and welcomed him inside. She tasted sweet, and a little spicy, and exactly as he'd always imagined Maggie would taste.

Damn. *Friends,* he reminded himself. He turned her loose and smiled.

She returned his smile with a saucy one of her own, and said, "Now why am I not surprised you're good at that?"

He laughed. Obviously, she hadn't been as affected as he had. It would be good to remember that. "You're not so bad yourself."

She gave him a cheeky grin. "I guess we need to talk about details. I'd like to do this as soon as possible. How long is the waiting period after you get a marriage license?"

"Three days. I looked it up before I came over." He checked his watch. "We still have time to go to the courthouse today and apply for it. Then we can get married on Friday. Are you going to talk to your minister?"

"I don't know, Tucker." She frowned and rubbed her

arm. "I'd feel like a hypocrite if I asked my pastor to marry us. Let's just go down to the justice of the peace and do it at his office."

That would be logical, he supposed. But if they wanted people to take them seriously, he thought a traditional wedding would be best. Still, for now, he held his tongue. "We can talk about those details later. Right now we should go apply for the license."

"Okay, let me change." She picked up her gun and equipment belt and took them with her.

Maggie came back a short time later in jeans and a lightweight sea-green sweater that turned her hazel eyes a soft, mossy green. She'd brushed her hair and left it down. Her hair was an amazing mix of colors. Everything from deep auburn to strands of strawberry blond. It was soft, too, as he'd discovered earlier. He controlled an impulse to touch it again, and decided not to think about what it would feel like against his bare skin. Much better not think about that, since it wasn't going to happen.

"I'll drive," he said. "We need to go buy you a ring after we go to the courthouse."

Maggie looked at him in surprise as they walked out the door. "You mean an engagement ring? I don't need one. All I need is a plain wedding band."

He opened the Mustang's door and let her in, then got in himself before he answered. "If you're marrying me you need an engagement ring." He started the car and pulled away from the curb.

"I don't see why. It's just a needless expense."

He shot her an amused glance. "Maggie, do you want everyone to believe this marriage is for real?"

"Of course. That's the only way to make sure the CPS doesn't get wind of the truth."

"Then you need an engagement ring. No one who knows me will believe I didn't buy my fiancée a ring."

She grumbled but she conceded his point. He had a feeling they weren't through arguing about the ring and knew he was right an hour later when they walked into a jewelry store in Corpus Christi.

Maggie strode in, every inch the officer in control. He regarded her with some amusement as she looked at the case the clerk pointed out and immediately zeroed in on a ring with a diamond so tiny he needed a magnifying glass to see it.

"This one looks good," Maggie said, pointing. "How much is it?"

The clerk looked disappointed and Tucker couldn't blame her. He caught the woman's eye and shook his head. "My fiancée is being thrifty, but I'm not." He gestured to another ring, a simple solitaire setting but with a decent-size diamond. It looked like Maggie, he thought. "Let us see that one."

"That's a lovely choice, sir." The clerk beamed.

"Tucker, that's too expensive."

He noticed the mutinous set to her jaw and smiled. "Excuse us a minute," he told the clerk and, putting his hand under her arm, led Maggie outside. She started arguing the moment they walked out the door. Leaning back against the planter in the center of the courtyard, he let her rant. Patiently, he waited as she made her case, which consisted mainly of her arguing that she didn't think a hunk of glass should cost so much and she didn't intend to pay for something so ridiculously outrageous.

"Are you through?"

"I guess." Her eyes flashed with annoyance.

He didn't bother to debate, but gave her the clincher to his case. "Maggie, if you get that dinky little ring everyone in town will know the marriage is fake."

"Why should they? No one will notice."

"Who are you kidding? We're living in Aransas City, gossip capital of the U.S. Besides, my parents would know the instant they saw it. You don't want them to know our real reason for getting married, do you?"

"No, of course I don't." She sulked. "If you didn't have so much money it wouldn't be a problem."

Tucker laughed out loud at that. "You really are one in a million. You're the only woman I know who's unhappy because her fiancé has money. Let me buy the ring for you."

"We'll split it," she announced. "And all the other expenses, too."

She couldn't afford half of what that ring cost. Not on a cop's salary. Besides, he wanted to buy it for her. "Nope. I buy the ring."

"Tucker—"

"It's a deal breaker. Take it or leave it." She glared at him. "Are you armed?" he asked. If that was the way she looked at suspects, he was glad he wasn't one.

"Always."

That surprised him. "You wear your weapon to the jewelry store?"

"My Glock is with me whenever I'm dressed." She reached behind her back and said, "It's either here or, if I can't conceal it, I have a purse with a hidden holster. I'm a cop. If I see a crime being committed I'm expected to intervene. Why do you ask?"

He hadn't known that, but then, he'd never dated a cop before. Or been engaged to one. And not being a criminal lawyer, he didn't know a lot of cops well. "Because you looked like you were about to blow me away."

"Ha-ha. No, I save that for the bad guys. You're merely annoying." She paced away from him a step, then turned back. "It's not right, Tucker. I don't want you spending your money on me. This marriage thing was all my idea."

"Yes, but I agreed to it. So we need to do it right. There's no point in our getting married if we announce to the world it's fake."

"I guess you're right," she said grudgingly. "You can always sell it once we're divorced."

*As if he would take the ring back from her. Not a chance in hell.* But wisely, he kept his thoughts to himself.

They went back inside and walked out with the engagement ring Tucker had chosen and two plain gold wedding bands that he decided he'd better let her have her way about. Maggie stated categorically that she wouldn't wear "the rock," as she referred to it, to work. She wanted something plain, that she felt comfortable with. Something that if she lost or damaged, she wouldn't have a heart attack over. So he gave in.

There would be other arguments, he felt sure. But he'd won the battle of the engagement ring. Oddly enough, he found he liked seeing his ring on her finger. Maybe this marriage wasn't as bizarre of an idea as he'd thought at first.

SURREPTITIOUSLY, Maggie looked at her left hand. The diamond sparkled, even in the dim, romantic lighting of the classy seafood restaurant Tucker had suggested they go to, to eat and discuss the rest of the wedding plans.

Tucker had told the clerk to put the ring in a small velvet box, then insisted Maggie let him slide the rock on her finger once they went back to his car. She'd been a little afraid that he'd kiss her. He hadn't, but instead of being relieved he'd acquiesced to her wishes, she was conscious of a vague feeling of disappointment.

The rock was gorgeous, the kind of ring any woman would kill for. A ring totally unsuited to a hardworking, firmly middle-class cop. Maggie had never felt more guilty in her life.

She shot him an irritated glance. Damn it, why couldn't he have been poor? Or at least middle class, like her? "I didn't ask you to marry me because you're loaded, you know."

Tucker looked up from the wine list he was studying and smiled. "I know. I wouldn't have agreed to marry you if I thought you were after me for my money."

The waiter came back and Tucker ordered a bottle of wine for them. White, because that's what she liked. Maggie had a feeling he wouldn't let her pay for half of dinner, either. "Is that why you haven't ever married? Because you think women are after your money?"

"I don't think all of them are. But I know for a fact at least one was."

"Sounds like there's a story there."

The waiter had returned and Tucker let him open the wine, pour out a taste and then, when he nodded, pour them both a glass. He took another sip of wine and set his glass down. Maggie sipped hers and sighed. Whatever it was, it tasted like liquid gold.

He smiled cynically. "Yeah, there's a story."

"You don't want to talk about it."

"Maybe some other time. Right now I think our time would be better spent talking about the wedding. We need to tell both our parents, obviously. Do you think your parents will want to have the wedding at their house?"

Maggie didn't have to think long about that. "No. They had my sister's wedding at the house and my mother swore never again. She was a nervous wreck and the house was in shambles afterward. On top of that, somebody's kid broke the TV and my dad was so angry he didn't speak to Lorna for a month. Let's just go down to the JP."

"I have a better idea. We'll have the wedding and reception at my parents' house."

Maggie goggled at him. "Are you insane? Have the wedding at the mansion?" She remembered his parents' home from high school, when Tucker had parties.

"It's not a mansion."

"In my book it is. Your mother will freak. She's going to freak anyway, isn't she?"

"They'll be surprised. But they'll deal with it. Don't worry, I'll handle my parents. We'll tell both sets of parents tomorrow night. We can plan the wedding and reception with my parents then."

She started to argue but he wore the same determined expression as when he'd decided to give her the rock. Damn, the man could be stubborn. "Okay, if it's all right with your folks we can have the wedding there, but there's no need for a reception. Aren't we just having family?"

"Family and a few friends. It won't be large. There's not enough time. We'll just call a few of our friends and ask them. I want to ask my partner and his wife and my secretary and her husband. You'll want to ask your chief and his wife, I'm sure. And whoever else you work with that you want to come. We can make out the list tonight when we get back."

Her head was whirling. She hadn't realized everything would be so complicated. She hadn't thought things through at all. For a smart woman she was starting to realize she'd been incredibly dumb about this whole thing. Fortunately, the waiter came back and took their order, which gave her a little time to compose herself.

She changed the subject. "Do you want to come see Grace with me tomorrow? I have a meeting set up in the morning and I thought you might want to be there, too."

"Sure. Let me know what time and I'll arrange my schedule. Have you made any headway locating her mother?"

"No, not yet. So far every lead has fizzled. The

woman could be anywhere by now. She's gone under-
ground and it's hard to find them when they do that."
Guiltily, Maggie acknowledged that she didn't want the
cops to find the mother. Grace deserved better than a
mother who had abandoned her.

"When do we start the process for applying to be
foster parents?"

"I have some of the paperwork, which I've already
started on, but I do need your input on some of it. We
have to take a course they call pre-training, to certify us
in child care. Then they'll want a caseworker to come
out and assess us, and our home. I have a long list of the
kind of questions they ask. It's pretty intense."

It occurred to her she hadn't thought their living arrangements through, either. "Do you mind moving into
my house?" She looked at him and her heart sank. He
just smiled and shook his head.

"Afraid not, Maggie. You're going to have to move
in with me."

"Why? Because your house is bigger?"

"Partly. It just makes sense to live in the newer house."

Newer, bigger and nicer, she thought, but she didn't
say it. "I'm not selling my house. I like my house.
Besides, I'll need it after we get divorced."

"I agree, there's no need to sell it. Why don't you just
rent it out?"

She could do that easily enough. Rentals were scarce
in Aransas City so they rented out almost immediately
whenever one came up.

The waiter brought their salads. They ate in silence

for a moment and then Tucker said, "Where do you want to go on our honeymoon?"

Honeymoon? "Oh, no," she said, laying down her fork. "No way. I gave in on the ring. I gave in on where we have the wedding. I even gave in on the house. I've given in on every damn thing you've mentioned. But we are not going on a honeymoon. Absolutely not."

He gave her a pitying look. "Yeah, babe, we are."

"Stop calling me 'babe.' It's annoying. Read my lips. No honeymoon."

Tucker put down his fork and looked at her with exasperation. "You're not being logical, Maggie. If we're getting married because we're in love—which, I have to remind you, is what we want everyone to think—then we'd want to take a honeymoon. It doesn't have to be long, just a few days. Are you working this weekend?"

"No." She snapped the word out, along with a death look.

"Good. Then ask your chief for a few more days off and we'll go on a honeymoon."

The waiter cleared their salad plates. "Your main course will be right out," he said, and poured more wine.

Maggie gulped some and glared at Tucker. Why had she never realized what a control freak he was? If he thought he was calling all the shots in this phony marriage, he had another think coming.

Preferring to brood in silence, she waited until the waiter had set their main course in front of them before she spoke again.

"We're not in love. In fact, I don't even like you right now."

Tucker laughed. "You're just mad because I'm right. Why don't we go skiing? Have you ever been?"

Maggie took another drink of her wine and tossed her hair over her shoulder with a twist of her head. "Oh, sure. I go to Switzerland every year and ski the Alps."

His lips curved. "Switzerland's too far. I like Steamboat Springs, Colorado. We can fly into Dallas Friday night and there's a direct flight out the next morning. I'll see if I can get us in at the condo where I usually stay. Failing that, my partner has a second home there and I don't think they're using it this weekend."

"I don't have any ski clothes. And I don't have time to buy them."

"Don't worry about it. My partner's wife is about your size. I'm sure she'll lend you whatever you need. And then we'll rent equipment for you there. You'll like it, you'll see. You're athletic, so I'm sure you'll pick it up quickly."

Maggie leaned forward and pinned him with the look she usually reserved for low-life scumbags she interrogated. "You're insane. Completely insane."

He laughed again. "Loosen up, Maggie. It'll be fun."

Fun? A romantic honeymoon with Tucker, the very appealing man she'd sworn not to go to bed with. What had she gotten herself into? And what had she dragged Tucker into?

"Tucker?" He looked up from his plate and smiled at her. "Maybe we shouldn't do this."

"Cold feet, Maggie?"

"Frozen. I hadn't realized it would be so complicated. I didn't think things through very well." She shook her head. "This is so not like me."

Tucker covered her hand with his. Her left hand, the one wearing the ring he'd insisted on buying her. "You've been focused on your goal. You want the baby, don't you?"

"You know I do."

"And you believe your chances of getting to keep her will be much better if we're married, right?"

"Yes, but—"

"Then let's get married. Maggie," he said, squeezing her hand gently. "I wouldn't do this if I didn't want to."

She stared at him for a long moment, then smiled reluctantly. "Okay. But I hope you don't regret it."

"I won't. And I don't think you will, either."

Maggie shook off her uneasiness. Focus on the goal, she thought. Keeping Grace. And don't think about the possibility that marriage with Tucker Jones might be nothing like she expected when she'd first proposed.

# CHAPTER SIX

"CAN I GET YOU something to drink?" Colleen Barnes asked late the next afternoon after she'd shown Tucker and Maggie into the living room. "Tea or something stronger?"

She looked a little bewildered, Maggie thought. And why shouldn't she since Maggie hadn't told her parents anything beyond she was bringing someone to see them. She'd kept the ring hidden, so she wouldn't have to explain immediately, but maybe that had been a mistake.

"No, thanks, Mom. We can't stay long." They had to face the dragon lady next, which was her private name for Tucker's mother. She knew she ought to be past it by now, but Eileen Jones had always intimidated her. It didn't matter that Maggie was a grown woman and a cop to boot, Eileen could make her feel like an unsophisticated kid with one condescending look. The last time she'd pulled the woman over for speeding came to mind.

"Frank, turn that TV off, you hear? Maggie wants to talk to us."

Maggie's father looked irritated but he muted the TV. It was tuned to his favorite station, the Fishing Channel. "What in Sam Hill is this about, Maggie?

You've never brought a man over here before. Not since you've been grown, anyway."

She shot a glance at Tucker, who was clearly struggling not to laugh. Great, her father was grumpy and her mother bewildered. She should have told them by herself. She decided just to get it over with. She thrust out her left hand to show them the rock. "I'm getting married. This Friday."

"Huh." Frank glanced at the ring, then sent Tucker a speculative look. "You don't say."

"Married?" her mother repeated blankly, staring at Maggie's hand. "To Tucker?"

Tucker took her right hand and squeezed it. She didn't dare look at him because they'd both burst out laughing. "Of course, to Tucker. Why else would I bring him?"

"Isn't this kind of sudden?" Colleen said, looking from one to the other. "We didn't even know you were dating anyone, Maggie."

"Say what you mean, Colleen." Her father looked at Tucker. "Is she pregnant?"

"Not to my knowledge," Tucker said.

Maggie squeezed his hand, hard. "Of course I'm not pregnant."

"I've been asking Maggie to marry me since I moved back to the area," Tucker announced, as if he wasn't speaking a bald-faced lie. "Yesterday she finally said yes."

"And we decided there's no reason to wait," Maggie said hastily. They had discussed what their story would be, but now that Maggie heard it spoken out loud she thought it sounded lame. Oh, well, she thought, that couldn't be helped now. "So we're getting married this Friday. At Tucker's parents' house. I'll let you know the details later." Unless his mother flipped out and they had to change plans. They should have eloped. Gone to Vegas and tied the knot there. Too late now, they'd chosen their course.

"Do you have a dress, honey?"

Maggie smiled at her mother. "Not yet. Will you go with me to look tomorrow? I'm working the morning shift, but we can go tomorrow afternoon."

"I'd love to. I'll make a list of bridal shops."

"It's informal. I want a short dress, so we can just go to a regular shop."

"Bridal shops have short dresses, Maggie."

The dress was the least of her worries. "Whatever, we'll decide tomorrow." She got up, pulling Tucker with her. "What's wrong, Dad?"

Frank frowned at both of them and rubbed his jaw. "Do I have to wear a suit?"

"Of course you have to wear a suit. You wore a suit to Lorna's wedding and didn't complain."

"Yes, he did," her mother said.

"Don't fit anymore." He sighed heavily. "I guess I could see if my burying suit fits."

She looked at Tucker and had to bite her lip. Great. Her dad was wearing his funeral suit to her wedding. Not a good omen, that.

They barely made it to the car before they both burst out laughing. "Oh, my God," Maggie finally said, wiping her eyes. "I don't know how I kept a straight face."

"It was tough," Tucker agreed as he started the car. "I was doing okay until the part about the burying suit. And his expression when he said it was priceless."

"At least that's over with," Maggie said.

"One set down, one to go."

Yeah, the ones she was worried about. "What if your mom freaks out?"

"She's not going to freak out. That's the third time you've said that. Why are you so nervous?"

"I'm not nervous." Terrified, maybe. She pulled out her cell phone and said, "Oh, look. The chief called when I had the ringer silenced. I'm sure he needs me to come in."

Tucker's glance was chock full of disbelief. "Liar. Good God, Maggie, you're a cop. You face down armed criminals. Telling my parents we're getting married should be a walk in the park to you."

"Huh. I'll take the criminal any day. I know what to do with them. I don't have a clue how to deal with your mother. I can't exactly throw her in jail because she makes me nervous."

Tucker laughed. "Cheer up. She's not as bad as you think."

*Wanna bet?* she thought. A short while later they pulled up to the mansion. It looked just like Maggie remembered. Big. Imposing. She glanced at Tucker, who was smiling at her. "Let's get this over with," she said.

"Okay." But he didn't get out. He simply looked at her, focusing on…her mouth. He was staring at her mouth and unless she mistook that gleam in his eyes… Oh, God, he was going to kiss her. And damn if she didn't want him to.

But he didn't. He dropped his gaze and said, "Let's go."

She'd imagined it, she thought, feeling foolish. They'd agreed they wouldn't have sex, so why would he kiss her? And why was she so disappointed that he hadn't?

"MOM, DAD, YOU REMEMBER Maggie Barnes, don't you?" Tucker said as they followed his father into the living room. Since Tucker had told his mother he was bringing someone with him, she had set out a tray of canapés, arranged almost perfectly on the antique silver platter she used to impress company. Someone—his dad, he was sure—had already eaten a couple, marring the perfect symmetry and no doubt incurring his mother's censure.

"Certainly. I hope you're not in trouble with the law, darling," she said with a laugh. She sat in one of the side chairs and sipped her wine.

His father offered Maggie a hand. "Harvey Jones. It's been a long time. Basketball, right? You were captain of the girls' team in high school."

Maggie smiled as she shook hands with him. "That's right. I can't believe you remembered that."

"I like sports," Harvey said. "Watched a lot of the games when Tucker was in school, although football was always Tucker's game. What can I get you to drink?"

"Maggie will have white wine and I'll take a beer."

"Coming right up," he said, and stepped behind the bar. "What's this about Tucker being in trouble with the law, Eileen? Am I missing a joke?"

His mother had caught sight of Maggie's left hand and was staring at it with a fascinated and, he admitted, slightly sour expression. "Maggie's a policewoman in Aransas City," she said.

"Are you, now?" He handed Maggie her wine and Tucker his beer. "Now that's an interesting career."

"Obviously, she hasn't stopped you for speeding or you'd know that, Harvey," his mother said waspishly.

Maggie rolled her eyes at Tucker. He grinned back.

"Well, Tucker, what is this about?" Eileen asked. "I had to cancel my meeting with the opera committee since you were so insistent on my being here."

"I think my news is a little more interesting than your opera committee." He reached for Maggie's hand. "Maggie and I are getting married this Friday. We wanted to talk to you about having the wedding here. And the reception, of course."

His mother choked on her wine. His father shot him a keen glance, then said, "Congratulations, son." He shook hands with Tucker and when Maggie offered hers, he smiled and took it, then bent to kiss her cheek. "Congratulations, my dear. His mother and I happen to think Tucker's pretty special."

"Thank you. So do I," Maggie said, surprising him.

"Married?" Eileen said faintly. "You and—and— You and *Maggie* are getting married?"

"Show her the rock," Tucker said to Maggie.

"Tucker." Maggie gave him a warning glance before turning back to his mother and smiling down at her a little anxiously. "I know it's kind of a shock."

Eileen stared at Maggie, then patted her lips with a napkin. "Yes, you might say that. I wasn't aware you and Maggie were even seeing each other, Tucker," she said, her voice having regained its strength. "This is very sudden, isn't it? Is there a particular reason you're in such a rush?"

"Relax, Mom. Maggie's not pregnant."

Maggie kicked him.

"Ouch." He rubbed his shin and grinned at Maggie, whose eyes were dark green and flashing him death threats. "I was only saying what she was thinking."

"Really, Tucker, that was uncalled for," Eileen said. "I thought no such thing. I simply wondered why I had heard nothing of this."

"Why don't we sit down and talk about it?" Harvey asked. Tucker and Maggie sat on the couch while his dad took the other side chair.

Tucker took Maggie's hand again and told his parents the same thing he'd told Maggie's parents. "I've been asking Maggie to marry me for almost a year now. Since shortly after I moved to Aransas City and we got to know each other again. It took me this long to convince her to marry me. I'm not waiting for her to change her mind."

Neither of them looked as if they were buying that lie. But neither Maggie nor Tucker could think of a better one, other than that Maggie was pregnant and they'd already blown that one by telling her parents she wasn't.

"If Maggie isn't certain about the wedding perhaps you should wait," Eileen said, looking hopeful.

"Well, Maggie? What do you say?" He tilted his head and considered her.

Her lips curved as she looked at him. "I'm sure. What about you?"

"Absolutely." Since it seemed necessary, he kissed her lightly.

"Sounds like we're having a wedding, Eileen."

"Yes, it does."

She sounded resigned. Maybe she wouldn't be as difficult as he'd thought.

"This Friday?" Eileen repeated. "And you want to have the wedding here? At our house?"

"That was Tucker's idea," Maggie said hastily. "It's no problem if we can't. We'll just go down to the justice of the peace's office."

Tucker nearly laughed. She couldn't have said anything more calculated to give his mother palpitations. Harvey and Eileen Jones's only offspring getting married at the JP's office?

Eileen gave a faint moan. "No, no. If you insist on getting married in this—this rushed fashion, you'll have it here."

"Thank you."

"How many people are you inviting?"

"No more than fifty. Maybe not that many."

"Definitely not that many," Maggie said, sending him a severe glare. "We just want family and a few friends."

His dad hadn't said much. He was still watching them closely, though. Sometimes Tucker wished his old man wasn't so observant.

"About the decorations, the flowers and such, do you have a theme in mind?" Eileen asked Maggie.

Maggie threw him a panicked glance. "Theme?"

"We just decided this yesterday, Mom. Maggie hasn't had time to think about all that."

She waved him aside. "Nonsense. Maggie's close to your age, isn't she? Surely she's thought about what she wants her wedding to be like. Haven't you?"

"Not exactly," Maggie said.

"Is this your first marriage?"

"Yes. Why?"

"Just curious, dear." She laughed again. "I can't imagine not having thought about my wedding at your age. Why, I had mine planned from the time I was fourteen."

"Tucker, would you mind looking at something for me?" Harvey said. "In my office."

"Sure, Dad." He hated to leave Maggie but his mother seemed to be behaving herself and Maggie was doing all right. "I'll be back in a minute," he told her.

"Take your time," Eileen said. "Maggie and I will get all these details ironed out."

Tucker followed his dad to his office. Harvey shut the door and said, "I don't have anything to show you. I just wanted to ask you what's going on."

"I'm getting married. I thought it was pretty self-explanatory."

Harvey crossed his arms and leaned back against the edge of his desk. "Not this time. You're not in love with Maggie, Tucker. And you said she wasn't pregnant. So I have to ask, why are you marrying her?"

Crap. He should have known his father would see through the lie. He wanted to tell him the truth, but he'd promised Maggie. Besides, he wasn't entirely sure his father wouldn't let it slip to his mother. And if she knew, that would be a disaster.

"You're wrong, Dad. I've been in love with Maggie for months."

"Which is why you've been dating a number of other women all this time," he said drily. "Including, your mother tells me, Isabella Jensen. Your mother thought you were serious about her."

"No, not at all. I told you Maggie wouldn't marry me. I was trying to forget about her." Tucker figured the less said about other women, the better. "I want to marry Maggie. I'm thirty-five, Dad, I know what I'm doing."

"You should, but I'm not sure that you do." He considered Tucker a moment, then smiled. "She's a beautiful woman. Unusual."

"Yeah." Tucker smiled, too. "Maggie's one in a million."

"Well, as you pointed out, you're a grown man. Let's go rescue your bride-to-be from your mother."

Tucker laughed. "Mom seemed to take the news pretty well. Better than I'd expected."

Harvey laid a hand on his shoulder. "With your mother you can never tell. I wouldn't be too complacent."

"Maggie's a cop. I'd back her against Mom anytime."

ARMED ROBBERS. Murderers. Thugs. Bangers. Psychos. Oh, why couldn't the chief call and tell her he had an emergency? Anything would be better than being interrogated by the dragon lady, Maggie thought.

That nice, slightly puzzled demeanor she'd displayed while Tucker was in the room had vanished the instant he left. She'd begun firing questions at Maggie like a general marshaling his troops. Oh, she hadn't been overtly rude, but it was clear from her questions that she thought Maggie was a damn poor choice as a bride for her precious son. Her attitude annoyed Maggie but she felt guilty, too. Eileen Jones only wanted the best for Tucker and she had no idea this so-called marriage was a sham.

"So we're agreed on white roses?"

"That's fine. I really don't want you to go to a lot of trouble, Mrs. Jones. I told Tucker we could—"

"Please." She raised a hand with a look of revulsion. "Don't mention the justice of the peace again. My son will not be married in an office."

Maggie bit her tongue. Eileen had pulled out paper and pen and started making a list. "Now, about the food. Did you have anything special in mind?"

Maggie looked at her blankly. She had no idea what to serve at a wedding reception. "I'm sure my mother could bring something. She loves to cook." Unlike Maggie, who considered it torture.

Eileen looked up from her list. "Home cooking?" She laughed, that short, high-pitched tinkle that made Maggie long for earplugs. "Really, Maggie, I hardly think that will be necessary. We'll have it catered. I'm sure I can find someone who'll help out on the spur of the moment."

Maggie fidgeted. "Have it catered? Won't that be expensive?"

"Expensive? What has that got to do with it?" She looked as if she'd never heard of the concept.

"I thought all this was the bride's responsibility." Maggie gestured to include the huge room. "You know, the reception and all that."

"Yes, I suppose it is. Traditionally. But yours is hardly a traditional wedding, now, is it?" She gave her a superior smile. "Don't worry, dear. We'll take care of it. I'm sure you can't afford this sort of thing on the salary of a *public servant*." She said the last two words with an audible sneer.

That fired Maggie's temper. *You're a cop,* she thought. *Where are your ovaries?* She stood. "Thanks, but no thanks. I'm paying for the reception. I'll order the flowers. And my mother can be in charge of the food. Tucker and I will deal with the drinks, too." She entertained a brief, but satisfying, image of a keg of beer smack in the middle of Eileen's elegant white living room. "You won't have to worry about anything except to tell people where to put things."

Tucker and his father came back into the room just then. Irrationally, Maggie wanted to kick Tucker. She contented herself with glaring at him instead.

"What's going on?" Tucker said.

"Why nothing, darling," his mother replied, unperturbed by Maggie's statement. "Maggie here is insisting on paying for the reception and arranging everything herself. I had merely offered her my assistance, but she obviously doesn't want my help." She sniffed, clearly offended.

Maggie gritted her teeth. She wasn't backing down on this one and if Tucker thought she would he could kiss her lily-white—

"We'll talk it over and let you know tomorrow, Mom. We need to get going. Maggie has the early shift in the morning."

Harvey gave her another kiss on the cheek before they left. Maggie really liked Tucker's father. But his mother was going to take some getting used to. It was a very good thing that the marriage was only temporary. Otherwise Maggie would have to face a lifetime of being detested by her mother-in-law.

# CHAPTER SEVEN

IT TOOK MOST OF the next morning for Maggie to fill out a report on a cow that liked to walk through town and drop cow patties along Main Street. She'd cited the owner repeatedly, but because the man had known her since she was in diapers, he didn't pay much attention to her. With long practice, Maggie ignored the almost continually ringing phones until Dottie, the receptionist, buzzed her.

She picked up the receiver, cradling it on her shoulder as she typed. "Officer Barnes."

"Maggie, dear, this is Eileen."

For a minute she drew a blank. "Hello, Mrs. Jones. What can I do for you?"

"I'd like to take you to lunch, if you're free. We can discuss some details about the wedding."

"I don't think Tucker—"

"Oh, no, just us girls. Why don't you come to the country club, around one?"

*Oh, right. In my uniform? They'd faint.* Glad for the excuse, she said, "I'm sorry, I only have a short lunch hour. Maybe we should try another—"

Again, she was interrupted before she finished her

sentence. "Then I'll come to you. Where do you suggest we meet?"

Why had she even mentioned having a lunch hour? Trapped, Maggie said, "We have a decent Mexican place and the Scarlet Parrot bar and grill. Oh, and there's a pretty good burger place." Which she could not see Eileen Jones going to, but it gave them another choice.

"I've eaten at the Scarlet Parrot with Tucker before. Let's go there."

"All right, I'll see you at one." Something told her she was not going to enjoy this lunch. But maybe that was just her suspicious mind. Maybe Mrs. Jones just wanted to get to know Maggie better. How bad could it be?

NATURALLY, she was late. Only by about ten minutes, but still, not the best way to impress your future mother-in-law.

"Maggie, hi," Delilah said when she walked in. "Are you alone?"

"Ah, no. I'm meeting someone." She looked around, spying Eileen by the windows. "There she is."

Delilah turned in the direction Maggie was looking as Eileen waved. "Isn't that Tucker's mother?"

"Um, yes."

"And you and Tucker were just here the other day."

"Uh, yes," she said again.

Delilah raised a brow and said, "Really. I know there's a story here."

*Oh, for God's sake,* Maggie thought, feeling her face heat. *I'm blushing and I never blush.* "I'll tell you about it later. I'm late." She hurried over to Eileen's table. "Sorry for keeping you waiting. I got tied up at work."

"That's quite all right, dear. Think nothing of it."

Maggie relaxed marginally after they ordered drinks and food. Eileen seemed to be going out of her way to put Maggie at ease, chatting away about nothing in particular. So why did she get the feeling that a Mack truck was about to hit her dead between the eyes?

The feeling persisted as their food was served. Maggie took a bite of shrimp, washed it down with a sip of tea, then said, "Was there something in particular you wanted to talk about? I mean, about the wedding details?"

Eileen had taken a bite of her shrimp salad and looked pleasantly surprised. "This is quite good."

"Best on the coast," Maggie said with pride, as if she owned the restaurant herself. "The owner and his wife are good friends of mine."

"Hmm. Yes, now about the wedding." She leaned forward and smiled, but it wasn't sweet. In fact, Maggie imagined fangs sprouting. "Why don't you tell me just exactly what you think you're doing, luring my son into marrying you when he's all but engaged to another woman?"

Maggie simply stared at her. She wasn't easily blindsided, but the accusation had come out of nowhere. "Tucker said nothing to me about being engaged to anyone else."

"He wouldn't. Not if you were pregnant and he felt obligated to marry you."

"He told you I wasn't. Are you calling your son a liar?"

"No, I know my son. And I also know lying, scheming, manipulative women." She sat back and sipped her tea delicately.

Maggie's temper blazed but she held it back. "Meaning me."

Eileen inclined her head regally. "If the shoe fits, and all that."

Carefully, Maggie laid down her fork, determined not to give the woman the satisfaction of losing her temper. "If Tucker was engaged he'd have told me."

"He wasn't engaged. Technically. But Isabella and I have been expecting him to ask her any moment."

Isabella. He had said he'd been going out with someone, but he hadn't implied it was serious. The opposite, if anything. "Maybe you should talk to Tucker. It doesn't sound like he's on the same wavelength as the two of you." And if he had been, she was going to clean his clock for saying he'd marry her.

Eileen's expression changed to one of bewilderment. "I don't understand it. Why on earth would Tucker want to *marry* you?"

Maggie put her hands together in her lap and squeezed. *You must not slap her, no matter how much she deserves it.* "As opposed to sleep with me and dump me?" she asked sweetly.

"That's not what I said, or meant. I simply wondered why he wants to marry you."

"Ask Tucker." She stared at Eileen as her lips tightened. "Oh, I get it. You're afraid to go after Tucker. So you thought you'd take me down and solve the problem."

"Take you down?" She looked horrified. "What a vulgar expression."

"Yeah, that's me. Just call me Officer Vulgar." Maggie got up, threw her napkin down, fished money out of her pocket and tossed it on the table. "That should cover my lunch. Just so you don't think I'm also a mooch. I suggest you talk to your son if you want the down low and dirty. You're not getting it from me." She marched out of the restaurant, head held high, holding on to her anger so she wouldn't have to admit to the hurt.

By the time she got home that afternoon, her anger, which she'd been forced to put aside while she worked, returned tenfold. What was Tucker thinking to tell her he'd marry her if he was involved with someone else? And even if that wasn't true, and she suspected it wasn't, what was he doing having a mother who was such a pain in the ass? Maggie had known Eileen didn't like her, but she hadn't honestly thought she detested her.

She pulled on her shorts, tank and boxing gloves and went to burn off some of her mad.

AS THEY'D ARRANGED, Tucker went to Maggie's after he left the office so they could work on the guest list. It still felt a little weird to think he was getting married in just a couple of days, but knowing he was helping Maggie made him feel good. Besides, it wouldn't last forever and then they could get back to their lives.

Maggie was undoubtedly right that they shouldn't have sex. I mean, how hard could it be? He'd just think of her as his buddy, as he'd done since high school.

Almost one of the guys. Simple. All he had to do was forget about the way she kissed him. And his reaction when he saw her at the restaurant. And… He shook his head. From now on any thoughts of Maggie in a sexual manner were strictly forbidden.

He heard the beat of the music through the front door. Finding it unlocked, he opened it and walked in. Really old, classic rock. He wouldn't have figured her for a classic-rock kind of girl, but the Stones' "Sympathy for the Devil" blared out amazingly loud. He found her in a bedroom she'd obviously converted into her workout room. Halting on the threshold, his mouth went dry. *Oh, Mama.* She wore a skimpy tank top, short shorts and boxing gloves and was whaling on a punching bag. She didn't look like one of the guys, that was for damn sure. She looked… Oh, man, she looked *hot.*

*Hands off,* he told himself. He watched her for a moment and since she obviously didn't see him, he walked over and turned the music down. She glanced at him with anything but a friendly expression in those amazing green eyes of hers.

He tucked his hands in his pockets. "Hey, Maggie."

"Hey, Tucker." She delivered a particularly nasty roundhouse kick to the bag, dropped her hands and shook out her shoulders. He glanced away, reminding himself that he didn't want to screw up their friendship.

"So, Tucker, why didn't you tell me you were *practically* engaged when you agreed to marry me?"

"Come again?" He stared at her blankly.

"Isabella. Does the name ring any bells?"

"Where did you hear about Isabella? And I wasn't engaged to her."

"All but, according to my source."

"Then your source is full of shit."

Maggie laughed and took a seat on the weight bench. "You shouldn't talk that way about your mother."

"My mother told you I was engaged to Isabella? Why would she do that?" Especially since she knew it wasn't true.

"Give the man a cigar. Yes, your mother and I had a lovely lunch today. Remind me to do it again, sometime. Like, maybe sometime in the next century."

He took a seat beside her and pinched the bridge of his nose. "Damn, I thought she took the news awfully well. I should have known."

"Looks like. Why didn't you tell me?" She struggled with her glove and Tucker took one of her hands in his to help her take it off, then tackled the other one, ignoring how she tried to jerk her hands free of him.

"Because I was not, and have never been, engaged or almost engaged to anyone, including Isabella. Before you, that is." Okay, there was one woman, but that was a long time ago and not relevant to the discussion.

Maggie stood and paced away. "Your mother hates me. We can't get married. It was a stupid, stupid idea anyway."

"It wasn't stupid. My mother doesn't hate you, she just doesn't know you. And she has some wacko ideas about who I should marry, but it's none of her business who I do or don't decide to marry."

She turned back to him, frowning. "I don't want to

cause trouble between you. Especially because of a fake marriage."

"You won't. Don't worry about it. I'll handle my mother."

"Tucker, are you sure you want to do this?"

He smiled. "Oddly enough, I am."

"Well, then at the least we shouldn't have the wedding at her house. Not considering how she feels about the whole thing. Let's just go to the JP."

"I'll talk to her," he repeated. "We're still having it at my parents' place. It will look better that way."

"Oh, yes, let's," she said. "Just what I want to do is say vows in front of a woman who hates my guts."

He walked over to her and put his hand on her shoulder. He turned her so he could scan her face and didn't like what he saw. There was temper in her eyes, but there was hurt, as well. "She hurt your feelings, didn't she? What did she say to you?"

She hunched her shoulder. "Nothing important. Just enough to let me know she isn't in favor of the marriage."

She wouldn't bad-mouth his mother, no matter how well deserved. It didn't surprise him, but it touched him. And it really burned him to know that his mother had chosen to hurt his bride, fake or not.

It took him a while but he managed to soothe Maggie's fears and joke her out of the bad mood she was in. By the time she went off to shower he figured he'd taken care of one part of the problem. His mother would have to wait until morning, but he intended to pay her a call, bright and early.

THE NEXT MORNING Tucker showed up at his parents' house so early he caught his mother in her robe. She looked happy to see him, fussing over him and asking if he'd eaten breakfast.

He sat down at the table. "Coffee's fine. I've got to get to work. I just came by to ask you what the hell you think you're doing, going behind my back to harass Maggie."

Her mouth opened and closed like a guppy's. "I did no such thing. I asked her to lunch to get better acquainted. If she's telling you lies—"

He held up a hand. "Can the innocent act, Mom. Maggie wouldn't tell me exactly what you said, beyond some damn lie about me and Isabella, but whatever you said, it upset her."

"I told her you were all but engaged." She sniffed. "Which is true, Tucker, you know it is."

"Mom, I had a few dates with the woman. Trust me, we weren't talking marriage." She started to speak but he cut her off. "But she's not important. Maggie, and the way you treat her, is what's important here."

Her face crumpled. "Tucker, you can't really mean to marry that woman. Maggie Barnes?" she said, with just enough attitude to really piss him off.

He stood up. "I'm marrying Maggie tomorrow. We can either do it nicely and happily here or we'll do it at the justice of the peace's office. In which case you won't be invited."

"Tucker!"

"You've got a choice, Mom. You can either accept Maggie and treat her with the respect my bride deserves or you can forget about seeing me anytime in the foreseeable future."

"Tucker!" Her eyes were wide with shock. "You'd disown your own mother?"

Since he'd vented, most of his anger had passed and he looked at her in exasperation. "Of course I wouldn't disown you. You're my mother, regardless of what you say or do that I don't like. But I won't put up with you disrespecting Maggie. Not now when she's my fiancée and not later, when she's my wife. Are we clear?"

His mother stood, as well, pulling herself together. "Perfectly. Your father and I insist you have the wedding here. I'll talk to Maggie and apologize for whatever I inadvertently said to upset her."

Inadvertent, his ass. But he let it pass. He had to admire how quickly and gracefully she'd bowed to defeat. "I'd appreciate that. I'll give you the number of guests who'll attend as soon as we know."

Getting married was more complicated than he'd realized. He wondered if *being* married would be just as complex. Or would it be worse?

## CHAPTER EIGHT

THE NEXT DAY, Maggie and Tucker recited their vows in the Joneses' living room. Maggie thought the whole thing had a little bit of a surreal feel to it. Almost as if it were happening to someone else.

"You may now kiss the bride," Reverend Crane said.

Tucker took Maggie in his arms and kissed her. It was brief, but it felt more real than anything else that had happened that day.

He smiled down at her and said, "You clean up good."

She laughed. "Flatterer."

"If you want the truth, you look gorgeous."

She ignored the note of sincerity in his voice. Best not go there. "All brides are beautiful. It's a requirement," Maggie said, getting her stride back. She couldn't help smiling. "But thanks."

"You're as beautiful today as I've ever seen you," he said and took her hand as they turned to face their families and friends.

*He's just being nice,* she told the fluttering in her stomach. *Don't make too much of it.*

"Maggie, you look stunning," Delilah said a short

time later as she hugged her. "Your gown is absolutely perfect for you."

Maggie was glad she'd listened to her mother and bought the long white gown that she'd seen at the first shop they'd entered. She'd fallen instantly in love with it. Strapless and slim-fitting, it was deceptively simple except for a little beadwork on the bodice. Though it wasn't traditional, she thought it suited her. And judging from the appreciative expression in Tucker's eyes whenever he looked at her, he more than agreed.

And she was glad she'd asked her pastor to marry them, after all. After thinking it over, she'd decided that she should. Once they'd decided against doing the deed at the justice of the peace's office, there really hadn't been a choice. First of all, her parents wouldn't have understood why she didn't ask him, and worse, the reverend himself would have been terribly hurt if Maggie, who'd grown up going to his church, didn't ask him to perform the ceremony.

If she'd thought about Vegas in time all this would be over by now. But neither she nor Tucker had. Maybe she was traditional, after all. She stifled a tiny pang, wishing that she could have been in love and getting married for real. *Focus on your goal,* she reminded herself. She shot a glance at Tucker, who was smiling at her. The side benefits weren't too bad, either, she conceded. It was going to be very interesting being married to Tucker.

"Thanks," she said to Delilah as Cameron hugged her and then claimed the right as one of her oldest friends to kiss the bride.

"You look incredible, Mrs. Jones," he said, his gray eyes twinkling. "And very happy."

"I am," she told him, realizing it was true.

"I'm really happy for you," Lana Randolph, Cam's sister-in-law, said as she hugged her. "But I'm still sad you're moving."

"I'm not moving very far. I'll still be living in Aransas City," Maggie said, returning the hug. She reflected that she was lucky to have friends like Lana and Delilah. Neither had said a word to her, although they had to suspect the real reason for the hasty marriage since they'd both seen her with Grace and, furthermore, knew she hadn't been dating Tucker. Lana, who was a doctor at the clinic in town, had even examined the baby for Maggie and pronounced her healthy. And Delilah witnessed the scene at the restaurant, so she definitely knew something was up.

But apparently, neither of her friends had given voice to their suspicions around their husbands. Gabe wouldn't have said anything, but Cam, at least, would have ragged on her about her decision to marry Tucker so suddenly if he knew the truth.

"But you won't be living next door to us. It's not the same," Lana said.

"Move over and let me kiss the bride," Gabe said, and did so as Lana talked to Tucker.

"You're a lucky man, Tucker," Gabe said a moment later.

Tucker grinned as he shook hands with Gabe. "You got that right."

Maggie wondered if he really felt lucky or he was just agreeing for form's sake. He seemed happy, laughing with their friends. He wore a navy suit with a white shirt and a beautiful silk tie, and he looked to-die-for handsome.

Later, they went outside to have a brief moment alone. "Have I mentioned how beautiful you look tonight?" Tucker asked her.

"Once or twice. Do you mean it?" Well, now she sounded pathetic. "Never mind. Forget I asked."

"I wouldn't say it if I didn't mean it. Come on, Maggie. You had to look in the mirror." He put his hand on her shoulder and rubbed it gently. "You know you look gorgeous."

She didn't know what to say to that, so she changed the subject. "Tucker, I don't want you to regret this."

"Marrying you?" He gave her a charming smile. "Maggie, the only thing I regret is that I'm not going to be taking that beautiful dress off my gorgeous bride tonight." He paused and added, "Am I?"

Maggie laughed. "You know the answer to that."

"Yeah," he said. "I was just checking to see if you'd changed your mind."

She smiled. "Nope. Why, are you having second thoughts?"

"It's hard not to when the bride in question looks like you do."

Gazing into his eyes set her stomach to fluttering. Tucker grasped both her shoulders gently and stared at her a long moment. She knew he was going to kiss her.

Instead of backing away, which was the smart thing to do, she stood still and willed him to do it.

"Tucker, really," his mother said from behind them, clearly disapproving.

"Just as well," he murmured so that only Maggie heard, and kissed her briefly. He smiled at Maggie and released her. "What's wrong, Mom? Can't a man kiss his bride?"

Maggie sensed a tension between them. She hated that she was the cause of it, and she knew she was even though Tucker would deny it if she said anything.

Maggie knew nothing less than the fear of losing her son would have made Eileen Jones apologize to her for "upsetting" her as she'd done the day after their abortive lunch. She had to give the woman credit. She'd swallowed her pride and begged Maggie's forgiveness very nicely. If Maggie hadn't been a cop who dealt with good liars on a daily basis, she might have believed she meant it.

Eileen didn't respond to his question. Instead she spoke to Maggie. "Were you planning on throwing the bouquet?"

"I hadn't, but I can do it if you think I should. There aren't many single women here, though." In fact, she could only think of three, not counting Maggie's spinster aunt, who was at least seventy-five. Oh, Lord, that would be a hoot to see. Aunt Martha would probably knock over the other women in her haste to get to the thing.

"That's entirely up to you. But if you're going to throw the bouquet and garter you'll need to do it soon. Tucker said you had to leave in an hour to catch your plane."

"Are you wearing a garter?" Tucker asked with interest.

Maggie sent him a mischievous smile. "Of course. It's my something blue."

"In that case, Mom, lead the way." He took Maggie's hand and they walked toward the living room.

"The house looks really beautiful, Mrs. Jones. I love the way you arranged the flowers," Maggie said, mindful of her resolve to get along with Tucker's mother. "Tucker and I really appreciate you letting us hold the wedding and reception here. It was so sweet of you and Mr. Jones."

Eileen smiled and for the first time Maggie didn't feel her disapproval. "Thank you, dear. We were happy to do it. And call us Harvey and Eileen, please."

It struck Maggie where she'd seen that smile before. Tucker looked like his father with the dark hair and blue eyes, while his mother was a petite blond beauty. But he'd inherited his smile from Eileen.

Just before they walked into the room Tucker released Maggie's hand and put his arm around his mother, hugging her. "Thanks, Mom."

She looked up at her son and placed a hand on his cheek. "I want you to be happy, Tucker."

"I am," he said and smiled at Maggie. "Trust me, I am."

"Then that's all that matters. I'll go gather the women for the bouquet tossing."

"Tucker, wait." Maggie put a hand on his arm to stop him from entering the room. "I don't want to cause trouble between you and your mom."

"I told you before, you won't. We're fine."

"What did you say to her, Tucker?"

"Nothing for you to worry about. I told her that you were about to become my wife and she needs to treat you with respect."

"That was sweet of you."

"Like I said, babe, anything for you. Let's go take that garter off," he said.

TUCKER HAD WANTED to stay at The Mansion in Dallas, but Maggie had vetoed it as too expensive and suggested they stay at one of the D-FW airport hotels. He gave in, even though he didn't intend for her to pay for anything involving the honeymoon. That part had been his idea and he was paying for it.

Tucker wheeled their bags in behind her and took them to the bedroom. One nice big bed. And a sofa bed in the other room, he thought regretfully.

What was wrong with him? He'd agreed to marry Maggie and live with her as a friend. He had no business thinking of sharing her bed, taking off her wedding dress… He shook his head to clear the image of peeling Maggie out of that long, slim, white dress. It's just the circumstances, he thought. Bride and groom, honeymoon, yada yada. Once they settled in to day-to-day life, he'd be able to see her as he always had. A good friend.

Who happened to be gorgeous and totally hot.

Damn. He left the bags and came out of the bedroom. Maggie had immediately kicked off her shoes and had gone to look out the window. Their room was on the side of the hotel that overlooked a garden, fortunately, instead of a parking lot.

She'd changed out of her wedding dress, much to Tucker's disappointment. She still looked great, though. She wore a short, sexy skirt and a V-necked sweater that clung to her amazing curves. Curves he needed to ignore. He'd changed into khakis and a button-down shirt, since he saw no point in taking a suit he wouldn't wear to Colorado.

He went to the minibar and popped the cork on the bottle of champagne, then poured a couple of glasses and walked over to Maggie.

"Did you arrange this?" she asked, accepting a glass.

"It seemed appropriate. It is our wedding night." He clinked his glass against hers and said, "Bottoms up."

She laughed and sipped. "Very romantic. Is that how you wow all the women?"

He smiled and took a seat. "No, but romance isn't the point of our marriage, is it? I should have said, to Grace." He raised his glass and they toasted the baby.

She sat beside him and sighed. "Are you sorry I got you into this?"

"No, I'm a big boy. I could have said no."

"Why did you agree, Tucker?"

He considered her. "Are you having cold feet again, Maggie?"

"No. Not really. But I'm wondering how you're going to deal with several months of celibacy."

He shrugged. "It's not that big a deal. I haven't had

a relationship in—" He stopped and thought about it. "Seven months. About. Maybe a little longer."

"You don't have to have a relationship to have sex," she said.

"I do. At least, I do now. I like to get to know a woman before we go to bed together." Her expression was so deeply suspicious he nearly laughed. "I told you I wasn't in to meaningless sex."

"What about Isabella? You dated her several times, didn't you?"

"Yeah. But we hadn't made it to that stage."

"Why?"

"Is this how you grill your suspects?"

"I wasn't grilling you. I'm just curious about the woman your mother said you were practically engaged to."

"She's a nice woman. But she wasn't anyone I wanted to be serious about. Which I think she knew. And that's why I didn't sleep with her. My mother—well, you have to take what she says with a grain of salt."

"Yeah, a grain she'd like me to choke on."

He barely managed to swallow his champagne. "I thought you two were getting along better?"

"We are. At least, she's nice to my face. But I know she's wishing I'd fall down an open manhole or something. Preferably before I get pregnant with any little Joneslets."

He laughed so hard he had to hold his side. "I don't think she's that bad," he finally managed to say.

"Huh." She took another sip of champagne. "So, who was the last woman you were seriously involved with and why didn't you marry her?"

"You believe in getting it right out there, don't you?"

"I think it's important that we know more about each other," she said solemnly.

"And besides, you're curious."

She dimpled and toasted him. "That, too."

Tucker's lips twitched. "My last relationship ended about seven months ago. She dumped me for a doctor, but I didn't want to marry her anyway, so it was fine by me. Now, what about you, Maggie? How are you going to deal with being celibate for months?"

She blew out a breath. "Trust me, it won't be a problem. My last relationship was six years ago. Right before I moved back to Aransas City. It didn't work out," she said briefly.

Apparently that's all she meant to say on the subject. He tucked that information away to talk about later, but zeroed in on one aspect he found hard to believe. "You haven't had sex in six years?"

She sipped her champagne, then set the glass down. "Six and a half."

"Good God," he said blankly. "That's a long time." Especially for someone as passionate as he suspected Maggie was.

She shrugged. "I'm not very good at picking the right man. So after the last one, I decided I wasn't going to sleep with anyone again until I was damn sure it wouldn't be a mistake."

"He must have hurt you a lot. I'm sorry."

"Do you mind if we don't talk about it? It's not my favorite topic of conversation."

He got up to pour them more champagne. "Okay by me. What do you want to do, then?"

"We've got champagne and a long night ahead of us. I know just the thing."

Somehow he doubted that what popped into his head was the same thing Maggie had in mind.

## CHAPTER NINE

"GET YOUR MIND out of the gutter, Jones."

He laughed, finished pouring and brought her glass to her. "I didn't say a word." He sat again.

"Trust me, your expression said it all." Not that she held it against him. Given her job, she spent the majority of her time around men. She understood very well the way their minds worked.

"What do you have in mind?"

"Movies. Old movies and champagne. How does that sound?"

He grimaced. "Okay. Only we swear we'll never tell anyone that we watched movies on our wedding night."

"It's a deal." She flicked on the TV and started channel surfing. "There doesn't seem to be much on."

"Why am I not surprised?" He took off his shoes and socks and stretched out his legs, propping them on the coffee table. "We could watch old episodes of *NYPD Blue*."

"Let's not and say we did." She continued flipping until she got to a repeat of *L.A. Law*. "How's this?"

Tucker gave her a thumbs-down.

"There's not even a decent movie," she said. "Here, you do it and I'll get us more champagne." She went to the bar and poured them both some more. "At this rate we're going to run out before we even find a movie to watch." She put the bottle back in the cooler, sat down and took a sip. "What's that? It's got Susan Hayward in it. My dad used to say I had hair the color of hers."

Tucker looked at her. "Yours is prettier."

She narrowed her eyes at him. "What are you after, Tucker?"

"Nothing." He raised a hand and said solemnly, "I speak the truth."

She punched him in the arm. "Ha. Do you know what movie this is?"

"Yeah. I saw it once when I was home with the flu. *Back Street* is the name of it. It's about a woman and her doomed love affair with a married man."

Her stomach pitched. Even after all this time, it still bothered her. "Can you change it?"

"Sure." He switched to another channel that was showing an Arnold Schwarzenegger movie. "How's this?"

"Fine." They watched Arnold blow up a compound in search of his daughter. Maggie wondered what it said about her that she'd rather watch an action movie than a romance.

"Maggie? Don't you like romances?"

"Not doomed ones. Besides, I don't think love affairs with married men are very romantic."

He took a sip of his drink and studied her. "Sounds

like there's a story there," he said, echoing what she'd said to him a few days before.

She didn't answer immediately. He didn't say anything. He wouldn't push her to share, she knew. But maybe it was time she talked about it. She never had, not once in all these years. She'd nearly told Lana one time, but the moment had passed and she hadn't. Maybe she shouldn't tell Tucker, either. It didn't exactly cast her in a good light.

"I was twenty-one," she said. "When I lost my virginity."

The segue didn't appear to bother him. "You waited longer than a lot of people do."

"Yeah, I did. I wanted it to be special."

"Something tells me it wasn't a great experience for you."

"Oh, the sex was good. He was very…skilled." And she'd been like a ripe plum just waiting to be picked. "I was fresh out of the academy and so naive I probably had a sign tattooed on my forehead that said, 'This girl's from Podunk and dumb as a post.'"

He frowned at her. "Aren't you being a little hard on yourself?"

Maggie shrugged. "No. You haven't heard the whole story yet. He was about ten years older than me. Smooth and very charming. Good-looking. And married."

"Ah. That explains your aversion to the movie. Did you know?"

He didn't appear judgmental, which made her feel a little better. "Not at first. Later I did. But—"

"Let me guess," Tucker interrupted. "He told you he was getting divorced."

Maggie nodded. "I told you I was naive. He said he was legally separated and he wasn't living with her and the divorce should be final, oh, anytime now." It still amazed her she could have been so gullible.

"It was a lie. Damn, Maggie, that's terrible."

"Yeah." She sipped her drink reflectively before continuing. "Two months after I first slept with him, his wife found out about us and called me. Seems she was six weeks pregnant and wanted her husband to stop fooling around with the slutty cop."

Tucker said something violent and obscene regarding what he'd like to do to the man. It perfectly described how she felt about the matter. To her surprise, she laughed.

"Well, I didn't do that, although I'd have loved to. But when he tried to convince me he'd only slept with her once and it really didn't have to ruin the beautiful thing we had together I wanted to throw up."

"What did you do to him, Maggie?"

Remembering, she smiled. "I threw him out of my apartment and locked the door. Then I flushed his keys down the toilet."

Tucker looked disappointed. "That's not nearly bad enough for what he did to you."

"It gets better. He had to walk home. It was ten miles. In Dallas, at night."

"Why didn't he just call a cab?"

She bit her lip, finding humor in the situation for the first time. "No money. I picked his pocket. And this was in the days before everyone had a cell phone. He broke into his car, I guess he was going to try to hot-wire it. But I called my station house and anonymously reported a car theft in progress when I heard the car alarm go off. Even though he got off eventually, he was hauled in and charged with attempted grand theft auto. No ID, no money. Very suspicious guy breaking into a BMW." She laughed. "That was much better than him just having to walk home."

Tucker smiled but then sobered. He reached for her hand and held it, squeezing gently. "I hate that he hurt you like he did. Damn it, he should be strung up. Your first relationship should have been good for you."

She shrugged, still angry at herself over the whole thing. "I hate that I was so stupid."

"You weren't stupid. You were naive and young and he took advantage of you."

She looked at him and shook her head, pulling her hand out of his. "Tucker, I had an affair with a married man. It was wrong and I knew it. Believing he was getting divorced makes it only marginally better."

"You're too hard on yourself," he insisted.

"Have you ever been with a married woman?"

He looked chagrined. "Yes."

Maggie said shrewdly, "You didn't know she was married, did you?"

"No, but that's beside the point. Even if I'd known I'd still have done it."

Maggie wasn't so sure of that. "You're just saying that to make me feel better."

"You're not the only one who's ever been gullible."
He reached for his drink.

"Tucker, the last word I'd use to describe you is *gullible*.
Just because you didn't know she was married—"

"No, not her."

He was silent for a long moment, so she said, "You
don't have to tell me."

He shrugged. "I'd been working in San Antonio for
a few years. She was a lawyer with the same firm.
Blond, beautiful. Ambitious. We started dating. I fell
hard for her. So hard I even started thinking marriage."
He laughed, not happily. "Fortunately, before I did
anything completely stupid, such as ask her to marry
me, I overheard a phone conversation she had with a
friend of hers. Seems I wasn't the only man she was
dating. She was juggling two of us. He was a wealthy
banker. She was trying to decide who had the most
money and was talking about hiring a private detective. She wanted to know who to dump and who to con
into marriage."

Maggie stared at him. "You're kidding."

"Nope. She said I was better-looking but she suspected he had more money and she had to be practical."

"God, that's cold."

"Yeah, tell me about it. I was a little cynical for a
while, but I got over it. The experience didn't do my ego
much good, though."

He acted as if it hadn't affected him, but she thought
it had more than he'd admitted. "You don't hate
women." Who could have blamed him if he had?

"No, I like women. I'm just very careful about who I get involved with now."

"I imagine you would be," Maggie said. "But, Tucker, she was the stupid one, not you."

"I was supposed to be out of the office that day. If she'd known I was anywhere near I'm sure she wouldn't have been talking so freely."

Maggie shook her head. "Not because of that. She was stupid not to realize there's a hell of a lot more to you than good looks and the bucks."

He stared at her a long moment, then smiled slowly. "Maggie, that's the nicest thing you've ever said to me."

She started to deny it but he was probably right. "Tucker, can I ask you something?"

"Sure."

"I asked you before but you didn't really answer. Why did you agree to marry me?"

"A number of reasons. But the main one is I care about you. I want you to be happy. Grace makes you happy. I wanted you to have a chance to keep her."

She wasn't sure that was the entire reason, but she didn't think he'd admit to anything else, so she let it pass. "We might find her mother. There's still a chance. And there's still a chance CPS won't let us have her, after all." Thinking about that depressed her. She could apply to foster another child, even without Tucker, but she didn't want another baby. She wanted Grace. "I guess the marriage would be even more temporary than we thought if that happens." That scenario also depressed her for reasons she didn't care to examine closely.

He moved nearer to her, then put his arm around her and hugged her companionably. "Don't borrow trouble. And another thing, I think we should stop referring to this marriage as temporary. It serves no purpose, and if we want people to believe our marriage is authentic, then we need to treat it like it is."

She leaned her head against his shoulder. "Is this a way of convincing me I should rethink my ban on sex?"

Tucker chuckled. "No." He was quiet a moment, his hand rubbing gently up and down her arm. "Why, are you rethinking it?"

She turned to look up at him. He wasn't smiling now, and he looked at her with a hunger she hadn't expected. She moved away quickly, before she did something stupid. Like kiss him. And she knew exactly where that would lead them. "Are you?"

His gaze zeroed in on her mouth. "If I said no, you'd know I was lying. I was the one who suggested we make it real in the first place. So, yeah, I've thought about it. But…I think you're right. It could screw up our friendship. And that's important to me. More important than a roll in the sheets."

"You looked at me like you wanted to…" Not wanting to say the words, she let her voice trail away. Damn it, she should never have started this conversation. What did it matter why he'd married her? He'd agreed, they were married, and that was that.

"Just because I might think about it now and then doesn't mean I'm going to do anything."

"Because going to bed together would be a mistake."

"Right."

"Right," she said, annoyed though she knew she had no right to be. "So, that's that. Why are we talking about it?"

"Because you asked me if—"

"Stop." She held up her hand, laughing. "I should know better than to ask a lawyer a rhetorical question. I've got an idea. You go pour us more champagne. I'm going to put my jammies on. And no, I'm not wearing what my mother packed for me to wear."

"Filmy nightgown?" he asked with a leer.

"Of course. But you'll just have to make do with the real me." Boxers and a T-shirt were infinitely safer. And she needed safe. Because Tucker Jones was very, very dangerous. To her peace of mind, at the very least.

*And what about your heart?*

She couldn't afford to fall in love with Tucker. She'd fallen for the wrong man before. Had her heart broken before. She'd been with three men and every single one had been the wrong man for her. She damn near hadn't recovered from the last one. Six and a half years ago, the breakup that had sent her running home, heartsick and convinced she'd never fall in love again. Dead certain she didn't *want* to ever fall in love again.

She was not going to fall in love with Tucker. That could only lead to disaster. A disaster she couldn't afford.

## *CHAPTER TEN*

IT DIDN'T SURPRISE Tucker that Maggie took to skiing like a natural. Although he knew how to ski, he wasn't too sure about his teaching capabilities, so he thought she'd be better off with a ski instructor, at least initially. Their first full day in Steamboat, Maggie took a lesson in the morning and then Tucker skied with her that afternoon. He liked sharing one of his favorite sports with her. He didn't even mind when she crashed into him and they both fell.

He liked watching her concentrate, liked seeing her deliberate movements as she focused on what she was doing. She was a natural athlete, not to mention extremely competitive. He couldn't help laughing at her frustration over not becoming a world-class skier instantly.

"Maggie, there's a learning curve in skiing, just like in everything else."

"I don't like the bunny slope," she grumbled. "Why can't I ski things like that?" She pointed to a run that was at least a single black diamond if not a double diamond. Expert. Steep, bumpy. He shuddered, thinking of a novice skier on one of those babies.

"Down, killer. Maybe next trip. Besides, you went down a run from the top. Most people don't do that their first day out."

"It was an easy one, you said so yourself."

He laughed at her pouting and didn't manage to get her to quit until the lifts closed. "Can you spell overachiever?" he asked her as they entered their condo.

"I'm not an overachiever," she said automatically, peeling out of her jacket and hanging it on the rack by the door. She linked her hands behind her back, stretched and groaned. "I have a feeling I'm going to be sore."

The way she did that thrust her breasts into prominent relief, something he didn't think she realized. But man, oh, man, he noticed. He shook his head. *Get a grip.*

"That's what hot tubs are for," he managed to say.

They had reservations that evening at one of Tucker's favorite restaurants, Café Diva. They soaked in the hot tub—another experience that brought him both pain and pleasure. Maggie in a bathing suit was something to see. It didn't matter how much he lectured himself about looking at her as a friend, he still had eyes, didn't he?

After they cleaned up, Tucker watched Maggie flip through a sheaf of papers and mutter. His stomach growled and he wondered if Maggie would ever put away the paperwork about foster care that she'd been absorbed in for the last half hour. She'd pulled it out the day before and had been reading questions to him that they would have to answer in an interview. It seemed invasive as hell to him, but Maggie had warned him that it would be.

"We're going to be late to dinner," he said as his

stomach growled again. She had to be hungry, didn't she? They'd both had water and munched on trail mix for lunch and hadn't eaten anything else.

Maggie glanced up at him and frowned. "Why do they want to know about our past relationships? I can see why they want to know about the current one, but my past is none of their business."

Maggie had been freaking out about the list of questions ever since she'd first looked at it. She said she'd only glanced at it before and this was the first time that she'd gone through all the actual questions the caseworker would be likely to ask.

"You don't have to tell them the whole truth, you know. Be vague."

"The whole truth? We're already going to have to lie like convicts about when and how and why we decided to marry, and about why we want to be foster parents and when we knew we wanted to do that. Now—" she waved a sheet of paper "—this is just more stuff to have to lie about."

"Why are you so worried? We'll work it out."

She ignored him. "I'm not telling them anything about him," she said. "I'm just going to act as if that whole…revolting episode never happened."

Tucker assumed she was referring to being with the married slime. "It happened a long time ago," he agreed. "That shouldn't have a bearing on your parenting abilities."

"Right. I was young, stupid and it has nothing to do with me now." She looked down and scribbled something on a piece of paper. "And I'm not talking about Spencer, either."

"Maggie?"

"Hmm." She wasn't looking at him, but frowned at the papers in front of her.

"Who's Spencer?"

She looked up and met his gaze. Her eyes narrowed suspiciously. "How do you know about him?"

"Because you just mentioned his name. Who is he? Not the man—"

"No. Not him."

He waited but she didn't seem to want to add to that. "Is this another story I need to know about?" he said when she didn't speak.

"No. I don't want to talk about it."

Ho-kay. Touchy subject, obviously. "Then why did you bring it up?"

"Because I wasn't thinking." She got to her feet. "Let's go eat. I'm starving."

He followed her lead, but he had to wonder about the other man she wasn't talking about. Should he push her to talk, or should he just let her be? Because there was definitely a story here.

Before long they were being shown into the Café Diva. A small, elegant restaurant with a gorgeous mahogany bar and a wood-burning fireplace, it had a cozy, romantic ambience. The snow falling outside completed the perfect picture. The walls were graced with paintings from local artists and it was also known for its wonderful food and an excellent wine list.

Tucker greeted the owner and their waitress by name, as he'd known both of them for several years. He introduced Maggie as his wife and they were suitably surprised and pleased to have the honeymooning couple eat with them.

"Do you know everyone in this restaurant?" Maggie asked him after the waitress left to get their drinks.

"Not everyone. But I've been coming to Steamboat for years now and always make sure to eat here at least once. It's one of my favorite places." He watched her reach behind her back and frown.

"What's wrong?"

"Nothing. I wish I hadn't left my Glock at home. I feel naked without it."

Tucker laughed. "Believe me, I'd have noticed if you were. I thought you said since you were going out of state it would be easier not to carry it." He realized she'd taken her customary position at the table, with her back to a wall and where she could see the door. He wondered if all cops did that and, if so, what did they do when a bunch of them got together?

Maggie shrugged. "It's still weird."

Tucker patted her hand. "Steamboat's pretty tame. I doubt you'll need it. There's a little crime around the mountain during high season, with all the transients and tourists, but not much. It's a lot like Aransas City in a way. In town the residents don't even lock their doors."

"It does seem like a nice town. When did you start coming here?"

"My parents used to come years ago when I was a kid and they'd bring me."

The waitress served their wine and brought them some crusty French bread and olive oil with balsamic vinegar. Maggie ate a bite and said, "Oh, this is delicious."

They talked a bit until the waitress came back and discussed the menu with them. After they ordered, Maggie said, "Why did you decide to move back to the Aransas Bay area? I heard you were doing well in San Antonio. Didn't you like it?"

"I liked it. I just decided I didn't want to spend the rest of my life there. I missed the coast, for one thing."

"I know what you mean. I missed it, too, when I lived in Dallas. I didn't expect to, but I did."

Before long their entrées arrived and they both began to eat. "Why did you move to Dallas?" Tucker asked Maggie. "Was it just to go to the police academy?"

She nodded. "That was part of it. Plus, I wanted to get out of Aransas City. I wanted out of the hick town and into the big city. I was all set to accomplish great things. That didn't exactly happen." She laughed and Tucker detected a note of bitterness.

"Did you like being on the Dallas police force?"

"Mostly. Some of it was hard. Some of the crime scenes we went to were…pretty brutal," she admitted. "But most of the time I liked my job."

"So you didn't leave Dallas to get away from police work."

She put down her fork and looked at him. "I came

back to Aransas City because I wanted to. Why don't we just leave it at that?"

Clearly, something had happened while she was in Dallas that she wasn't ready to talk about. He suspected it had something to do with the man she'd mentioned, Spencer. He wanted to ask her about him, but he figured she'd tell him when she was good and ready. He'd already discovered that Maggie could be very stubborn and closemouthed, so he let the subject drop.

"Whatever you say. Did you want to get some dessert? They have a dynamite crème brûlée."

Maggie sent him a grateful glance. "How about we split it? I don't want to eat a whole one. I'm already stuffed from eating the entrée."

They ordered the dessert and talked about skiing and their plans for the next day. While they were eating dessert, Maggie said, "Weren't you a partner in a big firm in San Antonio? Wasn't that hard to walk away from?"

Unlike Maggie, that wasn't one of the things that bothered him to talk about. He'd already told her the only thing about his past that still stuck in his craw. Admitting that he'd let Leila Anderson play him had been difficult. In fact, he was a little surprised he'd told Maggie about her.

Maggie took another bite of dessert. "You don't have to answer if you don't want."

He shook his head. "No, I don't mind. I got tired of the pressure, and the pace. You know the difference between a small town like Aransas City and a big city. I discovered I was tired of that more frenetic lifestyle, so I came back to the coast. I didn't want to live too close to my parents, which is why I chose Aransas City. There wasn't one instance that triggered the decision to move, but more of a gradual buildup of dissatisfaction."

"Do you think you'll stay in Aransas City?"

He smiled at her. "For the foreseeable future, anyway."

Her eyes darkened to a deep, mossy green. "I really appreciate what you're doing for me, Tucker."

"Believe me, Maggie, it hasn't been a hardship." Except one thing was becoming a hardship. Keeping his hands to himself. *It's just the honeymoon,* he told himself. *The romance of it. Once you get back home things will return to normal. Won't they?*

"That's what you say now, but that could change."

"I don't see why it should."

"You could meet another woman and…well, you'd be stuck because you're married to me. At least until we find out about Grace." She wasn't looking at him but had applied herself to the last of the dessert.

What was this about? "I'm not interested in another woman. Have I given you any reason to believe I am?"

She shot him a glance he couldn't read. "No, so don't get your shorts in a twist. But we both know the reasons behind our marriage. All I'm saying is you could have a change of heart and regret tying yourself down. Then what would we do?"

He stared at her a moment, trying to figure out where she was coming from. It dawned on him that this might have something to do with the mysterious Spencer. "Is that what he did? Have a change of heart?"

Her eyes had changed color, they were flat and very nearly gray, with no green to be seen. "No. His heart never changed. That was the problem."

The waitress came just then to ask if they needed anything else and to give him the bill. But Tucker wasn't sure Maggie would have said any more even if they hadn't been interrupted. It appeared that this story was one he would have to drag out of Maggie in bits and pieces. If indeed he managed to get the whole story out of her at all.

# *CHAPTER ELEVEN*

ONCE THEY RETURNED from their honeymoon and moved Maggie's belongings into Tucker's house, Maggie and Tucker became serious about becoming licensed in foster care. The preliminary training course wasn't a problem and they both soon completed it. As far as she could tell, the individual interviews that had been conducted at the CPS office had gone well. But the in-home joint interview loomed ahead of them and though Maggie wouldn't admit it to Tucker, she worried about it. And one of the major sources of her worry was that while they weren't sharing a bedroom, they had to make it look as if they were.

Of course, it had been her idea not to have sex, which she still believed was the right thing to do. And he'd agreed with her after he'd thought it over. But who knew it would be so difficult to live with a man platonically? she thought one morning.

He came into the kitchen just then, smiling that sleepy smile as he poured a cup of the coffee he couldn't function without. How was she supposed to ignore that every day? Bare-chested, wearing a pair of faded Levi's, his beard a sexy stubble on his cheeks, he made her…want.

Maybe she should just do it, she thought. She could talk Tucker into it, she was sure. They could do it, get it over with and then go on about their business.

She shook her head, marveling at how easy it was to rationalize. No, those were hormones talking. She ought to just go take a cold shower.

He sat and shook out the paper to read it, still not having spoken. She knew by now he didn't usually talk much in the morning, but how could he be so calm when today was their joint interview?

"Are you going in to work?" she asked him.

He glanced up. "Yes, why?"

"Today's the in-home joint interview," she reminded him.

He smiled. "I know. You've told me half a dozen times since yesterday. It's not until one. Plenty of time for me to get something done this morning."

"We have to do something to your bedroom. To make it look more like we share it. And the master bath, too. No woman in her right mind would give up that dream of a bathroom."

He looked really amused now, which irritated her. "I told you to take my bedroom."

"No, that wouldn't be right," she said decisively, if a bit wistfully. "I'll have to move some of my stuff in there. I should probably leave it, too, since they might visit unexpectedly. Probably will, if I had to guess."

"There's another option," Tucker said, waiting until she glanced at him to speak. "You could move into the bedroom with me."

"Oh, sure. I'm going to share a bedroom with you and not have sex with you. That's going to happen. It's hard enough to—" She broke off, annoyed at what she'd almost let slip. Tucker didn't seem to have any problems resisting her. His seeming lack of interest burned her, considering she was the one who had originally wanted to keep the marriage platonic.

He grinned. "Just a thought, babe."

A thought she was not going to explore. "Let me know when you're finished dressing and I'll start moving stuff in there. In the meantime, I'll clean up my bedroom. Don't you think it will be okay if I just shove everything into drawers and closets?"

"Beats me. I've never been interviewed for something like this. You've said they're pretty invasive."

"Invasive is one thing. Looking into a person's closets and drawers is just…sick," she decided.

Tucker laughed, reaching across the table to squeeze her hand. "Relax, Maggie. Everything's going to work out, I promise."

"I hope so."

"It will." He gave her hand a last squeeze and got up. "I'm going to shower. Maybe you ought to do yoga. Or go whale on the punching bag."

Not a bad idea, she thought. "Tucker?" He stopped at the door and glanced back at her. "Thanks."

He simply smiled and left the room. She watched him go, thinking that he looked nearly as good going as he did coming. Maggie turned her thoughts away from the tempting possibilities Tucker had brought to mind and back to the task of convincing the caseworker that she and Tucker were the perfect couple to foster a child.

THE INTERVIEW went better than Maggie had expected, and as far as she could tell, the caseworker had no problems with them. Tucker charmed her, spinning what, to Maggie, sounded like a believable story about why they wanted to be foster parents.

The woman had indeed peeked into all the rooms, but Maggie had worked hard on the master bedroom to make sure it looked lived-in by both of them. She'd even spritzed a little perfume in the master bath. She smiled, remembering Tucker's expression when he'd gone in there. He clearly hadn't expected that. Then Maggie had to show the woman where she planned to keep her weapon and assure her that it would either be locked up or on Maggie's person whenever she was at home, but she'd expected that.

The only thing Maggie hadn't anticipated, and she should have, she realized, was that the caseworker wanted to know how much interaction their extended family would have with them and the foster child, as well as their degree of acceptance. And she wanted to meet with both sets of their parents, though she said that wasn't urgent.

Maggie decided to talk to her parents that afternoon, but Tucker had wanted her with him when he told his parents about their plans. They had made arrangements to meet his folks for dinner, at a restaurant in Rockport.

She didn't expect to have a problem with her parents.

They might wonder why she and Tucker wanted to be foster parents, but they certainly wouldn't throw a wrench into the works. Her mother in particular spent a lot more time worrying about her younger sister than she did Maggie.

Late that afternoon, she went into her parents' house through the back door, which was unlocked, as usual. "Mom, Dad, where are you?"

Her mother came into the kitchen, her eyes sparkling. "I'm glad you stopped by. We have some exciting news to tell you."

"Where's Dad?" She wondered what kind of news would make her normally placid mother so excited.

"He's on the phone. No, here he is now," she said as Frank walked in the room. "Tell her, Grandpa."

"Hey, Maggie," he said, though he seemed preoccupied. He turned to his wife. "Colleen, we have a meeting with the Realtor at four-thirty, so we can't talk long."

"Realtor?" Maggie echoed. "Why are you meeting a Realtor? Are you buying a new house?" She couldn't imagine it. Her parents had lived in the same small brick house for longer than Maggie had been alive.

"We're putting the house on the market. Your father's finally agreed to move."

Maggie's heart sank. She'd known her parents had been considering moving to Florida to be with her sister and her family, but she'd hoped they'd decide against it.

"Why did you decide to move so suddenly? I thought you didn't want to leave here, Dad?"

Frank grunted and took a seat at the kitchen table.

"Well, Lorna's pregnant again and she wants your mother there to help her."

Pregnant? Again? "Summer's only six months old. You mean to tell me Lorna's having another baby already?" This one would make number four. Just how many children did Lorna intend to have?

"That's right. Isn't it wonderful?" her mother asked.

No, Maggie wanted to say, but she bit her tongue. "But you don't even know how long they're going to be in Florida. What if John gets transferred again?"

"Then we'll move to wherever they go." Colleen put her hand on Maggie's arm. "What's wrong, honey? Are you worried we won't see you? We can still get together at holidays and such. I know it's a big change, but Lorna needs us. With all those children..." Her voice trailed off, and she searched Maggie's face with a look of concern.

Maggie simply looked at her. She knew her parents loved her. But all her life it seemed she'd come in second to her baby sister. She didn't think her parents did it on purpose, or even realized they were playing favorites. But the fact remained, Maggie had felt like an afterthought in their lives for a long time. She moved away to stare out the window.

"Maggie, you understand, don't you? Lorna needs us."

She turned back to her mother. "Sure, Mom. I understand." She understood perfectly. Her parents might love her, but they loved her sister more. Why should it hurt? She was used to it, wasn't she?

"I was so excited I forgot you'd said you had something to tell us. What did you want to talk to us about, Maggie?"

"It doesn't matter," Maggie said. "I'll talk to you later. I've got to get back to work."

She didn't, but she couldn't stay in the house with them and pretend everything was hunky-dory when she was embarrassingly close to tears. What difference did it make what her parents thought about her becoming a foster parent when they wouldn't even be around? She'd simply tell the caseworker that her parents didn't give a tinker's damn about her, and were moving to freaking Florida, besides. So there was no need to worry about their reaction to any foster children Maggie might or might not have.

*I'm thirty-four years old,* she thought. *I've been grown and on my own for a long time now. The fact that my parents are moving shouldn't be a big deal.*

But it was.

TUCKER HAD LEFT WORK early so he could talk to Maggie about the best way to approach his parents when they told them about becoming foster parents. He wanted to be prepared because he had a feeling they were going to ask some difficult questions. Particularly his father, who Tucker knew was still suspicious of their motives for getting married. When he arrived at home, he only had to follow the music to find Maggie. He tracked her down to the room they'd converted into a home gym, with a weight bench, free weights and—since Maggie had moved in—a punching bag.

Extremely loud headbanger rock and roll blared from the stereo system he'd installed. Evidently Maggie had been doing some serious boxing. She wore a tank top, shorts and her boxing gloves and was barefoot and slick with sweat. His mouth started watering and he reminded himself they had things to talk about and seducing Maggie was not on the list of smart things to do. Damn it.

He watched her for a moment, a frown gathering as he realized how savagely she was going after the bag. He'd seen her at this before, but he'd never felt raw fury coming off her in waves. Even when she'd been mad at him over his supposed engagement, she hadn't been this angry. What in the hell had happened? He hoped it wasn't something to do with Grace. Maggie clearly had no idea he was there, so he walked over and turned down the music.

"Turn it back on," she snapped. She punched the bag with her right hand. *Smack.* Then her left, a quick double jab before returning to beat the bag with her left again.

He didn't do what she'd said, just watched her trying to decimate the bag. She apparently got tired of boxing and started with some Tae Kwon Do moves, a series of kicks interspersed with those repeated jabs.

"What's wrong?"

*Smack.* "Nothing's wrong." Another jab and a kick. "Turn the damn music back on."

"If nothing's wrong why are you beating the crap out of an inanimate object?"

"Because I like to." She kept at it, grunting with the effort.

"Did you talk to your parents?"

"Yes." She bit the word out as she sent a particularly

hard punch into the bag. "But not about the foster parenting. They're moving, so there's no need to worry about them."

"Your parents are moving?" That was the first he'd heard of it. "Where? Why?"

She whirled and delivered a roundhouse kick to the bag. "To Florida." She hit the bag with a combination one-two jab and kick. "To be with my precious sister—" she hit the bag twice "—and their precious grandchildren."

Her breath was coming hard and her words were jerky, but he heard her clearly. He walked over to her and put his hand on her arm. "Do you want to talk about this?"

"No, I want to beat the hell out of this punching bag." She shook him off and glared at him. "Don't mess with me, Tucker. I'm not in a good mood."

He wanted to gather her in his arms and comfort her, but she was obviously not in any mood to be consoled. "Come sit down," he said and took her arm.

She resisted at first but then she let him lead her to the weight bench and sit beside her. He took one of her hands and started to pull off her glove. "You're going to hurt your hands, if you haven't already."

Her eyes were stormy. A hard, brilliant green, but Tucker saw the hurt behind the anger. Again, he wished she'd let him comfort her. It surprised him how badly he wanted to console her. "Was this move a surprise? Or had you known about it? You haven't said anything."

She shrugged and let him take off the other glove and gently massage her hands. "It wasn't a total shock. They'd been talking about it, but I didn't think they were going to go. My mother wanted to do it but my dad had been resisting."

"Why did they decide to go now?"

Her eyes were bleak, not hot with anger. Gray and empty. "Because my sister—my younger sister—is pregnant again. With her fourth child. My mother's all in to the grandma thing."

A wealth of unspoken emotion lay behind those words. He didn't need a psychology degree to understand that. "Have you told your parents how you feel about them leaving Aransas City? About them leaving you?"

"No." Wearily, she lifted a shoulder. "What's the point? They want to be with Lorna. Lorna needs them, they said. Period. End of discussion."

"You might let them know you need them, too." He looked at her hands and imagined kissing them. Then imagined going right on up her arm. To her mouth. And— *Down, boy. What the hell are you thinking?*

"I don't need them." She jerked her hands out of his. "I'm thirty-four years old, Tucker. I don't have to have my mommy and daddy live in the same town to survive."

"It's not a matter of survival." He studied her a moment, not buying the supertough act she was putting on. "Maggie, there's nothing wrong with not wanting your parents to move. I wouldn't want mine to move away. And there's nothing wrong with wanting your parents' emotional support, no matter how old you are."

"Emotional support." She gave a short, bitter laugh and glanced away. Her voice was tight when she said, "That's a joke. It's always been Lorna. I love my sister, but…she's always been the needy one. I'm the self-sufficient one, the one who always knows what she's doing. At least, that's how they see me. And none of them, not my parents and sure as hell not my sister, even notice that occasionally I need someone, too."

"And you need someone now."

She nodded. "Yes. It's just like before. It never changes. When I moved back here from Dallas…my mother was so caught up with Lorna and her second pregnancy, I might as well not have existed."

It hurt him to hear the pain in her voice. "You needed your mother then."

She looked forlorn, something he'd never associated with Maggie before.

"Yes. I wanted someone to talk to. Someone who loved me, who cared about what happened to me. I…wasn't doing very well."

Again, he wondered what had driven her to leave Dallas. For Maggie to admit to anyone that she wasn't doing well was the same as another person telling the world they'd had a complete breakdown. "Did you find anyone else to talk to? A girlfriend, maybe?"

"No." Her gaze hardened before she rolled her shoulder and looked away. "There wasn't anyone. So I did what I always do. I sucked it up and moved on. I got over it. Talking is way overrated."

"Maggie?" He waited until she looked at him. "I know it's a long time after the fact, but you could talk to me."

Her expression softened. "Tucker, you're sweet, but I'm over that now." She blew out a breath. "I'm just overreacting to my parents moving, that's all. I'll be okay. It was just a surprise that they're actually going ahead with it."

She wasn't over it and he didn't think she'd be okay. But she didn't seem to want his help. He couldn't have said why that realization bothered him so much.

"If you ever do want to talk, come to me. Okay?"

"Okay." She put her hand on his cheek and smiled at him. "Thanks, Tucker. You're sweet," she repeated.

Sweet. His thoughts weren't so sweet. She was braless and the thin tank fit her like a second skin. He wanted to cup her breasts, take his thumbs over the peaks, strip her shirt off and see how beautiful they would be bare. Wanted to taste her, caress her, make love to her….

He raised his gaze to hers. Her breath came faster and she stared at him with parted lips, her eyes big and dark with emotion. "Tucker…I—I can't."

"Can't? Or won't?"

"It doesn't matter, does it?" She got up and walked to the door. "Sometimes I really wish I could just do what I want and not worry about the consequences. But I'm not built that way."

She left the room and Tucker blew out a breath. She was right. If they made love it would change everything between them. And he didn't want to change it, to risk… Damn it, he was falling for her.

## CHAPTER TWELVE

TUCKER THOUGHT Maggie was going to lose it waiting for CPS to make up their minds over the next couple of weeks. She was grouchy, touchy and despondent. Everything that was hard to live with. Even so, he was having a devil of a time keeping his hands to himself. He wasn't sure what that said about him, that he could find a woman so attractive in such trying circumstances.

Proximity. Maybe that's all it was. He wasn't falling for her. Not really. He was living with her, for Pete's sake. Seeing her in various states of undress. Looking but never touching. It was enough to drive a man crazy.

One day Tucker got a phone call just as he was about to leave the office.

"It's your wife," his secretary told him, handing him the phone.

He took the cordless phone and walked back to his office. "Hey, Maggie. What's up?"

He hoped it was good news. The wait was wearing on them both. He'd thought his mother and father had taken the news in stride when they first told them. At least, they hadn't said much that evening. But since then, every time he talked to his mother, she asked why Tucker and Maggie weren't starting a family of their own if they wanted children. And though he hadn't told Maggie, Tucker had the feeling that his father, at the least, suspected the truth.

"Tucker, it's—wait a minute."

He heard her say something to someone else and a short while later she came back on the line.

"I can't believe it."

"Where are you? You sound like you're at the bottom of a well."

"I'm in the bathroom at the station. I was afraid I'd cry and the guys would never let me hear the end of it if they saw me leaking tears."

"What's wrong? Have they found Grace's mother?" Tucker was growing more and more worried about Maggie's reaction if and when they found the woman. Since marrying Maggie, he'd done a little research. Enough to know that in child custody cases, especially those involving foster care, judges usually came down in the birth mother's favor, especially if there was no history of abuse.

He'd brought up the possibility of the mother being found or showing up and wanting Grace back a couple of times, but Maggie wouldn't talk much about it. She simply said she'd deal with the matter when it happened. It was how she planned to deal with it that worried Tucker.

"No, we haven't found her yet. Nothing's wrong." She paused, then burst out with, "Nina called. We get to have Grace."

"Maggie, that's great." He needed to bury his reservations and his worries. This was what Maggie had wanted all along. He had to be happy for her.

"I know. I can't believe it's finally happening. Can you meet me at the house? We can pick her up anytime, they said. I think it would be best if you went, too, don't you? They'll be expecting both of us, I imagine."

"I wouldn't miss it. See you soon."

Not long afterward, Tucker walked into the house calling for Maggie. She came out of the nursery holding the car seat, but when she saw him she dropped it and launched herself into his arms, laughing. "Can you believe it? I don't think I've ever been so excited in my life."

He spun her around and started to say something but she gave him a smacking kiss on the mouth, then smiled at him. So he kissed her back. Really kissed her, as he'd been wanting to do for weeks now. He crushed her in his arms, pushed his tongue inside her mouth, and she gave a low moan, her arms tightening around his neck.

He sank into her soft mouth, tasting, lingering, then slipped his hands over her curves and caressed her. Slowly, he became aware she'd wedged one arm between them and was pushing him away. He drew back and stared down at her. Her lips were wet from his kiss and he wanted nothing more than to drown himself in her and not come up until he was finally sated.

Then he looked into her eyes and knew it wasn't going to happen.

"Tucker—"

He shook his head and released her. "Let's go get Grace."

She didn't say anything else, just picked up the car seat and followed him to the garage where her car was parked.

Forty-five minutes later Maggie and Tucker walked back into their house with baby Grace and her belongings. On the way over and back, they both talked of other things and carefully avoided any mention of what had happened just before they left. But Tucker was damn sure not going to forget it and he didn't believe Maggie could, either. Now wasn't the time to talk about the two of them, though. Today was all about Maggie and the baby she'd wanted so badly.

"I've never seen you look this happy," Tucker said to Maggie. She'd carried the baby into the kitchen with her and didn't look like she intended to put her down for the foreseeable future.

"I'm not sure I ever have been," she said, smiling down at the baby in her arms. "No, that's not true. There was one time," she said. "But it didn't last."

"Want to talk about it?" Tucker asked.

She smiled again and shook her head. "No. Today's a happy day. I don't want to think or talk about the past." She paused and added, "But if I ever do want to talk about it, you'll be the person I talk to."

It should make him feel good that she felt she could confide in him. If she meant it. She was the most close-mouthed woman he'd ever known. Beyond the few things she'd told him on their honeymoon, she hadn't said much about her past. As far as he could tell, she didn't confide in anyone. Not her parents, not her girlfriends and certainly not her husband. Was that because their marriage was a sham? Or because she looked on their relationship—their friendship, even—as temporary? Or did she just not trust him enough to confide in him?

"Is the chief okay with you taking time off work so suddenly?" Maggie had said she would take a leave of absence for a while, maybe up to several months before she went back to work.

"Yes, he was great. He's known about it so he's been prepared to deal with me suddenly leaving. He said to take as much time as I need. I told him I'd fill in occasionally when he needs someone extra. Maybe ease into part-time."

"How do you think you'll like staying home?"

"I don't know. I've worked since I was eighteen and left home, so it will be a change. But I'll have to go back sometime. I have to figure out how to work and take care of Grace since once we're divorced I'll be a single mother."

He was really beginning to hate the sound of the D word.

Grace started fussing and Maggie picked up the bottle she'd been warming. "Here you go, sweetheart," she crooned. "Let Maggie take care of you."

Tucker followed them into the other room and watched Maggie feed Grace. She'd bought a rocking chair for just that purpose. "You're going to have to teach me about child care, you know. I mean, the course was fine, but I know there are things I didn't learn. So I can keep Grace if you need to go out. Or if you go in to work."

Evidently surprised, she looked at him. "I didn't know you'd be interested."

"I have to be if you want CPS to believe we're for real."

"True. Okay, you can help me bathe her tonight. And I'll let you give her the next bottle." She watched the baby drink for a bit then said, "I keep thinking about what it will be like, staying home full-time. I've taken care of my sister's kids but just for overnights or a few hours at a time. I've never stayed home with them, not for an extended period." She shot Tucker a wry look. "Besides, I'm not exactly domestic."

"Just because you don't cook doesn't mean you're not domestic."

She laughed. "Tucker, I don't do any of the things my sister does, and she's like the ultimate stay-at-home mom. The only thing I cook is rice. Oh, and canned sweet rolls. As for cleaning, I hate it. I'd rather face an armed robber than a dirty toilet."

Tucker laughed. "So would I. That's what cleaning services are invented for."

"You should let me pay for half that, you know."

"Maggie, we've been through this before." He wasn't about to take her money, but she kept trying.

"Isn't she sweet?" Maggie asked, looking down at the baby with an expression of pure love.

"Yes, she is. And so are you."

Maggie glanced at him and smiled. "Thanks, but sweet is about the last thing people think of when they look at me."

"They don't know you, then."

She smiled again but didn't respond further.

If ever he'd seen a woman with a whole lot of love to give, it was Maggie. She held nothing back from the baby. Apparently loving the baby didn't scare her as much as the thought of loving… Whoa, why was he thinking about love? Sex on the brain was one thing, but love? They had a friendly, practical, *temporary* arrangement that didn't include sex. Love had nothing to do with the two of them.

*But it could.* If he wanted it to. If he was willing to risk it. Even if he was, he thought, he was fairly sure Maggie wasn't.

It was crystal clear that while the marriage was temporary to Maggie, the baby was not. What would it do to her if she lost custody of Grace?

And what would it do to him when their marriage came to an end? Could he really just walk out of Maggie's life and go on as he had before? Did he even want to?

TWO WEEKS LATER Maggie realized that being a stay-at-home mom was harder than she'd ever imagined. She loved the baby and enjoyed being with her, but taking care of Grace full-time was no easy task, she soon discovered.

If it hadn't been for Tucker, she really would have gone crazy. But he came home from work every day and spelled her, taking care of Grace so she could exercise or just relax. Plus, he talked to her, about his day or current events or sports. Whatever she wanted to talk about. She'd never been quite so isolated before. She hadn't realized she'd miss the company of adults so much.

Even better, Tucker cooked. She felt guilty since it seemed the least she could have done was try to fix something for them to eat, but it was a skill she'd never mastered. She'd tried a couple of times, but the baby would start crying or something else would happen and the next thing you knew, she'd set off the damned fire alarm again.

It didn't seem to bother Tucker. In fact, nothing seemed to bother him, not even when Grace spit up on him. Maggie didn't think he had any more experience with children than she did. Probably less since she'd at least cared for her nieces and nephew.

He was a quick study. He was almost too good to be for real. The perfect husband. Temporarily.

Maggie refused to let that thought bother her. Just as she refused to think about what would happen if they found Grace's mother. Why borrow trouble? Trouble would find her easily enough without her looking for it.

And that was why she'd tried her best to ignore what had happened when she kissed Tucker the day they brought Grace home. If they hadn't been going to get Grace… If she hadn't reminded herself that theirs was a temporary arrangement and sex did not fit in with the plan… But the fact remained, resisting Tucker was becoming harder and harder for her to do.

As she'd been doing for the past two weeks, she pushed thoughts of that kiss out of her mind and went to get Grace ready to go out when Tucker came home. He'd called earlier in the day and suggested they eat at the Scarlet Parrot that evening. She changed Grace and put her in the crib so she could take the dirty diapers out. By the time she came back, Grace had fallen asleep. Maggie let her sleep, even though it was late for a nap, since she figured they'd be out later than her bedtime, anyway.

Tucker came home a short time later while she was folding the wash on the couch. "So, how was your day?"

"It was fine." She hated folding wash, which Tucker knew because whenever he saw her folding it he helped her. "What about you? You're early."

"A little." He picked up a shirt, shook it out and folded it. "Where's Grace?"

"She's in her crib. She fell asleep after I got her dressed to go out. Why?"

"Just wondered." He folded another shirt then said, "I want to talk to you."

"Okay. Sounds serious. Is it?"

He didn't answer. He moved the basket to the floor, then made her sit beside him. She couldn't judge what he was thinking from his expression, but the longer he was quiet the more worried she grew. "Just tell me."

He gave a half laugh and rubbed the back of his neck. "I'm not sure how to do this."

"You've met someone, haven't you? Damn it, I knew this would happen."

"No. Yes." He laughed again. "I have met someone. Someone I'm very interested in. There's just one problem. She's married." She started to say something but he put his fingers on her lips before she could. "She's married to me. And I'm having a hard time asking my wife if she'd consider dating me."

She stared at him for a minute as his meaning sunk in. "We agreed—"

"I know what we agreed. How about if, just for tonight, we go out on a date? See where the evening takes us."

"This is a novel way of getting me into bed with you. I have to give you points for originality."

"I didn't ask you to go to bed with me. I asked you for a date." He smiled at her, that heart-stopping smile that always made her wonder why she was so intent on resisting him.

God, he was cute. And he'd been so sweet to her. One date wasn't a big deal, was it? *Yes, you dummy, it is. When it's a date with Tucker.* But she wavered, anyway. "We don't have a sitter."

"My parents said they'd stay with Grace."

"Your mother doesn't approve of us fostering Grace."

"My mother likes babies as much as the next woman," he said. "She's the one who suggested keeping her."

Since Eileen and Maggie had spent most of the time since the wedding avoiding each other, she hadn't known that. For the life of her she couldn't think of any more objections. She should have a million, but she wanted to go. "All right."

"Great. I'll call them."

She watched him leave the room and shook her head. A date. With her husband. What harm could there be in that?

IT HIT HER OVER the popcorn at the movie theater, so hard and so clearly she nearly stopped breathing. She was doing exactly what she'd sworn not to do. She was falling in love. With her temporary husband.

She'd come to depend on him, not only to help her with Grace but just to be there. To talk to, to argue with. To be with. A hundred times a day she'd think, *I need to tell that to Tucker when he gets home.* Something Grace did or something she saw on TV or something that occurred to her.

It had been hard enough when she'd only lusted after his body. When she'd believed he was the player he'd always seemed like on the surface, he hadn't been nearly as hard to withstand. But there was a lot more to Tucker than that, and damn it, she should have realized it before she ever conned him into marrying her.

It had to stop. Right now, before she totally blew it and did something supremely stupid. Like making love with him.

"Maggie, are you all right?"

He spoke in her ear so as not to disturb the other moviegoers, and she felt his warm breath and shivered. "I'm fine," she whispered back. "I have to go check on Grace." *You can run but you can't hide.*

"Now? It's the climax of the movie."

She just shook her head and got up, earning annoyed glares from the people she had to tromp over to get out. Who cared about a stupid movie when she was one step away from complete and total disaster?

After she called about Grace, she waited for Tucker at the back of the theater rather than disturb everyone again by going back down the aisle. She didn't mind, it gave her some time to figure out what she was going to do.

Tucker found her when the movie let out. "Is Grace all right? I figured she must be since you didn't come get me."

"She's fine."

"Okay, then what's wrong with you?" he asked, taking her arm as they walked to the car.

"Nothing. It just occurred to me I needed to tell your mother which toy to give Grace if she couldn't get her settled. And I didn't want to disturb everyone, so I just waited."

He glanced at her as he opened the car door. "You told her that before we left. Along with leaving a list a mile long and phone numbers up the wazoo. Are you sure you're all right?"

"I'm fine, I just want to get home."

"I guess that means ice cream is out."

"Sorry. Do you mind?"

He didn't answer. After giving her a long, thoughtful look, he started the car and drove home. Once home, she checked on Grace, but the baby was sleeping soundly. She came back into the den in time to say goodbye to Tucker's parents.

Tucker shut the door behind them and walked over to her.

"It's still early. Do you want to have a drink or something?"

Oh, yeah, she needed alcohol to lower her inhibitions. "No, I think I'll turn in."

"Okay, but the date isn't officially over."

She stared at him blankly.

He put his hands on her shoulders and pulled her to him. "It's not over until you kiss me good-night."

Before she could object, or even react at all, he kissed her. His mouth was soft and knowing. His taste hot and tempting. His tongue probed her lips lightly and, heaven help her, she opened her mouth and drew him in even though her mind screamed *mistake*. This was exactly what she'd been desperately trying to avoid ever since she'd kissed him the day they brought Grace home. He kissed her slowly, lingering, making her breasts tingle and her legs weak. Making her head spin, making her wish...

*If he can do that to me with a kiss, what would going to bed with him be like?*

Wonderful. And too damn risky.

Maggie jerked back. "We need to talk."

He smiled at her and released her. "What do you want to talk about, Maggie?"

"Divorce."

## CHAPTER THIRTEEN

"YOU WANT A DIVORCE because I kissed you good-night? Don't you think that's a little dramatic?" Especially since she'd been as involved in that kiss as he was. What was going on in that gorgeous head of hers?

She had paced away, but at his question she turned to face him. "Don't be ridiculous. I just think it's time we talked about the divorce. Now that I have Grace."

"*We* are Grace's foster parents," he reminded her. "You said you wanted to adopt her."

"I do, but I don't know when I'll be able to do that. It could be a long time."

"Yeah, I knew that when I signed on. The original plan was to stay married until we found out about adopting Grace."

"Plans can change. I think we should discuss divorce."

This made no sense. What had spooked her to the point that she suddenly wanted a divorce? He stared at her, and then it dawned on him what was happening. "You're scared. I kissed you and it was good and now you're freaking out."

"You're putting way too much importance on a kiss. That has nothing to do with talking about divorce."

"Doesn't it? We're getting closer and it scares you. To the point that to keep me at arm's length, you bring up divorce."

"I'm not scared of you. I'm a cop; I'm not scared of anything."

"Oh, baby, you are so scared you don't know what to do. But not of me. Of yourself. Of your emotions."

She gave him a pitying look. "If it makes you feel better to think so, you go right ahead."

She put a good face on it, he'd give her that. But he hadn't imagined her response. Or the fact that every time they grew closer she reacted by putting as much space between them as she could. So he went to her, stood right smack in her personal space, and lowered his voice. "You weren't so cool a minute ago. When you were melting in my arms like warm honey."

"Please." She rolled her eyes. "I won't deny I enjoyed kissing you. So what? I'm a normal woman with normal feelings. But melting? In your dreams."

She had that right. He'd been dreaming about her for weeks now. She played in his head like a picture in HDTV, vivid and so real you could reach out and touch it. And he was tired of resisting, tired of pretending he only wanted her as a friend. "Prove it. If that kiss was nothing to you then kiss me again."

"No," she said abruptly, and moved back. "We need to work on putting distance between us. All this—this…cozying up has got to stop. Being close will just make things that much harder when we divorce."

"That's a pretty weak excuse, Maggie. I still think you're scared."

"I'm not scared, I'm being practical."

"So practical you won't even give us a chance." What would it take to get through to her? And why did he keep beating his head against this particular wall? He could have other women, just as soon as they divorced.

But he didn't want other women. He wanted Maggie. The woman who had married him and then spent every moment pushing him as far away as she possibly could. Rational or not, it pissed him off.

"Fine. You want distance, that's just what you'll get." He turned on his heel and left, knowing sleep was going to be impossible to come by that night. He was too mad. And too…hurt, damn it.

She didn't trust him. She'd married him, but only because she thought he would be easy to divorce. If she'd thought there was any potential of a real relationship, she would never have married him. She had never had any intention of having a lasting relationship with him. What's more, she'd been up front about that from the beginning. And he, God help him, had agreed. He'd been so sure that all he felt for Maggie was friendship, and maybe in the beginning that had been true.

But it sure as hell wasn't true now.

"ARE YOU STILL MAD at me?" Maggie asked Tucker a little more than a week later.

He glanced at her, then back to the road. They were

headed home from his parents' house, after attending a surprise party for his father's birthday.

"I'm not mad at you."

He'd gotten past the anger, but he wasn't happy, either. The conviction had been growing over the past few weeks that he knew just exactly what it was going to take to make him really happy. And he was fairly certain he wasn't going to get it.

"Right. You're not a bit mad. That's why you've hardly spoken to me in a week."

He shrugged. "Just giving you distance, babe. I thought that's what you wanted."

"I did, too. But…I didn't want you to be so angry with me. Maybe…maybe I was wrong when I said we shouldn't be close. I mean, we are still living together."

Still living together. And it seemed to him she was counting every moment until she could divorce him. Okay, he'd lied. He was still angry, damned angry, and he knew he had no right to be. He'd agreed to this crazy scheme of Maggie's. He'd agreed to marry her and live with her and not have sex with her. No one had held a gun to his head. Worse, he couldn't even say it was all about the sex, or the lack of it. It wasn't Maggie's fault that he was… Shit, he wasn't falling, he'd flat fallen in love with her.

"Tucker, I didn't mean to hurt you," she said, sounding troubled. "That's the last thing I want to do."

She had hurt him, whether she'd intended to or not. But no good would come of admitting that. "You didn't hurt me. Forget it, okay?"

"Can we at least go back to being friends? I miss you."

He glanced at her. Damn, he wished she didn't get to him. He wished he could go back to being just friends…but it was way too late for him. "Sure. And Maggie?" He waited until she looked at him. "For the record, I missed you, too." She gave her quick grin but didn't add anything.

He was quiet a moment, then changed the subject. "What did my mother want when she dragged you off with her?"

Maggie laughed. "I felt sorry for her. I think your mother's trying to teach me some culture. She introduced me to a lot of women on that opera committee of hers and talked about me joining. I didn't know how to tactfully tell her I'd rather bite off my hand than be on a committee like that."

"How did you get out of it?"

"I lied, sort of. I let her think I was going back to work sooner than I am. And I told her between my job and Grace I just didn't have the time. She didn't say anything else, but she can sure look disapproving."

"She'll get over it."

"I hope so. The redhead you were talking to while I was trapped with your mother? That was Isabella, wasn't it? I had to wonder if your mother strategically arranged that. Making sure you know what you're missing, you know."

"I haven't missed anything."

"Really?" She was quiet a moment, then asked, "You don't miss being with other women? Not even a little?"

"Have I complained?"

"No, but that doesn't mean you don't miss it. Most men would."

Tucker pulled into the driveway and put the car in Park. "What's going on? Did my mother say something to upset you?"

"It's nothing. I'll go get the babysitter and pay her. Do you mind driving her home or do you want me to?"

"I'll do it. I'll just wait in the car."

He watched her go inside. Something was definitely up with her. He hoped his mother hadn't been responsible for upsetting her. Since their talk before the wedding, Eileen had treated Maggie much better. At least, Maggie hadn't let on if she hadn't. But Tucker knew his mother still thought the marriage was ill-advised.

After he took the babysitter home he parked in the garage and came in through the kitchen. He found Maggie in the den, dressed in her favorite sleepwear, a tank top and shorts. He sighed, refusing to be distracted, though he found her just as appealing now as he had earlier when she'd been dressed up for the party. Not that it mattered. Besides, right now he wanted to know what had happened between Maggie and his mother.

"What did my mother say to you? And don't lie and tell me it's nothing."

"She didn't say anything, exactly. It's just… She hasn't come right out and said it, but it's pretty clear she thinks I'm the worst sort of wife for you."

"Why is that?" He took a seat on the couch, watching Maggie as she paced.

She stopped and turned to him. "Come on, Tucker. I'm nothing like the women you used to date. I'm not beautiful and poised and…whatever. I'm not into society. I don't like any of the things those women do."

"First of all, you are beautiful. Second of all, not every woman I ever dated was a socialite. Regardless of what my mother thinks, I dated a variety of women."

"Maybe, but I'm about as far from your mother's vision of the ideal woman for you as it's possible to get."

"Why are you so obsessed with what my mother thinks?"

"I don't know. I know it shouldn't get to me, but it does. It makes me feel, I don't know, inadequate."

"Well, you're not. Who cares what she thinks? You'll notice I didn't marry any of those women."

"You didn't marry me, either. Not for real."

He got up and walked over to her. "It feels pretty real to me. We live together. We have a baby to care for." He reached out and touched her hair, let the silky strands slip through his fingers. "We talk. We argue. We eat meals together. We work out together. The only thing we don't do that people in a real marriage do is make love." He moved even closer, leaned in and kissed her cheek, slid his lips along her skin to the corner of her mouth and kissed her there. "We could change that."

"Tucker—" She sighed but she didn't resist when he put his arms around her and pulled her even closer. "You're confusing me and I don't like—" He heard her breath catch as his lips cruised her jawline.

"What don't you like, Maggie?" He slid his hands up her waist to just under her breasts, flicked his thumbs over her nipples. "This?" She didn't say anything, just looked at him, her eyes huge and dark. "Or this?" Giving in to the urge he'd been fighting for so long, he cupped her breasts through the thin, silky fabric of her tank. Massaged her with his palms and wondered what it would feel like to touch her even softer bare skin.

Her lips were parted and her breath was coming harder but still she didn't stop him. "We shouldn't," she said. "But you're making it hard for me to remember why."

"Kiss me, Maggie. Don't analyze, don't think. Just kiss me."

She wrapped her arms around his neck and kissed him. She kissed like a fantasy. And she tasted like a dream. Sweet, with a hot, sexy taste beneath it.

Instead of devouring her as he was tempted to do, he let his tongue search her mouth, explore it, thrust and withdraw until her tongue answered his in a deep, stirring, sensual kiss. Long moments later, he raised his head and smiled at her.

Her mouth curved upward, too. "I'm not sure I care if this is a mistake."

"It's not. Trust me, it's not." She was warm and giving and he marveled that a woman as strong and capable as he knew Maggie to be could also be so soft and inviting.

Keeping his eyes on hers, he pushed up her tank and stroked bare skin. Her skin was like silk. He kissed her again, walking her backward until her knees hit the couch, then followed her down. He stopped kissing her long enough to push up her tank and draw it off over her head.

For a long moment he simply gazed at her, dry-mouthed.

"You're just as beautiful as I've imagined." Her breasts were full and lush, with tight coral tips that just begged to be kissed. He intended to give them a very thorough inspection. He touched his tongue to a peak, licked it, then very slowly, sucked it into his mouth.

Maggie moaned and put her hands in his hair. "Oh, that feels so good…don't stop."

"Wouldn't dream of it," he said, taking her other breast in his mouth. He sucked her nipple, tongued it. She leaned back against his arm, completely bare from the waist up, and Tucker drew in his breath in rapt appreciation. Smooth, creamy white skin, gorgeous breasts, her red hair spilling over her shoulders inviting him to do things he'd been fantasizing about for weeks, for months.

"Incredible," he said, and went to work again. Soon, she squirmed against him, arching her back to push her breasts into his mouth. He suckled first one, then the other, drawing the tight peaks into his mouth and tormenting them both, using his fingers on the one his mouth had just left.

She moaned again when he slipped his hand down to her shorts and slid his fingers between her legs to touch her through the skimpy fabric.

"Tucker…" She said his name on a sigh as he

skimmed his fingers over her again. She was damp with anticipation and it took all of his willpower not to strip those shorts off that instant and plunge inside her.

"Let's get rid of these." He started to tug her shorts down but Maggie put her hand on his wrist.

"Uh-uh," she said huskily. "First you have to lose the shirt."

"You do it," he told her.

She sat up a little and reached for the buttons, keeping her eyes on his as she opened them one by one. When she reached the waistband of his pants, she tugged the shirt free. Then she pushed the shirt down his arms and looked at him. She put her hands on him, slid them over his chest and nipples, then raised her eyes to meet his. The smile that curved her mouth was pure sin.

Her eyes had changed color and were now almost turquoise as she concentrated on him, stroking his chest with a light, deft touch. His nipples tightened and she moved closer and kissed his neck, then nipped it. Tucker groaned.

He cupped her and she moaned and pushed herself against his hand. She lay down on the couch and he followed, ending up between silky thighs. He rocked against her and she tightened her arms and legs around him. Nuzzling her neck, he asked, "Why are we on the couch when we have a nice, comfortable bed we could be in?"

"Because," she said as she ran her hands down his back to his butt and pulled him against her again. "I'm still not sure we should be doing this."

"I have to tell you, you're not acting like you're thinking this is a mistake."

She sighed. "You're right, I'm not."

He kissed her mouth again, slowly, then drew back and smiled at her. "Have I told you recently that you're beautiful?"

She laughed, the sound a sexy ripple, before her expression grew solemn. "I want you, Tucker. Inside me."

A cell phone rang. He glanced at the coffee table. "That's yours. Don't answer it."

She looked undecided. "It might be important."

"So is this."

"Tucker, I have to answer it."

Reluctantly, he moved off her and she sat up and reached for the phone, grabbing for her tank with her other hand and holding it against her chest. "I'm sorry," she said, then picked up the phone and flipped it open.

"Hello." She paused and said, "Yes, this is Officer Barnes." She paused then said, "Sara? Sara Myers?"

He watched her change from disheveled, about-to-be-thoroughly loved woman to pure cop in an instant.

"No, don't do that. It's too dangerous. Keep that door locked and I'll be there as soon as I can. Don't open the door, Sara, until you hear me or another officer. I'm on my way now."

She shut the cell phone with a snap, and yanked her tank top over her head and down to cover her breasts. "Shit, I knew this was going to happen. Tucker, I have to go." She jumped up and headed for the bedroom.

"What's wrong?" He followed her, watching as she

rifled through her closet for her uniform and then scrambled into it

"Remember that domestic disturbance I was called to the day I found Grace? The last time I pulled you over? I left the woman my number. I don't always, but I had a feeling about her.

"I was right. She just called. Husband's out of control again. She's had to lock herself in her bedroom to get away from him. He's already broken her nose. Now he's threatened to break every bone in her body if she doesn't let him in."

"Are you going to call for backup? You're not even working. You're on a leave of absence still. Maybe someone else should take the call." He wished she wouldn't go at all, but he knew she would.

"No, she's mine. She trusted me and she called me. Besides, I told you, I'm a cop. I'm always on duty. I'll call the station on the way." She strapped on her belt and added the gun. "With any luck I'll be able to arrest the bastard this time around. Last time she wouldn't let us press charges. Denied he ever touched her."

He walked with her into the kitchen. "Call me and let me know you're okay," he told her. Maybe he was overreacting but he had a bad feeling about this situation.

She smiled as she shrugged into her jacket. "Don't worry, Tucker. I do this kind of thing all the time."

He knew she did. That didn't mean he had to like it. "Just be careful."

"Always." She paused a moment before she left. "Tucker, about tonight…I'm sorry."

A moment later she was gone. And Tucker was alone with only a sleeping baby and a nagging fear for Maggie for company.

## CHAPTER FOURTEEN

MAGGIE AND A FELLOW officer named Ben Fairfield arrived at the apartment building at almost the same time. Ben had only been with the ACPD for a few months but Maggie had worked with him before and liked him.

"Glad you made it," Maggie told him.

Nodding, he said, "I thought you were on leave."

"I was. I am, but the victim called me and said she was locked in the bedroom with her husband threatening to break every bone in her body. Said he's already broken her nose, so he might just mean it."

Ben nodded again. "Apartment 3-D, you say."

"That's right. Third floor."

"Is he armed?"

"I don't know." Maggie glanced at the building with a worried frown. "She didn't say he had a gun, but that doesn't mean anything. She was scared out of her mind and might not have thought to mention it."

"One way to find out," Ben said. "Let's go."

A few minutes later Maggie pounded on the door. "Police, open up."

"I'm glad you're here. I think he may have killed her this time."

Maggie turned around to see a woman peering out of the apartment across the hall. "Why do you say that?"

"There was a lot of noise, hollering and cursing. Then it got quiet before starting again, even worse. He was throwing things around, from the sound of it. I think maybe she was one of the things he threw." She nodded, her face grim. "There was a huge crash and since then, nothing."

"Did you hear any gunshots?" Ben asked the woman.

"No, but I know he keeps a gun. Sara told me one time she was afraid the children would find it." She paused and added, "I called the police before on this man but you've never done anything."

Maggie stifled a pang of regret. *I tried,* she thought, but it hadn't been good enough. "Thanks for your help," she said and waited until the woman closed her door before pounding on Sara's again. "Aransas City Police Department. Open the door." She tried the knob, but it was locked.

Still no answer. She and Ben exchanged a glance. She took out her weapon and so did he. At her nod, he kicked in the door and entered the apartment with Maggie right behind him.

The place was a shambles, with broken dishes everywhere and a good bit of the furniture broken, as well. Apparently, he'd put one of the chairs through the TV screen. There was no sign of any people. The doors to both bedrooms were shut and there was an ominous silence. "Police," she called out.

Maggie pointed at the door of what she knew from her previous visit was the master bedroom. She and

Ben flanked it on either side. "Sara, can you hear me? Are you all right?"

A bullet came through the door and buried itself in the wall across the hall. They heard a wild laugh, then a man said, "She won't answer. The bitch got what she deserved."

Maggie's heart sank. Although she hadn't relished a standoff, at least that would have meant Sara had a chance. She nodded at Ben, for him to try again before they went in. Maybe the man was lying. Maybe—

"Sara Myers, are you all right?"

Another bullet through the door was their only answer. Ben counted to three with his fingers in the air and on three Maggie turned the knob and pushed the door open. Seconds later several shots rang out, though they all went wild and didn't hit either of them.

"Police! Put down your weapon," Ben shouted.

"That'll be a cold day in hell. Come and take it," the man invited. "That bitch won't be calling the cops no more."

Maggie went in low and Ben high, both of them aiming for the place they'd last heard the man's voice. Several shots sounded and Maggie jerked back, feeling a searing pain in her arm. "Shit, he hit me."

Ben didn't answer but she couldn't look at him until she made sure the shooter was taken care of. He'd been hit, that much was obvious, and he lay slumped over. Holding her gun on him, she walked over to him and checked his pulse. "Dead." A small arsenal of handguns surrounded him, yet by some miracle, they'd taken him out before he took them. She turned and looked for her partner, who lay on the floor, bleeding. "Damn it, you're hurt! Why didn't you say something? How did he hit both of us?" She rushed over to him.

"Just lucky, I guess," he said, grimacing. "He got my shoulder, but I don't think it's bad."

"No, I don't, either," Maggie said, inspecting it. She keyed in her radio. "Officer down! Officer needs assistance!" Then she went into the bathroom and grabbed a couple of towels, wadding one up to hold over Ben's wound.

He was hurt more than he let on because he allowed her to staunch the blood without arguing, which was totally unlike the man she'd worked with before. "You're bleeding, too," he said, a little faintly.

"It's just a flesh wound. I'll survive." And so would Ben, she thought, looking him over critically.

"Who do you think got him?"

"I don't know. Maybe you." She glanced around and caught sight of the very still form of Sara Myers, lying beside the dresser.

"Go to her," Ben said, brushing her hands aside to hold the towel. "I'm all right."

She was sure they were too late but she went to her, anyway. Sara looked…broken. She searched for a pulse but couldn't find it. She closed her eyes, hung her head and sucked in a breath. She looked at Ben. "She's dead. No gunshot wound. I think her neck's broken."

"Bastard probably did it when he threw her," Ben said. "You're bleeding like a stuck pig," he added. "Better put some pressure on that."

Maggie didn't argue. At least she was alive, unlike poor Sara Myers.

"We were too late. I wonder when he did it. If I'd gotten here faster…" She shook her head, then sat on the floor before she fell down.

"Don't beat yourself up," Ben advised.

She just shook her head, gazing at the dead woman.

"Maggie, don't take it so hard. We did the best we could."

"Yeah, I know. But it wasn't good enough." She'd failed, just as she'd failed weeks earlier to talk Sara into going to a shelter. And now Sara Myers was dead. There would be no chances of a new life for her.

THE HOUSE WAS QUIET when she returned, much later. She hoped Tucker had gone to sleep. After she left the hospital, where the doctors had assured them Ben would recover fully, she went to the station and called to tell him she was all right, but that she'd be a while and for him not to wait up. She hadn't told him about being shot or that her partner had been shot, as well. She figured she'd better tell him that in person. She wasn't too sure of his reaction, but she didn't think it would be good.

After putting her weapon and belt away, she checked on Grace but the baby was sleeping peacefully. So sweet, so peaceful, she thought, stifling the urge to pick her up and cuddle her for comfort. Instead she left her and went back to the den.

Going straight to the bar, she found a bottle of whiskey and picked up a glass. She splashed some liquor in it and tossed it back, shuddering as it burned its way down. Maggie didn't drink a lot, but she knew why so many cops did. Tonight was one of those nights when she could easily have crawled inside a bottle. She wouldn't, but she sure as hell intended to have a drink. Or two or three.

Her arm throbbed and she wondered if she'd been stupid not to take the prescription pain meds she'd been offered. Probably, but she'd decided to make do with over-the-counter pills and have a drink instead.

"I listened to the police scanner," Tucker said from the doorway. "I heard them say officer down. They didn't even have to specify, I knew it was you."

"It wasn't me. It was my partner." She gripped the glass tighter and downed another swallow. "He's going to be okay, though." Keeping her injured arm turned away from him, she glanced at him. "You shouldn't listen to the scanner. Especially if I'm gone."

"Right, that's going to happen. Looks like you had a rough night."

"Yeah." She laughed without humor and took another sip of whiskey. "It totally blew wide out."

He walked over to her, picked up the bottle and poured her some more. "Come sit down." He started to take her by the arm, then frowned, obviously noticing the bandage on her other arm for the first time. "I thought you said your partner was shot. What happened to your arm?" He rubbed her bare skin below the bandage gently. "You were shot, too, weren't you? Goddamn it, Maggie, you've been shot! Why didn't you tell me when you called?"

Maggie cursed herself. It looked worse than it was, she knew. They'd had to cut off her shirtsleeve to put a bandage the size of Aransas Bay on her arm.

"It's nothing. Just a flesh wound."

"Nothing? You were shot. That's a long way from nothing. I can't believe you didn't tell me. I'd have come to the hospital with you."

"And what would you have done with Grace? Besides, I didn't tell you because I didn't want you to freak out like you're doing now." She let him lead her to the couch and sat down.

"I'm not freaking out. But, yes, it upsets me to know that my wife has been shot and didn't bother to tell me." He sat beside her.

"I'm sorry." She set her glass down and rubbed a hand over her forehead. "I thought it would be better to tell you in person. Maybe I was wrong, I don't know."

"Tell me what happened."

She gazed at him before she began. He had that implacable look on his face. He wouldn't be put off this time, she knew. Besides, she wanted to talk to him. He was bare-chested, wearing only a pair of thin sweats that he must have pulled on when he heard her come in. He looked warm and strong and infinitely comforting. Tears stung her eyes and she resolutely fought them back. *Suck it up,* she told herself. *You're tough, you're a cop. Pull it together.* She took another drink before she started.

"He was holed up in the apartment with a small arsenal, but we didn't know that. We weren't even sure he was armed. Neighbor heard a lot of commotion, then nothing. We called out to the victim but she didn't answer." She skipped over the part about all the shooting, figuring the less Tucker heard about that the better. "We believe she was dead by the time we got there. The son of a bitch she was married to broke her neck. He threw her into the dresser. Like…like she was nothing."

Tucker put his hand over hers and squeezed comfortingly. "I'm sorry. I can't imagine how hard it must be for you to walk into that kind of a situation."

She shrugged, then winced at the jolt of pain. "At least I'm alive. Sara Myers is dead. And it's my fault."

# CHAPTER FIFTEEN

TUCKER STARED AT HER. She was serious. "Maggie, it's foolish to blame yourself for this." She didn't say anything. He didn't think she'd even heard him, she was so caught up in her grief and guilt. "What happened to him? Is he in jail? I'm assuming he's the one who shot you and your partner."

She nodded. "Yeah. He's not in jail. He's dead. Ben Fairfield shot and killed him but not before he'd managed to shoot both of us. At least, we think it was Ben's shot and not mine that got him."

"You could have been killed." Maybe it wasn't what she needed to hear, but it made him sick to think how close she'd come to— He shook his head, not wanting that thought in it. He knew the dangers of police work. Hell, anyone who watched the news knew them. It was just different when it was personal, when it affected someone you cared about. When it affected his wife.

"It's nothing. I got lucky. Sara Myers didn't."

"Why do you feel so responsible for her?"

"Because she trusted me. Because I couldn't get her into a shelter where she could get help." She got up and started pacing. Tucker could sense the frustration coming off her in waves. "I tried everything I could think of to get her to a shelter, but she wouldn't buy it. She was so damn sure he was a good guy underneath it all. I failed to convince her of the danger and now she's dead."

"Maggie, you can't possibly blame yourself over every case or every call that goes south. You'd be crazy by now. You couldn't function as a cop. So why are you letting this particular one get to you so badly?"

"I don't know." She rubbed a hand over her eyes. "No, that's a lie. I know exactly why she gets to me. Why this whole miserable situation gets to me."

"Tell me."

She came back and sat beside him, picked up her nearly empty glass and drained it.

"Do you want more?"

She shot him a look he couldn't interpret, then shook her head before setting down the empty glass. "I don't usually drink when something bad happens. I've known too many cops who slid inside a bottle and couldn't seem to make it out. But tonight... God, talk about ghosts of the past." She was quiet for a long moment, then she began.

"I met him for the first time when we went out on a domestic disturbance call."

"Met who?" he asked, but he had a feeling he knew.

"Spencer Whitman." She laughed bitterly. "The love of my life. I was in Dallas. It was my first call with the department and they gave me to him. He'd been around several years longer than I had and he had a rep for being a negotiator. He could talk anyone into anything. If we had a jumper, say, and couldn't find a shrink, he'd be the guy everyone wanted to talk him down." She smiled. "He really had a golden tongue."

"Were you partners?"

She nodded. "Eventually. That first time, I was just a rookie, following him around. Anyway, we went to a domestic disturbance. Almost exactly the same scenario as the one I walked into the night I found Grace. Sara Myers even looked a bit like that woman. But Spencer was able to talk the woman into going to a shelter. It was amazing, how he convinced her."

"And you feel like you should have been able to convince Sara Myers just because he got lucky that one time."

"It wasn't luck, or just an isolated incident. He had a gift. I saw him do it, time after time. And I learned from him, or thought I had. I've had a good success rate in these kind of situations until now."

"Maggie, it was Sara Myers's choice to stay with her abuser. None of this is your failure."

"You're wrong. My failure killed Sara." She put her head in her hands, then looked at him with tormented eyes. "My God, Tucker, I turned her into a sitting duck. I should have told her to run."

"And that could have turned out just as badly. Or even worse if other people had been hurt. You don't have a crystal ball. You can't say that if you'd done or said something different you could have saved her. As it was, both you and your partner were shot. One or both of you could have been killed. Or any number of innocent by-standers could have been hurt if the man hadn't been contained to that apartment."

She looked unconvinced.

"Did they have kids?"

Maggie nodded. "Three. They were huddled in the other bedroom, terrified to make a sound in case it reminded their father they were there. CPS has them now."

"At least the children weren't hurt. Can't you take any comfort from that?"

"Some." She frowned at him. "Okay, a lot. But I still hate that it turned out this way. I hate that she's dead and I couldn't stop him."

"I can understand that. But I don't understand why it reminds you so much of your past. Of Spencer."

She got up and walked back over to the bar, but she didn't pick up the whiskey bottle. Her shoulders squared and she turned back to him. "I don't know, exactly. It's like they're connected in my mind. I think failure connects them. Whenever I fail, especially if it's a domestic disturbance case, I think about Spencer. I feel inadequate again. Just like I felt with your mother earlier. I'm not good enough for your mother. I wasn't good enough to save Sara. And I wasn't good enough to make Spencer fall in love with me. No matter how much I loved him."

He'd thought he wanted to hear the story. Now he wasn't so sure. "Maggie, come sit down." He didn't care how minor she said the wound was, she'd been shot. She ought to be in bed, but barring that, she should at least sit down.

She crossed the room and sat beside him again. "I fell for him. Completely, madly in love. We had an affair. A red-hot affair that lasted about eight months."

"I thought cops weren't supposed to get involved with their partners."

"Technically they're not. In reality it happens all the time."

"Was he in love with you?"

"No." She shook her head, quick and decisive. "No, he never told me he loved me. Never lied to me or tried to make me believe what we had was anything more to him than something to keep the loneliness at bay. He cared about me, I know he did. And he liked the sex, but he didn't love me."

So big deal, the guy hadn't lied to her. He'd used her. And obviously, he'd hurt her. Tucker wished for just a few minutes alone with the man.

"I knew he was hung up on another woman, but I was so damn sure I could make him fall for me instead. She was the only person I ever knew of who Spencer couldn't convince to do what he wanted. He wanted her to leave her husband for him. She refused, said she wanted to save her marriage, so she and Spencer couldn't see each other anymore. They'd only been broken up a month or so when I met him."

"He hurt you. Badly."

"More like I hurt myself by not seeing reality. Then I got pregnant. I was so happy. I had all the fantasies that, once he knew, Spencer would marry me and the three of us would live happily ever after." She gave a short, bitter laugh. "We were both off duty and I went to tell him about the baby. But I found him packing. He said he'd been planning to tell me that evening. He was leaving Dallas. Seems he'd finally talked the woman he loved into leaving her husband and they were going to start fresh somewhere else. So, bye-bye, Maggie, it's been nice knowing you."

"Bastard."

"No, he wasn't." She shook her head. "Don't blame him for my problems. He didn't know I loved him. I never told him. And I knew all along he was in love with another woman. I just didn't want to admit I couldn't change his mind and make him fall for me. But you can't make someone love you. I learned that the hard way."

Tucker had a bad feeling he was going to have to learn the hard way, as well.

"Did you ever tell him you were pregnant?"

"No. I didn't see the point. It wouldn't have changed anything. I figured a baby with me would just ruin his life and he'd finally gotten what—who—he wanted. So I left Dallas and came back to Aransas City. I...wanted to be near family. I thought it would be better since I was going to be a single mother."

Tucker remembered when she'd said she'd needed her mother, and her mother hadn't been there for her. "What happened to the baby?"

Her expression was bleak. Her eyes huge and full of pain. "I had a miscarriage, not long after I came back. I told the chief I was pregnant but no one else knew. I thought I'd wait until I started showing. I never reached that stage."

He took her hand and squeezed it. "I'm so sorry, Maggie. You wanted it, didn't you?"

"Yeah, I wanted the baby. More than I'd ever wanted anything. The doctor said it was just one of those things. Nothing I did to cause it, nothing I could have done to prevent it. But I've always wondered...."

"Wondered what? That you were at fault?"

She started to shrug, then caught herself, wincing. "Maybe. I always wondered if the miscarriage was payback."

"Payback for what?"

"Remember my affair with the married man? The married man with the pregnant wife?"

Tucker just stared at her. She couldn't possibly believe what she was implying, could she? "Maggie, that's crazy. The whole situation was much more his fault than yours. He lied to you, told you he was legally separated. Besides, it's not like there's some kind of cosmic karma that says, 'Oh, Maggie screwed up so we're going to take her baby away from her.'"

"It was as good an explanation as the one I got from the doctor."

"Have you ever talked to anyone about this?"

"No. What would have been the point? I had a miscarriage. Wham, bam, no more baby. It was over and done with and I moved on."

But had she moved on? Suddenly her reasons for wanting to keep Grace became much clearer. As well as her fear of intimacy. At least two of the men she'd been intimate with had screwed her over royally. No wonder she didn't trust men.

"I know what you're thinking," Maggie said. "Grace isn't a substitute for the baby I lost. I feel a connection with her, that's all."

He didn't know what to say to her. How to comfort her. Because she needed comforting, no matter how much she believed she didn't. So he didn't say anything. Not yet. Careful not to jar her injury, he urged her closer and put his arm around her. "I'm sorry. I wish someone had been there for you when you lost the baby."

She put her uninjured arm around his neck and sighed, leaning against him. "Why are you so nice to me? You're always so nice. So understanding."

*Because I'm in love with you,* he thought. But there was no way he could tell her that. He'd only begun to admit it to himself. She wasn't ready to hear how he felt. Maybe she never would be.

"You deserve someone to be nice to you," he said lightly. "And you also need someone to put you to bed, since you won't go yourself. You're exhausted, Maggie. You need to get some sleep."

"I know." She sighed. "I shouldn't have drunk that whiskey on an empty stomach. I don't feel so good. And now if Grace wakes up— I'm just batting a thousand tonight for doing the wrong thing."

"I'll take care of Grace if she needs anything." And he intended to take care of Maggie, too. "Come on, I'll make you some scrambled eggs."

She sat at the kitchen table and watched him prepare the eggs, not saying anything. But her eyes were stricken and he knew she was replaying the events of the night in her mind. Torturing herself with what-ifs.

He put the plate in front of her. "Eat."

While she ate he steered the conversation to Grace, and what she'd done that day, and had the satisfaction of seeing the desperate look slowly leave Maggie's eyes as she talked about the baby and that she could now sit up. A milestone, Maggie said, and he'd even managed to snap a picture.

"I don't know why I'm so tired," Maggie said, laying down her fork. She'd eaten a little, though not as much as he'd have liked. At least she had some color back, but she looked exhausted still.

"It might have something to do with being shot." He led her to her bedroom, ignoring her when she tried to thank him and get rid of him. No way was he leaving her alone with her memories. Not tonight.

He picked up the tank top she'd thrown on the chair. "Can you get into this by yourself or do you need help?"

She took it from him. "Tucker, I'm fine. You don't have to baby me."

"Would you for once listen to me? Get undressed and get into bed."

He knew how exhausted she was because she didn't argue. She simply stripped out of her uniform where she stood and pulled on her tank and shorts. Then she crawled into bed. He got into bed with her, on top of the covers, with her uninjured arm against him. "Don't even try to argue with me," he told her.

"I won't. I should, but…I'm glad you're here." She snuggled against him, laying her poor injured arm over his chest.

"Yeah, me, too. Go to sleep, Maggie." She dropped off soon after, and just as he'd expected, she woke in pain, with a nightmare, deep in the night. Tucker gave her aspirin, then he held her, comforted her until she calmed down.

And his heart twisted when she said sleepily against him, "Tucker, you're my best friend," before she dropped off to sleep again.

She needed a friend, and he was happy to be there for her. But he wanted more, as well. A whole hell of a lot more. Because he'd finally admitted tonight, when he heard the chilling words "officer down" come over the police scanner and known it could be Maggie, what he'd tried to ignore for weeks now. He was totally, madly and, in all probability, hopelessly in love with his wife.

## CHAPTER SIXTEEN

MAGGIE WOKE EARLY the next morning, aware that her arm was throbbing and that her head rested on a warm, hard, masculine chest. Tucker's chest. She sat up suddenly, then had to bite her lip to keep from screaming at the dizzying rush of pain. Whoever had said flesh wounds weren't a big deal had obviously never had one. As she gazed at him, Tucker's eyes opened and he smiled at her sleepily.

"Hey."

"Hey yourself," she said, smiling in spite of the pain. "How's your arm?"

His voice was a deep rumble, rough with sleep. He looked as good as he sounded, all rumpled and sexy with his morning beard and those beautiful deep-water-blue eyes smiling at her.

"You didn't have to stay with me." She sounded ungracious, but damn, she'd been dreaming about him— sexy, sensual dreams, and then to wake in his arms… Still, no wonder she was a little shaken. The sexy dreams beat the hell out of the other dreams she'd had.

"You had a nightmare," he said, then rolled on his

side and propped himself on one arm. "Which isn't a surprise, considering."

The night before came back in a flood of memories. She and Tucker, about to make love. Then the call. The whole futile scene at the apartment. Sara Myers, dead. And when she'd come back home…

God, she'd told Tucker her whole miserable history with Spencer. How much had she drunk? And what in the world was the matter with her to spill her guts like she had? She never did that. Never. But then, for some reason Tucker caused her to do a whole lot of stupid things she didn't usually do.

She got out of bed, careful not to jar her arm any more than she had to. "Yeah, I remember. But you didn't need to sleep with me."

"Trust me, Maggie, it wasn't a hardship." He looked amused. And tempting. He'd gotten under the covers at some point the night before and now the sheet pooled around his waist. She tried not to look at his bare chest, to see the ripple of muscles as he got up and stretched. But that was impossible.

She took the coward's way out and dashed into the bathroom. He was gone when she emerged a few minutes later and she breathed a sigh of relief. Grabbing her rattiest, oldest robe, she went to get Grace and found Tucker there before her, talking to the baby while he finished changing her diaper.

"That's right, Gracie. Tucker's going to give you a bottle and then we're going to check out the newspaper."

Her heart simply melted. God, they were cute

together. Grace was kicking her feet and babbling that strange language only babies understand. Tucker had put on a plain white T-shirt and he looked…like a father taking care of his child, she realized with a pang of longing. Oh, damn, she had to stop this. "I'll take her if you want me to."

He glanced over at her and smiled, then put the baby against his shoulder and walked to the door. Grace peeped at her over Tucker's shoulder, all blond curly hair, big blue eyes and sweet as only babies can be. "I don't think so. Have you tried to pick up anything heavy?"

Maggie frowned. "I can manage. Besides, you're going to work, so you might as well let me have her." She reached out for her and sucked in a breath, then cradled her arm against her side. Okay, so taking care of Grace wouldn't be easy, but she could still do it.

Ignoring her, Tucker carried Grace into the kitchen and fixed her bottle of formula, then set out the cereal to give her when she finished. It annoyed Maggie that he was already at least as competent as she in caring for the baby.

"I'm taking a couple of days off work," Tucker said. "I already called Janice and told her to reschedule, so don't argue."

"You don't need to do that. I can take care of Grace." Maybe.

"Didn't I say don't argue? You'll have to go in to finish your report. And you'll have to talk to a lot of other people if they determine your shot killed that man, won't you?"

"Ben and I both think it was his. Anyway, what do you know about what happens when you shoot someone?"

"Just what I see on TV. But it's true, isn't it?" She didn't answer and he continued, "So let me take care of Grace while you deal with your business."

He'd left her with nothing to say or do, which irritated the heck out of her. She stalked over to the phone to call the hospital for an update on Ben's condition. Even though she'd expected good news or she wouldn't have left the night before, she still breathed a huge sigh of relief to hear they would release him later that day.

For the next few days, she and Tucker played house. At least, that's how Maggie tried to look at it. Because she sure couldn't afford to look on those days together, as a family, as something real.

SCHEMING HOW TO SEDUCE his own wife was more difficult than Tucker would have thought. He hadn't said anything or made a move since she'd been shot. First because she'd been hurt, and later because he wasn't sure how to approach her. He'd never expended so much time and energy on getting a woman into bed in his life. "Hey, how about a roll in the sack?" wouldn't exactly cut it.

So he decided to bring it out in the open. One afternoon they took a walk, with Tucker pushing the baby stroller and Maggie walking beside them. The weather was perfect, neither too hot or too cold, something that didn't occur often in this spot on the Texas coast.

One of the neighbors waved to them and Maggie waved back. "Tucker, my arm is fine now. I think you should go back to work tomorrow."

He glanced at her. "To tell you the truth, I've enjoyed the break. But I do need to get back. Janice has been phoning me daily with dire predictions of all my clients jumping ship if I don't come back."

"There you go. Your secretary doesn't strike me as the alarmist type."

Tucker laughed. "You don't know her very well, then. It's par for the course for her." They walked along in silence for a moment, then turned back for the house. "Grace is nodding off," he said. "We'd better go put her down for her nap."

"All right. I'll go to the store after we do. Otherwise we won't have anything for dinner."

"Why don't you wait on that? I want to talk to you."

She shot him a suspicious glance, but didn't protest. Once they'd put Grace down and left her room they went to the den. He noticed she'd grabbed her bag and was ready to head out the door the instant they finished talking. He had other plans.

"What do you want to talk about?" she asked when he didn't speak.

"Have you seen the doctor about your arm?"

"I told you, it's fine now. But yes, Lana looked at it for me. She says it's fine, too."

"Good." He walked over to her and before she could give him any flak, put his arms around her and pulled her close. "Because I wanted to be sure you were all right before I did this again." He kissed her. Her lips had parted in surprise and he took full advantage, slipping his tongue in and enticing hers to answer. After stiffening initially, her body softened and she leaned into him.

For a brief moment, she answered in kind. Her arm came around his neck and she kissed him back, blasting his resolve to go slowly into a zillion pieces. He put his hands on her bottom and pressed her against him, deepening the kiss when he did so. He left her mouth and trailed his lips to the pulse beating rapidly at her throat. Wild images filled his mind of stripping her where she stood and taking her, on the floor, on the couch, against the wall. Anywhere, as long as he finally, *finally* had her.

"Tucker, stop."

He hesitated, trying to wrap his mind around her words. But he couldn't. So he moved to her jaw and tasted her there.

"Tucker, we have to stop."

She wanted him to stop? Now? He raised his head and looked at her then. "Why?"

She pushed at his chest and he reluctantly released her. It gave him little satisfaction to see her hand was unsteady when she reached up to brush her hair out of her face. "I—we—we can't do this. We can't make love."

"We nearly made love the other night," he reminded her. Maybe she could forget that, but he sure as hell couldn't. He'd never forget the sight of Maggie, lost in passion.

"I know." She closed her eyes briefly, then opened them. "And it would have been a mistake."

"That's a matter of opinion." He reached for her, making sure to take her uninjured arm because he knew the other was still tender. "Maggie, look at me and tell me you don't want me. Tell me you don't want to make love with me. Do it, and then I'll leave you alone."

She looked at him with tormented eyes. "I can't. You know I can't."

"Then what's stopping you?"

"It's just sex, Tucker. Hormones." She paced away and waved a hand. "We've been living together and we find each other attractive and neither of us has had sex in months now. It's just convenience, that's all it is. Our marriage is temporary and if we give in to this…urge, it will just make divorcing that much harder in the end."

Did she really believe what she was saying? "What if that's not all it is?"

She stared at him. "What do you mean?"

"What if what we have between us is more than sex? For both of us."

"It's not. It can't be."

"You sound very sure of that." He studied her a minute. "Tell me something, Maggie. What exactly is it about the two of us making love that scares you so much? Because you don't trust me…or because you don't trust anyone?"

"You don't understand." She twisted her hands together, gnawed on her lip before she squared her shoulders and faced him. "I don't *want* to want you. And I can't afford to trust you. Not about this."

His mind blank, he stared at her. He felt as if he'd been punched in the gut. And then her cell phone rang. "Goddamn it," he snarled. "Isn't that just typical."

She didn't bother to say she was sorry. She checked

the number, then flipped open the phone. "This is Maggie. What's up, Chief?"

Tucker watched her face turn ashen as she listened. Devastated. He'd heard the word, used the word, but this was the first time he'd *seen* what it looked like.

"Here? In Aransas City? How do you know—" She listened impatiently, then said, "You're positive it's her? She has proof?" She gestured with her hand as if to cut him off. "I don't see how you can trust anything she says. You didn't tell her anything, did you? No, never mind, I know you didn't. I'll be right down. I want to question her myself." She didn't wait for an argument, just slapped the phone closed and looked at Tucker with pure terror in her eyes.

"What did he say?" Tucker asked, though he hardly needed to. Even what little he'd overheard didn't give it away as much as Maggie's demeanor. What she'd feared the most had finally happened.

Maggie passed a hand over her eyes and took in a deep breath. "Grace's mother—Carol Davis is down at the station right now. She just walked in, off the street, about half an hour ago."

"Are they sure it's Grace's mother?"

"They're sure. She had proof of her identity, and of Grace's." Eyes anguished, she looked at him. "Tucker, she wants Grace back. She said she gave up her baby to protect her, and now the threat is gone and she wants her back."

## CHAPTER SEVENTEEN

THE CHIEF STOPPED her at the door to the station house. "You just turn right around and go on home, Officer. Ralston is handling this case and you've got no call to be here."

"No call?" Maggie stared at him in disbelief. "I'm the child's foster mother."

"Which is exactly why this isn't your case. You can't be objective."

She bit off the hot words that bubbled on her tongue. She had to prove to the chief she could be professional. Calm, cool. Because she had every intention of seeing Grace's mother and questioning the woman herself. There was no way she'd trust that job to Ralston. He was a decent enough cop, but he wasn't very experienced, and certainly not in a case like this.

"Chief Corbitt, could we discuss this matter in your office?"

He eyed her for a moment, then jerked his head toward his office and turned around. Maggie followed him, formulating how she was going to convince him to let her question the woman. *Grace's mother.* God, the thought itself had her in a panic.

Chief Corbitt took a seat, steepled his fingers on the desk in front of him and said, "Go ahead."

"I know this case better than anyone else, and certainly better than Ralston. She won't know that I'm anything more to Grace than the cop who found her. You know me, Chief. You know I'm a professional."

"Normally, yes. But this is different. Maggie, you're crazy about that baby. That makes you just about the worst person to be involved."

"No, it makes me the best. Please, just let me question her. You can sit in and if I step over the line you can cut me loose."

He pondered that, then sighed. "All right. You'll just badger me until I give in. But mind you keep it professional and don't let your feelings get in the way. Any tiny sign I see that you're going to lose it and you're out of there."

"Yes, sir."

A short time later Maggie and the chief walked into one of the conference rooms. A thin, pale, young blond woman, about eighteen or nineteen, sat at the battered table dressed in threadbare jeans and a T-shirt. She looked down on her luck, but her clothes had obviously been washed recently and her hair was clean, so she'd made an effort to look decent when she came in. And while the way she twisted her hands together suggested nerves, she didn't show any telltale signs of drug use. Not at first glance, anyway.

Okay, so Carol Davis might not be a junkie. She'd still abandoned her infant, which didn't exactly make her an upstanding citizen. And since the child in question was not a newborn, the safe haven law didn't apply.

"Carol Davis?"

"Yes." She looked at Maggie and then her eyes lit. "You're the officer who found my baby. How is she? No one will tell me anything. Is my baby all right?"

"I'm the officer who found an abandoned infant beside my patrol car, yes. We haven't established that you are, in fact, the mother of that infant."

"Please." She reached out and touched Maggie's arm. "Is Grace well? Is she all right?"

"The baby is fine. She's with Child Protective Services." *And me,* Maggie thought. At least for the present. "We'll assume for now you are the mother of the infant I found. Are you willing to explain why you abandoned your child?"

"I'll do whatever it takes to get Grace back. You— you hate me," she said, faltering. "I can see it in your eyes. You can't understand how I could leave my baby the way I did. How I could abandon her. I don't blame you. But I swear, I did it for Grace. To keep her safe."

"Do you understand that you could be charged with abandonment and possibly child endangerment as well? Those are very serious charges, Ms. Davis. Felonies."

She paled even more but she made an effort to hold herself together. "I understand. I know it was wrong, but I was desperate and I didn't know what else to do. I couldn't protect her any other way."

Maggie felt a pang of sympathy, but she hardened her heart. Carol Davis hadn't proved yet that she deserved any sympathy for abandoning her child. "You dumped your child like so much garbage, Ms. Davis. You left her sitting out in the open in the middle of February in a parking lot, for anyone to take. That could hardly be called protecting her."

"No! I saw the patrol car and I thought the police could protect her. I thought they'd take her to CPS and find someone to care for her. And then I saw you go inside the building, so I—I put her beside your car for you to find when you returned. I hid in the bushes. I stayed right there and watched until you came back."

Maggie glanced at the chief, who hadn't said a word. "Why don't you tell us your story, Ms. Davis?" he said. "Start at the beginning and take it slowly."

Maggie sat down and opened her pad. She had a sick feeling in her gut that the woman's story was going to make her sound extremely sympathetic. And if that happened, Maggie stood no chance of retaining custody. If at all possible, CPS would side with the natural mother. As long as the child hadn't been abused…and Maggie knew full well that she hadn't.

"Grace's father left me when he found out I was pregnant. My parents had long since kicked me out. They didn't like Gerald and to be honest, they were just as glad to have an excuse to get rid of me. The morning sickness—" She shrugged and continued, "After I lost my job the only work I could find was at a bar in Corpus. A lot of bangers went there. It was bad, but I couldn't afford to be picky. Anyway, that's where I met Armand. He was nice. He tipped me and wouldn't let any of the others hassle me. At first, I just thought he was being nice. At first."

"This bar have a name? The gang have a name?"

She shook her head. "It's not important." She gave Maggie a sharp glance. "Besides, you know what happens to people who rat on bangers."

Yeah, she knew. "Go on."

"About six weeks after the baby was born, I was evicted. I found out later Armand had pressured the landlord to do it. He asked me to move in with him and I didn't have anywhere else to go, so I did." She halted, looked at Maggie and asked, "Could I have some water?"

The room doubled as a snack room, so Maggie got up, pulled a bottle out of the refrigerator and gave it to her before returning to her seat. She watched while Carol drank, then set the bottle down.

"Thank you." She drew in a breath and began again. "If I'd known what he would be like I would have chosen the streets. He didn't like the baby. He got angry every time Grace cried. He started talking about how he didn't want no 'other man's brat' around. I told him I'd leave. That's the first time he hit me. He told me I was never leaving him. If anyone left it would be 'that goddamn squalling brat.'" Her voice broke and she looked at Maggie with loathing in her eyes. "That's what he called my precious baby. I knew what I had to do. It took me two weeks to plan how to get away. During that time I did everything he wanted me to. I let him use me, I let him hit me, I let him do whatever he wanted as long as he didn't hurt my baby.

I prayed every day that Grace and I would get away. And finally, we did. I stole money for bus fare, took Grace and went to a friend, here in Aransas City. I guess I was stupid, because I didn't think Armand would bother to track me down."

Maggie could see it. All her words rang true. Carol Davis wasn't the monster of selfishness Maggie had imagined. She was an abused woman fleeing her abuser. Desperately afraid for her child. "What happened when he found you?"

"He said I was coming with him and that he was going to take care of my brat once and for all. He said he was going to kill her," Carol said stonily. "And he would have. I begged him to let me leave her with my friend, but he wouldn't hear of it. He—he wanted to kill her. To punish me." She stopped, drank more water, inhaled deeply and continued. "Angela wasn't home when he got there. She worked the late shift, so it was just Armand, me...and Grace. He said if Angela interfered, he'd kill her, too. And nobody could touch him, he said, because of his boys. He got really drunk and—" She halted, looking down at her hands clasped in front of her. "He raped me," she said flatly. "When he was finished, he passed out. I took Grace and walked out the door. That's when I saw the police car. So I left Grace there, and waited for you to come out. Once you did, I went back to the apartment and waited for him to wake up."

"Why didn't you wait for me and tell me what had happened? I would have helped you."

"He said he'd told his brothers where he was. If he

didn't come back, they'd come find me and Grace and kill us. And Angela, too."

"You believed him," the chief said.

"Of course." Her voice was dull, unsurprised. "Killing us would be nothing to them. Killing, that's their life." She was silent, then said fiercely, "I wished I could be like them. I wanted to kill Armand. To just make him disappear. He was lying there, passed out and stinking drunk. I could have done it. But I was afraid. Afraid of what they'd do to Grace, to Angela. To me. So I left Grace by your patrol car. And I went back with Armand. I told him I left Grace with a neighbor because if he killed her he'd get in trouble. He didn't care by then, he was just glad she was gone. Besides, he knew he had me to torture."

The chief didn't speak. He got up and left. And Maggie knew she'd already lost Grace.

"How did you get away this time? Aren't you afraid he'll come after you again?"

"He's dead. He died in a gang fight. The minute I heard the news, the minute I knew it was true, I left and came here for my baby." She touched Maggie's arm again. "Are you going to arrest me?"

"No." Even if Maggie had been inclined to, there wasn't a prosecutor in the world who'd take that case. Carol had been desperate, and she'd saved her child in the only way she knew. No one would condemn her for that, even if she hadn't chosen the best way to do it.

"And Grace?" she said quietly. "Will I get to keep Grace?"

"I don't know," she said, amazed she could sound so calm when her heart had been torn in two. "That's up to CPS."

Carol was openly crying now. "Do you think they'll give her back to me? I love her so much. It's been killing me, not knowing what happened to her."

"You'll have to prove you're a fit parent. That you can take care of her and that you won't put her in danger again. You'll have to prove to them you won't be in a gang situation again." And she was going to have to prove it all to Maggie, as well, though she didn't know that yet.

Carol wiped her sleeve across her eyes. "I won't. I swear I won't. Angela said I could stay with her. She needs someone to share the rent. She has some leads on a job, too."

"I'll go call CPS and see if they can send someone over as soon as possible. I don't know what they'll say, but I recommend you be honest with them. Be sure and let them know you're looking for work and out of your previous situation. And you'd better mean it, because they won't just take your word for it. And neither will I."

"I do mean it. Thank you for your help, Officer—" She stopped and laughed. "I don't even know your name and you've been so kind."

"Officer Barnes," Maggie said. She'd never changed her name at work, knowing the marriage wouldn't last. But now it looked like it was going to be over sooner than even she had expected.

"Officer Barnes, thank you. And thank you for taking care of my little girl when you found her."

Maggie couldn't speak, so she nodded and left. Before she broke down completely.

# CHAPTER EIGHTEEN

AN HOUR LATER, Maggie returned. Tucker took one look at her face—set, implacable, absolutely emotionless— and knew the news was really bad.

She laid her Glock on the table, then stripped off her equipment belt and laid that beside the gun, then started to leave the room. That alone told Tucker how upset she was. She hadn't left her weapon out since before they'd brought Grace home.

"Where's Grace?" she asked.

"She's asleep. Was it her mother?"

Maggie nodded. "Yes. I'm going to look in on Grace and then go work out."

Like hell she was. "Maggie, talk to me. Tell me what's going on. Are you charging the woman?"

"No." She didn't add anything else, just stood there looking blank.

"Why not?"

"Because she was an abused woman who protected her baby in the only way she knew how." She turned away from the hall and walked over to the window.

"By leaving her in a parking lot? Some protection."

Maggie turned back around. "It was the best she could do, given the circumstances."

Briefly, she told him the story Grace's mother had told her.

"So you're not going to do anything? You're just going to let this woman have Grace back as if she never did anything wrong? As if she never walked away from her without a backward glance?"

"CPS will handle it, but if she can prove she can provide a safe environment for Grace and take care of her properly, then yes, she'll get her back."

He simply stared at her. Maggie's mask slipped and he saw despair in her eyes. "No one would take the case, Tucker, if we did charge her. I saw her. Hell, I interrogated her. She was telling the truth. She was a victim and we can't condemn her for that. As for leaving Grace alone, she didn't. She hid nearby and watched me. She didn't leave until she knew Grace was in my custody."

"She could have just told you she waited. How do you know it's true?"

"She recognized me when I walked in the room."

"None of that makes what she did right. Why did she get involved with a gang member in the first place?" He went over to where Maggie stood, wanting to shake her out of her unnatural calm. No, he didn't want to shake her, he wanted to console her. Not that she'd allow it.

"She's young. Only eighteen. She was trying to survive. She met the banger at work and thought he was nice. He got her evicted from her apartment. She didn't know it was him, of course, so when he asked her to move in with him, she did. She had nowhere else to go."

He wanted to take Maggie in his arms, comfort her. But she radiated don't-touch signals. Afraid she'd break, he suspected. He remembered she'd said that after her miscarriage she'd sucked it up and gone on. That's what she was doing now. Alone. How could he make her understand she didn't have to do everything alone now?

Tucker put his hand on her arm and squeezed gently. "We could fight her. We could fight for custody of Grace."

"No. You didn't see her. She was a victim. I can't victimize her again, and that's what we'd be doing if we fought for Grace." She paused and added, "She loves Grace. It must have killed her to give her up."

"You love Grace, too."

"I'm not Grace's mother. I never was. And now I never will be."

"Maggie—" He started to put his arms around her, but she held up a hand.

"Don't, Tucker. I appreciate the thought, but just…don't be nice. Don't be…anything. I have to— I'm going to box," she said abruptly and left the room.

She hadn't said, "And leave me the hell alone," but that's clearly what she meant. She didn't want him, his comfort, his advice, nothing. She didn't want *him.* And it was too damn bad that he wanted her more than he'd ever wanted anyone in his life. Because he wasn't going to get her. Ever.

LATER THAT EVENING Maggie was giving Grace a bottle when Tucker brought her the phone, looking grim-faced. She'd heard it ring but hadn't answered. She couldn't think of a soul she wanted to talk to. All she wanted was to spend time with Grace, though that was a double-edged sword, since every time she looked at the baby she wondered how much longer she'd be able to keep her.

"Who is it?" she said, not taking it.

"Nina Baker," he said. "From CPS."

He held out his arms and she put Grace into them and took the phone from him. She got up and walked out of the room, leaving Tucker the rocking chair. The fact that her friend had called Maggie herself instead of letting someone else in CPS do it was undoubtedly bad news and she didn't want to be around Grace when she heard it.

"It's Maggie."

"Maggie, it's Nina. How are you?"

She saw no reason to lie. "Not so great. What have you heard?"

"We've talked to Chief Corbitt and he says the police are not bringing charges. I talked to Grace's mother myself and I'm going to recommend she be allowed to retain custody of Grace once she has employment and a place to live. I wanted to tell you myself. I'm so sorry, Maggie. I know how attached you are to the baby."

Maggie doubted that, but she didn't say anything. It was what she'd expected, after all. Nina knew she cared about Grace but she had no idea the full extent of Maggie's "attachment" to the baby.

Nina continued, "Would it be possible for you to bring Grace to the CPS office tomorrow so her mother can see her? I'd like the first visit to be on neutral ground, and with her CPS caseworker present."

"Of course. What time?" Maggie marveled that she could sound so calm when she wanted to scream and rage. But that wouldn't do any good, so she clamped down on her emotions and did her best not to feel anything. The only thing she did feel was...frozen. Everything inside her had frozen the moment she'd heard Carol Davis's story, and she hadn't thawed out yet. Maybe she never would.

They settled on ten the next morning. Maggie went back to Grace's room, halting at the door to watch Tucker with Grace. They were so sweet together. She could imagine Tucker with a child of his own. He'd be a good father. A wonderful father. She entertained a brief, desperate fantasy of herself with Tucker's child. Their child.

God, she was hopeless. He wanted to have sex with her. That didn't mean he wanted the same fantasy she did. Far from it. He'd married her as a favor, and now the favor was about to be unnecessary. Over and done with. If she wasn't selfish, she'd tell Tucker to start divorce proceedings right now. But she didn't. She couldn't face being alone, not yet. It wasn't fair to him, but she needed his support. The divorce would come soon enough, just as Grace would be gone soon. And Maggie would be alone, just as she'd always been.

"What did she want?" Tucker asked. He'd put the baby in her pajamas and now cuddled her against his shoulder as he patted her back.

"I'm taking Grace to see her mother in the morning. They want the first meeting to be at the CPS office."

"I'll go with you."

"You don't need to do that. I can take her myself."

"I know you can, but you're not going to. I'm coming with you."

She studied him a moment, then shrugged. She knew that when he had that face on he was unshakable. "We need to be there at ten."

The meeting with Carol the next day was every bit as hard as Maggie had feared it would be. Carol cried when she saw Grace, weeping unrestrainedly when she held the baby in her arms. Grace looked like her mother, Maggie realized, gazing at the two of them. And Carol Davis obviously loved her child. Emotion like she'd shown couldn't be faked.

After a while Carol calmed down and when she realized Maggie had been keeping Grace, she asked her a million questions about the baby's progress and all the things she'd missed over the past few months.

Tucker didn't say much but Maggie felt his presence and his support and was grateful for it. Because she knew that soon, not only would Grace no longer be in her life, but neither would Tucker.

Maggie was quiet on the way home, thinking about the visit. Carol had cried again when she'd had to leave Grace, but then she'd straightened her shoulders and wiped away the tears. "I'll have a job by the end of the week," she'd told the caseworker. When the woman had asked her what she'd be doing Carol had replied,

"Whatever it takes. I want my child back and I'm not afraid to work to make that happen."

Maggie wanted to hate Carol for taking Grace away from her, but she couldn't. Everything she'd told Tucker was true. And she admired Carol for facing the situation and trying her best to overcome it. She resolved to talk to Delilah and see if she and Cam had an opening of any sort at their restaurant. She also had the number of a woman who did child care in her home and had flexible hours. Maggie had thought about using her when she went back to work. Now she'd give the number to Carol Davis.

At least if Carol stayed in Aransas City, Maggie would be able to see Grace occasionally. Although she wasn't sure that wouldn't be worse than not seeing her at all. But she wanted to make certain that Grace was happy and cared for. Grace was the important one in this situation. What did Maggie's feelings matter as long as the baby was safe and happy and loved?

"You're awfully quiet," Tucker said, breaking in to her thoughts.

"I'm just tired. I haven't slept very well lately." Not since she got the news about Grace's mother.

"I know. I've heard you up during the night." He picked up her hand and squeezed it. "I watched you with her. With Grace's mother. You're amazing."

Surprised, she looked at him. "Why?"

"Because you're doing what you think is best for Grace and her mother, no matter what it costs you."

"She's barely more than a kid herself, Tucker. Carol Davis has been kicked just about every way there is, and she's still fighting. She's fighting to be with her baby. I'm going to help her do that."

"Even though it kills you," he said quietly.

"Even then."

## CHAPTER NINETEEN

THE DAY MAGGIE had dreaded finally dawned. It should have been dark and dreary to match her mood, but it was a beautiful day, crystal clear, mid-eighties, with a light breeze blowing and less humidity than usual. She tried once again to talk Tucker into going to work.

"I'm not going to fall apart, you know. You can go on to work. I'll be fine." And she would. She was blessedly numb. She only hoped she stayed that way long enough to hand Grace over to her mother. "Besides, I'm going to work as soon as Carol leaves." She didn't know if working would keep her mind off the baby, but at least it would give her something to do besides stare at the walls and miss Grace.

Tucker was sitting at the kitchen table, watching her give Grace a bottle. "I can go in later. Has it occurred to you that I'm going to miss Grace, too?"

It hadn't, really. She felt like a jerk. "I know you care about her, I just—"

"I love her, too, Maggie," he said flatly. "You can't be around a baby like Grace for as long as we have and not fall for her."

Now she felt like an even bigger jerk. "I'm sorry, Tucker. I'm sorry I dragged you into this and now you're hurting, too." She got up and put Grace in his arms, to let him finish feeding her. "I'm going to get the rest of her things ready."

Tucker came in with Grace a little while later. "Are you sure you know what you're doing giving her all the baby's furniture and toys?"

"I might as well. All Carol has is a crib and most of this stuff will be really useful for her. Besides, I'm not going to be using any of it."

"Ever?"

Her heart twisted but she said calmly enough, "I would want a husband to have a child and I won't have one for very much longer."

"It doesn't have to be that way."

Shocked, she turned to look at him. Surely he didn't mean that like it had sounded. "What do you mean?"

"We don't have to get divorced."

Her stomach rolled. If he was trying to make her feel better it sure as hell wasn't working. Because she realized she wanted more than anything to stay married to Tucker. To have a real marriage with him. But Tucker didn't want that. He'd only said it to comfort her. She'd already conned him into a marriage he hadn't wanted; the least she could do was stay true to her word and give him a divorce.

"Divorce was the plan," she said lightly. "I don't see any reason to change it."

He didn't say anything, just gazed at her for a long

moment before turning away and putting Grace down on the changing table. "What do you want her to wear?" he asked, and the moment passed.

Ten minutes later the doorbell rang. Her eyes met Tucker's. Wordlessly, he gave her Grace and went to answer the door.

"I love you," Maggie whispered to the baby and kissed her cheeks, then her soft, fine hair. Grace smiled and waved a chubby fist in the air.

Maggie walked out of the bedroom and put Grace into her mother's arms, then helped Tucker and Carol's friend load everything into the truck.

"I don't know how to thank you," Carol said when they finished. "Not just for this—" she gestured to the loaded truck "—but for everything you did for Grace, and for taking such good care of her. Will you come see us?"

Maggie nodded. Although she knew CPS was on the case, she'd check on them to make sure everything was all right, as well.

Maggie watched the truck drive away, standing there staring after it until they were long gone. Tucker came over and put his arm around her and watched with her.

"Come on," he said gruffly. "Let's go inside."

She let him lead her. She felt…nothing. Empty. Tucker still hadn't let go of her, she realized. He must think she was going to break down, but that was the last thing she intended to do. She moved away from him. "I'm going in to work. I should be back around dinner."

"Don't go in, Maggie. Stay here with me."

"No." Her throat closed up and she felt herself

losing it. "I need to work, Tucker. It will take my mind off…everything." Work had been her solace in the past. It would be again.

He walked over to her and took her limp hands in his. "Do what you need to do. But I want you to know, I'm here for you."

God, she wished she could accept his offer of comfort. Wished she could allow herself to depend on him, on his strength, on his caring. But she couldn't. She'd already committed the ultimate folly of falling in love with him. Depending on him now would only make it that much harder when he left. Because Tucker was going to leave her, just as Grace had. Just as her parents had. Just as everyone she loved left her.

TUCKER PICKED UP a pizza for dinner, even though he wasn't hungry and he doubted Maggie would be. But he meant to see that she ate something, regardless. He knew that taking care of herself was the last thing on her mind, so he'd try to do it for her. He hadn't been surprised that she'd gone to work immediately. That's how Maggie coped with what life threw at her. By sucking it up and going on.

Her lack of emotion wasn't natural, though, and he believed it was only a matter of time until she broke down. He'd meant what he'd told her that morning. He intended to be there for her, whether she wanted him to be or not.

He wouldn't think about how much he, too, missed Grace. Maggie was the important one here.

Her patrol car was in the driveway and her personal

car in the garage, so he knew she was home. He threw the pizza box down on the kitchen table and went in search of her. He could not only hear it, but he felt the vibrations of the music coming from the exercise room. Expecting to find Maggie beating the hell out of the punching bag, he opened the door and stepped inside. She wasn't by the bag.

He scanned the room and found her huddled in the corner with her knees drawn up to her chest. Crying. No, weeping. Passing by the boom box, he clicked it off, and in three quick strides he was beside her. "It's about time," he said. He sat down and pulled her into his lap, put her head on his shoulder and his arms around her. "Damn it, Maggie. I'm so sorry."

It said volumes that she didn't bother to fight him. She simply turned her body into his and continued to cry. It hurt him to hear her so desolate and not be able to help, but he thought crying it out was likely the best thing for her—the only thing that might make her feel even a little better. So he held her, comforted her, murmured soothing words into her hair as she sobbed.

She held something clenched in her hand. Something pink. One of Grace's socks, he realized. He felt a lump in his own throat, seeing the tiny reminder of the baby they would both miss so much.

A long time later, she finally ran down. Tucker still held her, not at all anxious to let her go. He picked up the towel lying beside them and wiped her tears, then gave it to her to blow her nose. Wordlessly, he took the sock in exchange for the towel and put it in his pocket, out of her sight.

"Better?"

"Not really. More like empty," she said, her voice hoarse with tears.

He tucked her hair back behind her ear, then, intending only comfort, he kissed her. For a moment she was perfectly still, then her arms went around his neck in a stranglehold and she kissed him back. He tasted salt from her tears. And heat, a river of it, flowing out of her.

She pulled back and locked eyes with him, hers still tormented. "Make love to me, Tucker."

Oh, God, he wanted to. But not like this, not with her so sad, so despairing. "Maggie—"

She interrupted him by kissing him. When he would have spoken she kissed him again, her tongue sweeping his mouth with desperate urgency. "Make me forget. Make me feel something, anything besides this pain that won't stop."

He was only a man, not a saint. And she was soft, yielding, reckless in his arms. He loved her and he wanted her so much. Had wanted her forever, it seemed to him.

He pushed her shirt up, cupped her bare breasts. Rubbed his palms over her nipples as they stiffened into taut peaks. Maggie reached for the hem of her shirt, tugged it off and tossed it aside. Her fingers reached for his shirt, swearing as she fumbled to unbutton it.

His mouth came down on hers, hard. Kissing her, consuming her, wanting all of her, as quickly as he could have her. Impatient with her progress, he jerked his shirt over his head and lay down with her, between her thighs. He kissed her mouth, then left it to suckle her breasts. Her hands were in his hair, urging him on, her hips bucking against his.

She moaned. "Tucker," she said on a sob.

He stripped off her shorts and panties, got rid of his own pants and came back to her open arms, lying between her silky thighs, pushing at the entrance to her body. She was wet, wild and shuddering and he sank inside her in one desperate push.

"Hurry," she said, her nails scoring his back.

He knew it was too soon for her, but he couldn't hold back and she clearly didn't want him to. Her body gloved him, stroked him with her muscles clenching as he drove into her and pulled back, again and again until he exploded inside her, in endless spasms.

Her eyes were heavy, slumberous, her lips puffy from his kisses, her hair messed up from his hands. She looked more beautiful than he'd ever seen her, even though she wore her sadness like another layer of skin. "More," he said, kissing her lips.

She kissed him, her tongue sliding against his and whispered, "More."

He carried her into his bedroom, lay her on his bed and followed her down. This time he took her slowly, seduced her until she writhed and quivered for him, and she climaxed screaming his name.

They drifted to sleep in each other's arms and he knew he'd do anything to keep her here, like this, in his bed, in his life, in his heart.

# *CHAPTER TWENTY*

EARLY THE NEXT MORNING Maggie woke in Tucker's bed, but he wasn't beside her. As she lay there, the night before came back to her in a collage of images. She and Tucker making love through the night, until they both fell into an exhausted sleep. Waking, eating cold pizza in bed, then making love again. He couldn't get enough of her, and she felt the same, tracing her hands over his lean, muscular body, letting him take her places she'd only dreamed about.

Nothing she'd ever experienced had compared to what they'd shared the night before. No one, not even Spencer, had made her feel what Tucker did. She loved him. Completely, totally. And she had to let him go.

Maybe it wasn't real, but it had felt real enough when he was loving her.

The night was a blur of lovemaking and she knew she would be sore. That would go away, though. There was one thing that might not. They hadn't used birth control. Not until they'd already made love twice.

After the second time, he'd asked her if she was taking anything. She'd said no, but told him it was the wrong time of month. Which it was...just barely. Tucker had taken some condoms out of his drawer and she'd seduced him again and neither of them thought about anything for a very long time.

One night. Just a couple of times. *It only takes once,* she thought, remembering her previous pregnancy. But no good would come of worrying. She'd put it out of her mind and pray nothing had happened.

The night before, when she was hurting so much, there had been some excuse for her lack of caution. But she'd been behaving irresponsibly from day one, when she cooked up the scheme to marry Tucker so she could keep Grace. She found it hard to forgive herself for any of her actions.

Tucker walked in and gave her a mug of coffee. "Thanks." Feeling self-conscious, she pulled the sheet over her breasts before she sat up and sipped the hot brew. "God, I love the first cup of coffee in the morning."

He smiled and sat down on the bed next to her. He wore a pair of jeans and nothing else. She couldn't help looking at his bare chest and remembering the feel of it beneath her hands. Remembering trailing kisses across his chest and down his abdomen....

"I know exactly how you feel," he said. "Are you going to work today?"

"Not until eleven, and I get off at four. The chief has me on limited duty." She took another sip and frowned. "I think he's afraid I'm going to lose it."

"I doubt it. He's just trying to give you a break."

His hand caressed her arm. She wished that simply

seeing him, much less having him touch her, didn't make her want him again. She had to call a halt to this newfound intimacy. "Do you want to file or should I?"

His hand still stroked her skin, making her shiver. "File what?" he asked absently.

"File for divorce."

His hand stopped its movement and he stared at her, a frown gathering. "Are you trying to piss me off?"

"No, I'm trying to be practical. The reason for our marriage no longer exists. Grace is with her mother now."

"You can ask me for a divorce after last night? After we made love—hell, I can't even count how many times? Are you kidding me?"

"Last night was about comfort, for both of us. You and I both know that."

"That's all you think it was? Comfort?"

He had dropped his hand but he still sat beside her. Too close. "I know that's all it was. So, who's filing for the divorce?"

"Neither of us."

"Tucker—"

He held up a hand to stop her. "There's no reason to rush into a divorce. I'm hurting, Maggie. Maybe not as much as you are, but I have feelings. I told you yesterday, I love Grace, too. Why make losing her any harder on us than it already is? Besides, you don't even have a place to stay."

True. Her house was rented for another several months. But there was no way she could stay with Tucker for too long. Not that it mattered. The damage was already done. She'd been in love with him for weeks now.

"All right, we can wait a little longer. But I don't think we should have sex again."

For a minute he simply stared at her and then a sly smile curved his mouth. "You don't think we should make love again," he repeated.

His dark hair was messed up, probably from her running her fingers through it a hundred times. The stubble on his face gave him a sexy, almost rakish air. Coupled with that devilish expression in those gorgeous blue eyes, she didn't trust him, not one tiny inch.

"That's right. I don't."

He reached for her mug and placed it on the bedside table. Then he stepped back and calmly stripped out of his blue jeans.

"Tucker! What are you doing?"

In about twenty seconds he stood in front of her, stark naked and very aroused. And smiling that same devilish smile. Maggie knew she was toast. Still, she tried.

"Put your clothes back on. This is crazy! We're not going to—"

He stopped her argument by leaning down and kissing her. Her body betrayed her. She wanted him, and he knew it, damn it. He got into bed with her, pulled down the sheet and stroked her breasts slowly. They had already tightened in anticipation, and she felt herself growing damp instantly, aching with need. "Damn you, Tucker," she murmured against his mouth.

"You might as well face it." His hand slid between her legs and he cupped her, exploring her boldly as he strung kisses along her jaw. "This particular Pandora's box has been well and truly opened. And it's not going to close anytime soon."

She pushed him onto his back, reached for a condom and sheathed him with it. Then she straddled him, teasing him with her body until they were both wild with need. "I hate when you're right," she said, and took him inside her. Seconds later, she came in a torrent of pleasure, then felt Tucker spend himself inside her with her name on his lips.

She couldn't move so she lay on top of him, boneless and exhausted. Tucker was right. Celibacy was out of the question now. She might as well enjoy him for as long as they had together.

Even if they couldn't spend every moment in bed together, at least there would be long periods of time when she wouldn't have to think about the mess she'd made of her life. And what she intended to do about it.

HE'D AVOIDED THE AX, Tucker thought a couple of weeks later, but each day was a new battle. Maggie still seemed determined to go through with the divorce. Even though he talked her out of it every time she mentioned filing, which was damn near daily, he felt pretty powerless to stop it ultimately.

*You can't make someone love you,* she'd once said. And he was trying everything he knew how to make her fall for him and so far, he'd failed spectacularly. It appeared Maggie was right on about that.

"Tucker, are you all right?"

He glanced up at his secretary. How long had she

been standing in front of him? "I'm fine. What did you need, Janice?"

Janice was in her mid-fifties and scarily efficient. She tapped the pad she held in her hands with a pen. "You called me in to discuss the Atkins file with me. But you've been out in the ozone for the past five minutes since I've been standing here."

"Sorry, my mind was elsewhere." On his wife. His soon-to-be ex-wife unless he figured out a way to convince her to drop that idea. "Can you get my father on the phone? We can take care of that business later. It will keep."

"Of course, I'll be glad to." She shot him a considering glance as she left.

He massaged his temples and wished he could concentrate on his work, but that obviously wasn't happening. It pissed him off, because he never neglected work and he didn't intend to start now. Even though he didn't have anything pressing currently, he still had clients and they still had needs. Now, if Maggie would just relax and let him— He wadded up the piece of paper he'd been making notes on and threw it across the room. Damn it, he was doing it again.

He arranged to meet his father for lunch at the Scarlet Parrot. He walked in at noon to find his father there before him. Delilah Randolph greeted him as he came in. They chatted briefly, then she put her hand on his arm. "I don't want to bring up painful subjects, but I was so sorry to hear about Grace. Not that I'm not happy for her mother, but I know how hard giving her up must be on you and Maggie."

"Thanks. It's worse for Maggie."

"I saw you with the baby, Tucker. It's hard on you, too. But at least you and Maggie have each other."

For now. And Maggie wasn't talking. Every night he tried to get her to talk about her feelings, but she refused. She'd let him make love to her, but she wouldn't talk. Not about anything important, and not one word about Grace. "Has she talked to you about Grace?"

Delilah shook her head. "Nothing beyond the bare fact that Grace's mother had returned and Grace was going to live with her. But you know Maggie likes to keep things close."

Understatement of the decade. They reached the table where his father waited. Tucker shook his hand and ordered an iced tea.

They talked for a few minutes and after the waitress dropped off their drinks and took their orders, Harvey said, "Is there something particular you wanted to talk about?"

"Yeah. And I'd appreciate it if you didn't tell Mom." His mother would probably advise him to divorce Maggie and forget about her. However, she'd been surprisingly sympathetic when he'd told his parents about Grace, and had even asked if there was anything she could do for Maggie.

"Not if you don't want me to. What's wrong?"

Unsure how to begin, he took a sip of tea. "I'm in love with Maggie," he blurted out.

"I could point out that you're married and supposed to be in love with your wife, but I take it that's a problem," Harvey said after a moment.

"Oh, yeah. She's not in love with me. She only married me because of Grace." He told him the story then, about the bargain they'd struck, including the part about no sex.

Harvey laughed. "I find it hard to believe you agreed to that condition."

"So, I was stupid. I'd convinced myself all I felt for her was friendship. That didn't last long, for me, anyway. Then, the night Grace left…Maggie was hurting and looking for comfort." He paused, thinking about that night. It hadn't been all about comfort, regardless of what she said the morning after. "I didn't take advantage of her, if that's what you're thinking. I tried not to, but I—she—" He broke off, shrugging, not wanting to go into detail. "Anyway, it happened."

"I think you were hurting as much as Maggie was, Tucker. I know you love the baby. There's nothing wrong with turning to your wife for comfort."

"Even if she isn't really your wife?"

"The marriage may have started out a sham, but it sounds like the real thing now."

The waitress returned with their food and after eating a few bites, Tucker continued. "That's the problem. It's not a sham, not on my part. But now that Grace is with her mother, Maggie says the reason for the marriage no longer exists. She keeps bringing up divorce, and that's the last thing I want."

Harvey ate a bite, then asked, "Have you told her you don't want a divorce?"

"Not exactly. So far I've just been dragging my feet."

And seducing her every night. He'd thought making love would strengthen their relationship, but even though Maggie clearly enjoyed the sex, Tucker knew she was holding part of herself back. He applied himself to his food without much interest.

"Let me take a wild guess. You haven't told her you're in love with her, either."

"No." He'd been picking at his food, but at that he glanced up at his father. "Do you think I should?"

Harvey blotted his lips with his napkin. "Frankly, Tucker, I can't figure out why you haven't already told her. How can you expect her to know what you feel when you haven't talked to her about anything?"

"I didn't want to know for a fact she isn't in love with me."

"That's a remarkably negative way of looking at it. And not like you at all."

Tucker pinched the bridge of his nose. "I haven't been myself since the day Maggie talked me into marrying her. She's making me crazy. Usually I'm good at reading people. But Maggie takes keeping her cards close to her chest to a whole new level."

"Tell her how you feel, Tucker. You might be surprised to find out she's in love with you, too."

Maybe. But what would he do if she wasn't?

# CHAPTER TWENTY-ONE

"MAGGIE, IT'S SO GOOD to see you," Lana said. "I can't tell you how many times I started to go next door and then realized you weren't there. Come on in." She opened the door wider and waved Maggie inside.

"Thanks. I hope you don't mind but I thought I'd catch you at home. I know you take off Wednesday afternoons."

"Since when have I ever minded you dropping by? Did you think that would change just because you got married?"

"No, but I didn't want to catch you in the middle of something."

"I'm not doing a thing." She patted her stomach, which was huge. "I'm supposed to be nesting. I'm due in a week and Gabe's been having a fit that I haven't quit work yet. He wants me to start maternity leave yesterday," she said with a laugh. "I just can't see sitting home waiting to deliver, though."

"Maybe it will happen sooner than you think."

Lana lowered herself carefully into the rocking chair. "I sure hope so. Gabe is driving me crazy hovering over me." She sighed and added, "He's even taken on more help at the shop so he can be with me more often now that my due date is so close. Which is great, don't get me wrong. But who knew he'd be such a mother hen?"

Maggie stifled a pang of envy. She didn't begrudge Gabe and Lana their happiness, she knew how much they deserved it. If only she hadn't made such a royal mess of her own life, she might have shared that same kind of happiness with someone. Not just someone, she thought. Tucker.

"Is Gabe here, then? I didn't see his truck out front. Don't tell me he cleaned out the garage enough to fit both cars in there."

"No, no," Lana said, laughing. "I thought since he has all this free time, he might as well be useful. I sent him to buy ice cream. He should be back any minute."

"I need to ask you something before Gabe comes back. And would you mind not saying anything to him? Or to anyone?"

Lana sat up straight and pinned her with a sharp glance. "Are you having a medical problem, Maggie? Why didn't you come to the clinic? Of course I wouldn't talk about your medical concerns."

"I didn't come to the clinic because I didn't want Tucker to hear about it. It would be just my luck that his secretary would see me go in or worse, his mother. I just need to ask you a question. How accurate are those early pregnancy tests you can buy?"

"Some are more accurate than others. How early are we talking? False negatives are fairly common if it's taken before you miss a period."

"My period is three days late and I'm normally regular as clockwork."

"They're about ninety-seven percent accurate at that point."

"What about false positives? Are they common, too?"

"No. False positives do occur, but they're rare. I could give you a blood test. They're extremely accurate. Do you think you're pregnant, Maggie?"

Maggie sat on the couch. Her head was reeling, even though she wasn't surprised. First off, she'd barely managed not to barf the last few mornings. After she took the test earlier that morning, she'd decided to check with Lana, just to make sure. If she was having a baby she wanted Lana to be her doctor. Unless… "Are you planning to go back to work after the baby is born?"

Lana smiled. "Yes. I'll take a couple of months off and then I'll go back part-time. So you do think you're pregnant."

She nodded. "The test I took this morning was positive. And I've been queasy in the mornings."

"I'd say you are most likely pregnant, then." Lana studied her a moment. "Forgive me, but you don't seem very happy about it."

"I am happy," Maggie said, fighting back tears. "But I'm miserable, too."

Lana leaned forward and grasped her hand. "Do you want to talk about it?"

Grateful for the support, Maggie shook her head. "I don't know. It's complicated." And how in the hell was she going to explain this whole debacle to anyone without sounding totally insane?

"Are you and Tucker having problems? You seem so happy together."

"It's hard to explain. Can I ask you something else? About pregnancy?"

"Of course."

"I had a miscarriage before. Does that mean I'm more likely to have one this time, too?"

"Not necessarily. It depends on the reason you miscarried."

"The doctor said it was just one of those things. It was early, in the first trimester."

"I can't say for sure without examining you, but again, I don't think you necessarily have to be concerned about another miscarriage."

Her anxiety eased up a bit. "Good."

"Does Tucker know you're pregnant?"

"No." And if she could possibly work it, he wasn't going to know until they were divorced. Or at the least, until after they filed.

They heard the back door slam and Gabe's voice came from the kitchen. "I bought four different kinds of ice cream. Well, three and a half," he said, coming into the room with a quart of ice cream in one hand and a spoon in the other. "I put the rest in the freezer."

Lana looked at her husband and said, "Gimme."

"Hey, Maggie. Long time no see," Gabe said. "There's a little matter of payment," he told his wife, leaning over and tapping a finger on his lips.

Lana laughed and kissed him. "Now, gimme."

He grinned at her and handed her the ice cream.

"I've got to get going," Maggie said. "Good to see both of you."

"Let me see you to the door," Lana said.

"No, don't get up," Maggie protested, but Lana ignored her. It took her a while to make it, but with Gabe's help she finally did and walked Maggie to the front door. "I mean it," she said in a low voice. "Anytime you want to talk you know I'm here. And whenever you're ready, make an appointment to see me so I can examine you. I'll tell our receptionist to get you in right away once you call."

"Thanks, Lana."

"Don't wait too long."

"I won't. I'll call soon." She definitely wanted Lana to be her doctor, but she doubted she'd take her up on the offer of talking. Lana was great, and she'd be understanding, Maggie was sure. But Lana was also about to have a baby with a husband who was crazy about her and their coming child. How pathetic would Maggie sound if she told Lana the story of her fake marriage? No, better to keep it to herself. Besides, there was only one course of action. She just hoped she was strong enough to follow it.

SHE MEANT TO TALK to Tucker as soon as he came home. Clean and quick and get it over with. But Tucker didn't give her the chance. He didn't so much as say hello when he came into the kitchen from the garage. Instead, he spun her around and kissed her to within an inch of her life. He tasted hot, potent. His hands fell to her hips and pulled her closer. Her breasts started tingling and her body went lax. She loved him so much. Didn't she deserve to be with him one last time? To make love with him?

No, she didn't deserve it. Not when she was about to lie to him. "Tucker, wait. We need to talk."

"Later." He reached beneath her shirt and cupped her breasts, then popped the front clasp on her bra and filled his hands with her bare breasts.

Maggie shivered at the feel of his palms on her bare skin. She should resist. But she didn't.

"I've been thinking about you all day," he said. "About making love to you." He kissed her again, thrusting his tongue deep inside her mouth, slow, wet and wild.

The next thing she knew he'd stripped her and boosted her onto the kitchen table. His mouth felt wonderful on her breasts. She should say something, anything, to stop him, but she didn't have the will. She loved him, she wanted to be with him, one last time.

He reached into his pocket and pulled out a condom. A condom he didn't need, but she didn't tell him that. Instead, she watched as he placed it on the table beside her, then put his mouth to her stomach.

"You are so beautiful," he murmured against the skin of her stomach. His lips trailed down, creating rivers of sensation, and then she felt the sweep of his tongue at her center.

"Tucker, wait," she said, putting her hands in his hair and pushing him away, even as her hips lifted to meet him.

His tongue slicked over her slowly, then he raised his head. "Why?"

She couldn't tell him that the last time he'd made love to her this way she'd barely maintained control. It had been too intense, too…shattering. And that had been deep in the night, in the darkness of their bedroom. How much more vulnerable was she now, in the light of day, naked with him still fully clothed? How much more vulnerable knowing that this was the last time they would make love?

"I want you inside me," she said. But she knew, no matter how they made love that she couldn't keep the distance between them. The only way to do that was to leave him.

Something flickered in his eyes. She couldn't tell if it was anger or hurt or something else entirely. He didn't say anything, but simply stood back and stripped, then sheathed himself and stepped between her legs.

She closed her eyes and waited.

"Maggie, look at me." His voice was rough and hoarse.

Though she knew it was a mistake, she opened her eyes. He lifted her hips and thrust into her with a smooth motion. She wrapped her legs around him, shuddering as he pushed into her and pulled out in a deep, driving rhythm. His eyes were shining and he kept them locked on hers as he made love to her.

Her body tightened. Her climax built, layer upon layer until it hovered just out of reach. Each time she thought she'd peak, he'd pull back, slow things down, then build her back up until she nearly screamed at the sweet torment.

His eyes still on hers, Tucker thrust deep inside her and she shattered, his name bursting from her in a sob of pleasure so intense she thought she'd died. Moments later, he followed her over, groaning her name as he spent himself inside her.

She didn't move. She couldn't. The most she could manage was to hold him until their breathing slowed.

"Why is it so hard for you to let anyone get close to you?" Tucker asked her long minutes later with his head resting on her breast.

She wanted to cry. "We're naked and you're still inside me. How much closer do you want to be?"

He raised his head and looked at her. He looked more sad than anything else. "You know what I'm talking about, Maggie. You share your body but since that first night we made love, there's been a barrier. Every time we make love. You wouldn't have dropped that barrier this time if I hadn't pushed you into it."

Her heart was breaking into a thousand pieces. "Leave it alone, Tucker. Please, just…don't talk about it."

He didn't say anything else. Simply moved away from her, picked up his clothes and walked out of the room. Maggie's throat closed up and she fought back the tears. When she gained control, she dressed. Then she went to find Tucker and tell him their marriage was over.

# CHAPTER TWENTY-TWO

TUCKER PICKED UP a heavier dumbbell and started another set. He'd rather be indulging in a nice, lazy post-coital glow, snuggling with his wife, but instead he was lifting weights, trying to get rid of the anger riding him.

He'd been primed to tell Maggie he loved her. And then he'd made love to her and sensed that damn distance she was always putting between them. She didn't want to be close to him. How many more times did she have to prove that to him before he believed it?

She enjoyed the sex. He knew that. But he wanted more. He wanted her to love him…and it was pretty damn clear she didn't.

"Tucker, we need to talk."

Glancing up, he saw Maggie in the doorway. She had her cop face on, which meant he couldn't read her at all. But he had a feeling he wasn't going to like what she wanted to talk about. He continued to lift, moving his forearm in a bicep curl. "So talk."

"Could you quit doing that?"

He finished the set, then put the dumbbell down and looked at her. She walked farther into the room but she

didn't sit down. But then, the only place to sit was beside
him on the weight bench.

"I'm going to file for divorce tomorrow."

Great. They made love and she decided to divorce
him. "I thought we'd agreed to wait on that."

"We have waited. Grace has been with her mother for
almost three weeks. It's time to do what we planned."

"Plans can change. I don't think we should get divorced
right now." Or ever, but he couldn't seem to say that.

"The only reason I can think of to stay married would
be if we were in love with each other. And we're not."

Not entirely accurate. One of them was. But why
should he lay his heart on the line when she'd only crush
it? "There's one other reason to stay married."

"I can't think of one."

"I can. Say, if you were pregnant."

She didn't say anything. Worse, she flushed and
looked away. *Oh my God.* Anger, and hurt, burned in his
stomach. "You're pregnant."

"It doesn't matter if I'm pregnant or I'm not. I'm
filing for divorce tomorrow."

He reached her before she could run out the door,
halting her with his hand on her arm. "When were you
going to tell me?" She didn't answer. "Goddamn it,
Maggie. Answer me. You owe me that, at least. Were
you going to tell me?"

She hesitated for a long moment, then she looked at
him, misery in her expression. "Yes. After we were
divorced."

He didn't trust himself to speak. She would have

denied him his child. Not permanently; he knew her better than that. But long enough to make sure they divorced before he knew about it.

"We are not getting divorced when you're pregnant with my baby."

"This is exactly why I didn't want to tell you until after we filed. I knew you'd fight me if you knew I was pregnant."

"You're damn right I will." Oh, to hell with it. He wasn't going to hang on to his pride when she was about to destroy their lives. He pulled her closer. "The baby isn't the only reason I don't want a divorce." She looked suspicious, angry. Not in the best frame of mind to hear his confession. But he plowed on, determined to say it. "I'm in love with you, Maggie." Even though he didn't think she loved him. Even though she'd hurt him more than he would have believed. He still loved her.

Her expression changed to one of disbelief. "Are you? Or are you just saying that because I'm pregnant?"

"I mean it. I love you, and it has nothing to do with the baby."

"It's a little ironic that you didn't think to mention this fact until after you found out I was pregnant. Not once before this have you ever said you loved me."

He started to yell, but forced himself to be calm. "I was going to tell you today. When I came home. And then I saw you and we made love and—" To hell with being calm. "Damn it, Maggie, I didn't tell you because you were doing your 'let me put as much distance between Tucker and me as possible' routine."

She shook him off and moved away. "I'm not trapping you in a loveless marriage simply because I'm pregnant. It wouldn't be right."

"We don't have a loveless marriage! I'm in love with you!"

She shook her head. "Don't. Don't do this, Tucker. Just let me file and don't fight me."

This was spiraling out of control so fast he couldn't possibly save it. But he had to try. "Do you think I'd lie to you about something this important?"

"You're damn right I do. If the lie resulted in you being able to do what you believe is the right thing. But it's not, Tucker."

She didn't believe him. Wouldn't believe him, no matter what he said. Or worse, maybe she did believe him and wanted to let him down easy. "You're not in love with me. That's the answer, isn't it? That's why you refuse to believe I love you."

"My feelings aren't the issue," she said. "I'm going to file in the morning." She walked out and this time he let her go.

It hurt, more than he would have believed possible, to know Maggie didn't love him and apparently didn't think she ever could. Their marriage had always been about the baby, not about the two of them. First Grace and now their unborn child. Maggie was pregnant. Unlike when she'd wanted to keep Grace, this time she didn't need to live with a man she didn't love in order to have a child.

"Tucker, wake up."

"Hmm." He cracked open an eye and realized

Maggie was standing beside his bed, shaking him. Every miserable scene from the night before came flooding back. He sat up. "What? What's wrong?"

"I think I'm losing the baby," she said, and burst into tears.

He reached for her. "Sit down. Come on, sit and tell me what happened."

She did as he said, wiping her eyes and trying to maintain control but she wasn't very successful.

"Take a deep breath," Tucker said, putting his arm around her and giving her a comforting hug. "And then tell me."

"I got up to go to the bathroom and I—I saw it. There was blood. I'm spotting."

He knew absolutely nothing about pregnancy. "I take it that's not normal."

"I don't know. All I know is last time…when I lost the baby, that's how it started. Bleeding, cramping, and then I lost it."

"We need to call your doctor. Is it Lana?" He figured she was, since the two of them were friends.

"Yes, Lana. But we can't call her now. It's two-thirty in the morning. She's due in a week and she needs her sleep."

"I'm sure she won't mind." He started to get up but Maggie clutched his arm.

"I'm so scared," she whispered. "What if I lose this baby, too? What if—"

He put his fingers to her lips. "Don't, Maggie." He put his arm around her again and hugged her, kissed her cheek. "Talk to Lana. It could be nothing." He didn't know if that was true or not, but he knew what she needed to hear.

He found the cordless phone, and after Maggie gave him the number, punched it in. Lana answered on the second ring. "Lana, it's Tucker. I'm sorry to call you so late, but Maggie's having a problem. She really needs to talk to you." He handed Maggie the phone.

He didn't hear a lot, partly because Maggie was crying and partly because she didn't say much after she explained her symptoms. Finally, Maggie said, "Okay, I'll come in tomorrow at eight-thirty," and handed him the phone. "Lana wants to talk to you."

He searched Maggie's face, but she didn't look as if Lana had reassured her very much. Damn, what had she told her? "Do I need to bring her to the hospital tonight?" he asked Lana.

"No. As I told Maggie, there's really nothing we can do at this point. She needs to try to calm down and take it easy. Rest, and try to get some sleep."

Tucker looked at Maggie. "Calm down? I don't think that's happening, but I'll try."

"Will you be able to come with her in the morning?"

"Absolutely."

"Good, she needs your support right now. I'm going to do a test on her HCG level tomorrow, and that might tell us a little more. The levels should go up exponentially at this stage of pregnancy. It will be another one or two weeks or so before we'll be able to see the baby on an ultrasound."

"And there's nothing I can do to help her? Nothing you can do?"

"Nothing other than try to reassure her. There are any number of reasons for spotting at this stage. Most of them don't mean she's having a miscarriage."

"But she could be."

Lana hesitated, then said, "Yes, it's possible. I'm sorry, Tucker."

He thanked her and hung up, setting the phone on the bedside table. Then he put his arms around Maggie and pulled her close. She didn't resist. Her arms went around him and she laid her head on his shoulder. Her cheek was damp against his skin. "I can't do this again," she whispered. "I can't lose another baby."

"You aren't going to lose it. Lana said there were all kinds of reasons for spotting."

"One of which is a miscarriage."

It was a fact he couldn't deny. They both had to face the possibility. "I wish I could promise you that the baby will be fine, but obviously, I can't. But I can promise you that whatever happens, you won't be going through this alone. You're not getting rid of me, Maggie."

She was quiet for a long moment, then pulled back and looked at him. "Why are you so good to me?"

"Because I love you." He kissed her mouth. "Don't even think about going back to the other bedroom. You're sleeping with me."

She didn't argue. She got into bed with him and let him wrap her in his arms. "Tucker?"

"Yeah?"

"I'm glad you're here with me."

"Me, too. Now try to get some sleep."

"I can't. All I can think about is what happened before. I don't ever want to hurt like that again."

"I don't want you to, either." He paused. Trying to comfort her, he blurted out, "Maggie, I'm hoping and praying you won't lose this baby. But if it happens... We could try again. On purpose this time."

She started crying again and he cursed himself for being a fool.

# CHAPTER TWENTY-THREE

"I DIDN'T MEAN—I know it wouldn't make up for losing this one, but— Damn, Maggie, don't cry. I'm an idiot. I'm sorry; forget I said anything." He patted her back. "Don't cry."

"It's so sweet," she said, finally managing to stop leaking tears. "You're so sweet. I know what you meant and I appreciate it, Tucker. I really do. But you don't have to do that. You've done enough for me."

He groaned. "You really don't get it."

Yes, she did. She understood perfectly. Tucker was a wonderful, kind man who wanted her to be happy. "You told Lana you were coming with me in the morning. You don't need to. I appreciate the offer, but I can go without you."

"You're not going alone. So do me a favor and don't argue about it. Get some sleep."

"All right." She was an emotional wreck. Sleep could only help. "Tucker? Thank you for being here for me."

"There's no place else I'd rather be than with you." He kissed her forehead and closed his arms around her. She felt safe…and loved. Was it an illusion or did he really love her, after all?

Maggie fell asleep pondering that question. And dreamed of Tucker and a sweet baby boy.

TUCKER INSISTED ON standing beside her and holding her hand while they waited for Lana to return with the HCG level test results. She didn't fight him since she'd been up since dawn and the waiting left her white-knuckled and desperate to know something. And hollowly uncertain of what she'd do if Lana confirmed she would lose the baby.

The door opened and Lana came in holding a manila folder Maggie assumed was her records. "Your HCG level indicates you're still pregnant, so that's good."

Hope bubbled in her heart. "I'm not having a miscarriage?"

"Unfortunately, we can't rule that out entirely. What we might do is take another level in forty-eight hours and then again forty-eight hours after that. If the HCG levels continue to increase that's a good sign that the pregnancy is progressing normally."

"So all we can do is wait?" Tucker asked.

"I know it's hard. But honestly, at this point there isn't much else to do." She smiled at him, then turned to Maggie. "Can you tell me anything else about your symptoms? Last night all you mentioned was the bleeding. Did you notice any more, or did it get heavier?"

"Nothing since last night. It was just the blood. Not very much, but it freaked me out."

"I understand. Last night did you have any cramping?"

Maggie shook her head. "No. Just the spotting." Lana wrote something down and Maggie asked her one of the questions that had been bothering her. "We had sex yesterday. Could that have caused it?"

Lana looked up and gave her a reassuring smile. "It might have caused some bleeding, but if you are having a miscarriage that wouldn't be the cause. However, to be safe, I would refrain until we know more about how the pregnancy is progressing."

Or about how it isn't, Maggie thought glumly.

"Don't worry," Tucker said. "We'll do whatever we need to."

"Cheer up. It's not for the duration. Just until we know more."

Unless she filed. The thought of not only losing the baby but of losing Tucker, too, depressed the hell out of her. To never make love with him again, or see him, or have him to talk to and tell about her day, to spar with, or even to hang out and watch the tube. No, she couldn't bear to think about that. Not on top of everything else.

She made an appointment to come in the day after tomorrow and then she and Tucker left. She thought about returning to work, but Tucker had a fit, so she didn't. After lecturing her about resting and taking care of herself, Tucker left for the office. She felt a pang of guilt knowing he'd been putting off taking care of his business yet again because of her.

She should do what she'd been talking about for the last several days and go file the papers for the divorce. That's what she should do.... But she didn't. Instead, she crawled into bed—Tucker's bed—and took a nap.

That night and the next day, Maggie carefully did not

bring up divorce, and neither did Tucker. She went back to work on a limited basis, trying hard not to run to the bathroom every few minutes to check that everything was all right. The second test set her mind a little more at rest, and Lana said the third, in two more days, should make them all breathe easier.

Once the pregnancy was far enough along, in about another week or two, they would take an ultrasound and continue to monitor its progress that way. They left the date for the ultrasound up in the air, though, since Lana was so close to delivery. Lana had said she wanted to do the test herself and insisted that it wouldn't be a problem, even if she'd had her baby. Even though she told herself not to count on anything, as more time passed Maggie began to feel cautiously optimistic.

The evening after the second HCG test she and Tucker went to see Grace and her mother. Maggie had deliberately stayed away, afraid that seeing Grace again would only make her feel worse, but she missed her so much she couldn't stand it. She'd kept an eye on Carol and Grace through CPS, and she'd heard they were doing well. But eventually, she had to see for herself that the baby was happy. Carol had agreed enthusiastically when Maggie had called the night before and asked if she and Tucker could come see them.

"You're sure this is a good time?" Maggie asked, as Carol showed them in.

"Anytime is a good time for you two." She smiled to include Tucker. "I know I have you to thank that Grace is so happy and healthy." She looked down at the baby in her arms and smiled. "Not to mention I know you're the one who helped me get me that job, Maggie."

"That was just luck that I heard about the cleaners needing help."

"But you didn't have to tell me about it. You know I wouldn't have gotten Grace back if I didn't have a job." Grace held out her arms, wanting to go to Maggie. Carol laughed and handed her over so Maggie could sit with her. "She's missed you."

"I missed her, too." Maggie looked at the blue-eyed, blond little girl cooing and babbling in her lap and felt her heart swell. "She's grown so much."

Carol nodded. "At this age even a few of weeks makes a difference."

Grace was obviously thriving. And Carol looked like a totally different person from the sad, desperate young woman Maggie had first met at the police station.

"Grace looks great," Tucker said. "How's she doing with day care?"

"She seems to like it. I had a hard time leaving her after just getting her back, but the hours are good at the cleaners. And her caregiver at the day care loves her."

They talked a while longer and played with Grace until it was clearly her bedtime. Maggie stood to leave and a wave of dizziness hit her so fast and hard, she nearly fell. If it hadn't been for Tucker grabbing her she thought she might have gone to ground. "I'm okay."

"The hell you are. Sit down. No, lie down. Do you mind if she stretches out on the couch?" he asked Carol.

"No, of course not. Are you all right, Maggie?" she

asked anxiously. "Is there something I can do? Get you a glass of water?"

"I'm fine," Maggie said, but she did sit down. "Tucker's overreacting."

"She's not fine, she's pregnant," Tucker told Carol. "And she's supposed to be taking it easy."

Maggie scowled at him. "I have been taking it easy. I only worked a half day today, and the chief has me on desk duty."

Carol went to the kitchen, returning with a glass of water, which she gave to Maggie. Maggie drank it and felt better. This time when she stood, the dizziness didn't return. Tucker insisted he would bring the car to the building since the lot had been full and they'd parked some distance away.

"I envy you," Carol said softly after he left.

Startled, Maggie looked at her. "Why?"

"Because you're having your child with the man you love. And he's obviously a good man who loves you very much."

"Things aren't always what they seem."

"Oh, don't get me wrong. I wouldn't take another chance of being with someone who would hurt my baby. Not ever. But if I could have a man like that look at me the way Tucker does you, I'd feel very lucky."

THE DAYS UNTIL the ultrasound passed slowly for Maggie as she suspected they did for Tucker, although the fact that the third hormone-level test showed increasingly elevated levels of HCG helped tremendously.

Maggie still hadn't brought up the divorce. She'd decided to wait until after the ultrasound to sort that all out. Maybe it was selfish of her, but she needed Tucker right now. She wasn't sure she'd have made it through without him.

Tucker didn't seem in any hurry to get rid of her. He wouldn't let her sleep in the other bedroom, but convinced her she slept better in his bed. And since she slept like a baby every night wrapped in his arms, she couldn't exactly argue.

Lana and Gabe had their baby, a healthy baby boy they named after his father. Lana still insisted she wanted to do the ultrasound and scheduled it for the week after she brought the baby home. She said baby Gabriel would be fine with his father for the hour or so it would take her to run the test.

Finally the day of the ultrasound dawned, when Maggie was about seven and a half weeks pregnant. Lana had told them that she expected to see a perfectly healthy pregnancy, since all the tests had been good and Maggie had experienced no worrisome symptoms after the initial spotting. In fact, she'd been sick every morning, which also made her hopeful.

Maggie clutched Tucker's hand while the technician spread gel over her stomach. Lana took the ultrasound device from the tech and placed it on Maggie's stomach. Maggie shut her eyes and prayed. Very shortly, Lana spoke. "There. There's the baby, and there's the heartbeat. Maggie, don't you want to look?"

Her eyes had flown open when she'd heard the word

*heartbeat*. She stared at the screen along with Tucker. "Can you see it, Tucker?"

"I think so." He didn't sound too sure, though.

She didn't want to admit it, but she couldn't really tell much. "Are you sure you see a heartbeat?" she asked Lana. "I can't see anything."

"I'm sure," Lana said. "I've had a bit more practice than you. It's hard to see this early." She placed a pointer on the area she wanted them to look at.

"I see it now," Maggie said, trying not to cry. "You think the baby is all right?"

"I do," Lana said.

"I can see it," Tucker said. "Wow, that's so cool. It's so tiny."

"Very cool," Lana agreed. "We'll do another one in a few weeks, but I don't think you need to worry. I think the spotting was simply spotting and nothing to be concerned about. You can resume all your normal activities."

"Everything?" Tucker asked.

Lana laughed. "Well, I wouldn't recommend skydiving, but pretty much anything else is all right."

"Does she still need to take it easy?"

"Only if she feels bad. I think things are going to be just fine." Lana patted his shoulder, then smiled at Maggie and left the room.

She and the baby were going to be all right. Along with huge relief, Maggie felt a growing depression. There was no reason for she and Tucker to stay together now. Except that she loved him and wanted to be with him.

But what if he really did love her and she'd just been

too stubbornly sure she'd messed up his life to see it? She thought about the past months, especially the weeks since Grace had gone back to live with her mother. Tucker had been there for her because he wanted to be. You couldn't fake something like that. And if he'd loved Grace, how would he feel about a child of his own? Was it fair to him to take the choice of raising his child with her away from him? Because she had decided he couldn't possibly want to be with her?

Didn't she owe them—she, Tucker and the baby—a chance to be a family?

# CHAPTER TWENTY-FOUR

"TUCKER, WHEN WE GET home we need to talk." She
planned to approach him cautiously. Start with the idea
of not filing for divorce just yet, since he seemed to want
to experience the pregnancy with her. Later she'd worry
about what to do once the baby was born. Maybe by
then she'd have a clearer idea of whether he really was
in love with her or just bent on doing the right thing.

Tucker shot her a glance she couldn't read. "My
thoughts exactly. I took the rest of the day off."

"I don't want your work to suffer because of me.
You've already missed a lot."

"Don't worry about that. I've rescheduled everything
and can catch up next week."

Once at home they went to the den. Maggie sat on
the couch, but Tucker didn't. Instead he stood by the
fireplace, rearranging stuff on the mantel. "I've been
thinking—" Maggie began but Tucker interrupted,
turning to look at her.

"I know what you're going to say."

"I don't think you do."

Tucker nodded. "Oh, yeah, I do. You're going to

bring up filing again. Because the baby is fine, et cetera, et cetera. But I want to have my say before you do."

"I wasn't exactly—"

"Maggie, are you going to let me talk or not?"

He sounded so stern it made her want to giggle. *Must be the hormones,* she thought. But he also seemed very agitated, so she shrugged and decided to let him go first. "Okay. Go ahead."

He didn't. Instead, he paced the room. She watched him a moment then said, "Tucker? I thought you were going to talk."

"I'm working on it." He came to a halt before her. "I've been trying to figure out a way to convince you I love you. I know I screwed up not telling you before you told me you were pregnant. But I can't change that."

"Tucker, let me—"

He shot her a "don't mess with me" look, so she relented.

"At first I thought about having my dad tell you what we talked about at the Scarlet Parrot earlier on the same day you told me about the baby. Delilah could have told you we were there. But I knew you'd think my dad would do whatever I asked him to, and he would. So that was out. Besides, I need to prove it to you myself."

She started to speak but he raised a finger. "I'm not finished." He put his hands in his pockets and paced again. "Then it occurred to me. You're a cop. You're a logical woman and when presented with the facts you'll listen. I'm not a trial lawyer but I took trial advocacy in law school. So I know how to present a case. And that's what I intend to do."

She stared at him for a moment. "You're presenting a case that you love me?"

"Yes." He held up a finger. "First piece of evidence, what have I said every time you mentioned filing for divorce? You started talking about it even before Grace's mother came back. When we had our date and I kissed you. Do you remember what I said?"

"Not exactly. I remember you talked me out of it."

"That's right. Just like I did every time you brought it up. After Grace left, I said we didn't need to rush into filing. When what I really meant was that I didn't want a divorce at all."

"That's not what you said."

"Out of order. I'm not finished presenting the evidence."

Maggie pressed her lips together, smothering a laugh. "Fine. Go ahead."

"All right. Here's another piece of evidence. Have I ever referred to us having sex as anything but making love?"

"I don't know. I don't remember."

"I remember and I haven't. Because it isn't just sex between us, it's making love."

She'd been a cop long enough to know when a person was lying. She'd bet everything she had, but most especially her heart, that Tucker was telling the truth. She got up to go to him but he stopped her words with his fingers on her lips. Then he gathered her hands in his and looked into her eyes.

"Maggie, I love you. I want you. I want to spend my life with you. I want to have babies with you. This one, another one, more if you want. I believe I can convince you I'm telling you the truth when I say I love you. If you'll give me a chance to prove it." He kissed her hands, then smiled at her. "But what I don't know is how you feel about me. It seems like every time I start to think you might love me, you bring up divorce."

Her heart had turned to mush as he spoke. She shook one of her hands loose and put it on his cheek. Gazed at him lovingly. "Are you finished presenting your case?"

"Did I mention I love you?"

Maggie nodded. "Yes, you did."

"Then I'm finished."

"Do you know what I was going to say at the beginning of this conversation?" He shook his head. "I was going to suggest we wait on filing until after the baby was born. And I planned to keep putting it off until I knew whether you loved me or you were staying with me because you thought it was the right thing."

"Really?" He looked so suspicious, she laughed.

"I don't want a divorce, Tucker. I only kept bringing it up because I believed that was what was best for you. I didn't want to trap you. I didn't want you to stay married to me simply because it was the right thing. I wanted you to love me."

"I told you from the beginning that I married you because I wanted to. I finally figured out I've been falling for you from the day we said our vows. Maybe before that."

"I love you, too. I have for a long time. For so long, I can't remember not loving you."

He pulled her into his arms. "Those are the words I've been waiting to hear." He kissed her, long, slow and loving. "I love you, Maggie."

"I know," she said, and laughed as he scooped her into his arms and carried her to the bedroom.

She looped her arms around his neck and strung kisses along his jaw. "There's something we need to do first."

He paid no attention, depositing her on the bed with great care. "Tucker, I mean it. We need to take care of something before we make love."

He had his shirt halfway unbuttoned but he paused and looked at her. "If you tell me you're having second thoughts—"

"No, nothing like that. But…I'd like to say our vows again. This time for real." She waited a little anxiously, unsure whether he'd think the idea was silly.

He smiled and sat on the bed. "Do you want to go first or should I?"

"I'll go first."

"Give me your hands."

She put her hands in his. "Tucker, when I first asked you to marry me I thought you'd be the perfect temporary husband. But it didn't take me very long to discover that you are the perfect husband for me and that I want our marriage to last the rest of our lives. You're my best friend, and my lover, and I want very much for you to be my husband. For always. Because I love you more than I can say."

He smiled at her, such a tender expression in his eyes she thought she'd drown in them. Tears started in her own eyes as he spoke. "Maggie, when you first cooked up this scheme I thought you were nuts. I told myself I'd marry you to help you out. I didn't realize that it would take me about a week to fall totally in love with you. So here's to crazy schemes and to the one woman in the world who is making my dreams come true. Dreams I didn't even know I had until I married you. I promise to love you, cherish you, and every year on the anniversary of the day you asked me to marry you, I promise to dream up something just as crazy for us to do together."

Maggie laughed through her tears. "I love you. You are such a nut."

He took her face in his hands and kissed her soundly. "I love you, too, Mrs. Jones. And that makes us perfect together."

*About seven months later*

TUCKER BENT DOWN to kiss the soft hair on his newborn son's head. "He's so amazing. He's incredible." He kissed Maggie and sat on the bed beside her. "And so is his mother."

"Isn't he perfect?" Love swamped her as she looked at her baby. "Look, his fingers are so tiny." She picked up one of his tiny fists and kissed it. "Do you want to hold him?"

"Absolutely." He held out his arms and she transferred the baby into them. "What are we going to name him? I have an idea if you don't."

She stroked the baby's cheek. "He looks like you, Tucker. And what makes you think I don't have any ideas?"

"Oh, maybe because you refused to discuss names the entire pregnancy."

"I do have an idea. But let's hear yours first."

"I thought since Grace is the reason we married in the first place, we should name the baby after her. But I'm not naming my son Grace."

Maggie laughed. "No, I think the other kids might tease him if we did that."

"Let's name him Davis, for Grace's last name."

"You must be a mind reader." She put her hand on the baby's head and smiled at Tucker and their son. "Welcome to the world, Davis Tucker Jones."

\* \* \* \* \*

*Mills & Boon® Special Moments™*
*brings you a sneak preview*

*Turn the page for a peek at this fantastic new story
from Karen Rose Smith, available next month in
Mills & Boon® Special Moments™!*

*Burned by her Greek tycoon ex, supermodel
Gabby McCord sought refuge in her work on the
glitzy PR campaign of her family's jewellery empire.
Finding refuge in the arms of new bodyguard
Rafael Balthazar was an unexpected perk!*

*Don't forget you can still find all your favourite
Superromance and Special Edition stories
every month in Special Moments™!*

### *The Texas Bodyguard's Proposal*
### *by*
### *Karen Rose Smith*

The door to the library at the McCord family mansion suddenly opened and an absolutely stunning woman with long, wavy, honey-blond hair rushed in—Gabriella McCord. Her face and figure had been on every fashion magazine cover in the free world…and in a few tabloids.

Rafael Balthazar's breath hitched, though he'd never admit it. He did not want to protect a socialite model who'd grown up with every luxury at her fingertips! But as security consultant for McCord Jewelers he had no choice, not when Blake McCord had asked him for this favor.

In a peacock-blue, figure-fitting dress, matching high heels and swingy gold earrings, Gabriella could take any man's breath away. Just not his. He didn't go for divas.

"I'm sorry I'm late," she began with a smile that added punch to her beauty.

Their gazes locked and, for a few moments, Rafe actually felt a shift in his universe.

No way.

"My…plane was delayed," she explained, her gaze still on his. "I just checked in and rushed over—" She stopped when she realized he wasn't smiling or crossing the room to greet her.

If she expected him to fall at her feet, she was going to be disappointed. "Miss McCord, I'm your bodyguard. My duties will begin tonight when you return to the Sky Towers. Blake assures me a driver will chauffeur you back to the hotel after his mother's birthday dinner. I'll meet you there and we'll go over your itinerary for the upcoming week."

Gabriella's small, well-defined chin came up and her back straightened. "It's so good to meet *you,* too, Mr. Balthazar. I just want you to know I don't feel I *need* a bodyguard. This is Blake's idea, not mine."

Nope, Rafe wasn't moving toward her. He had to establish an impenetrable boundary now. In a low, controlled voice, he responded, "You don't need a bodyguard? I understand there was a scene at the airport when you arrived." Blake had filled him in on *that* disaster. Rafe hadn't been available sooner. He'd been handling a security problem in Houston and had just returned in time to meet Gabriella before Eleanor McCord's birthday dinner.

Gabriella's cheeks flushed a bit. "Paparazzi somehow found out when I was arriving. I managed to slip away."

"More than paparazzi found out. There was a crowd waiting for you and it blocked the limo from leaving. Two things you'll learn while I'm guarding you. One, you have to be honest with me. Two, you must not put yourself at risk unnecessarily. Understood?"

Gabriella's golden-brown eyes sparkled with defiance. "Understood? I understand that you were once a Secret

Service agent, and a very good one. That's super. I commend your service. But I will *not* let you dictate where I go and what I do. Do *you* understand?"

He had to admit she was one beautiful, feisty package. Something he had to ignore…yet manage. "My job is to keep you safe."

"So you'll just have to do your job. As spokeswoman for McCord Jewelers, I'm going to do whatever Blake has planned for me and that will probably involve crowds. I also have a few engagements of my own and I can never predict what will happen."

"Like a stalker accosting you?" Rafe knew that had happened last year.

Gabriella's face drained of color, then she recovered her composure and gave him a new smile. "I haven't had any stalkers recently, so no worry there. And you only have to cover me for a few weeks. I'll be returning to Italy for a short time at the end of August. When I return to the States, Blake will have screened someone else and you can go back to your job concentrating on the security of the stores."

"In the meantime, we have to work together."

"No, Mr. Balthazar. You just have to make sure fans don't tear me apart."

Unbidden, an image took form in front of Rafe's eyes, a photo of Gabriella that had appeared in a tabloid last month. The paparazzi had snapped a picture of her dancing in a London club. It was a money shot because the clasp on her designer dress had malfunctioned. Just as the top of the dress had fallen—

Had the episode been an accident? Or had the whole situation been planned for publicity's sake?

This time Gabriella's face rapidly gained color, and he knew she was recalling the same image. Abruptly she turned away from him.

"Miss McCord…"

"We'll talk later," she murmured. "I don't want to keep my aunt waiting on her birthday."

And Gabriella McCord was gone.

"That went well," Rafe muttered and raked his hand through his short-cropped, black hair.

Gabriella McCord would be even more trouble than he'd expected, but he could deal with her. He'd protected the president of the United States. He wouldn't let one pretty model throw him off his game.

Not now. Not ever.

## *Do you dream of being a romance writer?*

Mills & Boon are looking for fresh
writing talent in our biggest
ever search!

And this time…our readers have
a say in who wins!

For information on how to enter
or get involved go to

# www.romanceisnotdead.com

 **SPECIAL MOMENTS™ 2-in-1**

## Coming next month

### THE TEXAS BILLIONAIRE'S BRIDE by Crystal Green

For nanny Melanie Grandy, caring for Zane Foley's little daughter was the perfect job...until she fell for him and her past threatened her newfound happiness.

### THE TEXAS BODYGUARD'S PROPOSAL by Karen Rose Smith

Burned by her Greek tycoon ex, supermodel Gabby McCord sought refuge in her work. But her attraction to new bodyguard Rafael Balthazar was an unexpected perk!

### KIDS ON THE DOORSTEP by Kimberly Van Meter

Put in charge of three abandoned girls, John Murphy is determined to protect them. Then their mother turns out to be all the woman this rancher has ever needed.

### COP ON LOAN by Jeannie Watt

Tony DeMonte didn't sign up to play bodyguard to a *librarian*. The big-city cop thinks he's out of place in this small town, but Jasmine may just change his mind.

### THE TEXAN'S TENNESSEE ROMANCE by Gina Wilkins

After a false accusation destroyed her career, Natalie's priority was getting her life back. The feelings that Casey awakened in her were distractions she couldn't afford...

### THE RANCHER & THE RELUCANT PRINCESS by Christine Flynn

Montana was the perfect hideaway for Princess Sophie Saxe. Until she found herself falling for a stubborn cowboy – and learning that the rancher always got his way!

### On sale 20th August 2010

Available at WHSmith, Tesco, ASDA, Eason and all good bookshops.
For full Mills & Boon range including eBooks visit
**www.millsandboon.co.uk**

# SPECIAL MOMENTS™

## Single titles coming next month

### LOVING THE RIGHT BROTHER
#### by Marie Ferrarella

When tragedy struck, Irena headed back to Alaska to console her ex-boyfriend's family – and began seeing his brother, her best friend from high school, in a very different light...

### A WEAVER BABY
#### by Allison Leigh

JD Clay didn't think she could get pregnant – or that wealthy businessman Jake Forrest could be a loving daddy. But Jake would offer JD and their miracle baby a love to last a lifetime.

### A SMALL-TOWN TEMPTATION
#### by Terry McLaughlin

When Jack Maguire arrives in Charlie Keene's small town, nobody's safe. Not Charlie and not the family business she's desperate to keep from this Southern charmer...

### A NOT-SO-PERFECT PAST
#### by Beth Andrews

Dillon Ward has a bad reputation and a shady past. But Nina needs him to repair her wrecked bakery – like, *yesterday*. And if there's one thing this single mum knows, it's that nobody's perfect...

## On sale 20th August 2010

# 2 FREE BOOKS
## AND A SURPRISE GIFT

We would like to take this opportunity to thank you for reading this Mills & Boon® book by offering you the chance to take TWO more specially selected books from the Special Moments™ series absolutely FREE! We're also making this offer to introduce you to the benefits of the Mills & Boon® Book Club™—

- **FREE home delivery**
- **FREE gifts and competitions**
- **FREE monthly Newsletter**
- **Exclusive Mills & Boon Book Club offers**
- **Books available before they're in the shops**

Accepting these FREE books and gift places you under no obligation to buy, you may cancel at any time, even after receiving your free books. Simply complete your details below and return the entire page to the address below. You don't even need a stamp!

**YES** Please send me 2 free Special Moments books and a surprise gift. I understand that unless you hear from me, I will receive 5 superb new stories every month, including a 2-in-1 book priced at £4.99 and three single books priced at £3.19 each, postage and packing free. I am under no obligation to purchase any books and may cancel my subscription at any time. The free books and gift will be mine to keep in any case.

Ms/Mrs/Miss/Mr _____ Initials _____

Surname _____

Address _____

_____

_____ Postcode _____

E-mail _____

Send this whole page to: Mills & Boon Book Club, Free Book Offer, FREEPOST NAT 10298, Richmond, TW9 1BR